The Trouble

Michael Martin

The Trouble is fiction.
Names, characters, places, events, and actual persons, living or dead, real or imagined, are used fictitiously.

The words from The Great Hunger by Patrick Kavanagh are reprinted from Collected Poems, edited by Antoinette Quinn (Allen Lane, 2004), by kind permission of the Trustees of the Estate of the late Katherine B. Kavanagh, through the Jonathan Williams Literary Agency.

Special thanks to editors Bernadette Kearns (Dublin), Averill Buchanan (Belfast), and Sian Phillips (Dublin), who strengthened this story immeasurably.

Published in the United States by Heart Beat Publications, LLC
Cover by Warren Design

Library of Congress Cataloging-in-Publication data available on request.

Printed in the United States of America.

One

An Garda Síochána Detective Adam Kincaid had the grave good fortune of being assigned three of Ireland's most notorious homicide cases at the start of the Troubles.

His first encounter with the All Saints Slayer, also known as the Crucifix Killer, occurred on a foggy morning in St. Patrick's Park, about one hundred yards from the Church of Ireland's cathedral. The year was 1968, the sun was rising, and Kincaid was a uniformed garda pursuing a single-minded quest, to one day join the Central Detective Unit, or CDU.

Up and down ladders, he and another garda lowered the X-shaped wooden cross, careful to keep the body from slipping through leather straps that bound the man's wrists and ankles to each rigid arm.

"Heavens he's stretched," the other garda said. "Must have been excruciating. Legs almost ripped from their sockets."

"What's that stuffed in his mouth?" Kincaid heard a Technical Bureau crime scene examiner ask.

"Gag?" CDU detective Philip Casey said.

The crime scene examiner removed it with tweezers. The detective slipped on rubber gloves and held the gag in the sunlight.

"Anything I can set this on?"

The crime scene examiner handed Casey a wide evidence envelope.

"Something bigger," Casey said.

The Tech Bureau lad glanced toward Kincaid, who had moved back. Casey's eyes followed. "*Anything* I can set this on?" he said.

Kincaid looked around. The other garda shrugged.

"Quickly," the detective barked.

Kincaid unbuttoned his jacket.

"Isn't that a bit drastic?" Casey asked.

"I can wash it," Kincaid said, as he lay his uniform coat on the lawn, where the detective spread open the moist cloth to an ornately-stitched phrase.

"A manutergium," Kincaid said.

"A which?"

"A lavabo towel. Hand towel. Used during Mass."

"You know so much—what's it say?"

The colorful stitching read: *O bona crux.* "Looks like Latin," Kincaid continued. "I think crux means cross."

The detective eyed the victim. "Well, this *is* a crucifixion."

As if on cue, the cathedral's bells started pealing.

KINCAID ATTENDED HIS FIRST murder conference that week, explained what he saw, being the first garda on the scene, learned why detectives considered both crime and scene "poorly-executed" and "amateurish."

"Chancing their arms, they were, hanging a man in that fashion in that place at that time," said Detective Casey, now the lead investigator.

Kincaid also heard the great wondering: Why? Why go to such trouble to exhibit a man who was dead before he was strapped to the cross? What was the manutergium trying to say? Why all the religious overtones?

He read media speculation, followed the story in the newspapers as it took on political overtones. Was the murder some sick message from a Loyalist paramilitary or the IRA? The Church of Ireland vigorously tamped down such talk, reminding that the victim was a beloved physician with no known political positions.

Kincaid interviewed witness after witness, ran down car plates, and did the tedious gumshoe work that would help prove his mettle. Still, there were no breakthroughs, no telling clues, like fingerprints, to celebrate, no eyewitnesses to anything more than an X-shaped shadow at dawn. The grim work may have been crude, but it was effective. The murder of Dr. Robert Boyd gradually joined the ranks of the likely-to-remain-unsolved.

"LUCKY LAD," DETECTIVE INSPECTOR John McDermott said two years later. "Getting out of Dublin Castle, just as things heat up."

"I thought it had been hot for a while," said Detective Garda Kincaid, no longer a uniformed beat cop but a full-fledged member of the CDU.

"They weren't shooting at us," McDermott said.

"No, they were bombing us."

"Did you read that bollocks statement from Saor Éire, or whatever they're calling themselves? Demanding an *official* investigation into Dickie Fallon's death?"

"I gathered they didn't like the headlines we placed."

"They don't shoot *us*," McDermott said. "They *never* shoot us."

"They do now."

ON HIS WAY OUT of Dublin, Kincaid called on his mother at the St. Francis Home, which he hated. He walked up a sidewalk, head down, only looking up to avoid a passing nurse or attendant assisting an elderly charge in a wheelchair or behind a walker.

"Mr. Kincaid," he heard.

"Good day to you, Mr. Kincaid," he heard again, each time raising his eyes just enough to politely acknowledge the greeting.

He walked up the stairs to the second floor, the odor of age and urine striking his nostrils. He tapped a door until it swayed back, to a dark room with the shades drawn.

"Mama?" he said, slipping in. He walked past a bed but didn't see his mother until he peeled back the gray drapes. She shaded her eyes with a grimace.

"Must you?" she said.

"You don't want the light?" he asked.

"No."

"The light's good for you."

"When are you getting me out of here?"

"When did we discuss?"

"You're leaving again," she said. "You always come by when you're leaving."

"I have to. Moving you where we both want you to be takes money." He knelt in front of her wheelchair. She set her withered hand on his and dug his flesh with her fingernails. He pulled away.

"Why would you do that?"

"Did I break the skin?" she said.

She shuffled the wheelchair to the bed and started to stand. Kincaid rushed over to hold the chair but she brushed him off, so he stood back, looking lost. With exaggerated shaking, she grasped the wheelchair arm and mattress and nightstand as she swiveled into bed. She slipped under the sheet and blanket and pulled them to her head.

"Get out of here," she told her son.

“**A MRS O'CONNOR FOUND** her,” Detective Garda Tiernan from the Sligo Garda station told Kincaid as they made their way into the bog wearing protective coats, boots, and gloves. “She and her husband. Cutting turf, they were.”

“Dry for a bog,” Kincaid said, as he looked at a stand of pine trees that edged the little wetland and caught the smell of death in the cool air. The preserved area lay just ahead, the breeze slapping a colored tape that stretched across four corners, roughly a square.

“Haven't had much rain since July,” Tiernan said. “Wet month, that. Mightn't have found the child if it kept up. Inspector—” Tiernan called out to a man peering over something Kincaid could not see. As they got closer, “the CDU detective is here.”

The smell intensified as they came upon a three-foot ditch between two banks of turf that allowed rainwater to drain from the bog. The ditch crossed a dirt path that connected two roads. Kincaid saw shredded clothing, bits and pieces of an anorak coat, blouse, vest and pinafore with only a left arm through its sleeve. A uniformed garda raised the tape and both detectives ducked beneath it.

“Kincaid, right?” the Tech Bureau Investigations Section (IS) detective said. “Dan Ryan.”

“Inspector,” Kincaid said.

“Your reputation precedes you,” Ryan said. “Welcome to my little corner of the murder squad.”

Ryan, Kincaid, and Tiernan peered at what Mrs. O'Connor had found. "Not much left of her, I'm afraid."

Kincaid bent closer. He looked at the girl's skull, neck, rib cage, part of the spine and left arm.

"Boyle Station take the call?" he asked.

"Yes."

"Uniform?"

"Garda Devitt," Tiernan said. "He'll be at the conference."

"She was ten?" Kincaid asked.

"Yes," Ryan said.

"Girl's birthday was just a few days ago," Tiernan said. "She would have been eleven."

"Any thought that the dismemberment was deliberate?"

"She was buried," Ryan said, "but shallow enough for animals to pull her out of that brush and maybe cart parts of her away. We're scouring the area and haven't found anything else, though."

"The case file you sent me mentions some medals," Kincaid said.

"We *identified* her with them, truth be told."

Tiernan handed Kincaid a large envelope. He peered in.

"Recognize any?" Ryan asked. When he didn't get an immediate answer, "You were in seminary."

"I recognize them," Kincaid said, handing back the envelope. "She was a devout little one," he said.

"IT WAS THE SMELL caught my attention," Margaret O'Connor told Kincaid for the first time, Ryan the second time. "I thought it was a dead sheep at first, then saw them crows a circling and walked over and saw the child."

Kincaid would never forget the first time he smelled death, the way it clung to every part of him, his hair and skin, his mind and spirit. It still clung—he never shook it. You never did.

"We had a few dry days—no rain for nearly a week," Mr. O'Connor said. "July was so wet—thought we'd best get after the peat while we could."

Detective Garda Tiernan caught up with Ryan and Kincaid outside the O'Connor's house as they were leaving.

"Pathologist can't say as to time or cause of death 'unless some miracle happens,' is how he put it," Tiernan explained.

"So we have to believe in miracles," Ryan said, patting Tiernan's arm.

THE GIRL'S MOTHER BROKE into sobs after Inspector Ryan, as delicately as possible, explained that she best not be looking at the body. He introduced Kincaid, "a top detective from a different unit who would like to hear what you can tell him."

"Katie's been missing since April," her father, James Dunleavy, said. "We been looking since April. I have it here." He paged backward through a calendar marked with Xs that stopped on April 17.

"Your other daughter found her sister's bicycle?" Kincaid asked.

"And my purse," Mrs. Dunleavy said. "Still had the money I gave her in it, ten shillings, two pence."

"The bicycle caught Mary's eye as she was walking the area," her father said. "We figured Katie had been snatched. Long gone from here after we found the bicycle. *Mary*." He called toward a bedroom door.

"We took the bike and purse into evidence," Tiernan told Kincaid.

"How old was your daughter—was Katie?" Kincaid asked.

"Ten years. Her birthday was last—" Her mother gasped.

"She was goin' on twenty. So precocious," her father said. "And such a dancer. You should have seen her dance."

"A dancer," Kincaid said. "Just around the house?"

"Oh, no," Mr. Dunleavy said. "School, ch—"

"This is just the kind of thing we feared in England," her mother interrupted. "Never talk to strangers, I always told my girls. Never take sweets. Never take a ride. We thought it was safe here."

"Is your other daughter about?" Ryan asked Mr. Dunleavy.

"*Mary*," Dunleavy called again. A door opened and a teenager emerged from the hallway.

"Can you tell Detective Kincaid where you found the bicycle, exactly?" Ryan asked.

"Up the hill, sir. From the Boyle-Ballymote road," the girl replied.

"And the purse?"

"On the grass between the road and the hill."

"It still had your mam's money in it?"

"Yes, sir."

"She and Annie Donnelly seem the only people who saw anything," Mrs. Dunleavy said.

"And the woman with the horse," Mary reminded.

"She only saw Katie bicycling by," Mrs. Dunleavy said. "There were people working fields. Any of them should have heard a car pass on such a quiet road."

"No one saw anything," Mr. Dunleavy said. "People don't want to get involved."

"People from all around helped you search," Tiernan asked.

"Help us, they did," Mr. Dunleavy said. "And we appreciated it."

"So they were willing to help," Kincaid said. "Is there anything, or anyone, might have scared them off?"

The couple looked at one another. "I can't think of—we—" Mr. Dunleavy said. His wife shrugged.

"Did she have anything else with her?" Kincaid asked. "Things you never found."

"We have the inventory at the station," Tiernan said.

"Her glasses," Mary said anyway. "They were pink, easy to spot. I looked all round for them."

"What about shoes?"

"She was wearing shoes," Tiernan said. "And a ring that went missing."

"Her gold ring," Mr. Dunleavy said. "Wore it on her right hand."

Kincaid envisioned the missing arm and stopped writing in his notebook. If animals tore apart the body, the ring may have disappeared in the bog. The eyeglasses maybe dropped in the killer's vehicle, as he was unlikely preying on foot.

But the shoes—where would they have ended up? He envisioned an animal dragging away a leg between its jaws. But how far would the leg go before the beast consumed it, leaving the shoe behind? So did human hands dismember her, and why?

"Will we get the things back?" Katie's mother asked. "The purse I don't care about. But the bicycle was Katie's favorite and no small expense. It was a very hoped-for gift."

"It was her independence," her father said. "She was on it constantly."

"Fingerprint section will want to examine them," Ryan said. "That's best done in Dublin."

"We already fingerprinted everything." Tiernan said. "Found Katie, Annie Donnelly, and a partial from Katie's sister," Tiernan told Kincaid.

"We appreciate your work," Ryan said. "But with our more advanced set up back in Dublin—"

"Sligo Station is perfectly capable," Tiernan interrupted.

"Me and the tech lads are going back in the morning," Ryan said. "We'll take the items with us."

"Is that a good idea?" Tiernan said. "If we lose chain of custody—"

"We won't," Ryan said.

"Gentleman," Kincaid intervened, looking at the family and Mary's wide eyes. "Do you recall the weather the day Katie disappeared?" Kincaid asked.

Father looked at mother.

"It was raining, sir," Mary said. "Lightly it was coming down, but it was raining."

"Rained all week, as I recall," Mr. Dunleavy said. "Typical April."

"What kind of monster would do this?" Mrs. Dunleavy asked.

Not a stranger, but someone who knew the community, Kincaid thought, based on knowledge of obscure side roads and the wet, consumptive bog.

Two

Inspector Ryan stood in front of the conference room table tapping his index finger on the Jobs Book, wondering as always if he'd missed any tasks, any assignments, any questions, any directions. As the members of his Garda Technical Bureau team took their seats, Ryan ticked off their respective roles in his mind: photography, fingerprints, questionnaire and documents, mapping, scenes of crime officer, press officer. Garda Devitt, Detective Garda Tiernan, Garda Kearney from the water team. And his expert on the intersection of Catholicism and crime.

"Now that we're all here, I'd like to introduce, from Central Detective Unit, Detective Garda Adam Kincaid."

Nods and welcomes circled the table as Adam leaned in and quietly returned the greetings.

"Ten-year-old girl, Katie Dunleavy, goes missing four months ago, after her mam sent her to a neighbors for haddock and spuds. Whole community mobilized to find her. Looked for weeks. Still looking, if you ask anyone around here. They never gave up on her. Katie turned up two days ago in the Limgahn bog. You all know by now Garda Devitt, who took that call at Boyle Station."

And so the case's first murder conference began, mostly going around the table and through a list of critical evidence the team had and did not have—yet, or maybe ever.

First up: the fingerprints of some six hundred area men over the age of fifteen. Dead ends so far.

Next, the team discussed the four interviews with the Donnelly family, where young Katie was riding that day to get "the messages for her mam," the fish and potatoes Mrs. Donnelly purchased at a store close to her house. When Katie didn't turn up, the Donnelly's teenage daughter Anne went with Katie's sister Mary to search for her, and remembered spying "something shiny" over a dirt berm off the road. Together the girls retrieved a "twenty four inch girl's Raleigh Space Rider bicycle, shown in the photos before you, along with the mother's purse," Ryan explained. No unidentified fingerprints detected on either, but "further examination in Dublin may yield something more substantial," an Inspector Ryan exclamation that brought a Garda Tiernan frown.

"No unidentified fingerprints on the girls' holy medallions, either," Tiernan said. "Which we done here at Sligo, just like the bike and purse."

Questionnaires were out in all the surrounding towns and villages and so on and so forth. From them, the detectives had so far learned that the last person to see Katie alive was a woman driving a horse cart. "She was goin' so fast, but she waved and shouted somethin'," the woman told the uniformed garda at her door. "I didn't catch what she said. The wind caught it first."

Water team searched the lakes as Garda Kearney explained during this report. Over two hundred uniforms searched farms, dug through manure, meticulously combed every strand of hay in every barn and open field within a twenty mile radius of the lost purse and bicycle.

"I understand footprints were not preserved as well as should be expected," Kincaid said, after raising two fingers to comment.

"That's what we understand," Ryan said. "Guards didn't mind the area of Katie's disappearance that night. We don't know how much was lost. Got some photos and one plaster cast, but made a bags of things otherwise."

"It wasn't Sligo," Tiernan volunteered.

"Wasn't Boyle," Garda Devitt said.

"Was," Tiernan retorted.

"Maybe now you understand why I want the evidence we *did* recover in Dublin," Ryan said. "But onto the next subject—why we brought in Detective Kincaid."

"The Father," Kincaid said. "Colm Kyle."

"Precisely," Ryan said.

A beige van cast suspicion on its owner, the McGuinn Seminary close to Katie's home, Ryan summarized. "Petrol pump attendant says a brother from the seminary filled the van the evening Katie disappeared," Ryan said. "Father Kyle then did a very strange thing by moving in with Katie's family."

"Father Kyle woulda been watching the crime unfold in real time," Detective Garda Tiernan interjected. "He was calling our offices, reciting what he was reading in sympathy cards that struck *him* as suspicious. He answered their door, telling dad to take a sit whenever a knock stirred. Even went so far as to follow a car from their house to around where Katie was found, better than twenty miles out, so he said."

"What's the name of his Order?" Kincaid asked.

"Order of St. Michael the Archangel."

"The patron saint of police."

KINCAID HEARD A MAN clear his throat and looked up from the dark wooden booth in the pub.

"Drinkin' alone, are ya?" Detective Garda Tiernan said, mug of stout in hand.

"Just Coke," Kincaid said.

"Coke? Without whiskey? What good's a public house?" He and his beer slid into the opposite bench.

"I shouldn't be in here," Kincaid said. He looked at the bar and the low lights and a few patrons talking and drinking.

"Gave up drinkin', did ya?" Tiernan said.

"Needed to get out of my room for a while," Kincaid said. "It's a nice night for some air. I've heard about this pub." He looked around the room.

"Better have," Tiernan said. "It's been here two hundred years. So when," he sipped his beer, "did you give it up? The drink?"

"Three hundred and forty five days ago," Kincaid said.

"Counting the days, are ya? Should I put this away?"

"I never liked stout," Kincaid said.

"Blasphemy," Tiernan said, bringing his hand around his mug in a faux guarding fashion. "Though if you're in AA—"

"I'm not."

"It's all right if you are. Thought about trying it myself. Once McQuaid got behind it—"

"Archbishop McQuaid?"

"Who else?" Tiernan said. "Member name of Conor F. started a Dublin chapter. British Army man, Sackville, took to proselytizing it. Got Maynooth College behind him. Later, the Archbishop himself."

"I went to Maynooth," Kincaid said.

"To be a priest?"

"That's where I went."

"McQuaid organized a conference, *The Priest and Mental Health*. At St. John of God's Hospital, as I recall. Sackville spoke there, about drinking, and what it does to the mind." Tiernan sipped his stout, used the rim of his mug to wipe foam from his lip. "Ironic, isn't it?"

Three men in camouflage and boots caught Kincaid's eye as they scooted into a booth across the room. "That reminds me," he said. "I wanted to ask Ryan if any paramilitary involvement was considered."

"Here? This isn't County Armagh, you know."

"Kidnapping *is* on the list of best practices."

"Ryan's certain it's the priest," Tiernan said. "Besides, how would kidnapping this particular child further any aims?"

"Good Catholic family. Good Catholic community. Protestant paramilitaries might consider that aim enough." Kincaid sipped his Coke.

"You were in seminary, right?" Tiernan asked.

"Ryan told you?"

"He did. Said you dropped out. Called to the Guards instead."

Kincaid snickered. "My mother wouldn't have called it that."

"Mam wanted a priest, eh? Don't they all?"

"So why the priest?" Kincaid asked.

"Father Kyle? He knew the child well. She danced at the seminary, for the retired priests, joined them for novenas to the Blessed Mother. Rode in the van to youth club outings now and again."

"So he's a pedophile?"

"Wouldn't be the first. Brenden Wryth scandal hasn't been outta the news."

"Where's the evidence?" Kincaid said.

"Spoken like a true ex-seminarian," Tierman said. "But at your question, we don't have any direct evidence. Just Ryan's hunch and rumors the Church plans to transfer him," Tiernan said.

Kincaid's eyes widened.

"Ryan didn't tell you?"

"Anything to these rumors?"

"Straight from the Archdiocese, I hear. That's *more* than anything. Surprised he didn't tell you."

Kincaid brought his hands together, interlocked his fingers, looked at the table.

"Ryan, I don't like him," Tiernan said. "He's murder squad, through and through and high and mighty, up in Dublin Castle lording his *specialness* over the rest of us."

"He take the bike today?"

"And the purse. And the money in the purse."

"Maybe they'll turn up something."

"What?"

"Always pays to be optimistic."

"I say the child got off her bike willingly," Tiernan said. "They won't find any fingerprints or partial fingerprints but what we already found. No hairs, no fibers, either."

"What was the girl doing while her bike was carted away and thrown in the ditch?"

"Fighting off her attacker as he dragged her along," Tiernan said.

"Or in the van with another assailant."

Tiernan sighed. "You want me to send a bangharda with you tomorrow?"

"Her mam will be there," Kincaid said. "No need for more uniforms."

"INSPECTOR," KATIE'S MOTHER SAID. "Do come in." She ushered Kincaid into the room. "Mister Ryan gone back to

Dublin, I understand. How long will he have Katie's bike, do ya think?"

"If they find anything on it, could be a while," Kincaid said.

"Well then—I'll pray they find something helpful. Mary," she called. To Kincaid, "I have tea, if you'd like."

"No thank—yes. Yes, I *would* like some tea. Thank you."

Kincaid and Mary Dunleavy sat in the living room with mother listening.

"Mam was getting dinner ready and she wanted to know where Katie got off to," Mary said. "I just got home from school myself. Katie was sick a couple days and stayed home."

"She was feelin' better and getting a little stir crazy," Mrs. Dunleavy said. "I thought the chore would do her good."

"I got the messages instead and Annie Donnelly asked her mam if she could help me look for Katie," Mary said. "Her mam said yes and we left on our own bikes and found what we found on the way back here."

"I rang everyone I could," Mrs. Dunleavy said. "The Guards, the hospital, everyone I knew."

"Is that how Father Kyle found out?"

"I suppose it is."

"You're not certain?"

"Well, no. He'd heard something, he did, but I don't know what," Mrs. Dunleavy said. "I didn't ring him or the seminary. Wouldn't have felt right about doing that."

"So *he* contacted *you*?"

"He rang right after."

"You remember what Father Kyle said?" Kincaid asked.

"Said he was sure Katie was all right, that God looks out for wee ones—more than a little, wee ones like Katie. He asked if we needed anything. Then he showed up at me door, which was surprising."

"Why was that?"

"Because I asked him to keep Katie in his prayers, and ask the other Fathers to keep watch for her, if he would."

"So you didn't invite him here?"

"Oh, no, no, Inspector. That would not have been proper."

"How far was the purse from the bicycle?" Kincaid asked Mary.

"A little ways. Closer to the road, it was."

"Any footprints? Tire tracks? Anything that suggested other people were about?"

"Yes, yes. There was footprints. And tire tracks. Ground was muddy. Raining it was, but not heavy."

"The Guards took note of all that, Inspector," her mother said. "They had cameras. I know they took photos. They poured plaster into the footprints. Even brought dogs down from Dublin, they did."

Kincaid leaned back and sighed. He let a silence he found awkward fill the void of fumbled footprints and missed opportunities. No wonder Tiernan was up in arms about the murder squad commandeering the little evidence they had.

"Would Katie get into a vehicle with someone she did not know?" he asked.

"No, never," sister and mother said almost at once.

"What about someone she knew?"

"I don't think so," Mrs. Dunleavy said.

"Someone she knew and trusted," Kincaid persisted.

"You mean Father Kyle?" Mary said.

"Mary! I'm sorry, Inspector, but these questions about Father Kyle have to stop. He's a wonderful man and done nothin' to hurt our Katie and everything to help her."

"She'd a got in the van with him, mam," Mary said. "But she woulda taken her bike. There's room enough for it."

"She loved that bike, she did," her mother said.

"Have you seen the van?" Mary asked.

"Not yet," Kincaid said. "It's a good point you make, though."

"It was *not* Father Kyle."

"Brother Carricker always drove the van, that I ever saw," Mary said. "Me and Katie went a few times in it to youth club."

Kincaid thumbed through the murder squad's notes. "Carricker, Carricker. Was with Father Kyle that night. Watching television."

"Wasn't Brother Carricker took Katie, either," Mrs. Dunleavy said.

Kincaid looked down the hallway, toward the bedrooms, a stairway, and around.

"Inspector?"

"Wasn't it crowded in here with Father Kyle?" he asked.

"Oh, well," Mrs. Dunleavy said. "It was a blessing, that. By our side every step of the way."

"Father Kyle led a search for her," Mary said.

"I read that in the interview notes," Kincaid said. "Near the Donnelly home."

"Had us praying, so convinced he was that Katie was near," Mrs. Dunleavy said. "If only . . . " Her voice broke. ". . . the good Lord had been listening."

"Why was she killed?" Mary said. Dread replaced the tears in her mother's eyes.

"We don't know," Kincaid said. "Not yet."

"Was she raped?"

"Mary! Dear God, what a question."

"We have to ask it, ma. I want to know. All my friends want to know."

"We don't need to know right now," mother said.

"If the person is still out there, close by," Mary said. "Was she raped, Mr. Kincaid?"

"We won't know until the postmortem, if even then," Kincaid said.

"Why not?"

"It's a long while Katie was out there." Kincaid set his note pad aside. "Tell me about her. I only know what I've read so far."

Mary looked at her mother, who deferred.

"She loved school. She wanted to be a teacher," Mary said, then caught herself. "What do you want to know?"

"All about her. Everything you can remember."

They looked at family photos and Katie's classroom notebooks, her other medallions and statues, pictures of her dancing, at school, at the seminary, on a stage in Boyle. Tears and sobs interrupted, but mother and daughter pressed on. Kincaid handed back the notebooks and Katie's stuffed bear and grasped Mrs. Dunleavy's hand and looked at her eyes. He drew his eyes back and stood. Mary walked him to the door.

"Mam wants Katie buried with her medals," she whispered. "She don't want them back. Dad, neither."

Three

Kincaid walked over the embankment where Mary and the Donnelly girl found the bike. He looked back at the road where the purse had lain, sizing up distances. He walked the area for an hour, taking in sight, sound, and smell.

From there he drove to the bog, donned protective shoe coverings, and walked into the crime scene, past the tape and a day-shift uniformed bangharda charged with preserving the area. He stood in the ditch where the body was found. The sadness was still here, a sense of premature death that clung to the soul sure as the smell clung to the nostrils. Despite how hard he tried to shake it off in the past, leave it at the crime scene, he could not, and like the death smell, finally gave up trying.

He eyed a structure through trees up a hill.

"What is that?" he asked the bangharda.

"Hay barn I think, sir. Owner was interviewed, that I do know."

"Have you been up there?"

"No, sir. But it looks to have a good view of the bog, it does."

Kincaid stared at the barn, and started toward it.

"Detective—sure you don't wanna take the road?" the bangharda called to him.

He waved her off. The grass and ground were dry and easy enough to traverse. No rain had fallen this week.

“**MIGHT I BE HELPING** you, sir?” a male voice called out as Kincaid emerged from the hillside onto the grounds around the barn.

“I’m with the Guards,” Kincaid said.

“I gathered, coming in as you just done,” the man said. “Little Katie Dunleavy’s been found, I hear. Been watching the commotion. What a terrible tragedy.”

Kincaid caught his breath and dabbed his brow with his sleeve. “Adam Kincaid,” he said. “I’m a detective.”

“Then detective, anything you’d be caring to see here?” the man asked.

“Maybe.”

“Come round then, if you’d like.”

Kincaid followed him into the barn, a horse stable. “I’ve got clients to feed.”

“Clients?”

“Boarded horses. You’re not gonna make me take them all out again, are you?”

“Guards searched the barn?”

“They did,” the man said. “They did.”

Something else Ryan did not mention.

“They say what they were looking for?”

"Something to do with the girl," the stable attendant said. "Something missing from her person, sounded like, might have made its way up here. They didn't find anything. I told them they wouldn't."

He picked up straw and a bucket of oats and started at the first stall.

"Every straw, they searched," the stable attendant said. "Every single straw. Are you finished down there yet?"

"Not entirely," Kincaid said. "Were you around the day Katie went missing?"

"Home watching the space landing, like everyone else."

"Is this *your* stable?"

"It is. Do a little farming, too. Barley, mostly. Have some livestock. Wish I had a piece of that bog. The prices they're getting for peat bricks—"

Kincaid followed the stable owner toward the next stall.

"Oats and straw, straw and oats," he said. "Ah, girl, you're low on water." He patted the horse's forehead.

"Was anyone else here the day Katie was taken?"

"Well, sir, Mister—"

"Kincaid."

"Sligo Station?"

"Dublin," Kincaid said. "Central Detective Unit."

"Ooh. Well, sir, I do hope you catch the bastards. Whoever done this."

"You were saying about someone else being here?"

"What day was that?" the stable owner said.

"April seventeenth."

"Might have been. Anyone boarding a horse coulda come by. I don't know who and I wouldn't remember even if I did. They don't have to check in with me. Guards are gonna interview all of them, my boarders. Probably all home watching the astronauts."

Kincaid looked beyond the door, through hay and dust in streaming sun. He walked out and looked across the narrow valley, then down, at the bog and the outline of the police tape, at the ditch where Katie's body was dumped, at the road beyond. He stared until the stable owner emerged.

"All done," he said. "And happy, everyone is." He walked toward his pickup truck.

"Do ya have," Kincaid called out, hurrying toward the truck. The stable owner was half inside the driver's seat.

"Did ya get any new clients?" Kincaid asked.

"How new?"

"Anyone after April seventeenth."

"I may have. Don't know off hand, though."

"Do you have a list I can see?"

"A list, a list. Might I be needin' a warrant from ya, too?"

"I can get one."

"I wonder if maybe you should."

"You said you wanted us to catch the bastards," Kincaid said.

Hand on the steering wheel, the stable owner stared through the windshield, a resigned smile crossing his lips. He reached into the glove box and pulled out a receipt book. "Starts in

January," he said, handing it to Kincaid. "Some are weekly, others monthly. Couple mighta boarded for the day, but not many."

Kincaid flipped to April, to Monday, April 20, 1970, where a *Philip Carricker* paid cash in pounds and pence.

"This horse still here?" Kincaid asked, his thumb against Carricker's name.

"No, no. Brother picked her up a few days ago."

"*Brother* Carricker? From the seminary?"

"He is. McGuinn's, outside Collooney," the stable owner said.

"Didn't know they kept horses."

"Have their *own* stable! But ran out of room until now. Brother was on a monthly plan here."

"What day did he pick up his horse?" Kincaid asked.

"Should be in that book," the stable owner said. "Last week. Matter of fact, about the time the Guards showed up down there."

"Do the Guards know he boarded here?"

"They just came round asking after my boarder list. Brother wasn't on it no more. But now you know," the stable owner said.

"AH, MR. KINCAID." THE innkeeper held up some small notes. "Rang for you. Hall phone's available, if you be needing it."

"I take it you're not starting anybody, at least not too much," John McDermott said over the phone.

"They've gone back to Dublin," Kincaid said. "Waiting on the postmortem. Ryan seems convinced a local priest is behind it."

"Now we know why he asked for you. What might your expert opinion be?"

"I don't know enough," Kincaid said. "I've gone over all the interview notes, the evidence file. Circumstantially, the priest makes an okay suspect. But no evidence points in his direction."

"I take it you haven't interviewed him yet?" McDermott said.

"Need my house in order first."

"Do his superiors have similar inklings?"

"They may. Tiernan says there's rumors about Father Kyle may be transferred."

"And we all know how that can play out, once the Church gets involved," McDermott said. "Honest Jack's Arms Crisis has gifted us a young, inexperienced hand at Justice. An inexperienced hand is an impressionable hand, particularly in the hands of a wily Archbishop with a phalanx of solicitors who doubtless know the fine points of Supreme Court cases like *O'Callaghan.*"

"Well put, though I'm not sure I agree."

"You don't follow politics the way I do. You'd best interview Father soon. And with delicate hands. Before they're tied."

"Tomorrow," Kincaid said. "I have some questions I haven't seen in the interview notes."

"Speaking of delicate hands. That lovely new document examiner with Technical was asking after you the other day. You made quite an impression, it seems."

"Hopefully Ryan won't speak ill of me," Kincaid said.

"She doesn't seem a fan of IS, so I wouldn't worry too much. How do you like murder squad, by the way?"

"Tell Greevey you overheard me praising the assignment."

"As you should," McDermott said. "You'll make inspector that much sooner. Never thought Tech would out pace us for career advancement."

"I wonder," Kincaid said. "Ryan isn't exactly forthcoming with everything they've been doing here. Tiernan doesn't like him, either."

"You know Ryan's reputation," McDermott said. "But you have some latitude, so use it."

KINCAID'S CAR CREPT UP the asphalt drive so slowly, he heard sticks and pebbles and gravel pop and crunch, stone by stone, stick by stick, beneath the tires. He parked away from windows and walked around the building, looking for the seminary's beige van. On his way back, toward the front entrance, he looked across a hillside vista toward the roads below, starting the journey to Katie Dunleavy's bicycle in his mind.

"You must be the detective with the Guards."

Kincaid jumped.

"Sorry to startle you. Brother Peter." The young man extended his hand.

"Adam Kincaid. Central Detective Unit."

"You're here from Dublin, too?"

"I am."

"The others, they had a different name."

"Technical Bureau," Kincaid said. "Investigations Section."

"Not what they're calling them in town," Brother Peter said.

"Murder squad, you mean."

"Sounds like a television show. This whole terrible affair—." He stopped. "You're here to see Father Kyle."

"And Brother Carricker," Kincaid said.

"Brother Phil. They're inside. Follow me, is it—detective or inspector?"

"Detective Garda, actually. Inspector is a few grades away."

"Like Brother and Father, some would say."

"YOU *CALLED* FIRST," FATHER Kyle said, extending both hands in a warm greeting. "I appreciate that. The other Guards just showed up at the door."

"I appreciate you're meeting with me."

"Do I have a choice?"

"Not—" Kincaid caught himself and thought about how to answer. "Not with the other group, perhaps. But I'm from a different division."

"I was beginning to think Brother Phil and I needed a solicitor, the way they were carrying on."

"Oh?"

"Sit, please. Can I get you anything?"

"No, no thank you."

"Let me get Brother Phil, then. He was just in the library."

Kincaid watched Father Kyle leave the room and looked around, through clear glass and stained glass on a morning that turned suddenly bright after a week of implacable gray. He breathed in the room, cooking odors and shaving kits, flowers in vases, remnants of a new carpet's factory smell. He let the stillness of the place settle over his thoughts.

Low, gruff voices emerged from the hall, Kyle first, Carricker frowning behind him. Kyle brought the two men together, hands on both shoulders.

"Detective, this is Philip Carricker. Brother Phil."

The younger man shook Kincaid's hand weakly and wordlessly, looking down just enough Kincaid thought him furtive.

"Let's all sit." Father Kyle directed them to a sofa and two large upholstered chairs next to a table with a floral arrangement. "We are at your service, detective."

Brother Philip broke his reticence when Kincaid mentioned the van.

"I did *not* fill it with petrol that day or that night," he insisted. "The station attendant's mistaken."

"There were other vans around that night," Fr. Kyle said. "We came forward when the Guards came round asking about vans. We were the only ones came forward, they said."

"You weren't forced to come forward?" Kincaid asked.

"By whom?"

"Youth club families who know the van."

"No, detective. Nothing like that."

"Where is the van, by the way? I didn't see it outside."

"Out for repairs," Brother Phil said.

"Have either of you been fingerprinted?"

"Why on Earth for?" Kyle said.

"They fingerprinted everyone about," Kincaid said. "But not you? Either of you?"

Kyle looked at Carricker. "No, detective. No one in the seminary, that I know of. We have thirteen men here."

Another Ryan omission Kincaid noted in his pad.

"I know you told Detective Ryan where you both were that day, but would you mind going over it again?" Kincaid asked.

"Of course. We were here," Father Kyle said.

"Watching the Moon shot return," Brother Philip said.

"Where was the van then?" Kincaid asked.

"I don't know. They keep a log," Father Kyle said.

"They?" Kincaid asked.

"We, I mean. We keep a log and the Guards checked it."

"There's nothing in the log between four and eight in the evening the day Katie went missing," Kincaid said.

"It was here, then," Carricker said.

"Several people saw it elsewhere," Kincaid said.

"As I said, *we* were here."

"Alone?"

"Together." Kyle gestured between him and Brother Philip. "Others came and went. Maybe one of them took the van."

"But you're vouching for one another?" Kincaid said.

Father Kyle looked at Brother Phil. "Yes," the brother said.

They spent nearly an hour going over Father Kyle's stay at the Dunleavy home, the mysterious car he followed that vanished near the bog, and Brother Philip's whereabouts before and after Katie's disappearance.

"That wasn't in the interview notes," Kincaid said about more than one omission.

"It wasn't?" Father Kyle.

"I told the Guards. They knew," Brother Phil.

Kincaid shifted in the chair, prompting Father Kyle to rise in happy anticipation.

"Would either of you have been riding a horse the day Katie vanished?" Kincaid asked.

Father Kyle slowly sat. "I don't own a horse,."

Brother Philip said nothing.

"The horse at the stable above the Limgahn Bog," Kincaid said.

"We have our own stable," Father Kyle said.

"Stable owner says he was boarded because you ran out of room," Kincaid said.

"She's a mare, not a stallion," Brother Philip blurted. "And no, I didn't ride her that day. It was raining."

Father Kyle glared out the window.

"Where was she boarded at that time?" Kincaid asked.

"Here, detective," Carricker said. "She was boarded here."

"When did you move her to the stable at Limgahn?"

Kyle and Carricker exchanged glances Kincaid thought suggestive.

“The Order doesn’t like the idea, but I wonder if we shouldn’t do with a solicitor,” Father Kyle said.

“That’s your right,” Kincaid said. “Though my questions shouldn’t be prompting you to exercise it.”

“No?” Kyle asked. “We’ve a young man here beginning his life and I would never forgive myself if I were to sit by and allow him to muck it up over a few misguided characterizations.”

“What might those be?” Kincaid asked.

The Father donned a fresh smile. “I think we must be finished here today, detective.”

Four

Mrs. Dunleavy collapsed into her husband's arms on the postmortem news that Katie was strangled.

"What about—what else?" her father asked. "You know?"

"If you mean rape—" Detective Tiernan said.

"I don't want to hear about this," her mother said. "I just—I can't."

"Wait," her husband mouthed to Tiernan and Kincaid. He took his wife to their bedroom and quietly closed the door. "Why don't we step outside?" he said.

"She was raped and dismembered," Tiernan explained.

"Oh, God," Mr. Dunleavy said. "Why would anyone do that to her? Isn't stealing her and raping her and ending her little life quite enough? Quite fucking enough?"

"We believe her assailant—or assailants—was hoping—" Tiernan paused, looked at Kincaid.

"What? You believe what?"

Kincaid swallowed, thinking about how to put it.

"Out with it," Dunleavy said. "You're believin' what now?"

"We believe they wanted to make it easier for animals to cart off the body," Kincaid said. "Postmortem found incomplete cuts on what was left. For whatever reason, they gave up. Had they not, it's doubtful we would have found her."

"Bloody awful," Mr. Dunleavy said. "I'm glad her mother isn't hearing this. And she never will, not from my tongue." He looked at Tiernan. "Are you gonna catch the bloody bastards did this?"

"We're doing our best," Tiernan said.

"I know ya are, I feel ya are," Dunleavy said. "But what if your best an't good enough?"

KINCAID BRIEFED RYAN, TIERNAN, and McDermott about his interview with the two clerics and the horse stable revelations.

"Interesting timing, them moving the horse while gardaí scouring the area," Ryan said. "Good work checking it out."

"I traipsed up there by chance," Kincaid said. "I thought it was an empty barn. I hadn't heard otherwise."

"Well, we did interview the stable owner. Right after the body was found."

"I heard," Kincaid said. "But not from you."

"Well, then. I haven't gotten to everything."

"So it seems."

"I expect to hear from the Archdiocese," Ryan said curtly. "I've asked Tiernan to keep an eye on the seminary. You, too."

IRISH DANCERS BEARING FLOWERS followed Katie Dunleavy to the grave a week after she was returned to the living.

She was happy in Heaven, the parish priest who buried her told the gathering, his eyes periodically falling on Kincaid.

Katie's journey began with the Heavenly host, those armies of angels who came to her family's aid, feeding them, staying with them, praying with them, saying special masses in their home, never leaving their sides, the celebrant explained, the reference to Father Kyle not lost on Kincaid.

How fitting that The Order of St. Michael, Archangel and chief among the Heavenly host, had seen to it that Katie Dunleavy could pass to eternal life unbound, by grief, by sorrow, by the selfish love that ties the dead to the living, the celebrant continued.

Kincaid watched Mrs. Dunleavy sway and nod, the Father's assurances a carriage of condolence.

"We ask why, why a child like this?" the Father said. "Kind and gentle. An innocent who harmed no one, who loved life, loved to sing and dance and learn. Loved her family and her church. Why an innocent whose whole life lay ahead?"

He let the words settle.

"I don't know," the priest said. "It is not in my power to explain the inexplicable, to second guess the hand of the Almighty. Why are innocents ever taken from us? The best we can do is live without grief, sorrow, anger, and remorse, so that they may bask in Heaven's warmth, free of worry over their loved ones down here."

A LETTER FROM THE Order of St. Michael, in an envelope addressed to Kincaid, arrived at the inn next day. The salutation addressed the Minister for Justice and the Garda Commissioner.

"We are shocked, outraged, and hurt by the promulgation of malicious rumours under the watchful eyes of the Guard," the letter began. "We have heard and read the most horrid things: that one or more of our resident clergy murdered young Katie Dunleavy and cut her up for wolves and wild pigs and anything else roaming about with a thirst for human blood. We demand our name be cleared, rumours stopped, and further interrogations halted, as they have left moral and mental scars on our innocent men."

Then an odd thing. "Mr. Kincaid," the innkeeper said. "This note was attached to the letter. I guess it fell off—I found it on the chair."

Fr. Colm Kyle felt "our interview went poorly, and we would like to set the record straight."

KINCAID CLEARED THE SECOND interview with Inspector Ryan, who spent more time saying "I told you so," than discussing strategy. Kincaid went back to the seminary, expecting Father Kyle alone, naively perhaps.

"Thank you for meeting us, Inspector," the Order's solicitor, a Mr. Harvey, said.

"I admit being surprised to find that note attached to your client's letter," Kincaid said. "And to find you here."

"I understand," he said, as Father Kyle and Brother Philip appeared from the hallway. "The Order is *very* concerned that nothing be misinterpreted or misspoken. They believe I can help. Father Kyle tells me he rather unceremoniously interrupted your line of questions."

"With threats of a solicitor," Kincaid said. Mr. Harvey smiled uncomfortably. "I was asking about the horse," Kincaid said.

"Father," the solicitor led.

"Actually, it's Brother's horse, so I'll let him explain," Kyle said.

As Carricker explained about how replacing rotted wood in the Order's stable forced him to temporarily relocate his mare, Kincaid noticed a stammer. Brother Carricker didn't remember the exact day he moved the mare to Limgahn, but it was in April.

"And the horse was returned to the seminary stable when?" Kincaid asked.

"This month," Brother Phil said, dodging the exact day.

"Katie was a wonderful dancer," Kyle intervened. "She used to dance here on Sundays. Why would any of us kill her?"

The interruption caught Kincaid off guard. He looked at Mr. Harvey.

"No one from the Guards has accused you of any killing, have they?" Mr. Harvey asked.

"No, and rightfully not." Kyle turned to Kincaid. "I have my own theory, and I think you should hear it," the priest said.

"Certainly," Kincaid said.

"I think the security forces kidnapped the child," Kyle said. "I seem them more and more. They seem to be everywhere since the start of the Troubles and the riots up North and all the masses streaming across the border."

"Which security forces, exactly?" Kincaid asked.

"Special Branch," Father Kyle said. "That's where I would start."

"Why would a Garda division kidnap a child?"

"Simple," Kyle said. "To instigate a search that might turn up a cache of weapons. IRA guns, due in the South from London. Your Special Branch is all up into this Arms Crisis. I read the papers, you know."

"You have to admit," Mr. Harvey said. "The idea does have merit."

"Special Branch informed the Taoiseach," Kincaid said. "Why the need for anything so elaborate and diabolical?"

"Why else?" Mr. Harvey said. "To fight the radicals."

"I also want you to know, I did use the monastery van that day," Kyle said. "I didn't sign it out. But it was earlier in the afternoon. And Brother—"

"I filled it with petrol," Brother Phil said. "That was all I did with it, in the morning."

"So you *were* at the petrol station that day?" Kincaid asked.

"I was," Brother Phil admitted. "But much earlier than the attendant says."

"Either of you ever offer Katie a lift?" Kincaid asked.

Father and Brother looked at one another and after Mr. Harvey gave the nod, "No," Father Kyle said. "She was never far from home whenever I saw her. No need for a lift."

"I hope this puts to rest to these horrid rumors" Mr. Harvey said, as he stood and shook Kincaid's hand.

"I hope so, too," Kincaid said.

"The Order will be pleased to learn that. The Archdiocese, as well."

GUESTS OF THE INN were either checked out or going about their business mid-morning when Kincaid settled into the uncomfortable chair next to the hallway telephone. He stared at a business card then dialed, stopped, hung up, dialed again, let the call ring, then hung up. Just when he thought he knew what he was going to say, he didn't know, so with each hang up came a renewed effort to gather his thoughts.

"Marta Carney," answered the voice on the other line.

"Bangh—I mean, Detective Garda Carney."

He took a deep quiet breath.

"Yes? And who might this be?"

"Adam Kincaid," he said. "From—"

"Central Detective Unit. I thought I recognized your voice."

"I—Superintendent McDermott said you were by his office and—he seemed to think—"

"I was," Marta said. "I don't get over to Phoenix Park much anymore and I saw John in the hall. He was my favorite guest lecturer at Templemore."

"John?"

"Oh yes. No one can turn the absurdities of life in the Guards into entertaining stories like Superintendent McDermott."

"I'm sure I've provided some grist."

"He never mentioned names," Marta said. "So you were saying about your boss?"

"I have a better question," Kincaid said. "What do you think of Dan Ryan?"

Kincaid thought he heard her sigh. She did pause. "You're out there with him," Marta said.

"I was. Technical has returned to the Castle."

"Dan's a good detective. But I can't work for him."

"Why not?"

"I don't mean him, so much as murder squad. I question why we need part of Technical devoted to investigations when we have CDU. It just doesn't work for me. But that doesn't mean—what do *you* think of Dan Ryan?"

"Good detective," Kincaid said. "Has the right instincts. I wasn't sure at first, I'm still not convinced, but his person of interest in this case gets more interesting by the day."

"And?"

"And what?"

"So he's a good detective. I hear you're a good detective. How are the two getting on?"

"He's not sharing enough. I don't know if it's an oversight or something else," Kincaid said. "Otherwise, the two are getting on."

"He may be testing you—see what you come up with on your own," Marta said.

"How long have you been with Technical?" Kincaid asked.

"Just crossed the two-year mark. But it seems like I just started. I feel like I still don't know anything."

"Why documents?"

"I love to read. And if you ask me why the Guards, police run in my bloodline."

"Guards?"

"UK. Bobbies and constables and high sheriffs. I was raised in London. Came here for school. But for Trinity, not Templemore. It's not a woman's job, you know. Unless of course you're a 'horse face.'"

"Which you are definitely not," Kincaid said.

"Why, thank you, Detective. I'll take that as an overdue vote of confidence."

KINCAID HEARD A NOTE slip under his door.

"Thought you'd want to know," Mr. Dunleavy told him later that day. "We heard through youth club. I left word at Sligo Station."

"They're both gone?"

"Both. And they didn't even say goodbye. Me missus is beside herself. It seems a real slight."

Before long, Tiernan, Ryan, and Kincaid were commiserating.

"Order had no answers," Ryan said on the phone. "Diocese no answer. Archdiocese neither."

GARDA TIERNAN RETURNED FROM the seminary with word the diocesan bishop had approved the twin transfers of Father Colm Kyle and Brother Philip Carricker, but to where they would not say.

"Do I have your consent then?" Kincaid asked Ryan.

"A delicate chore," Ryan said. "I'm tempted to say this is a ministerial duty, or at the lowest, Mr. Wymes."

"The bishop may not even see me," Kincaid said. "Nothing ventured . . ."

"What does McDermott say?"

"Told ya so."

"So he's not opposed?" Ryan said. "Figures. Never shies from rocking the boat, that one."

"He thinks it will go nowhere, but as long as I employ tact in the extreme. . ."

"Tact," Ryan said. "Maybe *that's* the secret to post-Macushla promotion."

Five

Church bells pealed, loud and brisk over the cold, gray river city. A small ferry approached a dock, a solemn-looking Kincaid grasping the side. The boat throttled to a stop and anchored and Kincaid stepped off.

"Can you point me the fastest way to the Sacred Heart cathedral?" he asked a dockworker.

"Up there," the man pointed. "North Hill. The monied district."

A SILVER-HAIRED WOMAN with a Parkinsonian tremor answered the door to the bishop's residence and office.

"What may I say is your business?" she asked.

"I have an audience.," Kincaid said.

"You mean an appointment." She smirked. "Audience. I haven't heard that in a while. Reserved for the Holy Father, it is. With whom, now, is your appointment?"

"Bishop Shannon."

She led Kincaid to an expansive foyer of hand-carved, polished oak. "Wait here while I get Monsignor," she said.

A small, stooped man opened a towering door.

"Mr. Kincaid. I'm afraid Bishop Shannon is unable to meet with you."

"I—"

"Not to worry," Monsignor said. "He's asked the vicar general to take his place."

"I've come a long way. I was hoping to interview the bishop."

"Yes, well. He's very busy these days, especially with the trouble up north. But he always cooperates with the Guards."

"We've talked to him before?"

"Yes, but not today."

"Then the vicar general it will have to be," Kincaid said.

The old monsignor led Kincaid past the large door into an office with seven-foot tall stained glass windows overlooking the river.

"John Brendan," said the vicar general with his hand extended. "You've come to inquire to about a Father Kyle, Colm Kyle, I understand.

"I have," Kincaid said. "And a brother, Philip Carricker."

"What can I tell you?"

"Why were they transferred? Where were they transferred?"

"Always pleased to cooperate—Inspector?"

"Detective."

"Always happy to cooperate with the Guards. Why are you interested in Father Kyle's whereabouts? I wasn't briefed about that part."

"He's a person of interest in a homicide investigation."

"Dear."

"Girl, age of ten. Near Collooney."

"Oh my. I'm so sorry to hear this."

"We understand both Father and Brother were transferred, with this office's approval."

"Is that what their order told you?" the vicar general asked.

"The Order sent me here," Kincaid said. "Their superior general did not feel they had adequate permission to provide details. Their solicitor insisted I look elsewhere."

"Solicitor. Hmm. Well, in any event, the Catholic Church is no haven for psychopaths, I hope you understand."

"Better than most. I was a seminarian."

"Is that so?" Brendan said. "Where, if I may ask?"

"Kiltyclogher."

"The border. Lovely church there, St. Patrick's."

"I know it well," Kincaid said.

"So you also know the Church doesn't harbor psychopaths, but rather, future gardaí. What possible sane motive would either of these clerics have for killing a young girl?" Brendan asked. "Or was it an unforeseeable accident?"

"We won't know any more until we can interview them further."

"I wish I could help you, detective. But—"

"Are you saying you don't know where they are?"

"I'm saying I'm not at liberty to discuss their whereabouts or their transfers. I'm afraid you've wasted a trip."

"Probably for the best," Kincaid said. "I didn't relish discussing the details of Katie Dunleavy's postmortem. Let the newspapers do that."

"Is that the wee one's name? How old did you say, again?"

"Ten," Kincaid said.

"And this postmortem—"

"It would be impossible to confirm any of the more disturbing findings that suggest a motive, without more interviews."

"Detective, you needn't play games with me. What will His Eminence be reading in the newspapers?"

"Which Eminence?" Kincaid asked. "The Archbishop may see it first, being in a larger city with more newspapers."

Kincaid turned toward the door.

"You think we're trying to hide something, is that it, Detective?"

"Father Kyle hasn't vanished because he witnessed the Archbishop jaywalking," Kincaid said.

"What happened to the child?" Brendan asked.

"Not until you tell me where I can find your missing clerics."

Without a word, Fr. Brendan vanished through another tall door, emerging momentarily with Bishop Shannon.

"Father Kyle and Brother Carricker are in Africa," Bishop Shannon said in a tone Kincaid found unceremonious. "Democratic Republic of the Congo. Now tell us, Kincaid is it, was the child raped?"

"Bishop Shannon."

"I am. And I am waiting."

"She was," Kincaid said.

"You'll be hearing from our solicitors should a word of the Church appear in any way connected with this tragedy," Bishop

Shannon said. "That includes further besmirching the reputations of Colm Kyle and Philip Carricker. Are we understood?"

KINCAID SAT ALONE IN a dark pub, hand around a glass of straight whiskey. The door opened to three men and a woman, laughing, boisterous, an intimate whirlwind of gaiety. They sounded French to Kincaid and they sat at a table a few feet away. He glanced over as a barkeeper took their orders and returned with a round. He lowered his eyes to a menu he'd already read.

"Hello."

Kincaid looked up. Was she addressing him from two booths over, male compatriots talking and laughing in the background?

"Hello?" she asked. "Yes. In fact, hello is just what I said."

"Hello," Kincaid said.

She spoke with her friends, slipped out of her seat, and walked to him. Her angular features, eyes, lips, cheekbones, narrowed into an alluring smile.

"My apologies," Kincaid went to stand.

"No, no, no," she said, her hand on his shoulder.

"I was preoccupied. Please." He indicated the bench opposite and she obliged. "I saw you come in."

"How could you have possibly missed us?"

Kincaid extended his hand.

"Adam Kincaid."

"Katerin Du Mond," she said, grasping his fingers. "A pleasure."

"I didn't expect to meet anyone here."

"One must always expect the unexpected. Pithy and obvious, I know."

"Not at all. I make my livelihood of it."

"The pithy and obvious?"

"The unexpected," Kincaid said.

"Really." She leaned in. "What do you do, if I may pry?"

"I'm with the Guards," he said.

"The Guards? You'll have to forgive me—"

"The police."

"The police! How fascinating. What do you do for the police?"

"I'm a detective."

"A detective? You solve murders?"

"And other crimes."

"Have you solved any murders lately?"

"Too—"

She stood and put her finger on his lips, went back to her table, grabbed her beer and returned.

"You were saying," she said.

"Too many murders."

"Any famous ones?"

"Run of the mill lot, mostly. Knifings, shootings, husband beating his wife to—" He sipped his whiskey.

"You can say it. Death. Which murderer brings you here?"

"The devil himself, I'm beginning to think."

"Does this devil have a name?"

"He does. But you wouldn't know him."

"I don't suppose I would," Katerin said. "But that's a good thing, no?"

The barkeeper lit a candle on their table.

"Katerin," one of the men from the other table called. He waved her back. She waved him off with a smile. "We've lost her again," he told his friends and they laughed.

"What do you do?" Kincaid asked, watching the candlelight dance on her necklace.

"Me? Nothing of much substance, I'm afraid. Not like a policeman."

"Now you have me even more curious."

"The detective in you."

"If I may pry."

"I sing," Katerin said. "I'm an opera singer."

"A diva?"

"To my circle of fans and friends, absolutely," she cooed.

"My mother sang opera," Kincaid said.

"Your mother? What's her name? I may have heard of her."

"Evelyn. Evelyn Doran. Before she married. She had more fans on the Continent than she did here. They called her Mademoiselle Papillon."

"Was that her favorite opera?"

"She played Suzuki many times, but always wanted to play Cio-Cio-san," Kincaid said.

"Tragedy runs in your family."

"How did you know?"

"Being a mezzo-soprano," Katerin said. "It's a curse. I long to play Lucia, but that role—"

"Goes to the soprano," Kincaid completed.

"You know your opera." She shot her eyes toward the other table. "You see my friends. We're performing tomorrow night. Will you be in town?"

"Now, I wish I could be."

"That sounds promising." She slipped out of the seat. "I really must go. Why don't you come and see us?"

"My business here was ended prematurely," Kincaid said. "I have to go back to Dublin."

"One more day? Perhaps to spend in quiet contemplation while we rehearse? Doesn't detection require contemplation?"

"I could make that argument."

"Then why don't you? Royal Theatre, seven. Tomorrow night. Your seat will be waiting."

She smiled and turned and faded back to her troupe.

DESPITE ITS NAME, THE Royal Theatre was small, nondescript, impoverished even, which its founders would argue kept the focus on the art, not the frame. Kincaid at first wondered if he was in the right place. He made his way through the crowd to a marquee that confirmed Katerin du Mond as Pitti-Sing in *The Mikado*, a role his mother played, and in her explanations, one of his early introductions to the power of satire.

In his seat in the dim light, the stage ready and bare in front of the curtain, Kincaid felt a hand on his shoulder and wheeled around.

"I can't wait for the encore," Katerin whispered, then disappeared down the aisle.

A TAXI DELIVERED THE pair to the front of a brick rowhouse, where Katerin took Kincaid's arm and steadied him as they walked up the steps.

"So you liked it?" she asked him in the hallway "You adored me?"

"Yes," he gasped. "I adored you."

She laughed as she unlocked her door. "A drink?"

"No, I—"

"I'll have one for both of us, then."

"You have a nice place," he said when they were inside. "Very warm."

"Thank you. The theatre provides it."

"How long are you here?"

"A fortnight this time. We come back in the spring."

Drink in hand, she tugged him to the sofa, moved her hand around his shoulder.

"Wh—I—where are you from? You never told me," he asked.

"I was born," she proclaimed, raising her drink as in a toast, "in Kiev. Ukraine. They call it Soviet something now, but it is Ukraine."

"Da—du Mond?"

"Try fitting Kateryna Myelovych Fyodorovna Tereshchenko on that little marquee."

She kissed him. Again. And again. Softly, playfully. Kincaid's body stiffened.

"I—I'm not sure," he said.

"Not sure of what?"

He backed away, almost imperceptibly at first. She moved closer.

"Where this is going," he said.

Kincaid felt a knot in his stomach, heat on his face, sweat on his hands. Katerin's fingers traveled to the top button of his shirt.

"Where is what going?" she asked. She pressed her hand against the top of his chest. "You're hot." She glanced his cheek with the back of her palm. "Hot, hot, hot. Do you have a fever?"

He opened his mouth to answer, but only a short pant came out.

"You don't look sick," she said.

He pushed up from the couch and stood.

"Adam?"

"I think I should go."

"Why? I won't bite. Maybe scratch, but only a little."

He grabbed his jacket and stumbled toward the door.

"At least let me call you a taxi," she said.

But he was out the door before she rose from the couch. He fumbled through the hallway, felt woozy as he looked down the stairs, grabbed the handrail and took it step by slow step. He crumpled two steps before the landing, choked as he tried to catch his breath, jerked away at the same soft hand on his arm.

"I'm sorry," Katerin whispered.

"It's all right," he said. "It's not you. I'm the one should be sorry."

"I wasn't listening," she said.

"You did nothing wrong. I'm just—"

Another tenant came through the door with a package and some letters. Katerin moved down the steps and out of the way. The woman smiled at both of them, walked up the stairs past Kincaid propped against the wall.

"If you wait, I'll call you a taxi. You're staying in a hotel?" Katerin asked.

"Yes," he said, staring straight. "That would be fine."

"Are you sure you're all right?" she asked.

"Yes."

As Katerin brushed past him on the way back up, "Why," he asked, "did you come over to me? In the pub?"

She stopped and he heard her breath. She didn't say anything, just stood and looked at him. She continued the rest of the way up and he heard her hand moving on the stair rail and her footsteps on the wood floor overhead, and her door not open, but close.

Six

"And I was calling you a lucky lad." John McDermott stuck his head into Kincaid's office, where the detective had his hand on a stack of paperwork.

"A year and a half later, and I'm still filling and filing," Kincaid said.

"You angered the wrong people. Just be glad they have another person of interest. Any word on that fisherman?"

"I haven't asked and Ryan hasn't said." Kincaid plunked an arm on the paperwork. "We both know who did it, why he did it, and why he and his accomplice were sent away. I don't want any part in charades just to keep the right people happy."

"I tried to warn you. *Delicate* hands."

"Yes you did. And I listened," Kincaid said. "Did everything by the book, I did. But delicate hands have no grip."

"What did Greevey tell you when the trip to Africa idea came up? What good would it do, right? Even if we could locate them. They wouldn't talk. And given the Church's status in the Congo, they probably have some sort of diplomatic immunity regardless."

"We'll take the Heavy Gang, then. Beat it out of them."

"There is no Heavy Gang."

"Marta says different."

"Adam." McDermott leaned in. "We will *never* know what really happened to little Katie Dunleavy. We have our walls of silence. The Church has theirs."

"MISSING PERSON'S INVESTIGATION," SUPERINTENDENT Greevey had told Kincaid in his Phoenix Park office.

"Why is the Murder Squad involved?"

"They believe the missing woman was murdered," Greevey said. "I'm not sure the preliminary investigation supports such a conclusion, but it's not my case. Higher ups want another set of eyes on the thing."

"And I'm the eyes," Kincaid said.

"It's also your turn at the border, Detective *Sergeant*. After this, I've no doubt we'll be calling you *Inspector*. How *is* your lovely mother, by the way?"

"More eager for the promotion than I am."

"Hah!" Greevey said. "I understand her excitement."

"I don't know if I'd call it excitement."

"Anticipation, then."

"This country has a terrible history with public care," Kincaid said. "But private care is hard to afford on a sergeant's pay."

"I don't blame you for wanting the best for your mum," Greevey said. "Find this girl or God forbid, her killers, and be done with the thing. We're tired of sharing you."

"Then promote me," Kincaid said.

KINCAID ENTERED AN INTERROGATION room where two Garda detectives—one standing, one seated—were so close to a young man they looked to be smothering him.

"Dick was just sayin' here he saw a certain kind of car in the area, weren't ya, Dick?"

"I was sayin' I didn't see *any* car there."

The detective punched his shoulder. "Don't start lying now there's a stranger in the room." The detective looked up at Kincaid, then back at the witness. "What kind was it again?"

"I didn't see any car," the twenty-something man repeated. "None of us did. You can ask us, any of us."

"We already have," the second detective said. "Your mates said it was a Zephyr."

"Where ya from, lad?"

"Already told ya."

"For the sergeant here."

The witness looked at Kincaid. "Can you tell 'em to stop hitting me?"

The seated detective slugged his shoulder again.

"Is that really necessary?" Kincaid said. "Lad's from right here in Conneskillen."

"Ya do your homework," the seated detective said to Kincaid. "DPP might not do his, then we get blamed, right O'Reilly?"

"That's how it's played," the standing detective said.

"I'm a sergeant and I outrank both of you and I say it's not played that way," Kincaid said. "Stop hitting the lad."

"What? Like this?" The seated detective backhanded the young man in the cheek where it wouldn't bruise. Kincaid lunged toward him. O'Reilly blocked.

"Okay," the witness said, rubbing his face. "It was a Zephyr."

"You don't have to say that," Kincaid said. "Not unless it's true."

"What are you, his solicitor now?"

"Best let it be, sergeant. Best let it be," O'Reilly said. "Two of us, one of you, and this chancer. Who they gonna believe?"

"No recorder's on," the sitting detective said. "Gonna be a body turn up and we already have our man."

"And who might that be?" Kincaid asked.

"Only one owns a Zephyr in the village."

O'Reilly's partner slid a paper across to Dick. "Sign it," he said.

"I have to sign something?" Dick said. "You never said I had to sign something."

"Sign it," the detective banged his palm on the table, "or I'll cut your bloody hand off and sign it for you."

Kincaid took a deep, distressed breath, as Dick's hand scrawled a shaky signature.

"YOU CAUGHT THEM ON one of their better days," Marta told Kincaid at lunch that afternoon.

"There have to be complaints."

"Oh, plenty," Marta said. "But they like to hit where it won't bruise."

"I noticed," Kincaid said. "They coerced that signature. I can't let that stand."

"I want to say something, too. But you know what will happen," Marta said.

"McDermott seems to get away with it all right."

"John's sense of humor I don't have," Marta said. "I can't deliver my blows to the brass with a smile. They'll as good as sack me. And I love my job."

"Who else can do whatever you're doing as well as you? I hear you're assigned something to do with Brenden Wryth," Kincaid said.

"Maps, Adam. I'm examining maps. It's not advanced mathematics."

"What does a serial child molester need with maps? Escape routes?"

"Not directly." Marta said. "We think he uses them as currency."

"Money or barter?"

"We think he's selling them to the Provisional IRA. He seems to have an uncanny knowledge of British troop movements in certain locales."

"How on Earth?"

"Simple, maybe," Marta said. "Combatant gossip, to the young, pretty women who work the mother and baby homes. The Magdalene laundries. Wryth is tied in to a couple of them.

Young men with puffed chests have big mouths around young women with puffed—"

"Sounds like Special Branch intrigue," Kincaid interrupted. "Serve Technical right if they lost you."

"Leaving may be my only choice. You know, I think this whole sorry Heavy Gang business was conceived over that *other* priest. The one you lost—not you exactly, but I.S."

"Ryan took it hard," Kincaid said. "He barely speaks to me."

"What about you?"

Kincaid stirred his coffee. "What about me what?"

"How did you take it?"

"I started drinking. Again."

"Drinking? You never drink. We've been out—"

"I drink alone," Kincaid said.

KINCAID CAUGHT HIS BREATH at the top of a rise in the hills, where photographers and crime scene mappers surrounded the discovery.

"Lady taking a walk found her," said Detective Inspector and lead investigator Christian Connolly.

"Ana Cairns," Kincaid said.

"Looks like it. She has a few teeth left. We should know soon enough."

Connolly looked at the naked body. "Nineteen, got off the bus just up the road there. Looks like she was dragged. Probably find the rest of her face down the mountain." He looked Kincaid square in the eyes. "We'll get the lad did this."

THE FIRST MURDER CONFERENCE was light on details.

"I understood a confession was in the offing," Kincaid said. "Everyone in the village seems to think we've our man, too."

"Corrigan wouldn't sign," Inspector Connolly said. "I thought you knew."

"I'm learning more about the case at the local pub than I am from other gardaí," Kincaid said.

"Sorry to hear that, I am," Connolly said. He looked around the table at detective O'Reilly and other Investigation Section staff. "We'll remedy it, won't we? Can't have our special guest from CDU kept in the goddamn dark."

TOP OF CONNESKILLEN STATION'S two-story stairwell, Kincaid heard groans and cries he followed down a dark hallway to a light beneath a windowless door. He rapped on it.

"Kincaid," he said.

"Well in hand, Sergeant."

"Connolly wants a look in."

The noise paused, the door opened to Garda Spencer, the seated detective. Kincaid looked past him, at Billy Corrigan, the reluctant suspect in Ana Cairns' killing.

"And what does Inspector Connolly need to see?"

Kincaid pushed past Spencer. Corrigan eyed him warily, weaving around, his eyelids drooping, closing, fluttering. He looked punch drunk to Kincaid, who propped him up in the chair, looked at his head, grasped a clump of hair that came up without resistance. Kincaid looked at the tile under his feet.

"Is there a reason half this man's scalp is on the floor?" Kincaid asked.

"I hadn't noticed," Detective Garda Spencer said.

"Why are you interrogating him this late at night?"

"I been up two fuckin' days," Corrigan slurred. "He won't turn the light off. And that atrocious music." He nodded toward a radio. "Real loud, he plays it."

Detective Spencer stamped over to Corrigan. "Don't you lie. Don't you fuckin' lie. You tell the sergeant what you did. Tell him! Before I beat the—"

Kincaid grabbed Spencer's arm. "There'll be no beating," he said.

Spencer shook loose.

"It's one on one now," Kincaid said. "Two on one, if you count him."

"I have work to do, Sergeant."

"Not tonight."

"Who says? Connolly tell you this?"

"Superintendent Greevey in CDU."

"Greevey?"

"You've heard of him."

"Who hasn't? I thought you said Inspector Connolly sent you."

"I answer to Greevey," Kincaid said. "And when I tell him what's been going on here for the past two days, Inspector Connolly will be answering to him, too. And the Commissioner. And the Justice Minister."

Spencer looked over at Corrigan, collapsed against the wall with a sick look on his face, mouth open.

"I'll follow you to Mr. Corrigan's home," Kincaid told Spencer.

"Home?" Corrigan said.

"To his bed, if necessary."

"My bed. I don't—"

"You want to stay here?" Kincaid asked.

"He doesn't want to stay here, do ya Billy boy?" Spencer said, a sinister grin on his lips. "Get ya right home, just like the sergeant asked."

"I don't want to go home," Corrigan said.

As Detective Spencer made ready to take Corrigan home, Kincaid slipped the still-unsigned confession off the interrogation room table.

KINCAID AND CONNOLLY PASSED a crude sketch of a noose on the road near Corrigan's house that wasn't there when Kincaid and Spencer dropped him off a week ago. It was big, red, prominent, easily seen in the street light and headlights.

"Warning?" Connolly said.

"Not a wonder."

Corrigan's sister Jenny answered the knock.

"William," she said. "I thought it was William."

"It's about William," Connolly said. "May we come in?"

As Connolly recited the news, Jenny gasped and fell, grabbing his hands on the way down. Through her tears she screamed about the Cairns' brothers blowing their car horn in the wee morning hours and screaming obscenities between blasts.

"I understand why you brought him home and I'm glad you did," Corrigan's mother said after she heard her son was dead. Her eyes bore into Connolly. "They'd have killed him at the station, sure."

"They wouldn't," Jenny objected. "You wouldn't have done that, right? You should have kept him. You could have protected him." Sobs punctuated every word. She was so short of breath, she could barely stand and panted between each sentence.

"I insisted," Kincaid said. "It was me. I insisted they bring him home."

"I know it was you and you didn't mean no wrong," Mother Corrigan said. "Jenny doesn't mean no wrong neither, do you love?"

Jenny shot Kincaid an angry glance and ran up stairs.

"SURELY YOU AREN'T BLAMING yourself," Marta said at dinner the following evening. "I'm not sure I disagree with his mother—had Bill Corrigan remained at the station that night—"

"They bloody well castrated him," Kincaid said.

"Terrible." She reached across the table and placed her palm atop his hand. "But a tragedy no one could have predicted."

"We didn't listen. I didn't listen. He tried to warn us—me and Spencer."

"How *could* you have listened? Or heard anything even if you did? The poor man was delirious from abuse. A policeman I know has confronted the same thing in the North. Forced justice is no justice at all, he likes to say."

"Now we may never know who killed Ana Cairns," Kincaid said.

"And we may. What I do know is you need some sleep. And lucky for you, we have a weekend." Marta looked around the restaurant. "Speaking of which, I'm afraid I need to be going." She put money on the table.

"First you won't let me drive you, and now you're paying?"

"Only for me," she said, standing and winking. She looked down at her dinner date, smiled, and at his side, bent down and kissed his cheek.

"You did the right thing," she said.

KINCAID DID NOT GO home that Friday night, but instead to a low-lit pub where he drank alone. He knew the place: he'd met sources and snitches here, closeted gay men who exchanged information for freedom. The 1861 Offences Against the Person Act and the 1885 Criminal Law Amendment Act, creatures of the UK Parliament and holdovers from the era before Irish independence, outlawed same-sex relations in the Republic. The heavy hand of the Church made the situation that much more unbearable.

The barkeeper slipped a note in front of Kincaid. "Says you'll know what it's about," the barkeeper said, nodding toward a blond man in a dark corner. Kincaid read the scrawl, got up and approached his contact.

"Ave a seat," the man said. He drew on a cigarette, blew a thin smoke stream. "I said—"

"I heard what you said."

"Well then?"

Kincaid eased down across from the man.

"Billy Corrigan didn't kill that girl," the man said.

"Is that so?"

"It is."

"Then who did?"

"Was the girl raped?" the man asked.

"Not that the pathologist can tell."

"Not much left of her face, I heard. Why would anyone do that to her? Rip off her identity like that?"

"Enough evidence points to Billy. That she rebuffed him. That's the theory," Kincaid said.

The man held the cigarette aside.

"A shite theory if there ever was," the man said.

"Why do you say that?"

"They cut his balls off. At the root." Before Kincaid could open his mouth, "Word gets round," the man continued.

"Because his killers thought he raped their sister."

"No."

"You seem pretty sure of yourself."

The man leaned into Kincaid. "Billy was with me the night Ana Cairns died," he said. "And believe you me, I wouldn't have castrated him."

Kincaid leaned back and sighed.

"They killed Ana because she was with Billy. And Billy because he was with me. Me, Billy, *our kind*, they calls it."

"Any way to verify this?" Kincaid asked.

"You mean come forward, out of the shadows?"

"Something like that."

"I've a better idea. Stop looking at her brothers. They weren't exactly fine with Billy, but they knew he'd never marry Ana."

"Have any names?" Kincaid asked.

"Just me own," the man said. "And I'd like to keep my head, if it's all the same to you, Billy being dead and all."

"I don't know if that's possible," Kincaid said.

"I could make it worth your while," the man said.

"Bribing a police officer—"

"No bribe." The man leaned forward. "No bribe at all. I seen ya in here. We all seen ya in here. Seen how ya look—at us."

"Not like that," Kincaid said.

“Exactly like that. When you figure it out.” The man scrawled his phone number on another scrap of paper. “I can be discreet,” he said, slipping the paper to the detective.

Seven

Kincaid and Connolly sat before the superintendent in charge of the Investigations Section, Technical Bureau, of which the murder squad was an informal division and the Heavy Gang was unacknowledged.

"You both know why I wanted to speak with you," Ray Bryant said.

"I'm not clear on it, no," Connolly said.

"Complaints. From the Cairns' woman's family and Billy Corrigan's sister," Superintendent Bryant said. "DPP is making it sound like Corrigan is as much a victim as Cairns. Commissioner's office wants answers."

"I read the letter," Connolly said, opening it. "'The suspect was subjected to very intensive and persistent interrogation that may have involved harsh and oppressive physical tactics unbecoming a garda.' I don't understand how the DPP came by this information if the family didn't supply it."

"Sergeant Kincaid?" Superintendent Bryant asked.

"Inspector Connolly and I have already gone over everything," Kincaid said. "You have what he has."

"I was given to understand our conversation was just between us," Connolly said. "That matters in the DPP's letter weren't substantiated enough to share."

"I'm just now learning about this DPP letter. My observations are in my answer to the Corrigan complaint," Kincaid said.

"Is that so?" Connolly said.

"You visited Mr. Corrigan while he was in custody," the superintendent said to Connolly. "Did you see what Sergeant Kincaid saw?"

"Which was?" Connolly asked.

"A bald spot where Garda Spencer or Garda O'Reilly tore out the suspect's hair."

"Of course not!" Connolly said. "If Sergeant Kincaid saw such a thing, either Corrigan tore out his own hair in frustration over being caught in so many lies, or he was going bald."

"Sergeant."

"A twenty-three-year-old man with a thick head of fiery red hair. Whose hair—was all over—the floor," Kincaid said.

His hands framing its two pages, Bryant frowned at the letter on his desk.

"What about bruising? Did you see any bruising? What was Corrigan's attitude when you were in the room?" the superintendent asked.

"No bruising that I saw," Connolly said. "His attitude I'd say was typical. He was always free to go at any time and he knew it. I thought he was just playing with Spence and O'Reilly."

"Your report says you had Corrigan in custody for more than the requisite twenty four hours," Bryant said. "But it doesn't specify *how* much longer."

"It wasn't quite forty eight. Chief Superintendent authorized it per Section Thirty."

"Which doesn't help matters, honestly," Superintendent Bryant said. "How long was this man kept awake?"

"I don't know," Connolly said.

"Sergeant?"

"He was awake when I came by at three in the morning," Kincaid said.

"The light was on, correct?"

"It was," Kincaid said.

"And this was what—forty hours into the hold time?" the superintendent said.

"*If* that's true," Connolly said.

"Why would you doubt me?" Kincaid asked.

"What about the planting of false rumors in the village?" Bryant interrupted.

"What rumors?" Connolly asked.

"About a witness seeing Corrigan's Zephyr near where Miss Cairns disappeared."

"Sergeant Kincaid report that, too?"

"Dick Duncan, witness, reported it. He says, and I quote, 'The Heavy Gang made me sign a lie. They were beating on me and wouldn't let up until I signed.'"

"The Heavy Gang again," Connolly said. "You know that's a myth, Ray."

“The Cairns family doesn’t seem to think so,” the superintendent said. “No one in the village seems to think so, either.”

“Where would they hear such nonsense?”

“Garda, *they* say. Same garda who spread it around that Billy Corrigan did Ana Cairns. Sergeant Kincaid didn’t use the term *Heavy Gang,* but he did corroborate the duress. Which he also reported to you, isn’t that true, Chris?”

Connolly uncrossed his legs, pulled his head in and glared at Kincaid.

“Inspector Connolly?” Superintendent Bryant repeated.

“He did. He told me,” Connolly said. “Informally, though. I told Spence and O’Reilly to take it easy.”

“I’ve spoken with Gardaí Spencer and O’Reilly separately and they deny the charges,” Bryant said. “So I’m not sure where this goes from here. Meanwhile, do either of you have any questions?”

“Are you concluded with me, Superintendent?” Connolly asked.

“For now.”

Both men rose, but “Sergeant” from the superintendent halted Kincaid. “A word.”

KINCAID LEFT THE INQUIRY with mixed feelings about his responses to the complaint. Honest they were, but political they were not. The voice he heard now encouraged his reservations.

"Ryan warned me," Connolly said, approaching from behind. "Said you'd fuck things up."

"I don't believe you." Kincaid kept walking. Connolly kept up.

"Whole investigation went down the jacks after you got involved. What's not to believe?"

"Ryan warned you and yet you insisted I help with this mess. Makes sense."

"Go back to CDU. We don't need you anymore."

"Fine," Kincaid said. "We'll follow up the new angle on our own."

"More shite," Connolly said. "Some drunk homosexual approaches you in a pub that caters to his ilk, and suddenly the Cairns homicide falls into place."

"That's your problem," Kincaid said. "You aren't willing to let a round peg slide into a round hole. You have to pound the square pegs until by some miracle, they fit."

"Interesting choice of words," Connolly said. "What else are we supposed to do?" he rasped. "I was at the student riots a few years ago. We had batons and nothing else. The press photos didn't begin to tell the story."

"Liam O'Mahoney's death—a frail drunk in a garda cell. The Dunnes Stores debacle," Kincaid returned. "Press didn't begin to tell the story on those, either."

"I wouldn't know," Connolly said. "Not my cases."

Kincaid continued out the front door.

"But Cairns is my case," Connolly yelled. "Leave it the fuck alone."

"ADAM." KINCAID TURNED TO Marta's voice under his umbrella in the snow flurries. She hurried across the street.

"You're working late," he said.

"I could say the same."

"Just wrapping up. I suppose you've heard."

"Vaguely," Marta said. They walked toward his car. "Why don't you have tea with me and tell me all about it."

"Too late for tea. What about whiskey?"

"I don't have any," she said.

"You don't have to. Pub—"

"I wasn't thinking pub," she said. And at his car door, "I'll even let you drive me."

"Your car?" Kincaid said.

"I walked," Marta said. "It was lovely this morning. Now." She looked up at the sky and the thickening snow. "All sins are forgiven."

THEY FOLDED THEIR UMBRELLAS and Marta opened the door to her flat. She took off her coat and gloves and took Kincaid's coat. She placed both palms against his red cheeks.

"Oh, bitter," she said. "I have just the thing."

"Not tea. I'll never sleep."

"Not tea." She held up a bottle of crème de cassis and a tin of cocoa powder.

"Chocolate?"

"With a spark," Marta said. "If you would." She motioned Kincaid into her little kitchen. "Dairy in the fridge. Grab the stout, too," she instructed. "Pots in the press. Two, please. Up there." She pointed to a cabinet over his head.

Marta poured the stout into the first pot. "About ten minutes." Kincaid moved around her toward the front room. "You're needed in the kitchen, Sergeant."

"You're boiling the beer?"

"I'm making a syrup," she said. "Now in this pot, cocoa, sugar, salt, milk. Whisk is in that drawer."

She combined the ingredients in the second pot and took his hand with the whisk and stirred. "Gently but continuously. Until it's nice and hot," she said.

She took down two mugs from another cupboard. "Now to combine things." She poured the boiled-down stout, syrupy now, into the chocolate mix, added the crème de cassis. "And now for the final ingredient." A bottle of green Chartreuse.

"Where did you come up with this?" Kincaid asked.

"Old recipes," Marta said. "I kind of combined them. Into the mugs now."

"Me?"

"Please."

He poured the spiked cocoa into each mug and she added a few tablespoons of Chartreuse. They raised the mugs to their lips.

"You're not drinking alone," Marta said.

Kincaid's smile was visible just above the steaming mug. He cooled the concoction with short breaths. "Sláinte!" he said.

"Sláinte."

KINCAID SPENT THE NEXT two weeks in a kind of interdepartmental limbo, still assigned to the Technical Bureau, Investigations Section, but effectively relieved of his duties therein "pending further investigation of various complaints regarding the section's handling of the Cairns homicide."

"Ahh, the prodigal son," McDermott told Kincaid on the latter man's visit to CDU headquarters. "Here to see Greevey, are ya?"

"I need guidance," Kincaid said.

"And *I* can't provide it?"

"Official."

"I'm as official as they come. Now where's the guidance wanting?"

"I have a solid lead in the Cairns homicide," Kincaid said. "Only trouble is, no one's listening."

"We are," McDermott said.

"Greevey asked to see *me*," Kincaid said. "Any idea why?"

"To announce your overdue promotion. And pick your brain about Cairns. Your lead asserts she and her friend Billy Corrigan were killed by thugs who hate homosexuals," McDermott said. "That's the gist of it, correct?"

"Specific thugs," Kincaid said. "I have names. We need to pick them up."

"And Connolly?"

"Won't hear of it."

"Bryant?"

"Told me not to interfere, that it was Connolly's case."

"Not if you're back here, it's not."

"They don't want this Heavy Gang stuff out," Kincaid said.

"How much does Greevey know about all this, do you think?"

"What he hears. I've tried to respect boundaries. I—"

"Fuck I.S.," McDermott said, stabbing his desk with an ink pen. "And fuck Connolly for thinking you owe him cover. It's not *you* who went to Wymes." McDermott set his pen down. "Let's talk about something more pleasant. Marta—"

"Marta. And?"

"Heard you gave her a lift. From the car park."

"I like her," Kincaid said. "I like her very much."

"So you're leaving Technical at a good time."

"Who said I was leaving?"

"WELCOME BACK," GREEVEY TOLD Kincaid that afternoon. "They don't want you anymore. Aren't you glad to have a family who does?"

"The Cairns homicide?"

"It's being sorted," Greevey said. "Just not by you. Anymore."

"I can't let her brothers—"

"I made sure the DPP got a copy of your response to the Cairns complaint. I don't know that IS would have forwarded it. Miss Cairns' brothers, meanwhile, should be in the clear."

"What about Billy Corrigan?" Kincaid asked. "He didn't kill Ana. William Hodgekiss—"

"Billy Corrigan is dead, Adam. He was never charged—"

"His name was sullied, dragged through the mud," Kincaid said. "The Cairn brothers accused of killing him."

"That's for Technical to sort. They have what they need on Hodgekiss and his friends. I don't want our name sullied."

"What about the RUC? Hodgekiss may go back to Belfast."

"Again, for Technical to sort."

In the silence that followed, Greevey changed the subject.

"How is your wonderful mother? I've been meaning to ask."

"Still waiting."

"And I think I know for what." Greevey stood from behind his desk. "Inspector," he said on his way to the door.

EVELYN KINCAID STARED OUT the third-story window from her wheelchair at a man walking through the snow, head down, face protected, something in hand.

Her son stamped snow from his boots in the foyer.

"Mr. Kincaid. What a pleasant surprise," the duty nurse said. "And you've brought—"

"A housewarming gift. To cheer her up," Kincaid said. "If that's possible."

"I'm sure she'll be delighted."

They walked the hallway, clean and white, no smell of urine, age, or death.

"I've been away again," he said. "How is she taking to the place?"

"I think all right," the nurse said. "Depression comes and goes, but that's nothing out of the ordinary."

They stepped into the elevator.

"Is she in the room we contracted for?" Kincaid asked.

"Not yet," the nurse said.

"Why not?"

"It is ready, that I do know. Maybe financial details."

"What sort of details? I've heard nothing."

"I wouldn't know, Mr. Kincaid. I've seen them hold things up until money is sorted. That's all I know."

Evelyn was still at the window when the nurse rapped on her open door.

"Evie. Your son is here."

She didn't look at them. Kincaid noticed the other bed, sheets wadded into a ball.

"He's brought you something. How nice of him to come out on such a cold day. Brr!" The nurse went to Evelyn's side and bent down to her. "How about we stretch you out on your bed? You've been up now for nearly two hours and we don't want muscle contractions." The nurse stood and looked at Kincaid. "She gets dehydrated." Evelyn grasped the nurse's hand in acquiescence. The nurse brought the wheelchair bedside, Evelyn keeping her head down. The nurse folded back the foot rests and moved to lift her.

"I can help," Kincaid said.

Evelyn made an incoherent protesting noise. He stepped back.

"Quite all right," the nurse said. "I'm big and strong and Eve isn't heavy at all, are you love?"

The nurse scooped up the thin, frail woman, laid her on the bed, trying to avoid the catheter line. Kincaid grasped it and held it aside. His mother didn't see him as he rested it on the bed rail. The nurse covered his mother with sheet and blanket.

"There we are," she said. "Anything else?"

Evelyn shook her head.

"Then I'll leave you two alone." The nurse pulled the door closed behind her.

"I got you something," Kincaid said.

He set the parcel on her nightstand. She didn't move.

"I met a very nice young woman, too," he said. "We talked about you. She's a mezzo-soprano in a traveling opera company."

Kincaid sat in a chair next to the bed. "You'd like her," he said.

His mother finally turned to him. "You don't look good," she said. "What's wrong with you?"

"I don't look good? In what way?"

"Like you're drinking again. Are you?"

"What a positive way to start off a visit," he said. "I was hoping we'd talk about how you like it here."

“I was promised a private room. They said you haven’t paid for it yet.”

“I have,” Kincaid said. “They insisted on it before we moved you.”

“Then you paid for the wrong room,” Evelyn said. She reached toward the neighboring bed. “Kept pissing herself, she did. They finally moved her.”

Kincaid felt a familiar hollow pang in his gut, as his mouth dried with the words that left him. He wanted to stand and leave, but instead he went to the window.

“Remember those nasty old barracks they forced you to live in?” she asked.

“Are you making a comparison? Because there is none.”

“I thought you had the money,” Evelyn said.

“I’ve already paid them, ma. Like I told you. They’ve got something to sort on their end.”

“I wonder what that might be,” she said.

“I don’t know. I will ask before I leave,” he said, staring out the window at the snow. “Will that suit you?”

“Will it suit me?” Evelyn said. “What kind of thing is that to say?”

He turned away from the window and she watched him go to the door. They said nothing to one another as he quietly slipped out.

“Miss, nurse,” he asked at the small office end of the hall.

“Leaving so soon?”

"I need to speak with whomever's handling my mother's arrangements. She's very unhappy."

"I'm sorry to hear that, Mr. Kincaid," the nurse said, standing from her desk. "You might try the main office. First floor, third door from the right."

"You have a name for this person?"

"I think Teri would handle it," the nurse said.

As he turned to leave, "It's *Inspector*, by the way. Not Mister. I'm with the Guards."

"Oh," the nurse said. "I didn't know that."

KINCAID SAT IN HIS dark apartment, nursing whiskey in a crystal glass, trying to take it slower this time, this time, this time, so as not to awaken again, again, again, in the wee morning hours, barely enough sleep to function. He had broken the habit, or so he thought, nothing to drink in over a year. He thought maybe he was seeing a pattern now, garda to sergeant, sergeant to inspector, mother on the move. He looked over at the black-and-white photo of the young woman clutching the roses when the telephone rang. He set the glass aside and leaned toward the receiver.

"Adam," Marta said. "I've been meaning to congratulate you."

"Thank you."

"How does it feel?"

"Honestly?" he said, leaning back on the sofa.

"Well, yes, of course."

"A bit like a consolation prize. Or maybe a hush payment. Say no more about the Heavy Gang or the heavy-handed bishop or the real reason Ana Cairns and Billy Corrigan met such untimely ends."

"I don't know, Adam. You really think the department is that cynical?"

"I think my promotion proves it."

"And I had hoped to celebrate," Marta said.

"I am celebrating." Kincaid audibly clinked the whiskey bottle against the glass.

"Maybe you shouldn't be," Marta said. "At least, not alone."

Eight

Detective Inspector Adam Kincaid watched other gardaí position a ladder. Flashbulbs lit the altar in the dim light from stained glass windows. He pushed aside the rope-and-winch assembly dangling from the oak crossbeams that spanned Our Lady of Perpetual Benevolence, bracing the exterior stonework that made this Irish Catholic church a model of Gothic sculpture in its working-class Dublin domain. Kincaid looked around the floor, along and under the pews. He walked up and down the center aisle.

"No blood," he said. "Or virtually no blood."

"No, Inspector," said CDU Detective Garda Tom Fields, eyeing the scene up and down. "It's a tidy brutality, for sure."

"What in the name of Janey Mac—"

Kincaid was staring when the voice startled him.

"Adam."

"Mr. District Officer."

"I worry when you get all formal like that," McDermott said. He looked at the altar. "As I was saying, what in the name—"

McDermott stepped up to the body.

"Monsignor Dylan Gwynedd, sixty years of age," Detective Fields said.

"These wounds are pretty precise," McDermott said. "Which is saying something with a scene this . . . elaborate."

Kincaid looked at the victim's left wrist and palm, below eye level in this upside-down configuration. "Nails?" he mused.

"When do you want him down?" Fields asked. "He's strapped to it pretty tight."

Kincaid leaned in and peered at the victim's other hand and palm. "Where's the sacristan?" he asked.

"Sacristy, Inspector," Fields said. "He needed to sit."

"Garda with him?"

"Yes, sir. His alibi checks, too."

"What about him?" Kincaid asked, nodding toward a priest, his hands folded in front, speaking with a bangharda.

"Sacristan and him come upon the victim together," Fields said. "Before morning Mass the monsignor usually handled."

"Where's the sacristy?"

Fields pointed. Kincaid followed his finger. "John?" he asked McDermott. They stepped down from the altar.

"Bring back memories?" McDermott asked.

"This one has nails."

WITH A GARDA AND the sacristan, McDermott and Kincaid seemed too large for the tiny sacristy. The sacristan stared at the wall.

"Poor bugger," McDermott told Kincaid. "Hell of a thing." He turned to the garda. "That'll be all."

"Mister—" Kincaid asked.

"Lanigan," the sacristan said. He pushed his way up to stand.

"Detective Inspector Kincaid. Detective Superintendent McDermott. Mr. Lanigan—"

"You can call me Patrick, if you like," Lanigan said. "I'm sorry. I had to sit." He looked at his chair, then at them.

"Please," McDermott said.

"Mind?" Kincaid asked Lanigan, indicating a chair.

"Oh no. Not at all," Lanigan said.

Kincaid sat next to him. "From Dublin?"

"Yes, sir."

"How far?"

"Ballybough thereabouts."

Kincaid jotted a note. "What happened?"

"I came . . . I told the other fella . . . detective."

"Fields?"

"I don't remember his name. Tall fella, red hair."

"Fields. You came where? Here?" Kincaid asked.

"Yes. I always tend to things before mass. Last night, I came in through that door." He pointed at the sacristy's outside entrance. "This morning, I came through the church. I had bell-ringing duty."

"Is the only way to the bell rope is through the front foyer?"

"It's the easiest way," Lanigan said.

"Can you tell me what you saw?"

"Well, again. As I already told—"

"I understand," Kincaid said. "But it's always been my practice to speak with our key witnesses. When something like this happens, we become a kind of family."

"A family?" Lanigan said. "Don't see that on the telly."

"So you went from the bell rope to—"

"The nave, sir. We saw it—him, the monsignor. I had to keep the people out, or I'd have collapsed straightaway. Father Kane—he was a rock."

"What did you see?"

"The cross. Inspector—" He leaned forward and lowered his voice. "The crucifix. I couldn't make him out at first. I never seen a cross upside down before. Of course, never seen a man hanging from a cross, either. Not a real man, anyways. I wasn't even sure it was Monsignor till Father Kane had a look."

"Where was Father—Kane, is it?"

"Yes, sir."

"Where was Father Kane when you met him this morning?"

"I come up to him outside."

"Where?"

"Bottom of the steps. He usually don't celebrate on weekdays."

"Why not?"

"He's our youth curate. Runs the youth club. Takes the teens on weeknight activities, wee ones on Saturday outings. Works with the schools on first communion and confirmation. Celebrates evening mass."

"But he was here this morning?"

"And a good thing, too. Parishioners were wantin' to get in, wonderin' where Monsignor was."

"So you found the body and you came to get Father Kane?"

"Almost ran out, till I saw the people. I tried to keep my cool."

"You both came back into the church from the front?"

"The big oak door, yes Inspector. Father Kane closed it, made sure it latched. I didn't say nothing other than prepare yourself, it's brutal. He blessed himself, Father, Son, Holy Ghost," he made the motion, "came into the nave, then gasped. 'We need to call the Guards,' he says."

"Then what happened?"

"Then?"

"Yes. What happened next?"

"Well—Guards came."

"No, I mean before we came."

"We waited."

"In the church?"

"Yes."

"Just stood around looking at the monsignor?"

"No, oh no, Inspector. Someone banged on the front door. I heard them tugging on it. Amazingly rude."

"It was locked?"

"Yes. Didn't I say that?"

"You said it was latched. But you can press the latch from the outside and open it, correct?"

"Yes. That's right."

"Then Father Kane must have locked it?" Kincaid said.

"I don't know, Inspector."

"But it must have been locked or the parishioners would have come in."

"That does make sense," Lanigan said.

"Do you know anyone who would want the monsignor dead?" McDermott asked.

"Oh, no sir. But I do know people will want his killers dead."

"So there's more than one, you think?" Kincaid said. "Killer."

"Seems like there'd hafta be, get that thing in the air like that," Sacristan Lanigan said.

KINCAID EYED THE MONSIGNOR'S body as a Technical Bureau detective with the Investigations Section, a forensics technician, and a pathologist with the Dublin City Coroner lowered the crude wooden cross to a white tarp on the altar floor.

"Bucketing down last night," he overheard the detective say as he approached.

"Murder squad?" Kincaid asked.

"Don't worry, Inspector," the detective said. "We know it's your case."

"Good." McDermott came up behind them.

"You hear," the murder squad detective said. "Marta's leaving."

Kincaid stepped back and looked at him. "She's leaving Technical?"

"That's what I said."

"Woman outside arrived for morning Mass." Fields came up to Kincaid with one eye on a notebook. "Says the sacristan told her and her husband to stay out. That Father was working on something."

Kincaid tried to focus over wondering what straw finally broke Marta Carney. He looked at the front door. "Were the doors locked then?" he asked

"She said they were, yes sir."

"Witnesses heard the bells when?"

"Around two thirty in the morning," Fields said.

"Like an announcement," Kincaid said, as he bent down to examine the body.

THE DETECTIVE APPROACHED THE priest after the interviewing bangharda finished. They shook hands.

"Cullen Kane, Inspector. Sorry to meet under such . . . awful circumstances."

"I spoke to your sacristan."

"Was he any help?"

"He said you were a rock."

"How kind of him," Kane said. "I don't feel much the rock. What can I help you with? Or should I say, what question can I answer that I haven't already?"

"You live nearby. Share the clergy house with Father Gwynedd."

"Yes," Kane said.

"Did you hear the bells?"

"Bells?"

"Two neighbors said they heard the church bells around two thirty in the morning."

"I would have been fast asleep then, Inspector. I sleep soundly, deeply."

"So you didn't hear anything?"

"As I said—"

"Did you see Father Gwynedd that evening?"

"Yes. I'm not afraid to admit I was probably the last person to see him alive. Not including whomever committed this atrocity."

Kincaid studied Kane. "Have we met?"

"That *is* a new question," Kane said. "Do you attend Mass? Not here, I mean. I've been curate in a few parishes."

"Where?"

"Cork, Tipperary. County Down."

"County Down."

"Yes."

"I haven't attended church in any of those places," Kincaid said.

"Then you are Catholic."

"Was," Kincaid said.

"I doubt we've crossed paths."

Kincaid kept looking at him.

"More questions?" Kane asked.

"Where were you last night?"

"Adam," McDermott scolded as he approached.

"It's quite all right. I've answered that question. Three times already," Kane said. "I was in my room. Writing."

"Anyone verify that?"

"I don't think that will be necessary, Father," McDermott said.

"In the greatest of ironies, Monsignor Gwynedd could have verified it," Kane said.

"You said you were writing," Kincaid said.

"Yes."

"What were you writing?"

Kane hesitated.

"Father?"

"A translation," he said. "Centuries-old Gaelic scripture into English and German."

"What about Latin?" Kincaid asked, remembering the manutergium with *O bona crux* left at the Dr. Boyd crucifixion.

"Too cumbersome," Kane said. "At heart, I'm a lazy man, Inspectors."

THE BELLS OF OUR Lady of Perpetual Benevolence chimed in the wind.

Church keys and a flashlight in one hand, Kincaid crossed the cobblestone street from the clergy house, fighting gusts with his umbrella as Monsignor Gwynedd would have fought rain the night he died. He hurried up the granite steps, grasping the handrail, unlocked and dragged open half of the big oak door. The door closed slowly behind him. The bells stopped.

"That took about three minutes," Kincaid told McDermott in the foyer, snapping off a stopwatch. He handed the keys back to Sacristan Lanigan. "Did Monsignor Gwynedd always come in through the front?"

"He would have last night," Lanigan said. "If he heard the bells."

"He was lured, then, Adam," McDermott said. "His killer lay in wait."

"But where?" Kincaid said. He brushed past the sacristan into the nave.

"Most obvious place seems behind a pew." McDermott said, following him.

"Where was the cross? Lying in front of the altar? If you saw something like that—"

"I'd want a closer look."

Kincaid examined the floor, the pews, all the surfaces around his feet. "If he was murdered here, why is there so little blood?"

Nine

"You're killing the oul fella. You've been killing him for years." The man leaned over to Kincaid along the bar. "Or is it your mam you're killin'?"

"Both," Kincaid said, fingering his whiskey glass.

"You keep killing them, they will, in the end, kill you."

Kincaid put the glass to his lips. "Pithy," he said.

"You wanted my frank assessment, I can tell." The man leaned over grinning and extended his hand. "Alexander Baldwin," he said.

"Adam Kincaid."

"And what do you do, Adam Kincaid?"

"I wait," Kincaid said. "For a friend."

"Be this friend male or female?"

"Female." Kincaid looked around Baldwin toward the pub door. Baldwin's eyes followed.

"Pretty?"

"I'd say so, yes."

"Blonde, brunette, or fiery?"

"Fiery blonde."

"Exotic, then," Baldwin said. "Have a name?"

"Marta," Kincaid said.

"Marta? I know a Marta."

As if on cue, Marta strode through the front door of Bloom's Public House.

"Marta," Baldwin declared.

Kincaid slipped off the stool and helped her slip off her jacket and scarf. She walked with him to the bar.

"Dr. Baldwin," she said.

"You know each other?" Kincaid asked.

"I've known Marta Carney since she was at Templemore," Baldwin said.

"Criminal psychology," Marta said, as she took a seat. "I take it you two have already met."

"So I've been spilling my guts to a shrink," Kincaid said.

"But you're not a criminal," Marta said. "Unless you've confessed something I don't know about."

"I never had a course in criminal psychology," Kincaid said. "When did that start?"

"With Conroy," Marta said.

"That sounds like shop talk," Baldwin said. "Are you—"

"A manic depressive with masochistic tendencies?" Kincaid said. "Yes, I am a garda."

"So you have had some psychology?" Baldwin said.

"Promotion course," Kincaid said. "Under Conroy. But general psychology, not the course about psychopaths, which I may be needing more and more these days."

"I take it you're not a traffic cop," Baldwin said.

"Detective Inspector," Marta said. "CDU."

Baldwin put both hands on the bar and leaned back in a gesture of astonished admiration.

"You're a criminal psychologist," Kincaid mused. He raised his voice over the chatter around them. "What do you make of a criminal who crucifies his victims?"

"Or hers," Marta added.

KINCAID TOOK OFF HIS glasses, leaned back in his chair, and closed his eyes.

"Sleepin' are ya," McDermott said at the office door. "Wake up, man." He tossed a dozen photos on the desk. "Take a look."

Kincaid opened his eyes, stared at the ceiling, then looked at McDermott.

"I insist."

"Where's the prose version?" Kincaid said.

"Prose my arse."

"You say that with some relish."

"I don't relish the idea of poring over pictures of human beings in that condition. But we've both seen worse."

Kincaid looked at his desk instead.

"Please, Adam. *Look* at the bloody things. We need you in top form for the murder conference. Technical will be at your every utterance."

"Don't forget the Church." Kincaid sat upright and peered at the images. "Someone had it out for him."

"Who? No enemies that we know of. Beloved in the parish. No mistresses. No angry wives."

"Doesn't look like woman's work," Kincaid said.

"No mistresses with angry fathers or brothers or boyfriends, either."

"What about the other priest?"

"They got on well, by all accounts," McDermott said.

Kincaid looked at the photos of the monsignor.

"Just like Dr. Boyd," Kincaid said. "Beloved."

"Repeat performance or copycat?"

"Seems a long time for a copycat to wait," Kincaid said. "I'll be dredging up some four-year-old records."

"Case is still open," McDermott said. "Maybe there's hope now."

"PATHOLOGIST'S REPORT?"

"Only preliminary." The pathologist slipped a document from a manila envelope with pictures and placed it in front of Kincaid. He thumbed through it at the head of the murder conference table.

"Side entry wound between ribs five and six . . . right side of body . . . oval shape—" Kincaid read, partly mumbling to himself. "Right side measuring approximately six inches from center of chest . . . lower left side . . . two point two inches."

"Why upside down? Do we know yet?" McDermott asked.

"An upside-down crucifix normally means two things," Kincaid said. "St. Peter, who asked for that position because he wasn't worthy to die as Christ did; or the cross of the Antichrist." Kincaid read the rest of the report. "C.O.D.: Asphyxiation. Cardiac arrest. Blood coagulants found in body."

"BLOODY HELL." KINCAID HELD a small tape measure against Monsignor Gwynedd's rib cage.

"Problem, Inspector?"

"Where were the straps?" he asked the pathologist's assistant (PA).

"Just finished that." He showed Kincaid a map of the body on a clipboard. "One around the forehead. One around the rib cage, 'cross that entry wound. One around the pelvis. The last one around the knees. Arms and feet penetrated, with those nails." He pointed to a stainless steel pan with four bent, rusty nails. "They couldn't have held anything up."

Kincaid took the pan and jostled the nails around in it. "Just for show, then." He set it down, eyed the corpse again. "What do you make of this?"

"Which, Inspector? Lots to choose from."

"Here. Between the ribs."

"Entry wound. Very near the heart. But didn't penetrate the heart. Actually, it's not very deep."

"Nail wound in the palm. And scratches—" Kincaid looked at the victim's forehead, where the marks from the strap showed. "So was this Christ? Or his opposite?"

"I wouldn't know, sir."

"Christ was crucified right side up."

"That I do know."

"St. Peter insisted on an upside-down crucifixion because it was the opposite of Christ's position. Here, we have a Christ figure—crown of thorns, side lance wound—but crucified like St. Peter."

"Did you look at the cross, Inspector? We have it downstairs."

"Yes. Gnarled sort of thing. What about the coagulants?"

The assistant took a file off a desk. "We found bovine pancreatic trypsin inhibitor and tranexamic acid in the victim."

"And they are what, precisely?"

"We call them anti-fibrinolytics," said the PA. "Used to control blood loss."

"Clever way to keep the crime scene clean?"

"Maybe. Poor créatúr would've bled out otherwise, being upside down."

"We can't have any bleeding horses," Kincaid said, a sly reference to the famous Dublin pub.

"You mean falcons, Inspector."

"I stand corrected."

Ten

Kincaid approached the altar at Our Lady of Perpetual Benevolence, genuflected, and ducked beneath crime scene tape across the railing. He compared a sparely-drawn blood-spatter map with the scene. He made the only two blood stains out with a flashlight, no luminol required. They had dried into the plush red carpet, depressing the fibers into little brown craters of despair.

Kincaid looked at the altar, a marble slab on oak legs shrouded with an altar linen. Luminol found no blood on the front of the linen—the altar frontal—nor its top or sides. Was it replaced with a clean version after the murder? How much did the coagulants help?

He looked at the credence table alongside the altar, where the trappings of Mass rested: candles, cruets for wine and water, manutergium and lavabo bowl for cleansing.

Behind the altar he looked the tabernacle up and down, an ornate golden safe that stored the Eucharist locked and out of sight until the next Mass. He bent and peered at the lock.

"Mightn't I help you, Inspector?"

Kincaid jumped.

Father Kane stood before the crime scene tape. "Sorry to put the heart cross ways in ya. Your men dusted that for fingerprints. Examined everything up there, in fact."

Kincaid looked up at the rope and winch. Then he looked at Kane. “Did they open it?”

“Open which, Inspector?”

“The tabernacle.”

“I don’t suppose they did. Monsignor’s key wasn’t on his person. I’ve got the other key and they didn’t ask me.”

“Would you unlock it for me?” Kincaid asked.

“Your warrant still valid?”

Kincaid withdrew the folded warrant from his coat pocket and offered it to the priest.

“I will render to Caesar,” Kane said, “but only if Caesar dots his eyes and crosses his tees.” He handed back the warrant. Kincaid raised the crime tape and Kane slipped beneath it, eyeing and avoiding the blood on the carpet. He unlocked the tabernacle and opened it. The silk-lined sanctuary was empty.

“You keep the ciborium elsewhere?”

“Monsignor must have removed it.”

“Why? Where too? We searched his rooms.”

“I wish I could tell you,” Kane said.

“What about the chalice?”

“Chalice?” He turned. “Covered, on the credence table. It’s not there.” He went to the table. “I hadn’t noticed.”

“No pyx, no paten, no monstrance,” Kincaid said. “In fact, nothing that holds body or blood.”

“I see you haven’t forgotten your catechism.”

“About—”

"I don't know any more, Inspector," Kane said. "I wasn't celebrating that day. Monsignor had his way and I generally stayed out of it. We celebrated together only rarely."

"Did you and he get on?"

"Professionally or socially?"

"Did you like him? Did he like you?" Kincaid asked.

"We got on, Inspector." He paused. "But I think—"

"Go on."

"He resented me. The Church blamed him for our dwindling numbers. I was sent to bring them up, especially the young ones. But this is an aging community. The young ones leave."

"How does a priest . . . resent?"

"Quietly," Kane said. "The chalice," he turned back to the credence table, "might go missing. The tabernacle," he marched up to it, "sit empty. But I'd been warned in seminary to rely on myself. I was dismayed, but never embarrassed."

"I don't follow," Kincaid said.

"I have my own sacred vessels, Inspector." He motioned toward the door.

"May I send a garda round to look at those?" Kincaid said. "With a warrant."

"By all means."

Kincaid stepped down from the altar, navigating around the forensic markings, and slipped under the tape.

"In so many words, then, everything sacred was removed from the scene of the crime," Kincaid pronounced.

Kane eyed the blood on the carpet again as he took in the idea. "I hadn't thought about it that way, but yes, I suppose that's true."

"Who would do that?"

"You mean, worry about besmirching the sacred with the sinful? We're in a church, Inspector. Your net will be a wide one, I would think."

Kincaid looked at a fresh scrape alongside and under the armrest of a wooden pew.

"Something else?"

"The rope." Kincaid looked at the winch assembly, grabbed the armrest. "Must have used this to leverage the body."

He looked up at the statues of Christ, on the Cross to the altar's left; Resurrected to the altar's right, nails in the wrists but nail wounds in the palms.

"So much understatement in the casual idol." Kane stared at the Resurrected Christ. "He looks unfazed."

Kincaid went to walk out, but at the foyer door turned back to see Fr. Kane staring at the altar carpet.

"How old are you?" Kincaid asked.

Kane didn't look up. "Thirty four."

"You're sure we've never met?"

"I can't imagine why we would have," the priest said.

"ADAM. COME IN. SIT down."

"Chief Superintendent." Kincaid closed the door and sat next to McDermott.

"John says you're working up a theory," Greevey said. "And revisiting the Boyd case."

"It may be premature."

"John's explained to you about the conference," Greevey said.

"Yes."

"So?"

"C'mon, Adam. Humor us," McDermott said.

Kincaid stretched and rubbed his neck. "Ritual homicide in both cases."

"It's more complicated than that, Chief Superintendent," McDermott said. "Tell him, Adam."

Kincaid raised his eyebrows with a touch of exasperation. "The crosses are not alike," he said. "But the leather straps that tied the bodies to the crosses are alike. The monsignor had forehead scratches, an entry wound under the ribs, nail wounds —Dr. Boyd had none of those injuries."

"So who was crucified?" Greevey asked. "Metaphorically speaking?"

"Saint Andrew in the Boyd case," Kincaid said. "Some mixture of Christ and Saint Peter in the Gwynedd case, though I've no idea what it means."

"The nails that bound Christ were in the wrists," McDermott said. "I remember reading that—and this whole mythology about the nails being in the palms, which would rip apart in that kind of hanging position. The nails we found in Gwynedd were through his palms."

"So our killer isn't historically astute?" Greevey said.

"He used genuine Roman nails, bent at the ends the way the Romans did it, to keep the body attached," Kincaid said. "Seems astute to me."

"What about the coagulants?" Greevey asked.

"Not sure," Kincaid said. "Simplest explanation may be the best: they were used to keep things tidy."

"What does it all *mean*?" Greevey said.

"Maybe our killer doesn't know what he wants to say," McDermott said.

"One other thing, sir."

"Go on."

"The sacred vessels went missing," Kincaid said.

"I'm not Catholic. You'll have to enlighten me."

"Chalices, wafer holders," Kincaid said. "Used to bless wine and bread on the altar."

"We're checking into that now," McDermott said. "The sacristan says he doesn't know. He had put them back, under lock and key as usual."

"Any theories as to why the killer, or killers, might have done this?"

"Father Kane had one," Kincaid said. "To keep the sinful from the sacred."

Eleven

Kincaid knelt before a bathtub with his fingers on the neck of a dead man. Flashbulbs snapped around him. Tech Bureau staff bumped him. He turned the victim's head, left cheek, right cheek.

"Marked putrefaction." Garda Fields bent down next to Kincaid. "Electrocuted. But a heart attack probably killed him."

"What fell in the tub?"

Fields nodded toward an electric razor. "What an eejit, pardon my sayin'."

"His face doesn't look shaved anywhere," Kincaid said. "He goes for the razor and it falls in right off?"

"Must've. Bad timin', too. They were havin' electric work done—replacing fuses and connections. Bypassed things till they could finish. Power stayed on till he was—well, done."

"The contractor committed this lapse?"

"Appears so, Inspector. We can't reach anyone at the business, it being Sunday. But we'll confirm."

"Talk about eejits."

"Anyone else around?"

"Victim's girlfriend," Fields said. "Fluthered when we found her. Woke up babbling about a child. I've gone round to the neighbors. If she's real, we'll find her."

KINCAID LEFT THE FLAT for a hallway between pockmarked plaster walls. The Technical Bureau's forensics team pushed past him, hurrying down two flights of stairs to a stoop outside the brownstone.

He gripped the wrought iron handrails and walked slowly down the concrete steps toward the street. He looked up at the building. Someone ran up the steps to the door. Startled, Kincaid didn't catch her, him before the door closed. He followed, and when he appeared up the stairs at the end of the hallway, he saw a child standing at the victim's locked apartment door.

"Who might you be?"

She turned and darted toward him, the only way out.

"Hey!"

She tried to get past him, but he grabbed her around the waist.

"Stop. Stop it," he said.

She scratched him and pushed at his chest and bit into his arm but got a mouthful of the coat he pulled back. He pressed her against the wall. Mucous pirouetted from her misshapen nose down a cut in her lip.

"Do you live there?" Kincaid asked.

She jerked her head away and turned and closed her eyes.

"Does your father live there? Your mother?"

She pushed the side of her head against the wall and stared out a window overlooking the street.

"Are you the daughter they were talking about?"

Nothing. Kincaid kept hold of her. "He's dead."

She closed her eyes. He felt her relax. Her head slowly bowed. Kincaid relaxed his grip and her feet touched the floor.

"I'm with the Guards," he said. He lowered his hands. "Do you have any idea what happened?"

She slid down the wall to sit on the floor, knees high, hands tucked. Kincaid saw bruises where her trousers rose from her ankles. He lowered himself down the other wall, got comfortable, looked at her.

"Who did that to you?"

"Eff off."

"You fell, I guess. That why the puss?" he said. "How long you been gone . . . today?"

She looked up the hall almost longingly, Kincaid thought.

"Man bein' thick?" Kincaid said. "What's that got to do with you?"

She wiped her nose and lips with her sweater.

"How old are you?"

"None of your business."

"You go to school around here?"

Nothing.

"I'm guessing Junior Cycle," Kincaid said. "You like school?"

Nothing.

"What's your favorite subject?"

She buried her head between her knees.

"Mine was math."

"So what?" she told the floor.

"You look smart."

She kept her head down.

"How'd you get them bruises?"

She tossed her hair back and blew the last strands out of her face. "Someone got rough," she said.

"With you?"

"Yeah, with me. Who else?"

"Who got rough with you? The man in the tub? Your—"

"He's not me da," she said. "Me da run off."

"Run off? On a lovely girl like you?"

"On me mam."

"Where's she?" Kincaid asked.

"In bits, I guess. I knocked."

Kincaid looked at his watch. "You hungry?" he asked.

"Why?"

"Pub—across the street."

Kincaid waited for an answer, as she looked down the hall, at the ceiling, toward the window on her other side. "I could eat."

"You won't run off, will you?"

"I might."

"Why? You do something wrong?"

She rubbed her hands up and down her legs. Kincaid heard her sniffling. He lowered his head and tried to look at her eyes. He slid across the floor in a couple of awkward lurches and pulled up next to her. "Ah, love," he said. She leaned against him and cried. He put his arms around her.

Garda Fields stepped into the hallway from the stairwell. He stood over Kincaid and the girl.

"What's your name?" Kincaid asked.

"Alyson," she whispered. Ah-lee-sun.

"This is Alyson," Kincaid said.

"Alyson. Pretty name. Are ya hurt, love?"

Kincaid shook his head.

"Shed any light on things?" Fields asked.

"Says her mam's the woman in the apartment."

Fields bent down. "She was hit, Inspector. Beat up," Fields said in a soft voice. He leaned down to Kincaid's ear. "We're rethinking cause of death. Sergeant Watts thinks homicide."

"Seems a little rash," Kincaid whispered back.

"Murder squad," Fields said. "You know—"

Kincaid felt Alyson tense. "Best not discuss this here," he said.

Twelve

"Can I have me church back?" Fr. Kane asked Kincaid on the phone.

"They're not finished?"

"You tell me. Crime scene markers are still up and I celebrate Mass tomorrow."

"I wish these things could be rushed—"

"What more could they possibly be needing?"

KANE AND KINCAID ENTERED from the back of the church. Kincaid went toward the altar. The ropes, the winch, the crime scene tape were gone.

On his way to a supply closet, "I appreciate your intervention, Inspector," Kane said. He approached the altar with rubber gloves, cleanser, brush, sponge, and a bucket of water. He knelt before the blood stains and scrubbed the carpet, wringing out the sponge in the bucket then scrubbing again, so hard the sponge blanched the carpet.

"You have bleach in that water?" Kincaid said.

"No, but I should." Fr. Kane sat on his knees and looked at the carpet. "Probably have to replace the bloody thing."

"Cold water should take it out."

"That may remove the *physical* remains."

Kane dumped the bucket in the bathroom sink and took it to the marble holy water font at the front of the church. But the bucket was too large for the font's mouth.

"Jaysus," he said.

"What are you after?" Kincaid asked.

"God's bleach."

Kane went into the church office and back to the font with a large coffee cup.

"You've a holy water container up here," Kincaid said, about a "Holy Water"-etched glass vessel on the credence table.

Kane went to dip the coffee cup in the font but stopped short. He set the cup on a pew and looked at the altar and the font. He lifted the marble font bowl from its stand and carried it to the altar, careful not to splash the water.

"Can I help with that?" Kincaid asked.

But Kane was upon the altar shortly. He set the bowl on the floor and took a deep breath and rested against the railing.

"Rather drastic," Kincaid said.

"I blessed this," Kane said. "I can't vouch for that other water."

He slid the bowl to the blood stains and tipped it and spilled the water on the blood.

"It's that important, who blessed it?" Kincaid asked.

"In this case."

KINCAID SAT BEHIND ROWS of pews reserved for family, friends, and clergy at the memorial Mass for Monsignor

Gwynedd, casket closed for the condition of his body. The detective looked around Our Lady of Perpetual Benevolence at the capacity crowd. Celebrant Bishop Gerry McCarthy said he admired "Monsignor's devoted parishioners," urging them not to let "the devastating circumstances" deter them from "love and service to Our Lord."

Father Kane sat in a front row pew near the aisle, turning his head and sweeping the room with his eyes. Other men of the cloth took their seats, some in front, some in back, all near the aisles.

"Inspector." Kane took Kincaid's forearm after the Mass on the front steps outside the oak door. People filing past grabbed the priest's shoulder or shook his hand.

"I'm so sorry for your loss," a woman said.

"He'll be missed, he will," a man said. "You've got big shoes to fill, young man."

"Only temporarily," Kane said with a smile.

"You have my condolences as well," Kincaid said.

"Thank you."

"Will they transfer you?"

"I've not heard yet," Kane said. "But that's a possibility. I don't think I'll be made the new parish priest."

"I was wondering, too—I noticed you didn't say anything."

"During the Mass?"

"Yes."

"I'm hoarse from saying too much as it is," Kane said. "The eulogies were in good hands."

Another priest passed the two men as he walked down the steps. Kane didn't reach out to him.

"I take it you don't know everyone here," Kincaid said.

"I know most, but not all," Kane said. "Monsignor originally hailed from Wales. I don't know many there."

"Did you ever know a Robert Boyd? A doctor he was, of families and children."

"No, Inspector. Should I have? I'm not a parent."

"But you are the curate in charge of youth."

"Again, no, Inspector. The name sounds vaguely familiar, but that's all."

"Could the monsignor have known him?"

"If only you could ask him," Kane said. "Ah—the ladies of the parish council. If you'll excuse me."

Kincaid watched a priest and a bishop step into a waiting car. He hurried down the steps and jotted the license plate number into his notepad.

"**WHAT CAN I DO** for you?" Lochlann Shaughnessy peered out the window of his room at the parish rectory, The Twelve Apostles of Ireland church. He turned to Kincaid. "Inspector."

"I saw you at the Mass for Monsignor Gwynedd," Kincaid said. "I wondered how long you knew him."

"I was a curate under his charge," Father Shaughnessy said.

"At Our Lady of Perpetual Benevolence?"

"Yes."

"And you said nothing at his memorial?"

"I came to pay my respects. Quietly."

"Still."

"What I had to say, I said to God."

"He was as well-liked as I've heard, then?" Kincaid asked.

"Yes, he was."

"How did you know? That he was well liked? I wasn't able to tell at the service."

"Every pew was full, Inspector. Surely you saw that."

"Yes, but—your silence, for instance. And others, including Father Kane."

"Father Kane isn't one to rock the boat," Shaughnessy said. "One always risks enemies when one goes against the grain."

"Do you know Father Kane well?"

"Only well enough to know he has the position Monsignor had when I was there. 'In charge of the children.' May I ask: Any leads? I've been wracking my brains—"

"We may have a connection to an earlier case," Kincaid said.

"Is that so? How much earlier?"

"Little over three years ago. You may remember it. Dr. Robert Boyd."

"Can't say as the name sounds familiar. What happened to this Doctor Boyd?"

"He was crucified, again in a bloodless fashion."

"Good Lord. And I assume his killer—"

"Never caught," Kincaid said. "The case is still open."

"Doubtless a message buried away in all this carnage," Shaughnessy said. "Know that I'm praying for you, Inspector. Gwynedd too, and the other man, even if for them, it's too late."

"Too late?"

"No prayer on Earth can change the fate of a dead man," Shaughnessy said.

"SO YOU'VE GONE AND done it," Kincaid said, as Marta slipped into his car from outside her flat.

"I told you I would."

"How did Fitzpatrick take it?" Kincaid pulled onto the road.

"Not well," she said. "I think he was afraid I might make noise."

"I think he understands the talent he's lost."

"That's sweet," Marta said, putting her hand on his wrist. "Almost as sweet as meeting your mam."

"Don't get the wrong idea," Kincaid said. "I'm taking you for moral support."

"They've assured you she has her new room. She should be in fine spirits."

"New job?" he asked.

"Me? Not yet. It's nice to have some free time, just to think, to plan."

"Any ideas?"

"Only one. Wherever I end up, it won't be law enforcement."

Thirteen

Kincaid took a seat near the front of the conference room at Dublin Castle. A young woman pointed to depictions of the Boyd and Gwynedd crime scenes. A religious medallion—St. Christopher, maybe—clutched the collar of her turtleneck.

" . . . hardly the usual configurations," she said. "I must admit to being somewhat stumped."

"Religious ritual," a detective sergeant said.

"Not necessarily," the woman said. As she talked, Kincaid leaned over to another detective. "What's this?" he whispered.

"Trying to get at that elusive theory of the case."

"Greevey?"

"Push down from the higher ups," the detective said. "I hear all the way from O'Malley," the Minister of Justice.

"Thrust down's more like it," another detective whispered. "Whole bloody country's talking about it. Nuthin' about the Troubles for a week."

"Crucifixion was a Roman invention, not connected with religion until Jesus and St. Peter," the lecturer explained.

"Who's she?" Kincaid asked.

"Outside expert," the first detective said.

"More blowback from the Conroy Report?" Kincaid asked.

"Lack of modern knowledge and techniques. Isn't that what Conroy said?" the first detective asked. "And what's the cure? Civilians. Non-police personnel. *Experts*."

"With the Boyd case still open—"

"Crucifixions." Kincaid spoke up. "And no religious ritual in them?"

"Maybe. But again, not necessarily," the expert said. "Detective—"

"Inspector. Kincaid."

"We can't be sure of a religious ritual angle," she replied. "The Medieval executioner availed himself of all manner of ungodly tortures like these. Minus any ritual."

"A side lance and a crown of thorns doesn't suggest it?"

"But Christ wasn't crucified upside down. And why the Cross of St. Andrew for the earlier victim? With such mixed symbology, the killer could be taunting us," the woman said.

"Or he could be a Scot," another detective blurted to laughter.

The expert waited for the room to calm. She cleared her throat, used a pointer at the photos.

"What I've never understood is how the feck they stay up," someone else in the audience said. "The bodies. Why their palms ain't torn."

"Nails in the palms are myth," the woman said. "They nail the wrists, between these two bones." She scrolled to a slide of an X-ray. "Radius and ulna, right here. And the feet are either placed on a foot rest, known as a *suppedaneum*, or nailed like this."

Another slide, of old nails through the side of a heel.

"This mummified artifact was discovered in 1968 near Jerusalem. The nail enters the side of the foot, here, near the heal, and, looking more closely." She enlarged the image. "The nail is bent. You see?"

"Our victims were strapped to their crosses," Kincaid said.

"Jaysus, Mary, and Joseph," someone else said.

"So what's the theory of the case? Greevey's panicking. It's all he talks about."

"I believe—"

"If there's no symbology, then our perpetrator is gone in the head," Kincaid interrupted, remembering the murder squad's aggressive methods. "Trying to get a theory out of insanity strikes me as insane."

The room went quiet. Coughs. Shuffling feet. Whispers.

"Thank you, Inspector," the woman said.

"INSPECTOR." THE WOMAN CAUGHT Kincaid in the lobby. She stuck out her hand. "Jane," she said with a slight pause and a distinct British accent. "Grey." She handed him a card. *Jane Grey, O.S.S.D., D. Phil.*

"OSSD?" Kincaid asked.

"You were rude back there," she said. "I realize you're light on clues, but—"

"So you run me down just to call me out?"

"Your interruptions were rude."

"I interrupted to prevent further misinformation."

"I think it stands to reason your perpetrator's 'gone in the head,' as you so curtly put it," Jane Grey said.

"I contributed that insight, yes."

"Stating the obvious seems like undermining, not contributing."

"I didn't mean it that way," Kincaid said. "Greevey said nothing about you and I would have preferred at the very least a consultation."

"Well . . . on further consideration . . . apology accepted, Inspector."

"I haven't apologized. What branch are you with again? Justice, Social Protection?"

"Order of the Sisters of Saint Dymphna," she said.

Kincaid's face changed.

"A nun?"

"Yes, Inspector."

"No—"

"Habit?" she completed. "Vestments can be intimidating, especially to someone who has committed a crime or who suffers mental illness. When I'm at work, these," she pressed the turtleneck and the silver medallion, "are the sum of my habit."

Kincaid looked at the medallion. "St. Die-mphna?"

"It is. And it's 'di'. Short *i*. Di-mfna. She's the patron saint of my profession and the people I work with. Ireland-born, too."

"Who are the people you work with?"

"The criminally insane."

Kincaid thought back to his musings about the need for a criminal psychologist. "I wonder if someone was listening?" he said. "Sister. If you thought me rude, I do apologize."

"I'm sure you didn't mean it." She smiled. "Would you be in a mind to grab a pint with me?"

"At a pub?"

"I think the wounds in the second case may be a signature, just like the kerchief in the first case," Sister Grey said. "The modus may indicate redemption as much as revenge. If I'm right, the cases are connected and there will be more."

"YOU WERE SAYIN' ABOUT redemption." Kincaid looked at Sister Grey over his beer.

"Couple of years ago in the States," she said. "Two boys—seven and ten—stomped a two-year-old to death. Beat him about the head with a brick, too. They wanted him to suffer."

"Brutal. But children—?"

"They stripped the tot and tied him to a cross where he died. The local constabulary found him in a basement after his killers confessed. One of them said they put him on the cross in hopes he might come back, like Jesus."

"A child's misguided imaginings. Child psychopath, but child nonetheless."

"Perhaps. But I still wouldn't rule out a redemption element in our killings," Grey said. "Victim suffers on Earth, descends into Hell, receives divine redemption."

"Or retribution."

"The torture itself would probably serve that element," Grey said. "The killer also seems to be telling us that the doctor and the monsignor were not worthy to die as Christ had, but rather, in some other fashion. St. Andrew and St. Peter felt the same way, and insisted on the different configurations."

"You're not running in circles, are you Sister?"

"No, but the killer may be. Confused, conflicted. He may know the victim and hasn't come to grips with how he feels. He wanted them to atone for something, while leaving open the possibility of forgiveness."

"Seems a convoluted theory."

"Crucifixion is almost unheard of in ritual homicide. Its most famous victims were saints," Sr. Grey said. "Most offenders don't see their victims as saints. So yes—using a cross as a murder weapon is a convoluted way to commit homicide."

"What do you make of the coagulants?"

"Keep the blood with the body, maybe," Grey said. "Blood and body are separated in the Catholic faith, reunited during the Eucharist. For some reason, the killer did not want the separation. Maybe. The missing altar hardware suggests something similar. No possibility that body and blood get separated."

"No blood in the park near the cathedral and hardly any in the church," Kincaid said. "What about limited defilement?"

"Of sacred ground? Yes, that makes sense. I hadn't considered it."

Kincaid looked at a menu, thinking about how to phrase his next question. He went with the blunt version.

"Who brought you in?"

"Brought me in?" she asked.

"Greevey, McDermott? Wymes? And all the way from—where exactly?"

"Just outside London. I usually work for Scotland Yard, but I'm known to An Garda Síochána. Why do you ask?"

"I don't mind telling you, we're on edge. Especially the detective units. Conroy report—"

"My order was working with the Guards before the Conroy Commission—"

"—labeled us incompetent."

"That's not the way I read it."

"It's had the effect of pitting department against department," Kincaid said. "I'm just now realizing how I was dragged into the middle of it all as a young, know-nothing cop."

"You don't strike me as the kind of man who could be dragged into anything,"

"Ever heard of Saor Éire?" Kincaid asked.

"IRA."

"Ex-IRA."

"What do they have to do with Conroy?"

"They killed a garda, Dick Fallon, during a bank robbery. Our first major loss to the Troubles. Dáil went crazy over it. All kinds of conspiracy and cover-up rumors. Like the government helped the bank robbers escape. Like our former Justice Minister,

Haughey, was selling arms to terrorists—five thousand handguns. Maybe Gardaí helped, too. SDU and CDU fought over the Fallon crime scene." Special and Central Detective Unit investigators "even missed a bullet some kid found and turned in," Kincaid continued. "What does all this look like, if not incompetence?"

"I understand," Grey said. "But I wasn't brought in to undermine you or make up for any inadequacies your politicians dreamed up."

"Is that so?"

"It is."

Kincaid mumbled his menu choice to the barkeeper beside them now. "Sister."

"Nothing else, thank you."

Kincaid's pager beeped. He took it off his belt and looked at the call-back number.

"I wish . . . I need to take this."

"Yes." Sr. Grey went to stand.

"No. No. I just need to make a quick call."

While he was gone, she motioned over the barkeeper and paid the tab.

Fourteen

Kincaid slipped between a line of gardaí blocking limestone steps to the Church of St. Columba in one of Dublin's posher neighborhoods. He walked up, stopped, and stared at the tall wooden doors.

"Gruesome, eh, Inspector?" Garda Fields startled him.

Kincaid squatted for a closer look. "Male?"

"From the Adam's apple," Fields said.

"Is this his . . . skin?"

"Fingerprints intact, at least," Fields said. "Teeth, too."

"That knife in his hand—" Kincaid studied it.

"Flensing knife, it looks to be, Inspector. For whales."

"Whale blubber." Kincaid stood and looked around. "And again, where's the blood?"

"Inspector." Another garda called to him from the side of the church. "Around here, sir."

Kincaid went around to the sacristy door. Inside the church, he saw another police officer.

"Sacristan let us in," the garda said. "We came upon it together."

The sacristan stood on the church altar. "This shouldn't be in here." He stared at a long, wide poster unfolded and hung across the tabernacle on the back wall. He looked at the police officers, then went up and reached for the poster.

“Don’t touch that,” Kincaid said.

“As I told the other guard, it has no business here.”

“Neither does the body at the door,” Kincaid said. He walked up the altar and eyed the unrolled portrait. “Take him out of here, please,” Kincaid said. As the garda led the sacristan out, Kincaid asked, “Who’s the parish priest?”

“That’d be Father Rob,” the sacristan said.

“Last name?”

“Parrodus. Father Robert Parrodus.”

KINCAID WATCHED THE TECHNICAL Bureau work the victim against the front door outside until the pathologist arrived. Kincaid raised the victim’s hand with a pen and looked at thumbs and fingers. All the skin was missing right up to the fingerprints.

“Bit less than we’re used to working with, eh Adam?” the pathologist said.

“Where’s the insides of him?” Adam asked rhetorically.

“He does look a bit like a deflated balloon.”

“Inspector,” Garda Fields called up. “Someone down there asking for you.”

“Down where?”

“There. Thought she was with the newspaper at first.”

“She?” Kincaid looked toward the pavement. When he saw Sr. Grey, he walked down the steps.

“Inspector.”

"Sister. How did you get here?"

"Drove."

"No, I mean—"

"It looks like another homicide." She peered over his shoulder. "That *is* a body, isn't it?"

"Yes, Sister." He motioned the gardaí to stand aside and she went up the steps with him. "You prefer sister or doctor?" he asked.

"Sister. And my friends call me Jane. But we're not there just yet. Oh, dear." She stopped in front of the body and forced herself not to turn away. "He's just sitting, almost casually. If he was alive when this happened—how awful. I can't imagine. And . . ." She looked around. "No blood."

"No splatter doesn't mean no blood." A Technical Bureau examiner turned around. "There *was* blood and lots of it. Body must have been cleaned thoroughly, then dragged up here on a tarp or something."

As Sr. Grey came through the sacristy and into the church, "Did you follow me?" Kincaid asked.

"I try never to follow, but to lead," Grey said. She looked at the unrolled poster on the back altar wall. "Michelangelo. *The Last Judgment.* I'd recognize it even in this crudely-commercialized form. It's a fresco in the Sistine Chapel. Behind the altar *there*, too." She stepped closer and looked it up and down.

"Sacristan who found the body said he's never seen it before," Kincaid said. He sighed and pushed his hair back from his forehead. "Greevey's gonna be breathing down our necks."

"Any idea who once inhabited that flesh?" Sr. Grey asked.

"No. But he has intact fingerprints. And good teeth."

"One thing seems clear, then," the sister said.

"What's that?"

"The killer wants him identified."

"ADAM." DISTRICT OFFICER MCDERMOTT motioned Kincaid into his office. He pointed at a newspaper on his desk. "The Return of the Crucifix Killer."

Kincaid looked at the front page. "Is *that* what they're going with?"

"The *Times, Cork Examiner, Independent, Evening Herald Evening Press*. Every gory detail they can wheedle out of unnamed sources and departmental leaks."

McDermott pawed through some files on his desk. "Another thing. Reading your report on that suicide-cum-homicide last week. Feels like something's missing."

"Missing?"

"Yes."

"You know how careful I am."

"I do. That's why it feels . . . like something's missing."

"Any idea what?"

"Seems straightforward to figure the girlfriend for it. Victim was abusive; never known to shave in the bath; neighbors reported hearing a loud argument; and she *was* the worse for wear."

"But the victim set up the negligent electrical work, not the girlfriend. Without the bypasses, fuses would have blown the second that razor hit the water. Probably saving his life."

"The family will sue about that," McDermott said. "Could the girlfriend have known?"

"That without proper breakers, a razor thrown into a bathtub could kill a man?" Kincaid said. "In her state, seems doubtful."

"She had motive and opportunity."

"Kid said different," Kincaid said. "Said her mam was passed out."

"Yes, I read that. Kid said that."

"Corroborated at the scene."

"Not entirely. Pathologist says he'd been dead a couple hours. Girlfriend could have got plastered in the meantime."

"Not what the child said."

McDermott looked at his desk. "What about the child?" he asked.

"I found her credible."

"I don't mean that."

"Oh?"

"Could *she* have done it. The child."

"John."

"I'm not codding ya, Adam. I mean it."

"She didn't confess, if that's what you're after."

"I don't expect she did," McDermott said. "What I expect is that she may have let on. Maybe you caught something. Something she said, the way she said it."

"I come upon a scared girl banging on the door of her flat," Kincaid said.

"Convenient."

"She'd been out."

"Where? Bangharda Thomas didn't get it out of her, either."

"In the street. Out of the house. No particular place. She's a kid, John."

"Out of the house because her ma was drunk, the man was beating on them, or because she just threw an electric razor into his bath." McDermott took a deep breath and pushed back in his chair. "We're under the gun here. Conroy breathin' down our necks, Justice Minister, right on up to the Taoiseach. And you know the line."

"That's the Troubles talking," Kincaid said.

"Screaming, more like."

"You have to push out the noise."

"Fallon would've lived if we were more like the—"

"We're not like the RUC," Kincaid said. "We don't have to be."

"We're understaffed, under-equipped, under-informed about this new state of things. Isn't that what they keep saying?"

"What's new about the state of things, John? It's been this way since the War of Independence."

"Long before that, if you believe the historians." McDermott leaned forward and took a pencil. He tapped it on his desk, then leaned back. "I been lookin' over my back since The Macushla. Helluva way to start a career. I've never had the luxury to feel steady ground beneath my feet. I'm always dancing."

"You really wanna go back to the days when bicycle thefts were all we solved?" Kincaid asked.

"I was labeled a union buster, Adam. Hell, we all were. Young recruits held up to the old guard with a big feck off, you're replaceable. Costigan sacked nearly a dozen of us."

"And if you hadn't done it, could you afford to be a policeman?"

"Without The Macushla? No. No way. We were bleedin' hands left and right for lack of pay."

"And you *were* reinstated."

"Only after the Archbishop intervened," McDermott said. "But I have never lived down the label Costigan appended to me, 'unfit for retention in the Garda Síochána.'"

"Yes, you have," Kincaid said. He reached across the desk and stopped McDermott from tapping the pencil. "You live it down every day."

"WE MEET AGAIN." DR. Baldwin brought himself up to the bar. "How goes the case of the Conniving Crucifix Killer?"

"We have a new addition to the team," Kincaid said.

"Don't tell me. A criminal psychologist."

Kincaid turned to the other man. "How did you know?"

"I didn't. But heard a rumor or two. Has he or she been any help?"

"Too early to tell," Kincaid said. "She's a nun, by the way."

"Talk about answered prayers." Baldwin raised his eyes facetiously, ordered a pint. "You a man of faith?" he asked.

"Faith, yes," Kincaid said. "Religion, not anymore."

"Which religion got sacked?"

"Catholic. Is there another?"

"Well, there are variations," Baldwin said. "Ireland loves its various flavors of Catholicism. Irish Catholic, Church of Ireland —"

"That's not Catholic."

"Oh, but it is," Baldwin said. "Pre-Reformation Catholicism. Which makes it a sort of hybrid: both Protestant and Catholic."

Kincaid stared at the wall, recalling Dr. Boyd's Protestant faith, and his crucifixion as a Catholic saint on Church of Ireland soil. "Hmm," he muttered, pondering the killer's possible knowledge of nuance.

"Sounds like you're in familiar terrain anyway," Baldwin said.

"I stumbled with the sister, our new team member. So much for familiar terrain."

KINCAID PICKED UP THE telephone in his office.

"Inspector."

"Sister Grey."

"We need you in the evidence room. I mean, well, *I* need you in the evidence room. If you wouldn't mind. I'd like to have a look at that fresco they took down from the church."

"They found nothing on it, Sister. No fingerprints, no hairs, no fibers, not a trace of its patron," Kincaid said.

"I wouldn't be looking for anything like that. It's a complicated painting," Grey said. "A lot going on. Pictures in the encyclopedia are too small to tell much. And the Vatican has no plans to fly me to Rome."

"BRING THAT LIGHT AROUND." Sister Grey knelt on a wheeled chair in an evidence room, *The Last Judgment* poster unfurled and held open with books, paperweights, and a stapler on each corner.

"Grand set up," Kincaid said with a smirk.

"As long as they don't fuss about me mucking about." She smoothed out a section with gloved fingertips. "So this, Inspector, shows the Second Coming of Jesus Christ. Here in the center is Christ. He doesn't have a beard, and he's a bit thick in the middle, so some people seeing this for the first time don't know who it is. But it's definitely Christ. On his left is his mother, Mary. Around him, various saints. On this side," she wheeled around to the lower left, "these are souls who've been saved. See how they're ascending toward Christ and Heaven above him."

Sister Grey moved to the center of the painting. "You can probably guess what this is," she said.

"The road to Hell," Kincaid said.

"The door, actually, coyly-situated right over the Sistine Chapel altar. Like a reminder."

"Or warning."

"And in this corner, the damned—see how they're all heading . . . down. Demons, here. Angels there. The souls come out of these Earthen graves, angels take the saved, devils grab the damned, and the soul cycle continues."

"I see lots of crosses," Kincaid said. "What's this big rake looking thing?"

"Instruments of torture," the sister said. "The Apostles, reminding Christ how they suffered. This one stands out." She moved the adjustable overhead lamp to a bald man with a beard to the right of Christ's foot, where His crucifixion wound was clear. Kincaid leaned in, stared, and chuckled.

"Yes?"

"Even Michelangelo got it wrong," he said, pointing to the holes in the top of Christ's feet.

"Yes, well—look closely at the bearded man. In particular, what he's holding."

"Appears to be someone's skin. It even has a face."

"And the bearded man has a knife."

"What do you know? A flensing knife," Kincaid said. "I can tell from the blade."

"He's our messenger, Inspector. He has to be. Saint Bartholomew."

"One of the Apostles."

"And a martyr. Maybe the most violently murdered martyr of all. Legend has it Armenian heathens flayed him alive."

"Legends."

"These legends come from something called the Apocrypha, kind of an unofficial New Testament."

"There's a face in the flesh, Sister. But it can't be Bartholomew."

"Most definitely not. It's said to be—" She picked up a magnifying glass and held it over the face in the flayed flesh. She bent down and studied it. "Hand me that book on the table over there. The encyclopedia."

Kincaid complied and she opened it to a two-page Last Judgment spread. She looked at the official photo, then back at the poster.

"I can see it from here," Kincaid said. "The faces—"

Sister Grey sat up. "The face are different," she said. "The face in *The Last Judgment* is supposedly Michelangelo, slyly announcing his handiwork. But this—" She turned to the poster, gave Kincaid the magnifying glass.

"It looks like the face of a child," Kincaid said.

DÉJÀ VU AGAIN. KINCAID sat in the first pews after the aisles reserved for friends and family at the memorial Mass for the St.

Columba victim, Deacon Ruadhán Moloney. The medical examiner had finally released his remains. With downcast eyes and a sheepish smile, Fr. Parrodus invited Kincaid to the memorial after an interview about the crime so light on details—the priest seemed to know nothing about his deacon—Kincaid called it "rather embarrassing, Father."

An organ played background chords in a loft over the back pews. Then *Soul of My Savior*.

"Soul of my savior, sanctify my breast." A strong, deep voice from the back of the church belted out the opening verse. Kincaid watched the line of celebrants walk up the center aisle toward the altar. Altar boys, deacons, two priests, and Bishop Gerry McCarthy, who owned the booming vocals.

"Body of Christ, be thou my saving guest."

But no Robert Parrodus. Kincaid looked around. The church was crowded; he couldn't make out many faces.

"Guard and defend me from the foe malign," the congregation sang, McCarthy leading. "In death's dread moments, make me only thine."

Kincaid was cold suddenly; goosebumps pricked his skin.

"In the name of the Father, the Son, and the Holy Ghost," McCarthy began. He said "Ghost" like "Ghast," the Old English version, which could mean angel or demon—or terrifying, as in "aghast."

"Peace be with you," McCarthy continued.

"And also with you," from the congregation.

The Mass proceeded, Kincaid glancing about. He saw the urn on the altar, cremation dispensation granted for the condition of the remains. He got up once discreetly for the foyer to scan the crowd. He made out clergy in the congregation. Black shirts, black sweaters, black trousers, black shoes, all men, in aisle seats.

"I think it . . . apropos, in light of the events that brought us here today, to speak to you about the nature of evil," Bishop McCarthy began his homily. "Evil comes to us, not wearing black, nor carrying a sword, nor galloping headless on a dark horse. It comes to us as it came to Adam, in the guise of goodness, in the guise of comfort, tempting us to sin and disobedience, leading us down the path of despair—"

The eulogies expressed bewilderment foremost. The victim's wife thanked the congregation for hosting the memorial. "Ruadhán so loved being a deacon here, working on matters for his church. He had a wonderful reputation and never turned anyone away who needed help. I don't understand—" She dabbed her eyes with a tissue and turned to the bishop with a longing look. Kincaid could tell she was crying, as she stepped down and retook her seat.

"Let me tell you about my brother," the victim's sister began. "He spent his life fighting for justice. He took on big, complex cases that set precedents for the way other cases would be decided. And he took on small cases, the man losing his farm to an unlawful repossession, the single mother deprived of her social welfare payments. He fought for the Church, too," she said. "I cannot fathom why anyone would have done such a thing—"

Kincaid slipped out of the Mass as the bishop said the final blessing. He passed an usher opening the front doors. Wind blew a light, cold rain so he pulled up his raincoat collar.

Bishop McCarthy positioned himself just under the doorway, an altar boy holding his umbrella. Kincaid pressed against the stone wall behind the bishop, watching faces as McCarthy pressed the flesh. As the crowd dwindled, Kincaid went around to the sacristy door. Locked. He looked in the back car lot. No cars, but fresh tire tracks on the wet earth. He returned to the front of the church and went inside.

"Your Excellency."

McCarthy stopped this side of the nave. "Yes? Come in, come in. You look frozen."

"Thank you." As the door closed behind him in the foyer, "Adam Kincaid, Your Excellency. I'm with the Gardaí. I was hoping you could answer some questions."

"I wish I could help you, but I was asked to celebrate as a prelate. Whenever a priest or deacon dies—"

"I saw you at Monsignor Gwynedd's memorial."

"Father Parrodus didn't hesitate to contact me."

"That's what I wanted to ask, Excellency. Where is he?"

"Robert?"

"I didn't see him at the Mass, but thought I'd catch him afterward. I did see other priests. But none came through the front door. Not one."

"I wouldn't know about that, Inspector," McCarthy said. "I don't know where Robert—Father Parrodus—is either, but it's possible he was called away to some emergency duty."

"I just . . . it just seems—odd, nonetheless."

"We're all scratching our heads, aren't we?"

"What did Ruadhán Moloney do for the Church? His sister —"

"Specifically? I don't know. That would be a matter for the Archdiocese, I suspect."

"His sister said he 'fought for the Church.'"

"What do solicitors do?" Bishop McCarthy asked. "The good ones fight for their clients. From what I gather, Mr. Moloney was an excellent solicitor."

"ARCHDIOCESE STILL STONEWALLING?"

"Yes," Kincaid said. "Won't return my calls. Right people out both times I've visited."

"I've a mind to take it up with Dermot himself," Chief Superintendent Greevey said.

"The Archbishop is out of town, I'm told," Kincaid said.

"Damned impossible, that crowd," Greevey whispered with a grin, in a rare moment of levity.

"Didn't used to be," Kincaid said. "John was telling me about the time the Archbishop saved his neck."

"That was McQuaid. And I'm suspicious he didn't have ulterior motives. A chit he might have planned to call in."

"What might that have been?"

"He's not a well man these days, so no fear of any called favors now. Diocesan finances are in chaos. Archbishop Ryan on the offensive. I wonder what else they're hiding." Greevey sighed, stood straighter, and recited, "We will wait and watch the tragedy to the last curtain," from Patrick Kavanagh's poem *The Great Hunger.*

KINCAID WENT TO STAND but Marta waved him off as she removed her coat to a heavy wool sweater underneath. She joined him at "their" two-person table in Bloom's Public House, with the James Joyce caricature etched into the front door's glass window. She noticed the manila envelope as she sat.

"You brought them," she said.

"Document, meet document examiner." He removed the crime scene photos of the stitched manutergium from the Robert Boyd homicide.

"I remember this case. You were on it?"

"As a uniform," Kincaid said. "It was my first homicide."

"Quite an introduction," Marta said. "Let's have a look." She slipped on a pair of reading spectacles and eyed the two photos. "*O Bona Crux.* But it's just the beginning of a longer prayer."

"Sister Grey mentioned that."

"Did she?"

"I said I was consulting with you. She didn't *quite* eat the head off me." He looked down. "So what's the unabridged version?"

Which Marta told, between barkeeper stops, a whiskey, and a pint.

"The prayer's medieval, attributed to St. Andrew," Marta said. "He recited it as he was led to his crucifixion."

Marta translated the entire Latin prayer, ending with, "He, who redeemed me through thee, shalt receive me through thee. Amen."

"Sister Grey *said* there might be a redemption element."

"I don't want her to think I'm crowding her," Marta said. "Just helping a friend, that's all."

"You need to meet her," Kincaid said. "I'm sure—"

"We've met," Marta said. "We worked a case together."

"So that's how the Guards know her."

The wind came in with the open door and Baldwin caught Kincaid's eye. He didn't look at them as he went to the bar.

"Should I ask him to join us?"

"Fine with me," Marta said.

"You can tell us the story of Jane Grey."

Kincaid went to the bar.

"Not tonight, lad," Baldwin said, looking downcast. "Another time."

Kincaid started to ask what was wrong, but something in Baldwin's tone stopped him and he returned to Marta.

Fifteen

The bell ringer and the deacon held the victim's feet until the bell stopped. Witnesses reported hearing it peal in the wee hours. Didn't recall exactly when. Bucketing down, so one woman thought it was thunder.

Kincaid jotted notes, ascended the tower, walked around the bell, studying its curvature, markings, position. He peered down, past the rope and the plastic crime scene flags fluttering along it. Down the tower stairs into the claustrophobic vestibule, he passed the rope, normally stored on a hook but hanging freely now, a crude noose at its conclusion.

"Victim's name is Terence Byrne," Detective Garda Fields explained.

Kincaid looked at the victim's mouth. "Another gag?"

"Maybe," Fields said. "We didn't want to remove it until the tech lads got here."

Kincaid frowned and with his pen, removed the gag.

"Man keeps his own counsel. That's what they say about you, Inspector," Fields said.

"They say that, do they?" Kincaid held the gag up to the light streaming in through a stained-glass window. "Another manutergium," he said. "May I borrow your pen?"

"You can *have* my pen if you need it for that."

With the two pens, Kincaid spread the cloth like a drape. An ornately-stitched phrase—*Ó, lógmar muince*—unfurled in gold letters with black borders.

"Looks like someone's name," Fields said.

Kincaid set the towel into an evidence envelope and pressed down the victim's shirt collar and looked at the rope burns around his neck. A Technical Bureau examiner cast a shadow behind him.

BYRNE'S OLDER BROTHER DELIVERED his eulogy, tearing and seething. "Me brother was a friend to every man," he said. "I pray for his executioners, only because Terry would insist."

A lifetime bachelor with only his brother as family, Byrne had been a staple in the diocese, paying bills, handling payroll, writing checks to heating contractors, plumbers, electricians, Kincaid explained at the murder conference. His office manager died two years ago. Byrne returned all his old accounting files to his clients after he retired.

"That's as much as I know," his brother told Kincaid. "Terry didn't often talk about his practice. Too boring, he always said."

"He wasn't despondent?"

"As happy a man as I ever knew," his brother said. "He would not have harmed himself."

"Notes left with hanging victims always suggest suicide," Sr. Grey said later.

"But since he didn't kill himself—" Kincaid said. "And we've seen this sort of note before—"

"Our perpetrator may have viewed Mr. Byrne's death as self-inflicted. It is fundamentally different from death by crucifixion." Sr. Grey said. Her tone turned cheeky with the next remark. "What does Marta think?"

"Thank you for reminding me to ask her." His tone sounded almost as cheeky.

"***Ó, LÓGMAR MUINCE,*" KINCAID** read the crime scene photo. "It may be some form of old Irish."

"Meaning what?" Greevey asked.

"I've asked Marta to have a look," Kincaid said.

"At Trinity now, right?" McDermott said.

"In the library," Kincaid said.

"Any chance we could woo her back?" Greevey asked. "To CDU—not IS. How is she keeping, by the way?"

"She's well."

"You still seeing her?" McDermott asked.

"As friends, colleagues."

"At least she didn't leave us *all* behind, eh?" Greevey said.

Kincaid looked at the newspaper headline on Greevey's desk. "*All Saints Slayer*, now?" he said. "Last two victims were a solicitor and a chartered accountant."

"Hardly saints in most people's books," McDermott smirked.

"But they did work for the Church," Kincaid said.

"The stuff of sainthood, eh?" Greevey said.

"Adam." Sister Grey appeared at Greevey's office doorway.

"Sister. You know Chief Superintendent Greevey."

"I do," she said. They shook hands.

"*Adam* is it?" Greevey said.

"Sister and I weren't on a first-name basis," Kincaid said. "At least, last week."

"If you can get me in to see the Book of Kells, you may call me anything you'd like," the nun said.

"The Book of Kells?" Greevey said.

"The manutergia," Kincaid said. "The stitching reminded Marta of the Book."

"That's some high-level planning on the killer's part," McDermott said.

"We're meeting in the Long Room," Kincaid said. "Marta arranged for an after-hours viewing. Just a page or two."

"Say 'hallo' for me," Greevey said. "Tell her we miss her."

BLOODY SUNDAY PUSHED THE All-Saints Slayer out of the headlines. British troops had shot twenty six unarmed Catholics in the Northern Ireland city of Derry—or Londonderry, depending on your politics. Now fourteen were dead and the occupying British government under a public relations siege.

"Guess Bloom's is out for a while," Marta told Kincaid over the phone. "Crowds are getting crazy around there."

"I won't be stopped by it," he said. "But I do understand if you'd rather not."

"It's not for lack of courage. You know me."

"What, then?"

"You sound annoyed," she said.

"Greevey says he misses you."

"And you?"

"Of course. Why do you think I keep asking you to Bloom's?"

"Or to see Evelyn."

"I only asked that once," Kincaid said. "I hope you didn't take it wrong."

"Of course not," Marta said with a barely-perceptible laugh. "It's work, Adam. I'm feeling every bit the impostor. I can't relax. At some point, it will all be over and then I can."

"Over? Are you leaving Trinity now, too?"

"My training. My orientation."

"Are we still on for the tour?"

"I'm never an impostor around the written word."

"And around me?"

"Be safe, please," Marta said. "That's what I'm thinking about when I think about you. And say hello to your lovely mother for me."

ON HIS WAY TO the bar from the pub door, Dr. Baldwin stopped when he saw Kincaid alone at a booth.

"You hear that out there?" he asked.

"Peaceful demonstrators," Kincaid said.

"Is that what the papers are calling them? Rioters, more like." Baldwin said. "To think the Brits asked me to consult on—what did they call it? Operation—started with D, I think."

"Demetrius."

Baldwin slipped into the booth. "I told them I didn't believe in interning people without trial. Now, look what they've got." He looked toward the door. "Marta braving the storm?"

"Not tonight."

"Don't blame her."

"New job," Kincaid said. "She's working overtime trying to get it mastered."

"Not with the Guards anymore?"

"Left us for Trinity."

"An academic post. She *was* one of my best students."

"Are you all right?"

"I will be." Baldwin waved toward the barkeeper.

"I mean, after the other night."

"Oh, that," Baldwin said. "Got some bad news, was all. Wasn't expecting it. What are you having?"

"Usual," Kincaid told the barkeeper. "What kind of bad news?"

"You're a garda." Baldwin leaned in close. "Maybe I *should* tell you."

Kincaid cocked an eyebrow.

"I was threatened," Baldwin said.

"Your life, your person?"

"I don't know exactly. They left a note. Told me to make the *necessary arrangements.* Got rather prurient after that."

"Any idea who?"

"None."

"How about why?"

Baldwin sipped his beer, set it down, leaned in even closer. "They seem to think—" He whispered. "That I raped someone."

"They accused you of rape?"

"Not that exactly. More like I was a party to it."

"Like a witness?"

"More an active participant."

Kincaid pushed back from the table. "Should you be telling me this?"

"It's complete shite, Inspector," Baldwin said. "But the threat may not be. I know I'm only an academic, but I do have some expertise in these things."

A brick smashed a window, wind, glass, and curtains blowing in. Kincaid instinctively jumped, slid out of the booth, and blocked the barkeepers from the damage. The crowd outside bleated, chanted, and screamed. The hairs stood on the back of Kincaid's neck. "Back away," he said. "Let's get back. *Way* back."

"Fuckin' arseholes," the barkeep said. "Nobody panic," he told the pub.

After the crowd—and any suggestion a bomb might be next —passed, Kincaid relented. "Come by Dublin Castle tomorrow," he told the barkeep. "We'll take a report."

"I'll do that, Inspector. I will. Thank you."

Kincaid went back to the booth as staff picked up the brick and swept up the glass.

"You, too," he told Baldwin.

"Me, too what?"

"I'll have CDU take a report from you. You might bring a solicitor, just in case."

"I don't need a solicitor. I've done nothing wrong," Baldwin said.

"Just in case," Kincaid repeated.

BALDWIN'S THREAT STORY STRUCK a dormant nerve in Kincaid, who remembered walking with a newspaper and an umbrella when he heard soft choking at a window too high for his then-twelve-year-old self to peer inside. He stayed beneath the window long enough to wait out any imagined sounds, then searched for a door.

As he passed along the building, the voice was a whimper, then a moan, then words that sounded like pleading. He stopped, tried to make out what she was saying, where she was saying it. The rain made it hard to hear.

"Hello?" he cried. "Can I help you? Are you all right?"

She screamed. He jumped then ran toward what looked like a door and grabbed the handle and pulled it. Locked, of course.

Kincaid felt the hairs on the back of his neck and an urgent pang seized his stomach. He wrapped the newspaper around his fist and smashed through a lower window and pulled his small body in, one wet leg at a time. He hopped on the first leg as he dragged the other across the sill, balancing on a chair. Next he was out an office door, down a hallway, past a line of offices, black name plates and silver lettering on each door, along paneled walls and stiff carpet.

She screamed again. Kincaid ran to the office at the end of the hall. He pushed the door back. "Hey!" he yelled. A man was on top of her, and either he was wearing white, or she was wearing white. He darted forward to pull the man off, but he swatted Kincaid back, blew the air clean out of him. Knocked against the wall Kincaid couldn't breathe. "I can't stop this, I can't stop it," he thought.

"I can't see his face. I can't see his head," he recalled all these years later. "I can't make her out. He'd got someone pinned down, but I can't make them out."

He tried to get up, but still couldn't breathe. So he sat. Then a weird thing happened. They stopped. The person underneath pulled off the man's mask. A mane of black hair flowed out. He turned around. But it was a woman. Olive skin, regal cheekbones, red lips. Very tended to.

And the screaming girl beneath? A boy—eight, ten—just a kid. He was looking at Kincaid. They were both looking at Kincaid, like "what the fuck are you doing here?"

Kincaid stepped back, stumbled, and hurried down the hallway and out the door into the rain. He never learned what he saw, didn't understand it, never reported it, and avoided the building on trips to get the newspaper or the messages or anything else his ma or da wanted.

Fresh out of Templemore, he felt guilty for the first time. He had witnessed a domestic violence of some sort, where victim and victimizer became allies in the face of his challenge, a pattern he would see time and again. And he had failed to report the crime, another recurring pattern in the life cycle of an investigation.

The only thing he did with the memory now was dream about it. He wondered, all these years later, if dream and reality hadn't somehow merged.

KINCAID LOOKED AT HIS mother, mouth open, gray hair, finer now but with hints of its former dark fullness, spread on the pillow. He looked at the gift, still unwrapped but on a dresser now in this single-occupancy room. He unfolded the newspaper he brought, saw another headline that relegated the All-Saints Slayer below the fold.

Embassy burns as mourning turns violent.

Twenty thousand people protesting Bloody Sunday, rocks and petrol bombs by the hundreds, the Union Jack in flames. Mere blocks from Bloom's Pub.

"Mister—Inspector—Kincaid." The nurse whispered as she slipped into the room. "I didn't see you."

Kincaid folded the newspaper. "When was the last time she was awake?"

“This morning, quite early.” The nurse went around to the other side of the bed. “Evie sleeps more these days.” She smoothed the hair out of Eve’s eyes. “Such lovely cheeks,” she said. “Even when she’s snoring.”

“Is she any happier?”

“When was the last time you saw her?”

“When I almost ate the head off your residency director,” Kincaid said.

“Oh, dear. I’m sorry to hear that.” She looked around the room. “Everything get sorted?”

“If she’s happier.” Kincaid took his mother’s hand and caressed it between his thumb and forefinger. “Then it’s sorted.”

“She’s happier for her, I’d say.”

“For her?”

“Nothing to make offense, but—she did ask about you the other day. Wondered when you’d visit again.”

Kincaid looked at his mother with a certain astonishment. “She asked about me, she did?”

“We could wake her. Gently, of course.”

Kincaid shook his head, leaned down and kissed her cheek.

He sat by the bed reading the rest of the news until sun became shadow through the partly-opened window blinds.

Sixteen

Sister Grey walked toward Kincaid as he faced the other direction in the empty, quiet Long Room in the Old Library at Trinity College.

"The face of a child," she whispered.

"Oh!" he gasped. "You startled me."

"Our *Last Judgment* messenger?"

"How could *that* be the handiwork of a child?"

They entered the famously-bookish two hundred thirteen-foot corridor of stalls, shelves, busts, arches, and shadows.

"So it's supposed to be Michelangelo's face, not a child?"

"That's the theory," Grey said. "Why Mister Angelo felt the need to announce himself is unknown. It may have had something to do with shedding guilt, sin, Earthly trappings. Scholars simply don't know." She turned her head toward the stalls and said breathlessly, "Perhaps we should ask Marta."

"Who said to wait here. Quietly."

Sister Grey took in the two-story book stalls. ""Eerie. All this silent erudition."

"Adam." Marta walked down an ornate wrought-iron spiral staircase near the front of the library. "I didn't hear you come in. Please." She motioned them over. Eighteenth-century Belgian sculptor Peter Scheemakers's busts of Homer, Socrates, and Plato stood watch near a stall labeled *C*.

"Sister." Marta took Grey's hand. "It's been too long."

"Marta was telling me about that," Kincaid said.

"We worked a bombing case—Ulster Revolutionary Front, or some such thing," Grey said. "Miss it?" she asked Marta.

"Not anymore," Marta said. "I thought I would, but I don't."

She guided them toward C stall, presented two old books with Latinate and Celtic texts open on a lectern-style book stand. Kincaid walked around a bookshelf ladder to see it.

Grey read from the first book. "*Ó, lógmar muince.*"

"As I explained when Adam asked, it's Irish, probably dating to either the Middle Irish or Early Modern Irish period," Marta said. "The language went through several transitions, starting with Primitive Irish, then Old Irish, Middle Irish, Early Modern Irish, and what we use today, Modern Irish."

"How old is this version?"

"Four to six hundred years, give or take. "

"And the rest?"

"*Lógmar,*" Marta pointed to the word next to a fanciful sketch of a jewel-encrusted crown, "means 'valuable'. 'Expensive'." She stared at the word. "Or more precisely, 'precious'. *Ó,* in this sense, appears to be an exclamation, like 'Oh, God!'"

"So, Oh expensive *what*?" Kincaid said.

"That's what puzzles me. This last word, *muince*, could mean a few things. 'Collar,' which doesn't sound expensive."

"Like a dog collar?"

"Or necklace, which could be expensive," Marta said. "You found this," she held up a crime scene photo of the *Ó, lógmar muince*-monogrammed lavabo towel, “with the hanging victim, right?”

“Correct.”

“Oh costly necklace,” she translated. “Or collar, if the noose is the collar.”

“A poor attempt at irony?” Kincaid said. “He bought the collar at the cost of his life?”

“Or another message,” Jane Grey said.

“The other phrase you sent me, from Dr. Boyd’s murder, is Latin. I found a reference to St. Andrew here,” Marta said, indicating the other book. “This is the *Legenda Aurea*. The Golden Legend. It’s a thirteenth century hagiography collection —basically an encyclopedia of saints—by the Italian archbishop Jacobus de Voragine. Very popular in its day.”

“Doesn’t look that old,” Kincaid said.

“The original is in Italy. This is an eighteenth-century copy.”

“*O bona crux diu desiderata et concupiscenti animo praeparata suscipe discipulum eius qui pependit in te,*” Sister Grey read.

“‘O good cross, long have I desired thee, and now thou art ready for my eager soul,” Marta translated. “As I was telling Adam, it was St. Andrew’s final prayer before he was crucified.”

“St. Bartholomew, St. Andrew, and St. Peter. All Apostles. All murdered,” Kincaid said.

“Martyred, Adam. A key difference,” Grey said. “My guess is that the fourth victim also has a martyred alter-ego.”

“I’ve been reading about these killings,” Marta said. “And remembering why I like the quiet life.”

“Apologies for dragging you out of it,” Sr. Grey said.

“Ah, but the rewards,” Marta said. She took the photos of the monogrammed lavabo towels. “We’re about to see one of them.”

The two investigators followed her out of the stall to a locked glass display case in the main corridor. They took sides and peered down.

“Is this—?”

“The Book of Kells,” Marta said.

“I’m getting goosebumps,” Sr. Grey said.

“Arguably the most famous manuscript in Western history,” Marta said. “This is one volume. The others aren’t on display this year.”

“Brilliant,” Kincaid said. “I’ve seen it before, but only in photos.”

“In all the years you’ve lived here?” Marta said.

“The Philistine detective,” Grey said.

“This style of calligraphy and adornment,” Marta pointed to the page. “It’s called the Insular style. I recognized it in the manutergia.” She held up the crime scene photos of the two altar towels.

“Someone spent a lot of time on this stitching,” Sr. Grey said.

"*Erat autem hora tertia,*" Kincaid read in the book. “Something about an hour.”

“Now it was the third hour, when they crucified Him,” Sister said. “The Gospel of St. Mark.”

"The Book of Kells contains the four Gospels—Matthew, Mark, Luke, and John," Marta said. "Best anyone can tell, the book dates to between the sixth century life of St. Columba—or as I prefer to call him, Colmcille—and the ninth century abbey his order founded, Kells Abbey in County Meath, where the great book was—"

A noise like something hitting the floor startled them.

"My. What—?"

It came from one of the stalls at the end of the corridor.

"You have a haunt," Sr. Grey said.

"Sounded like a book," Marta said. "And most of them are delicate!" She made a face and started down the corridor. But Kincaid took her arm.

"Sounded like it came from upstairs," he said, looking at the second floor of bookshelves that met the ceiling.

"Let me check." Marta moved out of Kincaid's grasp. She looked in the stall they had just visited. "Fine here," she said. She went in the other direction, to the front of the library. Kincaid started to follow. Sr. Grey stopped him.

"No need to panic her further," she said.

Marta vanished behind stall BB, next to the Shakespeare bust. They heard footsteps on the wrought-iron spiral staircase, footsteps on the second story, and the sound of something closing. Then a noise, a gasp, maybe a scream tailored for a library.

"Marta?" Kincaid called. He looked at the sister, went to the stall and started climbing the spiral staircase.

Footsteps, running, and Marta appeared out of breath.

"Marta? What's wrong?" Grey said.

Kincaid stepped off the stairs, came to her side.

"Are you all right?"

Marta opened her mouth but nothing came out.

"You look like you've seen the proverbial ghost," Grey said.

"It's back there," she said, partly turning and pointing. Grey started to move, but Marta grabbed her arm. "Adam," she said.

MCDERMOTT PARKED HIS CAR a few blocks from The Old Library. He crossed the cobblestone walkways and stopped outside the library at the sight of a horse tethered to a bicycle rack with reins, collar, and harness. He recognized the Irish Cob breed in the horse's long, heavy mane; lower-leg feathering; and spotted, or piebald coat. A uniformed garda motioned him into the building.

"Pony?" he asked Kincaid.

"There's more," Kincaid said. They walked down the corridor and the victim came into view. "There is blood," Kincaid said. "This time." They stopped short of the crime scene markers.

"What have they done?"

"Covered head suggests hanging for starters," Kincaid said. "Pathologist won't have him out of there until after lunch."

"Is Marta about?"

"Library Square, last I saw her. Walking near the Campanile with Sister Grey."

"How is she? Did you—"

"She's fine, though it was obviously quite a shock. And yes, I got a preliminary," Kincaid said, tapping the notebook under his jacket. "We'll meet for the longer version later."

They watched the Tech Bureau examiners photograph and measure and move the victim's covered head with a yardstick to avoid tramping in the blood.

"Cut into four pieces, about. Lashed to the book ladder," one of them said.

"I'm about to be sick," McDermott said. "I never get sick at these things."

"Superintendent, Inspector. A bit of room, if you please." The crime scene examiner motioned them back.

"How long until you remove the executioner's hood?" Kincaid asked.

"Not long, sir." The examiner peered under the hood with a flashlight. "Victim appears to be older," the examiner said.

"Appears?" Kincaid said.

"Late fifties, perhaps. Hard to say for sure. Hood's stuck to blood in the hair."

"Anything in the mouth, or can you see it?" McDermott asked.

"I knew you'd want to know, so I looked," the examiner said. "Didn't appear to be. But we'll know more after the autopsy."

KINCAID THUMBED THROUGH HIS notebook.

"She walked home alone," Sr. Grey said. "Quite suddenly, I thought."

"Harrington Street, near Synge Street. Here," he said. He looked toward a row of flats. "She just moved."

Kincaid recalled the low wrought iron fences, stone steps, and short stoops. Marta's new flat was two doors down from the electrocuted shaving man. Kincaid ran up the steps, into her building. He knocked at her door. "Marta. It's Adam." He pounded on the door. "Marta!" He came down the steps.

"Not home?" Sr. Grey said from the passenger's side window.

Kincaid looked around. He came up to the car. "She used to leave a key. At her other place." Kincaid looked at the shaving man's flat. "I've a mind to go—" He saw a familiar figure coming down the steps. "Alyson?" Kincaid called.

She looked at him, then ran. He slipped back in the car and followed her.

"A girl I interviewed about a possible suicide," Kincaid told Sr. Grey.

As the car pulled alongside the girl, Grey placed her hand on his sleeve. "Let me."

Kincaid stopped. Grey got out and chased Alyson. She grabbed her by the collar.

"Let go of me, bitch!" She hurled around trying to shake off the sister. But Kincaid grabbed her shoulders.

"Stop it," he said.

"Fuck you."

"That's a nun you're talking to," Kincaid said.

"I don't care what she is. Let me go."

"Why'd you run?"

She looked at them, past them, at any opportunity to take off.

"Why did you run?" he repeated.

"I didn't run."

"You saw me. You ran."

"You're that policeman. I told you what I know."

"And where did we leave that?"

She tried to yank free, but the two adults held her.

"I didn't arrest you or your mam, did I?" Kincaid looked toward Marta's flat. "You know a woman lives there?"

"No."

"She just moved in."

"Where?" Alyson asked.

Kincaid turned her toward the flat. "Short brown hair, early thirties."

"Why would I know her?"

Sister Grey leaned down. "She lives alone. She's a friend and we're looking for her."

Alyson looked like she was thinking. "She have a dog?"

Kincaid looked at Sr. Grey.

"She have a bloody dog?" Alyson said.

"I don't know," Kincaid said. "She didn't used to."

"Don used to chat up a woman with a dog."

"Don? You mean Dan?"

"Dan, Don, Dead. The dead man in our flat."

"How charming," Sr. Grey said.

"'She's a right lil' dinger,' he told my ma. I didn't hang around to hear the rest."

"When did you first notice Dan with this woman?"

"Couple weeks ago. Seemed like she was new, I guess. Hadn't seen her before. Hafta be new to put up with Don."

"And what do you think my next question's gonna be?"

"She looked like you said she looked, from what I saw of her," Alyson said. "I wish Dead Dan Don had taken up with her."

Kincaid lowered himself and looked Alyson in the eyes. "Did you kill Dan Faunt?"

She looked straight back at him. "If I'd a kilt him, there'd a been blood."

Kincaid looked at Sr. Grey. "I believe her," she said. "Though I have no idea who she's talking about."

"You see anyone else hanging around here? Your place, Marta's place?" Kincaid asked.

"Her name was Marta?" Alyson said.

"Yes."

"'Goin' to see Marta are ya?' I heard me mam and him argue about her. Sounded like she was Don's ex."

"Your ma around?"

"No," Alyson said.

"Mind if we check?"

"No," Alyson said. "I'll even let you in."

KINCAID APPEARED AT MARTA'S open front door two days later. She was declared missing at his urging, and he had barely slept in the days since the Long Room expedition, where Sister Grey left her in Library Park.

"Inspector."

He walked in and looked around. He slipped on a pair of latex gloves.

"No indication of a crime," the garda told him. "We rummaged around a bit. Got a broad warrant. Looked like she was still unpacking."

"Any sign of a pet? Dog, cat?"

"No, Inspector."

"No dog bed, leash, flea spray?"

"No, Inspector."

"Smells kinda doggy in here."

"Old building, sir. Musty."

"What's this?"

"Empty bowl, sir. That cabinet was open. We figure it fell out."

"Have it tested. Dog hair, dog food, dog slobber, dog anything."

"Yes, Inspector. So *the* Marta Carney, sir?"

"*The*?"

"Only the finest document examiner in the history of the Technical Bureau."

"I'll tell her you said that."

"Oh, sir. I wouldn't want to embarrass her."

Kincaid looked in the bedroom, bathroom, kitchen, closets. He took out a man's jacket on a coat hanger and held it against his chest. "Right now, I'd do anything to embarrass her," he said.

Seventeen

"Were you two an item?"

"What a question."

"Seriously. I'm dying to know."

Sister Grey drove through the gate at Gardaí headquarters in Phoenix Park. Kincaid nodded to the guard. They parked and he stepped out of her car.

"No," he said with the door still open.

"But you wanted to be?"

"Maybe." Kincaid looked around. "I met her right here, almost in this very spot."

"You were getting into your cars and she caught your eye."

He closed the car door. "She caught my eye inside that building," Kincaid said. "And my ear. She was challenging Greevey about some foul up with a handwriting analysis."

"Winning?"

"He never stood a chance."

"You admire a woman with brains," Sr. Grey said.

"And heart."

They took seats in a conference room abuzz with reporters, photojournalists, television cameras, and press badges before a podium and a few chairs at the front.

"Never seen a full-court press here," Grey said.

"More Conroy report fallout," Kincaid said. "Got our first-ever press officer last year. And," he looked down and whispered, "full-court press is an American basketball term."

"I'm a football fan myself," Sr. Grey said.

"Inspector."

Kincaid looked up at a reporter poised with a notebook.

"A few words?" the reporter asked.

"Can it wait?" Kincaid said.

"We were hoping—"

"The All Saints Slayer?" Sr. Grey interjected. "Where on Earth did you come up with that?"

"That's *The Sun*," the reporter said. "We have a policy—"

"This last victim was no saint." Another reporter joined them. "So I hear, anyway. Kincaid, isn't it?" He thrust out his hand. Kincaid ducked away as Sr. Grey intercepted.

"Jane Grey," she said. "Nun. Psychologist. You know, all this sensationalism can be an inspiration. To the wrong minds."

"Not from our paper. Nun?"

"Yes. Nun."

"Can we have your attention, please," from the podium. "Your attention."

The room began to quiet.

"If you'd all take your seats." The man at the podium, Superintendent Carey, smiled. "We have a lot to get through." When most of the standing-room-only crowd was seated, "I'd like to introduce Mary Feeney, with our press office. She will take your questions and, as *necessary* . . . " He let "necessary" settle on the room. " . . . refer them to the investigators we have in attendance. Mary."

"Yes. Good morning," she said. "We finally have a positive identification of the fourth—if not fifth—victim in this series of homicides."

Two hands shot up in the audience. "Fifth?" the reporter asked.

Feeney deferred to Superintendent Carey, who leaned into the microphone. "If you count the Boyd case from sixty eight," he said. "Check your press packets." He returned the podium.

"Regarding our latest victim," Feeney continued, "I'm very sorry to announce . . . he was one of ours. Alexander Baldwin. Dr. Alexander Baldwin."

"Baldwin?" Kincaid said.

" . . . a psychology professor who has worked with An Garda Síochána for the past ten years at Templemore—"

Kincaid stood, Sr. Grey's eyes following him up.

"He was strangled somewhere away from the crime scene, and we believe brought to the Old Library in the company of a horse—yes, Inspector?" Feeney said.

"Why weren't we told about this?"

Sr. Grey went for Kincaid's arm, then stopped and lowered her hand back to her lap.

"Why are we just hearing about this now?"

"I don't know, Inspector. Superintendent Carey."

The man in charge of the press office stood.

"No place for this, Adam," Greevey said from his seat alongside the podium.

"No, Chief Superintendent," Kincaid said. "It most certainly is not."

"Inspector, please take your seat," Carey said. Mary Feeney whispered into his ear. "Can we just please get through this," Carey added.

"This is no way to get through this," Kincaid said.

"We didn't know until this morning," McDermott said, sitting next to Greevey.

"This conference was already scheduled, Inspector," Carey said.

"Then you should have bloody well put the kybosh on it," Kincaid said. He picked up his coat.

"Adam." Sr. Grey tugged at him.

"Good for you." A plainclothes detective grabbed Kincaid's sleeve from a seat behind him.

"Adam!" Grey whispered. "You'll miss the best part, whatever it is." She tugged at him until he relented and retook his seat.

Carey and Feeney meanwhile tag-teamed media questions.

"To what the gentleman said earlier, why did it take so long to identify the latest victim?"

"It wasn't that long, not by coroner's standards," Mary Feeney said. "The body was not in identification-ready condition, and we needed to be sure. Especially in this case."

"How do you know these cases are all connected?" a television reporter asked. "I don't recall any horses involved in the other crimes."

"You're right. This homicide is different than the others," Carey said. "But it shares enough similarities. Its ritual nature, for instance. Yes, in the corner."

"Drawn and quartered. Didn't that go out in the Middle Ages?"

"Chief Superintendent?" Carey asked. Greevey went to the podium.

"It did," he said. "Crucifixions went out centuries earlier. Someone, we believe, is sending a message, with antiquated tortures."

"What was I saying about not jumping to conclusions about religious rituals?" Sister Grey whispered to Kincaid.

"Is it true someone on your staff vanished from Library Park that day?"

"No," Greevey said.

Scribble, scribble, scribble.

"What's the connection? Churches, then a library."

"Superintendent John McDermott might best speak to that."

McDermott took the podium, still looking flustered.

"All the victims . . ." he sighed, looked at Kincaid, looked at the audience. ". . . the first three, they, uh, worked for the Catholic Church. Dr. Boyd and Dr. Baldwin, however—no apparent connection with the Church. But," he looked at

Kincaid, looked down, sighed again, "three of the five victims, including Baldwin, *were* found with embroidered kerchiefs."

Kincaid sat up. "What?" he gasped.

"What kind of embroidery?" a reporter asked.

"Latin words."

"Baldwin had a manutergium?" Kincaid asked Sr. Grey.

"Adam," she said.

"When were you planning to tell us? Me?" Kincaid asked McDermott.

"*Diu desiderata,*" McDermott continued.

"Which means?"

"*Long desired,*" McDermott answered. "He was found in the Long Room, so—"

More hands went up. McDermott looked to Mary Feeney. She nodded. "Yes," McDermott said.

"What's a manutergium?"

"Hand towel a priest uses," Kincaid mumbled before a similar answer from the podium.

"What words again?"

"Latin for 'Long desired'."

"Embroidery?"

"In a manner of speaking."

"Belfast Telegraph," a reporter said. "Any connection to the witch burnings in the North?"

McDermott looked at Greevey, then Kincaid. "What witch burnings?" McDermott mouthed silently. Kincaid turned toward the reporter.

"In the North," the reporter repeated. "County Down way."

"Not our jurisdiction," Greevey interjected.

"They found those same kerchiefs," the reporter said. He looked at his notebook. *"et concubine animo praeparata—"*

Kincaid turned to him.

"Concupiscenti." Sister Grey chuckled. "Not concubine."

Rapid-fire questioning continued.

"What if they're connected?"

"Isn't it worth a look?"

"Shouldn't you be working with the RUC?"

"Aren't witch burnings medieval torture?"

Kincaid stared at McDermott and Greevey. "Where was this manutergium found?" he asked.

"With the victim, Dr. Baldwin," Carey said.

"But where? In the mouth—"

"In his hand, Inspector. It was wadded in his fist."

"ADAM." MCDERMOTT CAUGHT HIM in the hallway after the press conference. "What the fuck is wrong with you?"

"Marta's missing, Baldwin's dead."

"I understand Marta. But you barely knew the man, for God's sake?

"I was *getting* to know him," Kincaid said. "Met him at a pub near Merrion Square. Marta and I both met him, chatted it up. She took his class at Templemore."

"None of that justifies such an outburst."

"Gentlemen." Sister Grey appeared beside them.

The three stood silently. McDermott looked at the wall, Kincaid at the floor, Grey at the two men.

"He told me he'd been threatened," Kincaid said. "Baldwin. Last time we saw each other."

"Threatened about what?" McDermott said.

"I don't know exactly. It didn't make much sense, not to either of us. Something about a rape."

"Some kind of mistaken identity, maybe?"

"I don't know. I told him to report it to CDU."

Grey touched Kincaid's jacket sleeve. He looked up in time to see reporters, cameras, and a television crew heading their way.

"Time to flee the telly," Sr. Grey said.

They headed in the opposite direction. Reporters called out behind them.

"Inspector."

"Inspector Kincaid. How did you know the fifth victim?"

"Won't slow 'em down," McDermott said.

"Alexander Baldwin. He was a psychologist?"

"Was he *your* psychologist, Inspector?"

"I see they read their press packets closely," Sister Grey quipped.

"Did you really not know he was dead?"

"Marta Carney."

Kincaid stopped.

The reporter came up to him.

"What about Marta?" Kincaid said.

"Someone—nothing," the reporter said.

"What did you hear about Marta?"

"She used to work here, right?"

"No comment," McDermott interrupted, behind Kincaid.

Mary Feeney appeared. "No more questions, today, gentlemen," she said. "We've got to get back to things."

"Will you be investigating the witch burnings?" the *Belfast Telegraph* reporter yelled.

"Not our jurisdiction" Kincaid yelled back as they headed up a staircase.

"Greevey wants to see you," McDermott said on the second floor, a little out of breath.

"Of course he does."

"I'll wait for you downstairs," Sr. Grey said.

"Sure?" Kincaid said.

"You're going to get yelled at, maybe demoted, maybe even sacked," she said. "I prefer to remember you as the legendary detective you were."

"WHAT DID HE SAY?" Grey asked. They were walking out of the Phoenix Park building toward her car.

"We *will* be investigating the witch burnings," Kincaid said. "I will, anyway."

"What an idiotic name. '*Witch* burnings,'" Sr. Grey said. "At least you weren't sacked."

"No, exiled. I need a cooling-off period, Greevey says. We need to prove our mettle in the North, he says, followed by a discourse on the Saor Éire and the growing ranks of the Provisional IRA right here at home. By way of illustrating how fortunate I've been, Greevey took special care to note how many unmarried garda have been shipped to isolated Border divisions with no return ticket in sight. He also reminded me how much the Gardaí spent on my training with the Americans—"

"Americans?"

"FBI. Guards flew me to Quantico. Marta, too."

"Impressive," Sr. Grey said. "So where are the Guards sending you now?"

"A village near the witch burnings. Briar Lough, County Down."

"Sounds quaint. Inviting, even."

"It's majority Catholic."

"Well, then."

Kincaid stopped. "It's no place—"

"No place?"

He started walking again.

"No place?" she repeated.

"What did you mean, *inviting*?" Kincaid said.

"Don't try to distract from the disrespect at hand, Inspector."

"Well—it isn't. Any place for a—civilian."

"A civilian woman, you mean. Which doesn't explain why my order is working on a case there?"

"I didn't know they were."

"And you wouldn't. Hush hush. Top secret. Need to know basis, that sort of thing."

"Ridiculous," Kincaid said. "Nuns working undercover."

"I didn't say it was undercover," she said. "And I'd certainly not call anything we sisters do ridiculous."

"Then outlandish."

"Says the man assigned to the solve the witch burnings," Sr. Grey said. "Surprised they aren't getting more coverage here."

"Different victimology. All women, Greevey tells me. Maybe a copycat. And the Gardaí doesn't play well with the RUC."

"Why do you think that reporter brought it up?"

"Sell more papers. So unless Marta turns up burned at the stake—"

"Any news on her? Did Greevey say anything?"

"Nothing. I'm meeting with the woman next door tomorrow."

"The girl's mum? Alyson?"

"She promises sobriety and may have seen something. I'd welcome your help."

"But not in Briar Lough," Sister Grey said.

"WHAT'S SO TOP SECRET you can't tell a detective?" Kincaid asked Sr. Grey on the drive over to Alyson's house.

"You've heard the term 'Magdalene laundries.'"

"Where unwed mams work day and night."

"In terrible conditions," Grey said. "The governments in both North and South have turned a blind eye, but certain high-level church officials asked our order to take a closer look. I know of at least one Dymphnan working in such a laundry. But since the North is no place for a woman—"

"You said you worked a bombing case—with Marta."

"Terrorists—I call them terrorists, they call themselves *revolutionaries*—blew up a passenger train. Twenty three people killed. Mothers, children, tourists, workers. Just regular people. Marta and I analyzed some unsigned letters claiming credit, me looking at psychology, her looking at handwriting. The two can be closely aligned, especially under stress."

"William Flynn," Kincaid said.

"William *Henry* Flynn," Sr. Grey said. "His brand of narcissism insisted on the *Henry*. I heard he committed suicide."

"Just as the Guards were honing in," Kincaid said.

"Must have killed him to leave all those letters unsigned."

"Whole thing left a bad taste," Kincaid said. "Lingering to this day."

"That why Marta eventually left?"

Kincaid pulled the car in front of Alyson's house.

"It was an early straw," he said.

"I TOLD THEM I wouldn't speak to anybody but you," Alyson's mother Marisol told Kincaid. She looked at Sr. Grey. "I don't know her."

"Jane Grey," she said, extending her hand.

"Well. Care to sit?" Marisol asked.

They looked around the disheveled flat. Kincaid made a place for them on a sofa.

"Have a tea? Anything to eat?"

Both declined. Marisol slumped into a chair across from them.

"Marta is a good friend," Kincaid said. "When I found out she lived across the way—"

"I don't blame you," Marisol said. "She seemed like a nice person."

"Is this her—the woman you saw?" Kincaid took a Polaroid from his jacket.

"That's her. The other investigator had a different picture, but that's the same person. Said she used to work for the Guards."

"She did," Kincaid said. "She was one of the best."

"Your daughter . . . is she—?" Sr. Grey asked.

"Working. She helps an elderly woman around the house."

"Good for her," Sr. Grey said.

"Do you two . . . work together?"

"On a different case," Sr. Grey said. "Adam's—Inspector Kincaid's—friend Marta vanished after we visited her about it."

"You think someone kidnapped her? Killed her maybe?"

Kincaid fidgeted. "We don't know," he said. "She's simply a missing person at this point."

"I don't understand this country," Marisol said. "I don't understand how people can be so cruel."

"Where are you from?" Sr. Grey asked.

"Spain. A little town outside Madrid."

"What brought you to Dublin?"

"Dan. We met in Madrid."

"Your daughter said Dan spoke with a woman who matches Marta's description," Kincaid said. "That she might have had a dog."

"Oh," Marisol said. "I wondered about the dog. It wasn't her dog."

"No?"

"I think it was a friend's."

"Male or female friend?" Sr. Grey asked.

"Male."

Kincaid sat up. "Boyfriend?"

"Don't know. But I do know it was a male friend because Dan would have gone on about her otherwise. He loved rubbing my nose in his way with women."

"Did you ever see him, Marta's friend?"

"No."

"Your daughter said you and Dan argued about Marta," Kincaid said.

"Your friend wasn't interested in Dan," Marisol said. "But that didn't stop him."

"Were you arguing about her the day Dan was killed?"

"I don't know. Maybe. I was too drunk to remember."

"I'M NOT COMFORTABLE LEAVING before Baldwin's memorial," Kincaid told Chief Superintendent Greevey. "And of course, there's the matter of Marta. Sending me away in the middle of such chaos surrounding the people I care about—"

"I'm hurt, Adam," McDermott said.

"*Some* of the people I care about," Kincaid said.

"What can you do here, for either of them?" Greevey asked.

"I'm your best homicide investigator."

"If you weren't so close to both of them. And Marta's not dead. At least, not that we know of."

"And if she turns up dead, what then? You call me with the tragic news?" Kincaid asked.

"CDU is on it. Special Branch, too. And Murder Squad—"

"Wonderful."

"Given Marta's connections with Technical, I wasn't going to put them off."

"I'll call you when they release Dr. Baldwin's body," McDermott said. "You'll have time to return. It's not like you're going back to the States."

"Higher ups want to set an example," Greevey added. "How can we justify forcing young, married recruits to leave their wives and kiddos for border towns if we don't also send the occasional veteran that way? You'll be up there a few weeks, at most. Something of a goodwill gesture. Our best man for their hardest case."

"So it's political," Kincaid said.

"Fianna Fáil is playing defense," Greevey said. "Rumor has it Fine Gael has a new man, Cosgrave, who can halt the violence at the border. May put him up for Taoiseach, *if* they prevail. We won't halt the violence—as if that's even possible—without the cooperation of the RUC."

"Consider yourself an ambassador," McDermott said. "God and Country. Patriotic duty."

"Good lord," Kincaid said.

"Him, too."

"You know how irascible I can be."

"You're well-regarded in the North, Adam. Did you know that?" Greevey said. "I suspect you'll be too flattered to be irascible."

Eighteen

The Dublin-Belfast Enterprise slowed as it approached a railway curve near the Boyne Viaduct in Drogheda, County Louth and County Meath near the border.

"If any town embodies the tragedy and travail that is Ireland, eh?"

Kincaid looked at the woman beside him, reading a story in the *Irish Times*. "Ritual murders grip Dublin," the headline announced.

"The two Olivers," he responded.

"One a saint and one a scoundrel," she went on. "Which was which depends on who you ask though, don't it?"

"Isn't that Ireland?" Kincaid said.

"We're still shooting ya over it. Depending on your answer. *That's* Ireland."

He watched the trusses pass the window as the train trundled across the viaduct bridge over the Boyne River. He laid his head against the window and nodded off recalling the time he and his mother visited the shrine to St. Oliver Plunkett in St. Peter's Catholic Church, Drogheda. He was a boy and the martyr's preserved head seared his conscience.

Kincaid awakened as the train slowed across the border, to his mother's pale face still peering at him over a blanket the afternoon he said goodbye for this journey.

The woman beside him sighed as the train stopped.

"Not again," she said. She motioned with her eyes to a conductor walking down the aisle, stopping at each row of seats.

"Slight delay," he said. "Underway soon. Slight delay. Getting underway soon."

"Code for bomb threat," the woman told Kincaid.

"The train? Or the tracks?"

"They've never had the nerve to blow up anything. Why bother when the threat will do? You're not from here, are you?"

"Dublin," he said.

"Ahh. Me aunt lives there. She wants to visit, but I won't let her." She sat up and looked out the window.

"Who makes the threats?" Kincaid asked.

"Take your pick," the woman said. "South Armagh Brigade, Gusty Spence's group, IRA. Even the RUC, some would have us believe. Where you headed?"

"Briar Lough."

"Newry Station, then," she directed.

The roving conductor stopped. "Inspector?"

"Yes?" Kincaid said.

"Would you be so kind as to come with me."

"Why?"

The conductor leaned down and whispered. "Police business, sir. I've been asked to be discreet."

The woman watched Kincaid rise from his seat. “Inspector. Well,” she said. She stood and moved aside as he slipped past her into the aisle.

KINCAID AND THE CONDUCTOR navigated a slope to a clearing away from the train. Wind blew across early-blooming wildflowers, low grass, mossy stones, and the hydraulic gasps of relaxing gears and pistons.

They came upon four armed men wearing balaclava masks and green camouflage. One smoked through the opening in his mask.

“These men won’t let the train cross until they speak with you,” the conductor said.

“Let’s see some ID,” the shortest man said.

“Who wants to see it?” Kincaid asked.

“*Who* is not important,” the short man said. “What’s important is *why*.”

“Best give it him,” the conductor told Kincaid.

The short man looked over Kincaid’s ID and handed it back.

“Pat him down.”

Another man patted Kincaid from neck to shoes. “Nothing,” he said.

“Unarmed?”

“CDU doesn’t carry,” Kincaid said, though his RUC contact would provide a firearm as needed.

"The Guards have someone we want," the short man said. "He belongs here. He's one of ours. He's fled justice and we aim to get him back."

"We won't release a terrorist," Kincaid said. "You can blow up a bridge, kill me, kill everyone on that train. But it won't matter."

"You ain't hearing me right. I said he's one of *ours*, not one of *us*." The man sat on a stone wall, pulled a rifle onto his lap. "Big difference."

"He's a priest, man," one of the others said. "Name o' Brenden Wryth."

"He fled to Ireland after Monsignor Mulvaney started making noise," the short man said. "RUC might've arrested him. Now, they can't find him."

"We don't have him," Kincaid said.

"You do."

"If we did, I'd know about it. How did you know I was on the train?"

"You're here about those women been killed," the short man said. "It's around. Wryth worked with one of them."

"First one kilt," another man said.

"Maybe you oughta let me do what I came here to do," Kincaid said.

The men talked among themselves.

"Tell your bosses either they return Wryth, or we take action. On Republic soil."

"Haven't you already?" Kincaid asked.

"Which time?"

The short man waved his head at the conductor back toward the train. His group gathered their arms and started toward a dirt road.

The conductor took a deep breath. "Thank you, Inspector," he said.

"For what?"

"Humoring them. We never know, you know."

He took Kincaid back up the slope to the train.

ROYAL ULSTER CONSTABULARY CONSTABLE Iain Brugha greeted Kincaid at Newry Station.

"Constable." Kincaid shook his hand.

"Train was late."

"It got held up. Men in masks making threats."

"Sergeant O'Connell has a Walther PP at the ready for you," Brugha said.

"What caliber?"

"Twenty two." Kincaid caught a smirk. He picked up his luggage and followed Brugha to an armored Hotspur Land Rover.

"YOU KNOW THOSE MEN who stopped the train?" Kincaid asked, as the Rover cruised along an asphalt road. Brugha didn't respond. "Looked like Provos to me."

"Take your pick," Brugha said.

"But IRA."

"You can talk to the sergeant about it."

He slowed toward an approaching red sign with white lettering—*Stop. Check Point. Headlights Off*—resting against two orange traffic cones that peeked above it. The legs Kincaid saw dangling from a military Hotspur belonged to a British soldier in green camouflage who slipped out and walked toward them with a machine gun.

"VCP," Brugha said. "Take but a minute." He rolled down the window and the soldier, a look of recognition dawning, leaned in.

"This the guest?" he asked, eyeing Kincaid.

"I wouldn't call him a guest," Brugha said.

The soldier eyed Kincaid with a languid grin. "Should we search him?"

"I'm with the Guards," Kincaid said. "But you already know that."

"All the more reason to search ya," the soldier said.

"Sarge would have my arse," Brugha said. "Chief Superintendent would have his."

"It's your arse, not mine," the soldier said. "Any weapons, Mr. Garda?"

"No."

"Wait here." The soldier walked away.

Brugha struck his head out the window. "C'mon now," he yelled. He frowned at Kincaid. "You're already causing trouble and you just got here."

An interminably long time seemed to pass before the soldier returned with a mate, stood at the rover's window peering down.

"What now?" Brugha asked.

"We need to make sure he's not armed," the soldier said, this time without bending.

"He won't be armed unless Sarge wants him armed," Brugha said.

"We need to make sure."

Brugha turned to Kincaid. "I tried," he said.

Kincaid pulled on the door handle, ready to step out, saw the machine guns go up.

"Take your hands off the door," the soldier yelled. "Just wait till we come around."

They ushered Kincaid out of the vehicle, patted him down, pawed through his luggage, kept grave countenances Brugha knew were suppressing smirks and laughter.

"Guess he's not armed," the soldier said. "What good is a cop without a piece?" With his rifle, he waved Kincaid back into the truck.

Brugha eyed Kincaid with a mix of suspicion and consternation.

"I understand," Kincaid said. "Never argue with a man whose gun is bigger than yours."

They continued down the road.

KINCAID AND BRUGHA HEARD voices behind a door marked "Kevin O'Connell, Sergeant" in Briar Lough's RUC station.

"I *am* tellin' ya straight. Darren Larkin was up there. Lann was still alive."

"That's not what he says."

"I don't care what he says. He looked like he'd been hit. On his head or somethin'. I came up the hillside—"

Constable Brugha tapped on the door.

"Can it wait?" O'Connell said.

The constable peered in. "The Gardaí inspector, sir."

"They sent him, did they?"

"Yes, Sergeant."

"All right, then. If we must, we must. Let's meet the esteemed investigator from the South."

Brugha motioned Kincaid into the room. After niceties, Kincaid told him why the train was delayed.

"They told you about Father Wryth?" O'Connell said.

"In so many few words."

"What I doubt they told you is the very pressing role he's now playing in north-south relations. It's political—out of my wheelhouse."

Kincaid looked at the teen boy O'Connell was questioning.

"More police," Conor said with a sardonic stare.

"Conor here was just explaining what he saw at the latest crime scene—what are they calling it your way?"

"A witch burning?"

"A burning, at least," O'Connell said. "The man he saw, Darren Larkin, claims to have found the victim—young woman named Lann McLaughlin—lashed to one of the stones. Old Druid piece. We have bunches of them around here. Mr. Larkin —"

"I don't care what Darren said," Conor barked. "He was up there, with Lann."

"She was dead?" Kincaid asked.

Conor looked down at his hands.

"Go ahead. Answer the man," O'Connell said. "Was she or wasn't she dead?"

"Couldn't a been dead," Conor said. "They was talking, sounded like arguing."

"Conor says he told his da after Lann turned up dead," O'Connell said. "His da brought him here."

"This—may I?" Kincaid asked.

"I understood you were just to be observing," O'Connell said.

"That's true. I'm not trying to interfere."

"What else do you want to know?"

"Who's the other man? The boy mentioned—"

"He's at our hospital," O'Connell said. "Claims he slipped on a mossy rock."

"She hit him with a rock, is more like it," Conor said.

"He have any motive to kill this woman?" Kincaid asked O'Connell.

"Sure as hell did," Conor volunteered. "They was seein' each other. Lann broke it off."

"How do you know?"

"Everyone knows."

"Small town," O'Connell said.

"So he kills her. Why go to the trouble of making it look like the other murders?" Kincaid asked.

"I don't know," Conor said. "Pin it on the other killer, maybe."

"Darren isn't that sophisticated." O'Connell sounded exasperated. "And this particular murder didn't exactly go as planned."

"OBSERVER MY ARSE," O'CONNELL told Kincaid, on their way to the clinic.

"After the train—" Kincaid said.

"Yes, well. They usually don't warn us beforehand. And they didn't harm anyone, correct?"

"Didn't they?"

In Dr. Irwin's waiting room, his nurse motioned them back.

"May we?" O'Connell said at an exam room door.

"Yes," Dr. Irwin said. "Of course, Sergeant. Come in."

Darren Larkin tried to stand from the exam table.

"No, no. Please," O'Connell said. "This is Inspector Kincaid. From the Guards. Here to *observe* our work on these burning deaths."

"The South?" Larkin said.

"Not exactly a burning, this last one," Irwin said.

"That's partly why we're here."

"You think I killed Lann," Darren said.

"I don't think anything at this point," O'Connell said.

"That shit Conor Clarke—"

"I need to advise you that you're not obliged to say anything unless you wish to do so," O'Connell said.

"Heard it before," Larkin interrupted.

"But anything you do say will be taken down in writing and may be given in evidence. So—" O'Connell took a wire bound notepad from his jacket. "Conor says he overheard you and Lann arguing. Saw you up there that afternoon."

"When was this?" Kincaid asked.

"Nine nine nine call came in Wednesday around four," O'Connell said.

Darren sighed, sat forward. "I already told ya. I *was* up there. Trainin' me dogs."

"Darren trains sheep and cattle dogs," O'Connell told Kincaid.

"*Champion* sheep and cattle dogs," Darren said. "International Sheep Dog Trials. I'm training some new handlers, too."

"Tell Inspector Kincaid what you told Constable Brugha."

"Kelty was keeping a close eye—"

"Kelty?"

"One of my dogs. He noticed her first."

"Lann McLaughlin?"

"Yes."

"Was she alive?" Kincaid asked. "Dead?"

"I don't know. I called to her. I ran up to her and must've been screamin'. I patted her cheeks, smoothed the hair out of her eyes. I tried to untie her but the binds were too tight. Looked like someone used wet leather that shrunk up. I tried to listen for her heart but couldn't hear. Too much wind." He looked at O'Connell for a cue.

"Go on," the RUC sergeant said.

"I ran down the hill to get help," Darren continued. "Slipped on a stone, banged me head. But I made it home. Started getting really sleepy and me mam brought me here."

"His mam called us," O'Connell said.

Kincaid went to open his mouth, then hesitated. He looked at O'Connell.

"More questions?"

"If you don't mind."

"I suppose," O'Connell said.

"Had you been out of sorts with Miss McLaughlin?" Kincaid asked.

"No," Darren said. "We were getting on just fine."

"So you weren't breaking anything off?"

"Nothing to break off. We were just friends."

"She didn't want to stop seeing you?" O'Connell asked.

"Why would she?"

"You pushed yourself on her. She refused. You became hostile—"

Darren pushed off the table and stood on shaky legs in his exam gown. "Are ya daft? I told ya, we had nothing to break off."

"You said something about this crime being different from the others," Kincaid said. "Not a burning."

"A failed burning is more like it," O'Connell said. "Either the wood wouldn't catch or the wind was too strong. Lann was bound, the bottom part of her dress and shoes were scorched. But the killer seemed to have given up."

"What was the cause of death?"

"Blood loss," O'Connell said. "She was stabbed in the throat."

"But she was not stabbed or burned when Darren found her."

"Finally," Darren said. "Takes a policeman from the Republic to understand."

O'CONNELL AND HIS SISTER Mattie carried tea and small sandwiches into their living room. Kincaid stood from an ornately-stitched chair. "Certain I can't help?" he said.

"Not at all," Mattie said. "I'm quite enjoying this. Guests these days are rare."

"I was certain you'd be annoyed by my presence," Kincaid said as O'Connell sat next to the fire.

"I am," O'Connell said.

"Kevin!" Mattie exclaimed from the kitchen.

"But I've been asked—no, *told*—to be cordial. Cooperative."

"Me, too," Kincaid said. "I resisted coming. I have plenty to do at home." An official-looking folder on an end table caught his eye.

"Autopsies, crime scene reports," O'Connell volunteered.

"May I?"

"During tea?"

Kincaid withdrew his hand. O'Connell suddenly grabbed the folder and tossed it on his lap. "That's me, being cooperative," he said.

Kincaid looked at photos. "Just when I thought it couldn't get more brutal."

"Victims were alive when they burned," O'Connell said. "Gagged, but far enough out of the village that no one would have heard them anyway."

"What kind of gags?"

"Rags, oil cloths. Not like those fancy-stitched things you found," O'Connell said.

"Manutergia," Kincaid said. "Otherwise known as lavabo towels. Used during Catholic mass."

"They told me you were Catholic."

"One referenced the crucifixion of St. Andrew," Kincaid said. "The second, a precious collar. The last one we found, something long desired."

"You also found a painting."

"*The Last Judgment.* Cheap knockoff, but left with a victim —"

"Who was skinned alive," O'Connell completed. "That detail has fortunately eluded our newspapers. These sundry items lead anywhere they haven't told me about?"

"Here," Kincaid said.

"I don't mind telling you," O'Connell leaned back, "I don't want you here, my sister's hospitality aside. We don't need the Guards. It just causes—"

"What?" Kincaid asked.

O'Connell set his half-empty tea glass on the end table. "We're under the cosh here," he said. "The burning victims were all Catholic. One of them—a nun, Mary Theresa Mongilly—worked for Brenden Wryth."

"We don't have him, by the way," Kincaid said. "I told those Provos, but I doubt they believed me."

"Why would you hide a notorious child molester?" O'Connell said.

"Is that why they want him? Bring him to justice?"

"Did they tell you that?" O'Connell asked. "Because if they did—"

"They implied it."

"He's been making maps for the British Army, some of the Loyalist paramilitaries. Maps of IRA movements. Uses them in exchange for protection. Now that the Guards—"

"Let me stop you," Kincaid said. "I was told just the opposite: that Wryth was selling maps to the IRA of British troop movements."

"Would that surprise you? That he'd sell to both?"

"Maybe not."

"And why not sell maps or information to the Guards? The IRA has become a big thorn in the side of the Oireachtas, Justice —"

"We don't have him. I'd know if we did.

"Well." O'Connell let out a chuckle he was trying to restrain. "Wryth *has* vanished. Doubtful he's dead. *In cognito* is probably more accurate."

"So this nun who worked for him got burned at the stake."

"Ulster Loyalists employing a new form of terror to flush out Wryth for betraying them?" O'Connell said. "Or nationalist insurgents doing the same? Being in such a Catholic village, I tell the journalists who come calling we favor the former theory."

A *Belfast Telegraph* on a foot stool caught Kincaid's eye. Just above the fold, and beside a different story with photographs of a graffiti-covered wall behind a barricade and a raggedy Shorland armored truck, *Witch burner claims second victim.*

O'Connell looked down at the paper, too. "Something our countries have in common for a change."

A CAR DOOR SLAMMED. A woman in a uniform skirt and service jacket walked toward Kincaid and O'Connell, next to O'Connell's car on the narrow dirt road.

"Mich Doherty," O'Connell called out.

"Kevin O'Connell," she replied.

"This is—"

"Detective Inspector Adam Kincaid," Doherty said. "Your reputation precedes you. Michelle Doherty. Friends call me Mich." They shook hands. "Woman Constable one jurisdiction over."

"Constable," Kincaid said. "The honor is all mine."

"Mich is a celebrity—she was one of our Ulster Week participants a few years past," O'Connell said.

"Celebrity my arse," Mich said. "Don't let him fool you."

"She was an ambassador, our Mich, to exotic foreign lands," O'Connell said. He rubbed her sleeve between his finger and thumb. "In this lovely shamrock green."

"Ulster Week?" Kincaid said.

"I went to the exotic foreign lands of England and Scotland," Mich quipped. "Thought Stormont might see fit to drop the *Woman* part of my title. We all did. Maybe someday."

O'Connell looked up the hillside. "Shall we?" he said.

WOMAN CONSTABLE DOHERTY LOOKED at the monolith and the crime scene around it. "So this is where Miss McLaughlin was found," she declared.

"Mich is here to compare notes. The murdered nun, Mongilly, was closer to her barracks," O'Connell said.

"Which they are closing, by the way," Mich said. "Not enough stills and cockfights left to bust. They were supposed to build us a Type A barracks, but we got left with the older model. I'm in Greene, Inspector Kincaid, a county town about nine miles north." She walked around the rock. "They did not burn her."

"They tried," O'Connell said.

"Cause of death was a knife wound?" she asked.

"In the throat," O'Connell said. "But we have a witness says he saw her before that. Tied up 'ere, maybe unconscious, maybe deceased. So either *he* knifed her or someone else—"

Constable Doherty looked at Kincaid, then at O'Connell with an urging in her eyes. O'Connell cleared his throat.

"Any ideas so far, Inspector?" O'Connell asked Kincaid, who was examining the scorched grass and half-kindled pyre around the slender stone monolith. He smelled the burned wood. He saw blood on the stone, wood, and dirt.

"Not much petrol," he told O'Connell. He looked up at a herd of bleating sheep on the nearby hillside. "This area seems protected from the wind."

"A poor imitation?" O'Connell said.

"Maybe," Kincaid said.

"Darren lying?"

"Maybe."

"He said he couldn't hear her heartbeat," O'Connell said." "Too windy."

"Might be true," Kincaid said, looking down the hillside. "Too windy to hear, but not too windy for a fire with enough accelerant. Maybe they didn't want her to burn."

"What sense does that make?"

"I looked at the autopsy," Kincaid said. "The angle of the knife wound does not fit either witness. Someone about the size of the victim came around the rock and pressed it into her neck. It went straight through. Conor Clarke and Darren Larkin are tall men. They would have had to squat in an awkward position. Why do that?"

Doherty nodded. "A short man, then. Wonder if I should have another look at a fella we pulled in."

"First I've heard of that," O'Connell said.

"Name is Brian Campbell," Doherty said. "Does some shepherding. care-taking, other odd jobs. How tall was this young woman?"

"About five feet and seven inches," O'Connell said.

"I *will* talk to Campbell again," Mich said.

Nineteen

The mirrors were covered, the grandfather clock on the other side of the room stopped. Rory McLaughlin sat next to his wife Niamh. Kincaid and O'Connell sat in opposite corners.

"Lann was our only child," Mr. McLaughlin said. "Inspector Kincaid, was it? As I was saying to our priest—"

"Lann," Kincaid said. "A lovely name."

"Thank you, Inspector."

"We are having the wake this weekend, guests on Sunday," Niamh McLaughlin said. "They have released the body."

"We would find it very comforting if you could attend," her husband said. "The both of you."

"You are in from Dublin?"

"I am," Kincaid said.

"They think our daughter's—" Her mother brought a handkerchief to her eyes. "What did she ever do?"

"We don't know much at this point," O'Connell said. "If you would not mind again, can you tell the Inspector some of what you've already told me."

"Yes, certainly," Rory said. "What would you be wantin' to know, exactly?"

"Let's start with when was the last time you saw your daughter?" O'Connell asked.

"Wednesday morning," Lann's father said. "I thought she was headed into the village to pick up some fur samples."

"Driving?"

"Yes. But the car never left."

"Where were these samples from?"

"Local mink farms. Some fox," Mr. McLaughlin said. "I grade pelts before they're sold to the coat makers, milliners, what have you. Clients in Belfast, Dublin, London, Paris, even Moscow."

"You do this here?" Kincaid said. He looked at O'Connell for approval. "If I might ask."

O'Connell nodded.

"I travel some, too," McLaughlin said.

"He was in Dublin last month," Mrs. McLaughlin said.

"Ireland and the UK are thinking about banning fur farming," Mr. McLaughlin said. "Sales have picked up more than a wee bit in anticipation."

"Ghastly, that one human being could do this to another," his wife said.

"Lann—your daughter—had no enemies? No angry boyfriends, no spurned lovers—" Kincaid asked.

"If you mean Darren Larkin, they did see one another for a bit," her father said. "But she had not mentioned him in a couple weeks, and never said anything about falling out."

"Did you see them together?" Kincaid asked.

"Sometimes. Darren came here to visit," Niamh said. "Seemed like a lovely young man."

"Anyone else?"

"Who might be an enemy, are you meaning? We are republicans, Inspector. We have a goodly number of natural enemies."

His wife took Rory's hand and shook her head.

"She doesn't want me talking about it. But I have been threatened. Any of us speaks our minds gets threatened," Mr. McLaughlin said. "That they would take it out on our daughter—that's their way, Inspector. It's their way."

"He means the loyalists," O'Connell said.

"Damn right I do."

"Hush," his wife said. "You're having no cause to use such language here."

"These men need to know," he said. "My grandfather lost his leg in the War of Independence. My father fought with the resistance during the border troubles. Our family bleeds republican green."

"You have any names of these enemies?" O'Connell asked.

"You have 'em, Constable. I've reported this before."

"You gave me group names: Ulster Revolutionary Front, South Armagh something. I need individuals."

"James Glenn is one, and a noisy one at that," McLaughlin said. "Might also be callin' himself Glen Mitchell, Mitchell Glenann. He hails from up around Markethill."

"I'll look into it," O'Connell said, jotting down the names.

"That's what you been saying," Mr. McLaughlin said. "That's what you always say. You and the rest of the B-men."

"I'm not a B-man."

"Your daddy was."

"Well, then," O'Connell said. He stood up.

"We know, Constable," Mrs. McLaughlin said. "Plenty of your men lost their lives in these Troubles. Rory means no offense."

KINCAID SAT IN A hard metal chair with a worn upholstered seat in Sergeant O'Connell's office. He turned when he heard footsteps outside, footsteps inside, a foyer hidden from view, where O'Connell hung up his damp raincoat. He came into the office.

"My apologies for the tardiness," O'Connell said. "Car fire."

"I can smell it." Kincaid sat up. "Was anyone hurt?"

"Made a bags of the owners finances, and a family of modest means besides. They only had the one car." O'Connell picked up a pipe and pressed tobacco in it. "Mind if I smoke?"

"Better than the smell of burning upholstery. Arson?"

O'Connell smiled as he lit the pipe and drew in. "What else."

"The village is mostly republican?" Kincaid asked.

"And this part of Newry is mostly Catholic," O'Connell said.

"I don't understand this conflict," Kincaid said. "Is it a civil war or a revolution?"

"Why of course, it's a revolution," O'Connell said. "Rebels hereabouts are Catholic and republican nationalists who want to break with Her Majesty. Up Armagh way, Belfast, and the like, rebels are Protestant loyalists who say, 'God Save the Queen and

Keep the Union.' The Crown, I believe, is terribly put out that it didn't remain a proxy war."

"You think these murders are part of the Troubles?" Kincaid asked.

"What? The bombings, shootings, burnings, ambushings are not enough?" O'Connell sat down at his desk across from Kincaid, drew on his pipe. "You married?"

"No."

"You say that with a certain finality."

"I've been close," Kincaid said.

"Hasn't happened for me, either," O'Connell said. "Late night bombings tend to be incompatible with matrimonial harmony."

Kincaid chuckled. "We were both police," he said.

"You and your missus?"

"Yes."

"Do not have many women on the force up here," O'Connell said. "Mich Doherty is a standout, and would be a sergeant or an inspector now if not for her sex."

"And the late-night bombings?" Kincaid said. "Any thought of leaving them behind?"

"Tis the family business, so I grit my teeth and go on," O'Connell said.

"My mam wanted a priest," Kincaid said, with a dismissive stroke in his tone.

"And?"

"I left the seminary for the Guards."

"What's that old saying, for the blessed ones, there is more than one calling?"

"You're Catholic?"

"I am. And I've paid a price for it," O'Connell said. "A Catholic constable is a traitor to the cause. IRA almost succeeded in killing me, back when I was stationed in Armagh."

"What changed?"

"Michelle Doherty. Her brother's a leader in the South Armagh Brigade. They don't talk, but he *has* put out word that she and I are off limits."

"Your mam must've wanted a constable," Kincaid said.

"Of course. Like I said, family tradition, started by a distant Catholic cousin, Paddy O'Connell. Royal Irish Constabulary."

"Name sounds familiar."

"Soloheadbeg Ambush that started the War of Independence. IRA succeeded in killing him. Shot him dead."

"He was your cousin?"

"A few times removed, he was. But the Constabulary—" He pounded his heart. "Right here. Paddy and my grandfather. Uncles, cousins. Dad was a B-special. Died a year after the Hunt Report stood them down."

"I'm sorry to hear that. Distraught, was he?"

"Heartbroken. Goddamn bureaucrats taking me life, he said."

"We're strangling on a report of our own."

"Conroy," O'Connell said.

"You've heard."

"And read. The high points, anyway. You have my empathy."

Kincaid watched the aromatic smoke rise from O'Connell's pipe. "That why McLaughlin called you a B-man—because of your father?"

"That term is derogatory to some. Like a B-movie actor. B-men—the B-Specials—were the Constabulary reserve. Da didn't qualify for full RUC. It wore on 'im."

O'Connell went to a closet, returned with a coat on a hanger. Kincaid sat up. "Me dad's old B-specials uniform," he said. "They thought they got 'em all. Supposed to turn 'em in. But—he fought in the feckin' Border Campaign. Was the least they could do, let him keep his uniform. So Matilda and I kept it for him."

"**HOW DO I ADDRESS** this fellow?" Kincaid asked. "High Sheriff, Most High Sheriff, Excellency? Or just Sheriff?"

"That's right," O'Connell said. "You don't have High Sheriffs in the South. Not since, what, the Twenties?"

"Something like that," Kincaid said.

"I call him Chief Superintendent. He's retired RUC. I was under him for a time."

"Will I meet the Chief Constable?" Kincaid asked. "I was told that might not be possible. But no reason why."

"Simple enough reason," O'Connell said. "Chief Constable Shillington is recovering from a heart attack. He may not make our fiftieth anniversary celebration."

"He's all right?" Kincaid said.

"He is. Which is surprising," O'Connell said. "Chief Constable has had his hands so full with the Troubles—he had to bring the troops in, you know—it's a wonder he hasn't dropped dead."

ON THE DRIVE INTO Newry, they passed roving British troops and through security checkpoints and beneath the sound of helicopters.

"You see him?" O'Connell asked, at the vehicle checkpoint where the soldiers stopped Brugha.

Kincaid shook his head.

"Good thing," O'Connell said.

The soldiers waved them through.

Crude barricades drew Kincaid's eyes, beneath written proclamations scrawled on walls and bricks and stone, where soldiers leaned and smoked, their eyes following the sergeant and his guest as O'Connell's Ford Anglia crept into the city.

A woman greeted them at the door of a two-story stone house, and led them into a parlor where the High Sheriff of Down was turning and being turned by a tailor with needle, thread, and tape, before two mirrors.

"Mr. Leery," the woman said. "Sergeant O'Connell. And—" She looked hopefully at the guest.

"Kincaid. Adam Kincaid."

"Yes, gentlemen. Please. Make yourselves comfortable," the High Sheriff said. "I hadn't intended this distraction. We're having no small trouble getting these measurements right. Kevin."

"Good to see you again, Chief Superintendent," O'Connell said. "Mr. Kincaid is the Detective Inspector with the Gardaí. He's here about the burnings."

"Yes, terrible. Graham and I discussed all that when his office called. Got me wondering if some of our combatants haven't moved to a more high-profile means of getting their messages across."

The Sheriff frowned at his tailor, who sat on a footstool and put down the thread and tape. He reached out to shake hands. "On behalf of the Crown, we appreciate your assistance, Inspector Kincaid. I'm sorry Graham couldn't meet with you."

"Thank you," Kincaid said. "It's an honor."

"The court dress I'm donning is for a welcome luncheon and more than one parade. While I appreciate the political side of law enforcement—" He slipped a ceremonial sword out of its scabbard and held up the hilt. "I'm not as comfortable with the pretense." The tailor adjusted the white lace at the Sheriff's throat, and brushed his dark blue velvet coat. "I understand you have a counterpart to our witch burnings in the South."

"All staged in a ritual way," Kincaid said. "A reporter from the *Belfast Telegraph* remarked on the similarities at one of our press conferences."

"And so, here you are. Any leads? Any new information?"

"No new leads," O'Connell said. "But the Inspector does have a suggestion."

A helicopter soared overhead and the rapid tat-tat-tat of nearby gunfire intruded.

"Already helping," the High Sheriff said with some irony.

"You've heard of Father Wryth," Kincaid said.

Leery and the tailor stopped. The tailor lowered his needle. "Hasn't everyone?" Leery said.

"Sergeant O'Connell and I are considering the idea that he is somehow tied to these killings."

"Rumor is he's fled to the South and that the Guards have him under wraps," O'Connell interjected.

"Do they?"

"No," Kincaid said.

"I believe you. Though North and South be at odds, we keep no secrets from one another," the High Sheriff said. "Too many spies."

The tailor rose from the footstool. "Just look at the cut a ya," he said, eyeing his client in the mirror.

"Is Special Branch investigating these witch burnings?" the High Sheriff asked.

"I try to avoid Special Branch," O'Connell said. "But I've seen no indication they're involved."

"Over time, I came to think them a necessary evil," High Sheriff Leery said. "They *have* been helpful with our Orange walk problems."

The tailor raised a hat to the Sheriff's head and adjusted it.

"One of the Orange Parades in July?" Kincaid said.

"Yes. Nationalist group—the Republican Resistance Guard, better known as the RRG—threatened to disrupt our July Twelve parades. Special Branch made a deal with the RRG not to interfere. Of what that deal consisted—ouch!" The tailor stuck the Sheriff through his breeches with a needle. "We don't select our Sheriffs with pricking anymore," he said.

"Unlike England and Wales," Kincaid said.

"You know about that?"

"The Queen pricks a paper with the name of her High Sheriff selection among the nominees," Kincaid said. "Dates to Queen Elizabeth the First. But only in England and Wales."

"They *did* send the right man."

"I'D SAY YOU MADE a positive impression," O'Connell said, as he looked under his car in the street, first this side, then that side, front, back, walking around it. Two British soldiers watched the ritual.

"Seemed a good fella. Easy to like," Kincaid said.

"The High Sheriff occupies an enviable perch," O'Connell said. "Neither side is trying to kill him. At least, not yet." He stood up. "Never open my boot, either. Go in through the back seats." He nodded toward them.

"They could wire your car this quickly?"

"They could and they have."

"From car bombs to stake burnings. Seems improbable," Kincaid said. "But how would we follow that up?"

"Delicately."

"*How* delicately?"

"Do not want to stir up anymore than we hafta."

O'CONNELL SLOWED THE CAR and pulled over to the roadside. It was quiet and barren out here.

"What I take it you're saying is, that my police work won't be up to snuff unless we do it your way," he told Kincaid.

"*My* way?"

"The way that could get us both killed. Or worse—innocents caught in the crossfire. I thought you understood."

"I do prefer the straightforward to the twisted."

"Which I'm already doing."

"With Darren Larkin? A *maybe* copycat killer?"

"Or this Brian Campbell. Or James feckin' Glenann, whoever —" O'Connell turned his red face to the windshield. He stepped on the gas and the two men sped out of the gravel back onto the road.

"Forget something?" Kincaid asked.

"Remembered something—someone, actually. Back from my days in Armagh."

They pulled onto two-lane Bessbrook Road and in about fifteen minutes pulled into a farm with a white two-story house, barns, concrete warehouse, and grain bins.

"Home of James Mitchell. Knew my father. Hates Catholics."

"And in the village of Glenanne," Kincaid said. "McLaughlin's tormentor?"

"Maybe a coincidence," O'Connell said. "But worth a look." His car crept up to a muddied Hotspur Land Rover dimpled from gunfire.

"More coincidence?" Kincaid asked.

O'Connell pulled ahead of the Land Rover and parked alongside a tractor. "Brugha got you armed?"

"Should I be?" Kincaid said.

"You are, right?"

Kincaid pulled back his jacket to the holstered pistol. "Never used a Walther twenty two."

"It's the best we could do."

They got out of the car and looked inside and around the Land Rover.

"Pistols, Rugers, rifles. Looks like a Special Patrol Group truck," O'Connell said.

"SPG?" Kincaid said. "What's it doing here?"

"Me da knew ol' Jimmy from the B-Specials. B-Specials and Special Patrol are cousins."

Kincaid felt the hood. "Cold. It didn't just arrive." He saw a man walking away from the house. "That him?"

"Jimmy?" O'Connell called out. The man turned, looked, then kept walking. "Jimmy!" The man picked up his pace. Kincaid started after him, but O'Connell grabbed his arm.

"Delicately," he reminded.

"Jimmy. It's me, Kev. Gordon's boy."

"Whaddya want?"

"Ya doe naw remember me?"

"I remember ya," Jimmy called back. "You armed?"

"Yes," O'Connell said. "You know that."

"Take it out. Put it on the ground."

"I cannot do that. You know that, too."

"Then get the fuck off my land."

"Hafta bring you in then, Jimmy."

"You got no jurisdiction here."

"I can bring in others."

"Fine, then."

The man went around a barn. "I've got a gun," he called back.

"You come out with a gun, I will shoot you," O'Connell said.

"Just stay where you are," Jimmy said. "We can talk from here." He stayed out of sight around the barn.

"That's all right," O'Connell said. "I'll get backup."

They backed away. As O'Connell reached for the car door handle, they heard a shotgun cock. They turned and saw the barrel around the barn.

"No need for backup," Jimmy said, pointing the weapon at them. "Whaddya wantin', Gordon's boy?"

"What's the SPG doing here?" O'Connell yelled.

"Dunno anything about it."

"How can that be?"

"Truck's been here a couple days," Jimmy said. He fired the gun into the air. A flock of birds flew out of a tree. He didn't move from behind the barn. "I asked you what you wanted."

"Your name come up," O'Connell said, keeping his sidearm poised.

"Who brung up me name?" James Mitchell asked.

"No one in particular."

Kincaid walked around the car and raised his hands.

"Adam!" O'Connell said.

"Why don't you put that goddamn thing down?" Kincaid told Jimmy.

"And who might you be?" Jimmy asked.

"Adam Kincaid. Detective Inspector with the Gardaí."

"Gardaí? Here ta turn over Father Wryth, are ya?"

"I don't know anything about Father Wryth. I'm here about the witch burnings."

"Father Wryth's doing, too," Jimmy said. "They's Catholics, republicans, correct?"

"Who?" O'Connell said.

"The burning victims."

"Yes."

"Then damn 'em all, they deserved it."

"AH. MR. KINCAID," SAID the innkeeper at his guest house about a mile from the O'Connell home. She grabbed a note for Kincaid. "She called while you were out."

"She?" Kincaid said. He called back from the hallway phone.

"Adam! So very good to hear your voice," Sr. Grey said.

"Likewise." He leaned forward uncomfortably in the little chair at the phone table. "You don't know how much, in fact."

"I've some news for you. I didn't want to leave it in a message. Alex Baldwin's wake is on Sunday. "

"This Sunday?"

"Yes."

"Terrible timing," Kincaid said. "I'd planned to attend another wake here."

"Oh?"

"Most recent victim. Furrier's daughter."

"You stay there," she said. "I'll represent both of us."

"It would be easier," he said. "Though I hate to miss it."

"Have you learned anything?"

"Oh, yes," Kincaid said. "Rebel group stopped my train on the way in."

"McDermott mentioned as much but never said why."

"The Gardaí is hiding a fugitive, so they say."

"A fugitive?"

"Some kind of cover up, the rebel group thinks."

"Sounds like an important fugitive," Sr. Grey said.

"It's a priest, a Father Wryth."

"Brenden Wryth?"

"You've heard of him?"

"Everyone in my business has heard of him, Adam. He's a major source of patients. I heard he was dead."

"Apparently not." Kincaid sighed and ran his hands through his hair. "I try to keep my head down, you know. But our countries are crawling with spies and informants. They know what's happening before it happens. I hate feeling ignorant of anything that affects the Guards. But I may be, in this case."

"Could Father Wryth be one of them? An informant. So the Gardaí is protecting him," Sr. Grey suggested.

"That's one theory." Kincaid heard rustling on the line. He heard Sr. Grey put the phone down.

"There were libel suits," she said, calling to the phone away from the line. "I have some old notes about them."

"Was your order involved?"

"No, no. Father Wryth's order, rather. They sued a victim who had come forward. And a victim sued the Church, for calling him or her a liar in the newspapers." Now back on the line, "They shopped the suits to London. Some of the stories ran in our tabloids," she said. "I don't know the verdicts, or if there ever were any. Could have settled, I suspect."

"You just happened to have notes on this man?"

"It's good to know the enemy," Grey said.

"I'll ask McDermott. 'Are we hiding a fugitive—?'" Kincaid said.

"No—not McDermott," Grey interrupted. "Greevey. You have to go higher."

"You want me staying up here, don't you? Have you heard anything about Marta? I know McDermott would have telephoned, but—"

A long pause.

"Sister?"

"You can well imagine," she said. "The entire department, from what I can see, is working overtime looking for her."

"And nothing."

Another long pause.

"How the feck—pardon me, Sister—does someone just up and disappear like that?" Kincaid said. "Someone like Marta, especially?"

"Could she have left on her own?"

"Why? She had the job of her dreams. A new place. The stress of her old job long gone."

"And—"

"And?"

"Well, there *is* something," Grey said.

"Something what?"

"Marta. She may have been seeing someone."

"Seeing someone?" Kincaid stiffened.

"They don't know, Adam. They're not even—"

"Bloody hell. The missing boyfriend."

"There's no evidence of foul play," Sr. Grey said. "If anything, they ran away together. Of their own accord."

His breath came in short bursts. "How did this come up?"

"Detectives found a note, presumably to her. 'To my room shark,'" Kincaid thought he heard her say.

"Room shark?" he asked.

"Roon. With an 'n'. Roonshark."

"What, praytell, is a roonshark?"

"A rúnsearc," Sr. Grey said, "is a secret lover."

Twenty

"Reposing at . . . " the notice announced. At the McLaughlin's home, the men spoke in low, careful tones. The women were silent and forlorn. Kincaid read about Lann McLaughlin's love for her family, especially her grandfather, her respect for God's kingdom, her devotion to church and country.

On a table he left a sympathy card he'd signed the night before, with an offhanded doodle that became an hour-long obsession, the Gardaí insignia or shield, a Celtic cross inlaid with a G and an S that intertwined one another like delicate spring vines. Around the perimeter, "Garda Síochána na hÉireann," he drew.

Guardians of the Peace of Ireland.

"Very nice," O'Connell said, peering over his shoulder. Kincaid turned to him. "Brugha is minding the manor."

"Mr. Kincaid," Lann's father said. "If you would."

He followed Rory McLaughlin to the living room where they had earlier discussed the case, through a crowd eating cakes and finger sandwiches and sipping tea, brandy, and wine. Drawn curtains made the room almost pitch black, except for one open window through which a breeze teased and flicked napkins and candles.

"You have my sincerest condolences," Kincaid said. "I cannot imagine what you must be feeling."

"Thank you," McLaughlin said. "It means a lot, that you'd stay like this. Kevin told me about your doctor friend. You have *our* sincerest condolences."

Kincaid looked at Lann, hands clasping a cherry red rosary, folded over her heart, face pale, almost gray, scarf and turtleneck covering her mortal wound, a handmade quilt tucked from chest to feet. He looked at the compressed pillow on the chair beside her casket, where her father had sat for the past three days, only breaking for the toilet and a leg stretch when his calves cramped so badly he could barely stand.

A woman touched Lann's hand and kissed her cheek and stared at her alongside the Inspector. She looked at Kincaid with wide, bright eyes. "You're with the police?" she said. "I hope you catch the miserable bastards what did this."

Another woman asked Kincaid if he'd known "little Lann." He recited what he knew of her, and asked subtle questions.

How long did she work for her father?

Did she go into Dublin often?

Did she have friends in the area? Any reason to travel to Portadown? Markethill? How about Glenanne?

"Lann went into Dublin a few times recently," a man who appeared about sixty said. "I know she dreamed some day of going to the big city, living there. We all thought Belfast till the Troubles."

A veiled woman wearing a diamond brooch and black-lace armband appeared beside Kincaid as he turned away from the body. In the gray light from the open window, her arms looked strong under sheer sleeves. She looked at Lann, blessed herself, and mouthed a prayer. She turned to Kincaid.

"Inspector," she said. She raised the veil.

"Constable."

"Mich, please. Have ya been learnin' anything?"

He looked uncertain.

"I heard your questions," she said. "I've questioned witnesses before, but never at a wake."

"I hope you don't think me indelicate."

"Not the way you were asking."

"Sergeant O'Connell advised me to tread carefully."

"Against your better instincts?"

"Against the clock. Who's next, and when?"

"I interviewed Brian Campbell," she said. "Twas a dead end."

"He had an alibi."

"And several witnesses to it."

Out the window, a cellist and two violinists stepping out of a car caught Kincaid's eye.

"We're starting the laments," Lann's aunt announced. "If you please."

Kincaid and Mich Doherty filed out with the group. They passed O'Connell in the foyer, talking with a neighbor.

"They're burying her today," Mich whispered into Kincaid's ear.

LANN'S FATHER AND NEIGHBORS raised the sides of Lann's casket and walked it out of the house and set it onto a makeshift stand of chairs in the yard. The cellist opened her instrument and steadied it on its end pin in a small round stand in the dirt. She sat in a chair beside the two violinists, a young man about Lann's age and a young woman. Doherty motioned with her head toward Darren Larkin, standing alone, watching distantly.

"Well," O'Connell said.

Niamh McLaughlin looked at Darren, too. Stared. Stood alone and stared. Her husband came to her side and put his arm around her shoulder, where she let it rest and then walked away. She walked toward Darren, beyond the crowd, and Kincaid watched her approach, stand, and say something, and take Darren's hand and walk him toward her daughter.

The violins joined the cellist's trilling drones in A, B flat, and C, as Darren stared at Lann. Kincaid bowed his head but raised it when he saw Mich Doherty out the corner of his eyes dabbing tears beneath her veil.

Behind her, up the damp dirt road along the greening hedge and the budding trees and the gradually-verdant valley, Kincaid saw men stepping out of a dull white van, boots, green sweaters, and camouflage, moving in a slow-motion trance. He watched them go around the van, then saw the first barrel emerge. He gasped to Doherty, "guns" and felt himself ramming O'Connell against the shoulder. "Guns," he yelled, and saw the men running, boots stamping the ground as he ran from person to person gasping, not screaming.

"Go, go, go. Guns. They have guns."

The bullets cut down first a violinist, then a neighbor, then another neighbor. Bullets hit the ground low and flew up and burst the cello as though a grenade had exploded from inside. People ran toward the house and O'Connell had his sidearm in both hands and was firing but Kincaid saw him fall. Mich Doherty's head flew back as she spun around into a row of tall plantings near the house. Kincaid was not armed that day.

The men were upon them now, shrouded in black ski masks, machine guns and pistols ripping the air, gunfire filling Kincaid's nostrils with that smell, that firing-range smell, burning, sharp, unforgettable.

He grabbed Mich by both arms and dragged her around the house. He felt a sharp sting, another sharp sting, before he dropped. Through a haze of blood, smoke, and fire, he saw the white van spin mud and gravel and speed away.

He crawled over bodies, one man screaming in a way Kincaid had never heard, a woman's strained puffs grasping air. He felt a hand grab his wrist. The cellist's hand was cold but her gaze peaceful. Her grip relaxed and her gaze became a stare.

He kept crawling, and weakening, blood soaking his trousers. He saw O'Connell against the McLaughlin's front door, the sergeant's gun in the bushes beside his limp hand. Kincaid crawled on both elbows and O'Connell saw him through sweat, pain, and dissipation.

Kincaid looked at him, then the door. He raised his hand and started to open it, but as the door moved in O'Connell went backward against it. The Royal Ulster Constabulary Sergeant shrieked.

"Leave it, Adam. Leave it," he said.

Kincaid struggled to pull the door closed again, against O'Connell's weight. "I'll be back. I have to call for help."

Kincaid started crawling away.

"Don't leave."

"I need to call for help," he said.

"Don't leave me."

"I'm bleeding out," Kincaid gasped. "I won't last."

Kincaid crawled across cold, wet, rough dirt past one car, then another. He raised his hand and tried to open O'Connell's car door, but his hand shook. Through clouded vision, he turned against the car door and breathed and looked at his legs. He turned and tried the door handle again. He pressed the handle and tugged at the door until it opened. He pulled himself in, and past a locked rifle, he reached for the car radio, grasped the hand speaker, and pressed the call button.

KINCAID OPENED HIS EYES to a nurse beside his bed in Daisyhill hospital, about ten miles from Briar Lough in Newry, County Armagh side. He overheard the nurse talking to a doctor about the "new hospital" and "how nice it will be," something about "the old workhouse".

"You're awake," the nurse said. "How are you feeling?"

He looked past her at dull walls and old equipment.

"O'Connell. What—"

"How are you feeling?"

"What . . . There was music."

"I need you to focus," the nurse said. "How are you feeling? We need to know."

Kincaid looked at the aluminum blinds, dusty, parted to the sun.

"Mr. Kincaid. How—"

"Thirsty."

"Any dizziness? Headache?"

"No," he whispered.

The nurse put a water cup with a straw to his lips. "You have a visitor," she said. "Are you up to seeing her?"

"What happened? Are they—did they—"

"I don't know," the nurse said. "Your visitor. Maybe she might know."

He raised his eyes above the straw and looked at the nurse.

"She?"

"I think she works with you."

Sister Grey walked in after the nurse left. Kincaid tried to sit up.

"What are you—"

"Can't leave you alone for a minute," she said. "Let alone a fortnight."

"You can't be here," he croaked.

Her shoes clicked along the tile floor as she came to his bedside. "But I am," she said.

"How did you know? Did someone tell you to—"

"Everyone in the Guards knows," she said, gently pushing his shoulder down until he stopped trying to rise.

"How did you get here?"

"Train. And no one held it up."

"Aren't you lucky."

"You're the lucky one," Sister said. "You lost a lot of blood."

"I don't remember."

"They found you slumped across the constable's car."

"Mich Doherty. How is she?"

"No, no. I meant the constable you were with."

"Sergeant. O'Connell. What about him? What happened to him?"

She took his hand, looked at him.

"How are they? Are they all right?" Kincaid said.

"No," Sr. Grey said.

"Oh, God." He looked down. "How many others?"

"I don't know," Sister Grey said.

"One, two?"

"A few."

Kincaid grabbed his blanket and sheets. "Innocents. Just innocents."

"There's a Mr. Brugha—"

"Constable," Kincaid said. "He's a constable." He sounded defensive.

"My apologies. I didn't know his rank."

"Can you—" He indicated the water. "I'm terribly thirsty."

She held the straw to his lips.

"Thank you," he said. "I'm sorry if I sounded perturbed."

"It's all right," she said. "There's a *Constable* Brugha who's taking over temporarily, I think. He's the one who found you."

"What did they tell you . . . about O'Connell and Doherty?"

"She died instantly. He held on but passed in the operating room. Massive stroke, I'm afraid."

Kincaid stared at the wall, the window, the blinds. "So fucking senseless." He looked through the nun, then at her. "I'm sorry, Sister. I didn't mean—"

"Always apologizing for bad language," she said.

"Me mam would slap me face if she heard me swearing around a nun."

"They say you'll be released in a few days," Sr. Grey said. "They got both bullets out."

"I'm weak as a pup," he said. "Can you do me a favor?"

"Of course."

"Will you pay my respects to Mattie O'Connell? The sergeant's sister."

"I will," she said.

"If it's not an imposition."

She put her hand over his. "I'm staying at a convent just outside Briar Lough. Believe me, it's no imposition."

TWO OTHER VISITORS APPEARED in Kincaid's hospital room two days later, accompanied by an RUC constable.

"Chief Superintendent. John!"

Kincaid tried to push himself to sit up in the bed.

"Francis," Greevey said. "Until we get you home, it's Francis."

McDermott set aside a package he was carrying and cranked the head section with a lever at the foot of Kincaid's bed.

"That good?" he asked.

"Perfect," Kincaid said. He looked at the constable, who was either frowning, scowling, or looking serious. McDermott and Greevey took up positions on either side of his bed.

"We took the opportunity to arrange some meetings," McDermott said. "Partly to make provisions for this extension of your visit."

"I can't tell you how sorry we are this happened," Greevey said. "Everything gone to shit, in one horrific moment."

McDermott took Kincaid's hand. "I take it the good sister has already been to see you," he said.

"She has," Kincaid said. "And now that she has, you need to take her back with you."

"Oh ho!" McDermott said.

"We'd have to arrest her, Adam," Greevey said. "Cuff her, tie her feet, straitjacket even."

"Not to distract from this fruitless topic, but—" McDermott picked up the package and handed it to Kincaid. "We thought you might find this useful."

"You still need to take her back with you." Kincaid pressed apart the tape and tore back the wrapping to a large sketch pad and a set of gray and black drawing pencils.

"Remember when you were laid up with that broken leg?" McDermott said.

"Painfully." Kincaid smiled. "Thank you," he said to McDermott. "Both of you," he turned to Greevey. "This means a lot."

"Can't have our best homicide investigator letting his skills go to rot," Greevey said. "I remember more than one occasion you've grabbed the pad from the sketch artist and made an impressive correction."

"She didn't think it was impressive. Neither did he."

"They were the best we had until you came along," Greevey said.

"Don't get any ideas about changing departments," McDermott told Kincaid.

"Where are you staying?" Kincaid asked.

"Little inn, here in Newry," Greevey said. "The RUC has been right accommodating. The higher ups I've spoken with—their voices shake. Chief Constable Shillington sent word that you are to be personally thanked for what you did. I wasn't aware until now that he'd suffered a heart ailment."

"How is he?"

"Heart wise, on the mend. Morale wise, devastated," Greevey said. "To lose two men, and during such an awful year."

"One man," Kincaid said. "The constable from Greene was a woman. And I did nothing to save either of them."

"You did what you could," McDermott said. "What any good Gardaí officer would have done."

"This insanity must be extinguished," Greevey said. "We cannot have it crossing the border."

"It's already crossed the border," Kincaid said.

"Mountjoy's filling up," McDermott said. "Provisionals. You know, *An Phoblacht* had the audacity to criticize prison conditions there."

"I didn't mean the paramilitaries, specifically," Kincaid said.

"We aren't immune from the shootings and the bombings. You know that."

"Father Brenden Wryth," Kincaid said.

"Rumor and innuendo, Adam," McDermott said.

"So you've heard of him."

"Of course."

"Paramilitaries stopped my train over him," Kincaid said. "To deliver a message that An Garda Síochána is hiding the most notorious child molester in Irish history, at least that we know of."

"Outrageous," Greevey said. "Even if we had him, or knew where he was, we have a minefield called the Extradition Act to navigate."

"He claims Republic citizenship, Adam. So say the rumors. The District Court will not issue an order—"

"I know the rules, John."

"Then you also know Part Two, Section Eleven: 'Extradition shall not be granted for an offense which is a political offense or an offense connected with a political offense.' Brenden Wryth has committed as many political offenses as—alleged—heinous offenses against the general morality. Where do the lines get drawn?"

"These rumors about Wryth are just more republican propaganda designed to excuse homicidal impulses," Greevey said. "Bunch of damn serial killers, the whole lot of them."

"Do they know who shot me?" Kincaid said. "Who killed all those innocent people?"

"No," McDermott said. "Sergeant O'Connell gave detectives a name before he died, but unless something's changed since then, it's been a dead end."

"A name?"

"A man he went to Church with."

Greevey sighed. His face looked drawn and tired. "I need to step out," he said. "Get some air. No need to hurry on my account."

"Jaysus," McDermott said after Greevey left the room.

"He seemed defensive," Kincaid said.

"He's not lying about the Gardaí hiding Wryth."

"He can't *know* for sure, can he?"

"Why would we hide a child molester?" McDermott asked.

"Several reasons."

"Name one. Just one."

"Intel. On loyalist activities," Kincaid said. "We've never had good loyalist intelligence."

"So you think he might be tied up with Special Branch?"

"Maybe. The Special Branches answer to no one, not in the South, not here," Kincaid said. "We found RUC Special Branch arms on a farm not far from here. A civilian-owned farm. Parked in an armored lorry."

"Who found?"

"Sergeant O'Connell and I."

"We both have our dark sides," McDermott said.

"I may have been shot over this feckin' priest," Kincaid said. "Most of these killings have Church connections—"

"I can't believe the Guard—any branch—would suborn keepin' a vicious criminal from justice," McDermott said.

"But if he's a political criminal . . . helping our side—" Kincaid looked at the sketch pad. He picked up the clear plastic pencil case. "I hear you think Marta ran off with a boyfriend."

"What?" McDermott said.

"I heard that theory. I don't buy it."

"I don't know anything about it. Where did you hear it?"

"Probably nothing," Kincaid said. "Marta would no more run off with a man than she would rejoin the Guards. She's worked too hard to get where she is."

"Yes, well," McDermott said. He looked at the door. "I should rejoin our boss. Don't want him committing a cross-border incident."

"Baldwin's wake? I was—"

"No way you could have known, Adam," McDermott said.

"I wish I could have been there. Doctors say I'm fortunate I wasn't paralyzed."

"You'll be up for a Scott Medal," McDermott said. "I'd say you're a shoo-in."

"They bloody well better not," Kincaid said.

Twenty One

Sister Grey and Constable Brugha steadied Inspector Kincaid by either arm as he limped on crutches into his room at the inn in Briar Lough. Mattie O'Connell followed with his overnight bag from the hospital. Kincaid hop-walked into the living area where Sister Grey led him to a chair.

"I'm too much of a burden," Kincaid said.

"I wouldn't allow you to be so impolite," Grey said.

Mattie looked around the little room. "Where are you sleeping?"

"Normally, through there." Kincaid nodded toward a closed door. Mattie opened it and looked up the stairs.

"Upstairs you're going? Good heavens," she said.

"They can bring a cot for me down here," Kincaid said.

"A cot?" Sr. Grey said. "How dreadfully hospitable."

Mattie climbed the stairs. "No room here even if you could get up the steps," she called down.

"Sister—I appreciate you're visiting me. Really, I do," Kincaid said. "But you have to go back."

"Sister Mongilly's convent has invited me to stay for the time being," she said. "Can't very well turn them down now, can I?"

"Sister's been a welcome presence," Mattie said, emerging from upstairs. "I'd be sorry to see her leaving our little village." She looked around the room again. "And I'm not seeing for the life of me how you can stay in our little village. Is this the only room available?"

"Yes," Kincaid said. "At least for the next week."

"Maybe Constable Brugha has some alternative suggestions."

"I'm afraid I do not, Miss O'Connell. Me wife and I and our —"

"I wasn't meaning you, Constable. But anyone *else* you might know."

"I wish I did," he said. "But—"

"But what?" Mattie asked.

Brugha hesitated.

"Come on. Out with it."

"It's all right," Kincaid said. "I'll be fine here."

"There's already too much talk," Brugha said. "A garda, here."

"A garda who tried to save my brother's life," Mattie said.

"Not meaning any disrespect to Sergeant O'Connell." Brugha stared at Mattie, then at Kincaid. "But I've talked, too."

"What do you mean, *you've talked too*?" Mattie asked.

"Just what I said," Brugha explained. "We, none of us, has liked it much."

A cold gripped Kincaid, a cold of vulnerability, an old feeling. "It doesn't matter," Kincaid said. "I'm fine here."

"I'd expect it of some in our town," Mattie said. "But not from you, Iain. Kevin—?"

"Sergeant O'Connell knew," Brugha said. "He talked, too." He looked at Kincaid. "I'm sorry, Inspector. But our countries are separate for a reason."

MOURNERS FILLED THE O'CONNELL house, friends from the village and the RUC, but with both parents dead and no other siblings, only a cousin from the family. Mattie's eyes were wet when people approached and hugged her. "I never thought I'd lose my baby brother to a death like this," she said. "I always thought it would be in the line of duty."

"It was," people said.

"If you mean him trying to protect innocents from senseless killing, then I suppose you're right."

"Where's the man who tried to protect Kevin?" folks asked. "The Gardaí Inspector."

"In a little room in the village," Mattie said.

"Will we be meeting him?"

"The sister he's working with is to pick him up and bring him," Mattie said. "He's in a wheelchair."

"Poor man, and all for Kevin and Lady Constable Doherty."

"It's not permanent," Mattie said. "He took a bullet in his back and leg, but nothing worse than broken bones and flesh wounds."

"I'LL NOT HEAR OF it," Mattie said to Kincaid after everyone but Sr. Grey was gone. "You're takin' our downstairs room and that's where you'll stay until everythin's fixed and working."

"I don't think that's a good idea," Kincaid said.

"Sister—"

"Are you sure?" Grey asked.

"You can't very well take him to the convent, can you?" Mattie said. "I've got only myself, no other kin but a cousin. We lost our parents to age and infirmity. If a wounded man in a wheelchair gets the tongue's wagging, then so be it. But it's what Kevin would have wanted, despite what Constable Brugha thinks."

"Thank you," Kincaid said.

"Then I can leave?" Sr. Grey asked.

"You're still taking us to Constable Doherty's wake?" Kincaid asked.

"Tomorrow," Grey said. "I'll bring your luggage round from the inn meantime."

After she left, Kincaid tried to rise from the sofa with crutches. Mattie took his arm. He steadied himself with her help and cautiously stepped forward.

"Are you all right?"

"I think so," he said.

She went toward the stairs. "Inspector."

He stood straight and looked at her.

"I appreciate your bein' here." Her lips quivered. Her face looked ready to cry. "It gives me comfort."

His mouth creased into a restrained smile. "Thank you for having me," he said. "And it's Adam."

"I like 'Inspector'," Mattie said. "After hearin' 'Constable' for so many years, it feels like a promotion."

GREAT BUILDINGS OF GREAT BRITAIN. Kincaid pulled the coffee-table book onto the bed and looked through historical black-and-white construction photos and sketches that gave way to color photos of the structures as they are today.

Westminster Abbey, London
Rievaulx Abbey, North Yorkshire
Liverpool Road Railway Station, Manchester
Tower of London
Windsor Castle
Westminster Hall, London
Stonehenge
St Martin-in-the-Fields, London
Canterbury Cathedral

"Stonehenge. Wiltshire. Possible burial ground. Myths surround its pagan rituals, ancient human sacrifice, Druid healing powers," he read.

"Tower of London. A fortified castle on the River Thames. Built by William the Conqueror to intimidate the conquered. Royal palace turned notorious prison."

"St Martin-in-the-Fields. One of the most famous churches in the world. Medieval construction. Elaborate reconstruction 1720-26. A primary anchor of Trafalgar Square."

"Westminster Hall. Seat of English law. Site of many famous state trials where its vast size accommodated spectators. Sir Thomas More sentenced to death here for opposing Protestant

Reformation and King Henry VIII supremacy over Church of England. Other notables sentenced at Westminster include Guy Fawkes for the "Gunpowder Plot"; Oliver Plunkett for the "Popish Plot"; King Charles I, for High Treason. The sentences often ended in gruesome executions."

Kincaid stared at that last phrase. And another following it: "Westminster Hall is without a doubt the most solemn spot in all England." – Sir Charles Oman.

He turned to panoramic pictures of the Hall's "magnificent hammer-beam roof, the largest medieval timber roof in Northern Europe." It was an "architectural masterpiece" commissioned by Richard II almost six hundred years ago. "Giant oak beams supported by gargantuan buttresses span the hall eighteen metres, or sixty feet across. Wooden arches atop the beams hold the arched roof . . . The effect is one long room with not a single pillar in the center."

Kincaid stared at the arched ceiling and the architectural drawings that conceived it. *One long room.* The somber wood, the darkness gazing from the floor. Twenty six oak angels held each beam upon their wings, and Richard II's coat of arms in their hands. *One Long room.* The detective looked at the light entering the front door and the windows above it. He closed the book, set it aside, and lay back, staring at the ceiling. He picked up his sketch pad.

One Long Room.

He called Sr. Grey after he finished the sketch.

MATTIE SAT IN THE living area staring at a mirror draped with two uniforms on clothes hangers. Kincaid stopped in the downstairs bedroom doorway.

"Where's your wheelchair?" she said. "You need to stay off those legs."

"Hard to maneuver in here."

"Then your crutches. I can get—"

He motioned her back. "I hate crutches. And wheelchairs."

"Then come over here and sit on the sofa," she said.

Kincaid hobbled over, grabbing a doorknob and the sides of furniture—anything he could grasp. She reached out to help but he waved her aside. She made way for him to sit on the sofa. He looked at her face in the soft light of the end-table lamp. Her cheeks were red, her eyes bloodshot. Her lips seemed less set than they usually were. Part of her seemed to be trembling. She sat in the adjacent love seat, and had to turn to see the mirror.

"Kevin's old uniform," she said. "I had it let out a bit. He'll be buried in it."

"And his father's?"

"I would like it buried, too," she said. "Neatly folded, at Kevin's feet. He showed it to you?"

"He seemed very proud of it," Kincaid said.

"Oh, yes. Gordon loved the old Constabulary—Ulster Special Constabulary. It crushed him when the Hunt Commission disbanded it. He died not more than a year later. Kevin blamed the great Lord Hunt, conqueror of Mount Everest."

"Climbing by committee," Kincaid said.

"Why in fact," Mattie said, "that's exactly what it was. Poor Gordon just another step on the path to the top."

"Tinkering bloody bureaucrats," Kincaid said.

"Kevin hated them. It really boiled over when they tried to change the uniform color—to blue. 'Bunch of feckin' army castoffs,' he said. I guess the Brits were trying to offload their blue surplus."

"The Crown treating Ireland as a castoff," Kincaid said. "Never."

"Shh. The loyalists will hear you." She looked back at the uniforms. "What do you think? Should I bury both of them?"

Kincaid looked at her as though the question were rhetorical.

"I'm so thankful—" Mattie looked at her hands, then at Kincaid. "I'm so thankful Gordon O'Connell didn't live to see his son die."

She was crying now and Kincaid worked to slide himself over and take her hand. He squeezed it and she steadied herself with her other hand and bawled. He tried to move closer, started to stand and sit next to her. But she squeezed his hand and looked at him and he knew he was close enough.

KINCAID ANSWERED THE O'CONNELL'S door on crutches. Mattie came up behind him.

"I'm going into town for the messages, so you're on your own," Mattie said. "Sister knows where everything is." She took

Sr. Grey's hand and whispered, "Watch him he doesn't do too much" on her way out.

"So," the nun said, as they sat down.

Kincaid opened *Great Buildings of Great Britain* and set it on the coffee table in front of her. He opened his sketch book and set it alongside. She looked at the photos of Westminster Hall and his sketch resembling Westminster Hall.

"Did you draw this?"

"Yes," he said. "What do you think?"

"It's an excellent rendering," she said. "You've missed your calling." She went to set the sketch pad down.

"Please," he said. "Have another look."

"It's quite detailed," she said. "But you seem a little off. Here, see. The photographs show about a dozen arch supports. Your sketch has twice as many."

"Anything else?"

"Well. Here." She pointed. "The arch supports are smaller in your sketch. And the entrance. Also smaller. And there's no window over it. Still, though—a remarkable likeness."

"It is remarkable, isn't it?" Kincaid said.

"Getting back in the hang of—"

"The photographs are of Westminster Hall," he said.

"Yes. Of course. I've been there many times."

"My sketch is of the Long Room, in the Old Library. At Trinity College."

Sister Grey picked up the sketch pad.

"Now that you say it . . . You drew this from memory?"

"Yes," he said.

"I never would have seen it. You think—"

"I think if someone wanted a stand-in for Westminster Hall in Dublin, Ireland, the Long Room would get the part."

"And why would anyone want such a stand in?"

"To re-create an execution."

"Westminster Hall was a library of barbarity. Any trial in particular?"

"Thomas More, Oliver Plunkett," Kincaid said.

"And of course, Guy Fawkes, for the Gunpowder Plot."

"Remember, remember—"

"The fifth of November," Sr. Grey said. "I know of no reason why the gunpowder treason—"

"Should ever be forgot," Kincaid interjected.

"Fawkes was supposed to be hanged," Grey said. "But he ran, fell, and ironically, broke his neck. So—not a match for our dramatist."

"Thomas More?"

"Merely beheaded," Sister Grey said.

"That seems to leave Dr. Baldwin standing in for our own Oliver Plunkett, hanged, drawn and quartered. And soon to be canonized, I've heard."

"As a Catholic martyr," Sr. Grey said. She looked at the sketch of the Long Room again. "You're making me want to visit the library. Not in Dublin. Here."

"I'M GOING. I NEED to be there," Kincaid said.

"Really, Inspector. You're a love for wanting to attend. I know Kev would feel the same way. But you need to stay off your feet."

Mattie O'Connell fussed over a raincoat and umbrella. She answered the door when the bell rang. Sr. Grey walked into the living room where Kincaid impatiently sat.

"We're to go with Constable Brugha," she said.

"Where is he?"

"In the car, sulking. I wanted his help with your wheelchair, but—"

"I can help you get it," Mattie said, pushing it out of the bedroom.

"I'll *hobble* to the car," Kincaid said.

As the women folded the wheelchair and put it in the trunk, Brugha reached back and unlocked the door. Kincaid slipped in, crutches first.

"Thank you," Kincaid said. He leaned forward. "What's the chance of something bad happening?" he whispered.

"Bad, like someone attack the procession?"

"Yes."

"With police, it's always a concern," Brugha said.

"What about them?" Kincaid said.

Brugha looked at the women, closing the trunk, walking around the car. "They must stay to the roadside," he said. "It's the marchers more likely to get attacked. And if anyone knew you were a garda—"

"I'll keep it as quiet as possible," Kincaid said.

IN TWO HEARSES AT the head of a crowd, Kincaid saw the caskets, flags and wreaths dominating their centers. He overheard RUC uniforms talking beneath umbrellas. The downpour had become a drizzle.

"Spitting out here earlier."

"Gonna get a soft day after all."

"Fathers Flynn and Gillum are co-celebrants?"

"Yes, Chief Superintendent."

"I knew Kevin as a Catholic. Devout, before the Troubles."

Kincaid rolled up in his wheelchair with Brugha behind him.

"Chief Superintendent," Brugha said.

"Yes. Constable Brugha. Very good to see you again," the Chief Superintendent said. "You have my sincerest condolences. Kevin will be sorely, sorely missed."

"Yes, sir," Brugha said.

The Chief Superintendent looked down at Kincaid. "And you sir, you have our enduring thanks."

Brugha looked bewildered and uncomfortable. "Are you planning to formally introduce us, Constable?"

"Yes, yes Chief Const—Superintendent. Inspector Adam Kincaid—Chief Superintendent Mitchell Gallagher, CID, Criminal Investigation Division," Brugha said.

"Pleasure, Inspector." They shook hands. "The Chief Constable and I were just talking about you. What you did when Mich and Kev were shot—"

"It wasn't nearly enough," Kincaid said.

"As I was saying, you have the RUC's gratitude," Gallagher said. "I want you to know that. I'm just sorry we had to meet under such atrocious circumstances."

"Thank you," Kincaid said. "It was an honor knowing both your constables."

A solo snare drum brought the crowd to attention as pallbearers took the coffins from the hearses. The empty hearses moved to the front of the procession.

"Mind if I walk with you?" Sr. Grey came up beside Kincaid and Brugha.

"You shouldn't be here," Brugha said.

"But I am."

"I have to agree," Kincaid said. "The car might be safer."

"Miss O'Connell is with the family," Grey said. "Not enough room."

"The only family is her cousin," Kincaid said.

"It's still too crowded," Grey said. "Emotionally crowded, if not physically."

"Should you hear anything that sounds like fireworks, duck and run," Brugha said.

"With all these police?" she said.

"The lads don't care," Brugha said.

The procession was silent except for the occasional snare drum and the sound of walking in the rain. Taunts started as the group rounded a corner near a traditional Protestant neighborhood.

"Nationalist scum," a woman yelled.

"Feckin' fenians," a man yelled from the other side.

"Shut your fuckin' mouth, Prod vermin."

"Who you tellin' to shut up, ya Taig cunt?"

Sister Grey raised her eyebrows and sighed.

"Lord, please get us through this," she said.

The procession arrived at the church, with the hearses parking and the pallbearers approaching narrow steps. The crowd watched as O'Connell's pallbearers ascended the steps first. After they were in the church, Mich Doherty's pallbearers started up the steps.

CRACK!

Gunfire. People screamed and everyone ducked. The pallbearers lowered the casket. The church door shut. Kincaid grabbed Sr. Grey and pulled her down as Brugha crouched beside the wheelchair.

CRACK! CRACK!

More gunshots from more than one weapon as police fanned into the crowd. A loud male voice's command echoed. Kincaid couldn't tell from where it came.

"Warning shots," Brugha said.

CRACK! CRACK! CRACK!

"Makes me wonder if it's not Mich's brother," Brugha said. "He could never attend the funeral unless well armed and ready to shoot."

"Why do you say that?" Kincaid asked.

"He's an óglaigh with the South Armagh Brigade. Subject to immediate arrest."

More hollering and the shots stopped and after enough time, Brugha rose, as others around him stood. Sister Grey started to rise, but Kincaid kept her down.

"It's all right," the Chief Superintendent's second in command announced. "It's over. It's over."

"It's never over," Brugha whispered.

KINCAID WAS STILL IN his suit when Mattie approached with a cup of tea and a pad of entries titled *Occurrences, Reports, and Complaints Book*.

"Kev must have brought this home, though you're not supposed to take it out of the office. He did sometimes. Constable Brugha was asking after it."

"You didn't give it to him."

"Not when his new calling in life seems to be foiling you," she said. "I don't care what Iain says, Kevin would not have approved. I wanted you to see this before I returned it."

Kincaid opened the book on the coffee table.

"You best be movin' it, though," she said, as she set the tea beside it.

"Thank you."

"How are you liking the room?"

"The room is fine. But I feel guilty," Kincaid said. "For imposing."

Mattie sat. "I appreciate the company," she said. "You and Sister."

Kincaid reached for the tea and as he clasped his fingers around the cup and handle, she clasped his hand, tears welling in her eyes.

"I can't believe he's gone," she said.

Twenty Two

Brugha pulled the Hotspur alongside a hill that rose from the roadside in a mottle of greens and browns before it vanished over a low plateau in the lifting fog. Kincaid heard hounds baying and barking.

"I don't suppose you wanna be trying to climb?"

"No, Constable. Just take good pictures."

Brugha got out of the truck and Kincaid watched him crest the hill. He turned to a book Sr. Grey checked out of the Newry Free Public Library, *Reformation Saints: Catholic and Protestant Clergy and Dissidents Who Lost Their Lives to Religious Persecution.*

She had one biography marked.

"Oliver Plunkett, Archbishop of Armagh, Ireland. Declared a martyr by Pope Benedict XV 17 March 1918. Beatified by Pope Benedict XV 23 May 1920."

Brugha knocking on the passenger-side window startled Kincaid. "Hand me that Polaroid if you would, Inspector," he said. "A bit gray out here, but you'll get the gist of things."

"What *is* the gist?" Kincaid asked.

"Hard to tell at this point."

Brugha left with the camera. Kincaid looked down at his legs and tried to move them but winced. "Fuck!" he said and smacked the dashboard with the side of his fist. He sighed, looked out the window, then at the book. He turned to the index.

"Burnings," led to page 76 and an entry that began, "Made famous by the executions of Joan of Arc in the Middle Ages and the 17th-century Salem Witch Trials in America," and continued, "John Foxe's *Book of Martyrs* reports that over three hundred Protestants, from high-ranking clergy to peasant commoners, were burned at the stake for heresy under the reigns of Henry VIII (1509–1547) and Mary I of England (1553–1558).

"Women guilty of heresy and other crimes against either the Catholic or Anglican Churches were almost exclusively burned, to avoid the 'indecent' exposures which might occur during those execution techniques reserved for men, notably quartering and beheading. Follows a tradition established during the earlier days of crucifixions."

Kincaid could not recall any crucified women.

Brugha startled him at the window again. "CID's in from Belfast, you know, given our short-handedness." He slipped a handful of Polaroid photos to Kincaid. "Brutal."

"Looks like someone set a scarecrow on fire," Kincaid said.

"Also found this," Brugha said, producing a long, slender book covered in plastic. "Told 'em our guest from the Guards would want to see it."

"And they consented?"

"You're the most famous detective on the island, or so I keep hearing," Brugha said. "They had no choice but to consent."

THE BELL AT THE O'Connell's house rang.

"I rushed over the minute I heard," Sr. Grey told Mattie in the foyer. "Another killing. Adam—terrible, terrible news. Do they know who it is?"

"By the looks of things," Kincaid said with the ledger open before him on the coffee table, "a bookkeeper."

"A bookkeeper?" Mattie said. "Why on Earth—?"

Mattie peering over her shoulder, Grey looked at the entries, all next to amounts in pounds sterling.

MD, Op Banner—uniforms

MD, Op Banner—shirts, trousers

MD, Op Banner—P.O. 1987765

Hotel Tyrone—linens

Hotel Tyrone—linens

Belfast Transport—driver uniforms

Belfast Transport—driver uniforms

SB—dress and press*

SB—dress and press*

"If I didn't know better, I'd say this is a collection of laundry tickets," Sr. Grey said.

"Ministry of Defence, Operation Banner," Kincaid said. "Code name for British Army operations up here."

"And SB?" Grey asked.

"Sisters and Brothers," Kincaid quipped.

"The asterisks refer to this footnote." She pointed. "*Uniforms.* SB wears uniforms."

"Special Branch," Mattie squeaked.

"*That* is a possibility," Kincaid said. He held up a transparent evidence envelope. "This was in what was left." He looked at Mattie and whispered to Sr. Grey. "Of the victim's mouth."

Sister Grey picked up the clear baggie and read the inscription on the wrinkled cloth inside: *suscipe discipulum.* "Take up the disciple," she said.

"The North has its first manutergium," Kincaid said.

"And Saint Andrew's prayer continues." Sr. Grey noticed Mattie staring and trembling. She took Mattie's hand.

"Having all this evidence about—it feels like Kevin never left," Mattie said. "The pictures he had out earlier—"

"You saw those?" Kincaid said.

"I've seen enough not to let it bother me. Or so I think until I see more."

"May I see them?" the sister said.

"Official police business," Kincaid said.

"For which the Gardaí is handsomely compensating my order."

"Didn't you take a vow of poverty?"

"I did. But my order did not. Most orders are self-sufficient. We don't have the benefit of weekly church collections or other forms of priestly tribute."

"Any idea which place was doing the washing?" Mattie asked.

"Nothing in the book," Kincaid said. "Must've been an internal ledger."

"About those crime scene photos," Sr. Grey said.

"I'll leave you to it," Mattie said. "Had enough brutality for today."

Kincaid handed Grey a manila envelope.

"Oh!" she said, turning away. "Her face."

"Probably why the book was left," Kincaid said. "Only clue to the victim's identity." He sighed. "Had enough?"

"THE HOTEL TYRONE AND Belfast Transport send their laundry to a convent," Brugha told Kincaid on the phone.

"A convent?"

"Yes, Inspector. Housekeeping supervisor at the hotel says it's a big operation. Washing, ironing, folding, pressing—industrial scale. Says he feels bad for the women. Hot as hell in the place."

"Name?"

"I don't know."

"Can you get it for me, please?"

Kincaid heard Brugha thumbing through papers.

"Constable."

"I said I don't know," Brugha said.

"You didn't ask?"

"Not during that conversation."

"Does that mean there were subsequent conversations?"

"No."

"I find it hard to believe you wouldn't know all about the laundry." The conversation paused again. "If you feel you can't trust me—"

"Sisters of the Atonement. In Belfast," Brugha croaked.

"OH!" KINCAID'S HEAD JERKED up from the backrest of the living room sofa where he'd fallen asleep.

"Long days gettin' to ya," Mattie O'Connell said. "Don't blame ya. The McLaughlin family's funeral—"

Kincaid pushed his hair back and the sleep out of his eyes. "That may rank as the saddest experience of my life," he said. He looked around. "You didn't hold a wake."

"I didn't cover our mirrors or stop our clocks," she said. "If that's what you're meaning."

"Partly."

"I don't care to be a martyr to my sorrows. Kevin wouldn't have wanted that. He was a man who faced things, head on. Anyways, we had hardly the family for a wake." Mattie went into the kitchen, talking all the way. "Sorrows is why you're havin' those bad dreams, I'd be certain of it," she said. And on returning, "You remember any of them? The dreams?"

"Didn't know I was having bad dreams."

"You don't wake yourself up?"

"No," Kincaid said. "What am I doing?"

"Calling out."

"Loud enough to wake you?"

"If I were asleep."

"I'm sorry. I had no idea."

Mattie sat across from him. "You were shot, Inspector. It was a terrible trauma. Maybe you need someone to talk to."

Kincaid looked ahead, beyond the window.

"I'm prying, I know—"

"The person I was talking to was killed," Kincaid said.

"Oh—"

"Maybe by the same person behind these burning deaths. Or persons."

"Because he was talking to you?"

"I hope not," Kincaid said. "I don't think so." He picked up the laundry ledger on the coffee table. "Your husband ever mention the Sisters of the Atonement?"

"No. But he had looked into some of those mother and baby homes. Several Catholic orders run them. Anglicans and Presbyterians, too. He knew a great deal about them. I was surprised at what he learned."

"I thought Sisters of the Atonement was a laundry."

"That's how they earn their keep," Mattie said. "Unwed mams, some with babes. Sisters work 'em to death, Kev said."

"What was he—"

The phone rang.

"I don't know," Mattie said on her way to answer it.

"If it's for me—" Kincaid said.

"It's Sister," Mattie said. "She's bringing a visitor by."

BEFORE KINCAID STOOD A stunning young woman in a magnificent shroud of spiritual grace.

"Mother Superior Stephanie Teresa, Inspector Adam Kincaid," Sr. Grey announced. "He's the Gardaí investigator we've been speaking about."

She extended her hand. "Welcome to RUC territory, Inspector."

"Mother Stephanie is abbess where I'm staying," Grey said.

Kincaid said something warm but indiscernible.

"And this is Mattie O'Connell."

"I knew your brother," Mother Superior said. "He met with me at the station, several times."

"You were Sister Mongilly's abbess," Mattie said.

"For only a few months," Mother Stephanie said.

"Please, everyone. Do sit," Mattie said.

"Miss O'Connell—thank you so much for having us," Sr. Grey said.

"I understand no men at the convent," Mattie replied.

"If the inspector was a priest," Mother Stephanie said.

"Can I get anyone anything?" Mattie asked.

Everyone politely declined.

"I was sorry to hear of your brother's passing," Mother Stephanie said. "He was a guardian angel after Mongilly's death. Advised me on steps we could take to better secure ourselves. And the abbey."

"Thank you. I'm missing him dearly," Mattie said. She dabbed her eyes with her sleeve and through a sniffle said, "Did you know him before—Mongilly's death?"

"No. But my predecessor did."

"Really?" Kincaid said.

"Sergeant O'Connell mentioned talking with her," Mother Stephanie said. "He didn't say about what."

"Perhaps Constable Brugha will check into that if I ask nicely enough," Kincaid said.

"You'd need a saint on your side for that," Mattie said.

Kincaid cleared his throat. "Sister Grey said you might have some information about this." He held up the ledger.

"May I?" Mother Stephanie said.

"Please."

Mother Stephanie took it and read. "Entries suggest a Magdalene Laundry."

"The laundries that double as homes for unwed mothers," Kincaid said.

"Or young women cast out of their families for some moral offense—drugs, alcohol, boyfriends. I don't like them, Inspector. The women are little better than indentured servants, desperate for a roof over their heads, often trading one abuse for another."

"Magdalene, I take it, refers to Mary Magdalene," Kincaid said.

"Of the Crucifixion," Mother Stephanie said. "Biblical lore has cast her, unfairly I believe, as a fallen woman. These laundries profit on the backs of *fallen women*, who are powerless against the moral and dare I say physical authority of their convent overseers. Since the labor is free, a Magdalene Laundry can undercut the competition quite considerably."

"Brugha thinks this ledger came from the Sisters of the Atonement."

"It very well could have," Mother Stephanie said. "Mongilly got entangled with their headquarters. When Grey mentioned that ledger—"

"Entangled?"

"I didn't like what she was doing for them, and I said so," Mother Stephanie said. "It was bookkeeping, just like that." She indicated the ledger book. "They sent their monthly bills, Mongilly made ledger entries, sent the entries back."

"Couldn't find a bookkeeper in Belfast?"

"Seems strange, doesn't it? But then, everything about her life got strange after Father Wryth appeared."

"The notorious Father Wryth again," Kincaid said.

"He arranged the laundry job, after Mongilly stopped working for him," Mother Stephanie said.

"Doing what, exactly?" Kincaid scribbled in a notepad.

"Same sorts of things. Bookkeeping. Travel arrangements. I'd call her a *girl Friday*, but her adventure was hardly as romantic as Robinson Crusoe's."

"You don't allow men at your convent," Kincaid said.

"True. But we are not a cloister, Inspector," Mother Stephanie said. "Our sisters are free to come and go, associate with whom they wish, for the most part. Where priests are concerned, 'strict' is stricken from 'restriction.' Male orders have a latitude denied female orders. If a father asks a sister for assistance, the request is considered to issue from the mouth of God."

"Why did Sister Mongilly stop working for Wryth?" Kincaid asked.

"My predecessor, may she rest in peace, was outraged," Mother Stephanie said. "So Mongilly broke it off. Monsignor Mulvaney had come forward with his charges by then, and the Archbishop—"

"Archbishop Conway?"

"Archbishop Conway sent a letter, a stern letter, mind you. Since the trouble with James Chesney, Monsignor Mulvaney has had the Archbishop's ear."

"Chesney?"

"Father Chesney. Monsignor had proof he was working for one of the republican brigades," Mother Stephanie said. "His Eminence saw this proof and got rid of Chesney."

"This Monsignor Mulvaney—where is he based?"

"Belfast. But you're unlikely to find him there."

"Why not?"

"He hasn't been seen nor heard from for the past six months."

"YOU LOOK LIKE YOU'RE in hot pursuit of a fleeing question," Sr. Grey said.

Kincaid smiled. "I've been reading that book you gave me. Says burnings were reserved for women and Protestants."

"Do we know any more about the third victim?"

"Every bone in her body was ripped from its joints and sockets. Before she was burned."

"Sounds like she was racked," Grey said. "How ghastly. And still no idea who she is. Was, rather."

"M. E.'s hoping for a dental match."

Kincaid picked up *Reformation Saints*. "Speaking of racks, Baldwin's killer or killers used the bookshelf ladders in the Long Room to replicate the rack Plunkett was drawn and quartered on. 'Dragged, usually by horse, on the rack, to the place of execution,'" Kincaid read from *Reformation Saints*.

"The horse outside the library," Sr. Grey said. "Oliver Plunkett, Archbishop of Armagh. How much do the current archbishops know about all this, I wonder?"

"Might not hurt to inform them," Kincaid said.

"Or warn them," Grey said.

SISTER GREY DROVE THE cramped Ford Zephyr with her eyes up and her head down, lowered reflexively when the first helicopter buzzed overhead.

"You're getting into the routine of things," Kincaid said.

"And you're not crouching low enough," she said.

She raised her head when they approached a checkpoint, where a British soldier stuck his nose in the car demanding their business and any papers they might have to support it. Variations on, "A garda? Here? Why?" were the most common questions Kincaid answered, some delivered with more seething than others.

"I lay in bed, hearing bombs or bullets somewhere," Grey said as they continued onward. "The other sisters count them like sheep. The first question at breakfast repeats like the machine guns. 'Who did we know was killed last night?' They always know someone."

She parked on Castle Street in Armagh and looking up the street and down it, again and again, unloaded Kincaid's folded wheelchair from the back seat. She looked through the fence at the cathedral.

"I'm sorry I'm not much help," he said.

"It's light and I'm strong," she said. "And you can still be a sentry."

She helped him into the chair and they went around to the open gate and along a flat, narrow drive to the entrance. The cathedral's verger met them near the tall, arched front doors.

"Inspector Kincaid, Sister Grey. Welcome."

"Thank you for arranging this."

"I can't take much credit," the verger said. "Archbishop Simms was eager to meet you. He's been following these killings." He looked beyond the gate to the roadside. "Any trouble getting here?"

"Of the shooting kind?" Kincaid asked.

"Well, to put it indelicately—"

"None," Sister Grey said.

"Good then. Follow me."

Kincaid wheeled himself into the church. The archbishop walked toward them down the long central aisle in the nave. He was a brisk, sharp man, early sixties. He extended his hand.

"The Most Reverend George Simms," the verger said. "Adam Kincaid, Inspector with the Gardaí, and Sister Jane Grey, of the Catholic Order of St. Dymphna."

"Your . . . Grace?" Kincaid said.

"George, please. Or Bishop, if you're in a formal mind. Welcome to the Hill. And on such a lovely day."

"Lovely church," Kincaid said.

"St. Patrick, did you hear that?" the archbishop announced, looking up and around. "It's been rebuilt I don't know how many times. Always good to hear preceding generations got it right."

"Most certainly," Sister Grey said. "It's stunning, Your Grace."

"Come, sit," he said.

They took aisle pews, eye level with Kincaid.

"I read you're a student of the Book of Kells," Grey said.

"I am," the archbishop said. "Started when I was in Dublin. The victims—the ones with the notes. I have to admit, that piqued my interest."

"Any insights?" Kincaid asked.

"The writer of the notes knows insular calligraphy," the archbishop said. "Intimately, I would surmise. The stitching alone is quite a feat, certainly attention getting. These killings, I must say, are giving the Troubles a go for top billing, as if such a thing were possible. And here you are, about another."

“A pattern has emerged,” Sr. Grey said. “They may be staged to look like medieval executions.”

“Of religious leaders and clergy,” Kincaid added. “Oliver Plunkett brought us.”

“Does Bill know about this?”

“Bill?”

“Archbishop Conway. My spiritual brother a few blocks down.”

“We’re meeting him after we leave here.”

“Finding us both in town on the same day is an act of Providence, certainly. What can I do to help?”

“Get word out,” Kincaid said. “Ask your clergy to keep their eyes open. And if you should hear of anything—” Kincaid handed him Constable Brugha’s card. “He’s handling the case in Briar Lough and vicinity, and knows it well as anyone.”

“Other than the Middle East, no place on Earth has a more confusing Babel of faiths and creeds than we do,” the archbishop said. “But bombs and bullets are the weapons of choice, not nooses and pyres.”

“We may have found a connection to the conflict,” Kincaid said. “At least, a tangential one.”

“Oh?”

“Would you happen to know anything about the laundries?”

“The Magdalene homes,” Sr. Grey clarified.

“We’ve generally stayed out of that business,” the archbishop said. “One or two have come and gone over the years, but from a practical standpoint, we don't have a population of nuns to operate them. From a moral standpoint—"

"What about the Bethany House?" Sr. Grey interrupted. "When you were Archbishop of Dublin." Archbishop Simms frowned and turned to Kincaid.

"We're closing the Bethany Home, if we haven't already. My successor in Dublin, Archbishop Buchanan, would know more. But back to the Book of Kells."

He stepped around the pew and past the choir and organ section and disappeared behind the altar. Grey looked up when she heard his shoes striding back across the stone floor. He handed them a newspaper with photos of the manutergium from the first Dublin murder.

"Whoever did this," Archbishop Simms said, "spent a lot of time with the Book."

"MARTA," KINCAID TOLD SR. Grey as she pushed him down Dawson Street on the way to the Catholic archbishop.

"The idea wasn't lost on me," Grey said. "But Marta a serial murderer?"

"Or Marta, perhaps coerced, to do something short of serial murder," Kincaid said.

"To aid and abet? An accomplice of some sort?"

Kincaid said nothing.

"Adam?"

"Why?" he said. "Why would she do that, help in a killing?"

"Maybe someone stole her work."

"What work? I don't remember Marta ever doing embroidery."

Grey smiled, picked up the pace, looked forward, and mused.

"Did you know the Primacy of All Ireland is invested in both these men?" Grey said. "They are both Primates."

"Aren't we all?"

"Not that kind of primate, but I fear you know that already," Sr. Grey said. "The clerical kind. Men, inevitably, charged with leading their flocks. Across the island, in this case."

"There's not a Primate for the Republic?"

"There is. He's called the Primate of Ireland. Just Ireland. Not *all Ireland*."

"And me family wondered why I left."

"The Church?" Sister said.

"Yes. This church. That church. Any church. I'm an avowed agnostic."

"Rather like being a confirmed bachelor," Sister said. She saw two men across the street whose eyes seemed to follow them. "I hope the verger was right."

"About what?"

"When he said walking was safe."

"You know how to use that thing?"

"What thing?"

"The derringer in your purse," Kincaid said.

"You've been going through my purse?"

"No need. I felt it when you brushed against me."

"Inspector!"

"I assume you have some sort of permit? From the RUC, presumably?"

"I do. Special dispensation for persons whose, and I quote, 'lives may be endangered by virtue of the work they do, the service they perform, or the position they hold, especially if related to government or law enforcement.'"

"They gave you all that?"

"I do have friends in high places." She looked up to the sky. "What about you? What sort of concealed firearms are you permitted?"

"Sergeant O'Connell provided me a Walther P22," Kincaid said.

"Rather an inferior weapon," Grey said.

"More than I usually have. My department doesn't carry."

"The Republic takes a dim view of my derringer, I'm afraid. But no need to pack heat there—or at least, not nearly as great a need."

"Speaking of that need," Kincaid said.

One man stopped in front of them.

"Understand you might be needing an escort," he said.

"Where did you hear that?" Kincaid asked.

"To St. Patrick's."

"Who's escorting us?" Grey asked.

"Us," the confronting man said. He addressed Grey. "Who are you?"

"I'm a Catholic nun," Sister Grey said. "Here." She reached into her purse.

"I'll take that," the confronter said, but not before she retrieved her card. She handed purse and card to him.

"Never heard of this order," the confronter said. "Or one that carries guns." He held up her derringer with a grin.

"Are you Catholic?" Sr. Grey asked.

The man just stared at her.

"If you are Catholic, then surely you've heard of St. Dymphna. One of the most famous saints in all Ireland."

"I'm not Catholic, but I am republican," a second man said.

Kincaid pushed himself forward and reached around to his back pocket. The second man pulled back a jacket to reveal a revolver strapped around his chest.

"I'm not armed," Kincaid said. "My wallet."

"We know who you are."

A third man emerged from the shadows of another building. He walked toward them and Kincaid looked up at Sr. Grey. The man walked right up to Kincaid and squatted down to eye him.

"Michelle Doherty was my sister," he said.

"I'm—"

"You're in this chair because of her."

"No," Kincaid said.

"So it's not true?"

"I'm not in this chair because of Constable Doherty."

"You took a bullet for her."

"I pulled her out of the way," Kincaid said. "But I'm not in this chair because of anything she did."

"I was at her funeral. You might have heard me." Mich's brother stood. "I'm Rowan," he said. "This is Seamus. This is Sean."

"You were the ones firing the shots? Some kind of volley?" Kincaid asked.

"A warning," Rowan said. "My sister—" He stopped suddenly and put his hand to his forehead and his voice cracked. "It cost Michelle her life," he said, in tears now. "They killed the furrier to shut him up. Killed his daughter to shut her down. Killed my baby sister because she was there."

"They don't know who killed Lann McLaughlin," Sr. Grey said.

"Shut up! Ya do too," Seamus the confronter hollered.

"And they don't know why," Grey continued, unfazed.

Rowan Doherty turned and whistled twice through his fingers. Men in balaclavas or hats with visors pulled over their eyes emerged from door and alley ways.

"You'll need help," Rowan said, looking at Grey then Kincaid. "Getting to the church."

"I think we'll be fine," Kincaid said. "If you'll just let us pass."

Rowan motioned his men back, motioned Seamus to return Sr. Grey's purse. She joined Kincaid as he pushed the wheelchair onward.

"You'll never get up them steps," Rowan called out.

The sister and the inspector stopped.

"Without an assist, that is."

A SOLEMN WALK LATER, they appeared at a gate on Cathedral Street that opened on a steep flight of thirty or so steps to a magnificent cathedral with Gothic twin spires. A woman in low heels carrying a file folder paced down the steps toward them.

"Inspector? Detective Inspector Kincaid?"

"Yes," he said, as she stopped, out of breath.

"I didn't know," she said. "When Simms' office called us . . . We would have had you come around back. There's plenty of parking."

"We walked," Sr. Grey said.

"Walked? Oh, Good Lord. Well, then, What are you men doing here?"

"They were kind enough to escort us," Kincaid said.

"Wasn't a kindness ' tall," Rowan Doherty said.

"You're not supposed to be here," the woman told them. "You know how His Eminence feels."

"We had nothing to do with Father Chesney," Sean said. "Told him to be on his way, in no uncertain terms."

"It doesn't matter," she said. "His Eminence condemns your actions and unless you intend repentance and confession—"

"We're intendin' no such things," Rowan said.

"Then you need to leave."

Doherty looked at the cathedral. "This man can't very well walk up them steps," he said.

"We can make it around back," Kincaid said.

"Well, actually, it's still a bit of a hike from here," the woman said.

"What's a bit more?" Sr. Grey asked.

"Our journey's not finished, madam," Doherty said to the woman. He took the handle of Kincaid's wheelchair and motioned Seamus to take the other and Sean behind.

"I will call security," the woman said.

"And they won't be tussling with us," Doherty said. "Just let us get your guest to the top of these steps and we'll be along."

She moved toward them with her mouth open, but Sr. Grey gently took her arm.

"Mr. Kincaid took a bullet for his sister," Grey told the woman.

"He's the one?" she said.

"Yes."

"Well. Very well." She stepped aside. "But no farther than the top of those steps," she called, as the men carried Kincaid up to St. Patrick's *Catholic* Cathedral, one step at a time.

Twenty Three

Kincaid, Sr. Grey, and Constable Brugha watched young women dressed in drab skirts and aprons load washing machines taller than they were; steam iron white shirts; press blue trousers; and fold king and queen sheets and pillowcases into tight, bright squares.

"Our operation, such as it is," said the prioress standing with them at the industrial laundry room's wide doorway.

Sister Grey noticed a worker looking at her, turning away, looking again, a furtive stare. The woman walked through another doorway, then returned pushing a cart piled with folded sheets.

"Will you need to interview any of them?" the prioress asked.

Brugha set his briefcase next to Kincaid's wheelchair and started into the room.

"We generally don't allow the public—"

"Police business, Sister," Brugha said.

"Constable," Kincaid said. Brugha stopped. Kincaid motioned him to eye level. "Maybe we should wait. Focus on the business office first," he whispered.

"Givin' orders again, are ya?" Brugha growled.

"No. Just recommendations."

"I'm not in your chain of command. I don't need your recommendations, advice, or any other interference," Brugha whispered, loudly enough that Sr. Grey looked over at them.

"By all means," Kincaid said. "Do it the RUC way."

Brugha stood straight, caught Grey frowning at him, reluctantly acquiesced. "Your business manager, Sister," Brugha said.

The prioress looked at her watch. "Should be back. If the bank opened on time."

They started down the hallway.

"Have you had many problems here, at the convent?" Sr. Grey asked.

"Troubles related? No, thank God, though my thanks may be misplaced."

"How so?"

"Without us, the republicans wouldn't have clean uniforms," the prioress said. "Or whatever they call what they wear. Pardon my saying so, but they protect us like soldiers do whores."

"Really?"

"God forgive me. But shrinking from the truth has never been my way."

"You've contracts with the British Army and something called SB—" Kincaid said.

"And the Guards. Yes! Our Dublin sisters wash gardaí uniforms."

"I've been plainclothes for so long I don't remember getting shirts and trousers back," Kincaid said. "How long has your order done our laundry?"

"Ms Nic Cionnaith can fill you in. By the way, I almost joined the Dymphnans," the prioress said to Sr. Grey. "I'm very impressed with the work you do."

"Thank you," Sr. Grey said.

The prioress knocked at an open office door. "Good morning, Siobhan."

"Mother Catherine. Good morning. Come in."

"I've brought the visitors. Inspector Kincaid, Constable Brugha, Sister Grey."

"Siobhan Nic Cionnaith." She extended her hand. "Pleasure to meet each of you." She eyed Kincaid. "I've seen you in the papers."

"Doubtless standing," Kincaid said.

"It was something about a murder," Ms. Nic Cionnaith said. "But in the South."

"Inspector Kincaid is on loan from the Guards," Brugha said. "Sister Grey, too."

"Sister?"

Grey extended her hand. "My order doesn't wear habits," she said. "Thank you for seeing us."

"Which order?"

"Saint Dymphna."

"Ahh," Nic Cionnaith said. "The mind readers."

"Hadn't heard that one before," Grey said.

"You had something you wanted me to look over."

"Yes." Brugha opened the briefcase and handed her the murder-scene ledger. Nic Cionnaith's face changed. "Miss?"

She looked at them.

"Do you recognize it?" Kincaid asked.

"This belongs to Mary Clery," she said. "Where did you get it?"

Kincaid sat forward on hearing the name. "Clery?"

"Yes, Inspector. Mary Clery. She's a part-time bookkeeper."

"Is Ms Clery about?" Brugha asked.

"Not for a few days. She only comes in at the end of the week. Friday, sometimes. Saturday most times."

"To do what, exactly?"

"This." She took the ledger. "Does work around Belfast. We found her through an agency."

"Which agency, Miss?"

Kincaid squirmed around in his wheelchair, watching Brugha, wanting to assure he hadn't heard "Marta Carney." Given that there was no such thing as a coincidence—

"We just know it as The Agency. I could look it up." She went to a file drawer.

"Can you describe Mrs. Clery?" Kincaid asked.

"She wasn't married," Nic Cionnaith said. "That's the first thing."

"Height, weight, complexion," Brugha asked.

"Pretty lass. Five four, five five. Eight, maybe nine stone."

Marta. Or a million other Irish women. Kincaid's stomach dropped nonetheless. Brugha leaned down to him.

"Well?" the constable whispered.

Kincaid cleared his throat. "Anyone have any reason to harm Ms Clery?"

"Harm her?"

"Anyone you can think of. Did she have any enemies?"

"Oh, goodness. No, none that I could imagine," Nic Cionnaith said. "She was quiet, bookish."

"Like a librarian?"

"Adam," Sr. Grey said.

"Yes. Rather like a librarian, but without the stern demeanor."

Kincaid looked at Sister Grey, who raised her eyes despairingly. "How long had she been working here?" he continued.

"Why—how long would you say?" Nic Cionnaith asked the prioress, Mother Catherine.

"A month?"

"No, no. Less than a month. Definitely less than a month."

"A pretty lass, you said. Brown hair, blue eyes?" Kincaid asked.

"Can't say about her eyes. But she did have dark hair. She was ever' bit of Irish," Nic Cionnaith said. "Witty, smart, quick on her feet."

Kincaid leaned back, looked away, and took a deep breath.

"Has something happened to Mary?" Mother Catherine asked.

"We don't know," Brugha said. "Would you have an address for her?"

"Yes, of course," Nic Cionnaith said. "I think the agency included it on her resume."

"I KNOW WHAT YOU'RE thinking, Adam, and I think you should stop thinking it," Sr. Grey whispered as Mother Catherine escorted them down down the hall to leave the building.

"We'll soon find out."

"Oh—!" Sister Grey collided with the laundry worker, now exchanging more than eye contact. The woman dropped a pile of folded sheets.

"You stupid—" Mother Catherine said to the worker. "I'm so sorry," she said to Sr. Grey, as they collected the sheets.

"It's quite all right. Are you all right?" Grey asked the woman.

"Yes, ma'am."

The prioress eyed her until she hurried off with the sheets.

"Should you need anything else," the prioress said, "you know how to reach me. Go in God's love."

IN THE CAR AS they pulled away from the convent, "If she's home. If she wasn't the latest victim. If, if. You have Marta on the brain," Sr. Grey said. "Did you notice that?"

"Which?" Brugha said.

"The way the prioress snapped at that laundry worker."

"She's a nun," Brugha said.

"Which is supposed to mean what?"

"Stern. Like a librarian."

"Constable Brugha—" Sr. Grey saw something in her purse. She took it out: a slip of paper. She opened it.

"My God," she said as she read it. "She's a Dymphnan."

"Who?" Kincaid asked.

"The woman who ran into me. She dropped this in my purse." She handed him the note.

"'Don't read until out of building,'" Kincaid read on the fold. "'Here on assignment. Need to talk. Will be in touch. Sister Francisca Patron de la Guerra, O.S.S.D.' Assignment?"

"Remember I told you my order was having a look at the Magdalene laundries? Sister de la Guerra is apparently, what was the term you used: an undercover nun."

Brugha smirked.

"I didn't mean any disrespect," Kincaid said.

"Could have fooled me," Grey said.

Kincaid grasped Brugha's arm and directed his eyes to a cemetery on the way out of convent grounds where a backhoe was digging a grave.

"Just another suggestion," Kincaid said.

"Fine, Inspector." Brugha pulled the car to the curb, behind a white van marked "Kellen and Sons, Funeral Directors." A small tractor pulled a cart stacked with burlap sacks away from the van and up an embankment toward the plot.

"What are you thinking?" Brugha asked Kincaid.

"What are they burying."

Brugha got out with a notepad. Kincaid opened the passenger door.

"Kinda hard to navigate this hill with a wheelchair," Brugha said. "Why don't—" But Kincaid swung out two crutches.

"Are you quite sure about that?" Sister Grey said.

"If I slip, will you catch me?" Kincaid said.

"If God doesn't," she quipped.

Kincaid hobbled around the car and gradually ascended a cobblestone path, stumbling but not falling in ruts and crevices. Brugha or the sister intercepted each fumble.

"We been workin' for the convent about ten years," Mr. Kellen told Brugha. "No one else wanted the contract. O'Shanes, Kelly Brothers, Mercury and Deal. None of the big houses."

The tractor parked next to the grave.

"Bodies?" Kincaid said.

"You're with the Guards, eh?" Kellen said. "RUC can't handle a simple murder."

"Just answer the question," Brugha said.

Kellen looked up the hill as the tractor backed up. "Bodies they are—Inspector."

"Six to a grave?"

"Looks to be."

"Thought the limit was four," Brugha said.

Kellen looked ahead and started to walk.

"So—what about it?" Brugha asked Kellen.

"They're small," Kellen said. "Children. And some of the sisters, when they get up in years. Well, they whither."

"By children, you mean of the mams who come here?"

"Yes. So again, if you don't mind me askin', what's a Gardaí man doin' in Norniron?"

"Special assignment," Brugha said. "And the limit *is* four. To a grave."

"I'll tell the sisters," Kellen said. "My understanding' was they had special dispensation, since they own the grounds."

"You ever have occasion to deal with the office manager? Ms Nic Cionnaith?" Kincaid asked.

"Oh, yes. A sharp eye she keeps."

"Go into her office?"

"I have. Went in last week to pick up a check."

"Did you?" Brugha said.

"I did. Anything wrong with that?"

"Was anyone else in the office with her?" Kincaid asked.

"No."

"Have you ever seen her with anyone else?" Brugha asked.

"Well, let's see. Mother Catherine I've seen with her," Kellen said. "Other nuns. And mams."

"What about a young woman, about this woman's height?" Brugha indicated Sr. Grey. "Not a mam or a nun. Someone who comes and goes."

"A young woman, young woman. Cannot say as I have. Let me ask my boy." Kellen whistled up the hill, waved his son down. He had seen a person matching the description of Mary Clery.

"When was the last time you saw her?" Brugha asked.

"In the office, last week maybe," Kellen's son said. "In the carpark, a few days ago. Arguin' with a fella, she was."

"Any idea about what?"

"No. But he had his hands on her, and I started down to see what was wrong until she pulled herself away and drove off."

"You describe this man?" Brugha said.

"He was taller n' her. Black hair."

"Dressed how?"

"Grand. Sharp."

"I mean, what color?" Brugha said. "Were his clothes."

"Dark."

BRUGHA WALKED BACK UP the steps from Mary Clery's cottage wearing latex gloves. He leaned through the car window.

"No one about," he said.

Kincaid sighed and turned to Sr. Grey in the back seat.

"That young woman's face was obliterated," Kincaid said. "How can I not think it could be Marta?"

"*Why* is Marta mixed up in this? *How* is Marta mixed up in this?" the sister said. "Why do you *think* she's mixed up in this?"

Brugha stood there listening.

"Because she vanished the day we found Dr. Baldwin. And because I have an intuition," Kincaid said.

"I saw her last, remember?" Grey put her hand on his shoulder. "She's not dead, Adam."

Kincaid raised his eyes to Brugha.

"I'll brave the steps," he said. "And the courts."

"I've got it handled, Inspector," Brugha said. "No need to brave anything."

"Why don't you let me decide that?"

"Because you'll be decidin' for the both of us. And her, too."

"I'm quite all right with that," Grey said.

"Well, you would be," Brugha said.

Kincaid opened the door as Brugha reluctantly stepped aside, put out his crutches and started to stand. Sr. Grey stepped out and helped, Brugha held off. Out of the car Kincaid emerged, to navigate another stone walkway. "Is there a smooth path in all Eire?" he asked.

"The policeman's lament," Sr. Grey said. "Constable—would you be so kind?"

Brugha stomped ahead of them and as they approached, opened the back door to Clery's house. "Been through. No trip wires. Nothing out of the ordinary. But I didn't search anything because I have no warrant."

Kincaid peered in. "I don't plan to search," he said. "Just peek." He hobbled into the kitchen, eyed neatly-stacked dishes, a drooping plant on a dining room table, a radio, pots and pans hanging from hooks over the stove, clean Formica counter tops.

"Almost doesn't look lived in," Brugha said.

Kincaid looked at letters, bills, snapshots, and a parking ticket attached with magnets to the refrigerator.

"Here's a license number," he told Brugha.

Sister Grey looked at the photos with him. "Recognize anyone?" she asked Kincaid.

"If you mean contemporaries of Marta's—no."

Kincaid circled the living room, eyeing its cramped but neat furnishings. He ran a tissue across an end table and a mid-century credenza. No dust. He followed Brugha into the bedroom and watched him stoop to look under a dresser and next to it, a dressing table. On rising, he looked at Kincaid.

"You don't look so good," Brugha said.

"Leg's killin' me. All of a sudden."

"Sit, then."

Kincaid looked at the bed.

"I'm sure she won't mind," Brugha said. "Then we'll go."

Kincaid lowered himself to the bed.

"Better?" Brugha asked.

"Yes."

"Adam," Sr. Grey called from the living room.

"I'm resting," he said.

"I may have found something."

Brugha went into the living room.

Kincaid looked at the mirror above the dressing table, where from it he saw broken glass near an aluminum casement crank handle on the bedroom window. He took his crutches and positioned them but stopped when he saw something else in the mirror. He looked down, at blue, red, green, and yellow wires snaking from beneath the bedspread to under the bed.

Brugha appeared at the door with something in his hand. “Inspector—”

“Stop,” Kincaid said. “Don’t come in here.”

“Why—”

Kincaid looked down.

“You were saying about trip wires.”

“Bloody hell,” Brugha said.

Sister Grey appeared next to him.

“Get out of here,” Kincaid said.

“What’s—”

“Turn around and slowly, quietly walk out. Both of you.”

“Sister, go,” Brugha said. “Now. Go.”

“I’m—”

“Don’t argue!” Kincaid said, resisting the urge to yell. “Go.”

“Go to the car, use my radio, tell them we need bomb disposal,” Brugha told the sister. “Explosive Ordinance Disposal. EOD. Remember that. EOD.”

“*You* tell them,” Kincaid said. “You both need to leave.”

“I’m not leaving,” Brugha said.

“I won’t know what to tell them,” Sister Grey said.

“That’s why you both need to leave. As long as I don’t move —”

“I’m no coward,” Brugha said.

“I know,” Kincaid said. “Now get the hell out of here.”

Brugha took Grey's arm. "We'll get you out, Inspector," he said.

BRITISH ARMY BOMB DISPOSAL experts in padded suits surrounded the bed, watching as one of their own emerged from beneath it with a transparent case of gray clay.

"No tellin' what's gonna happen when his weight comes off," the Army lieutenant said.

"Couldn't get it all?" His captain knelt for a better look.

"Got the C4. Simple enough bloke," the lieutenant said. "But there's something else in the mattress. Chemical detonator, probably. Some kind of contact explosive."

"What's this mean for me?" Kincaid asked.

The Army captain stood. "What it means is we're gonna have to grab you and run. Suit him up."

The men got a thick, padded bomb disposal suit around Kincaid's head, torso, and up both legs to the edge of the bed.

"Here's the plan: One man on either side. They grab you by the suit and pull the rest of it over your arse as you dive toward the door."

"A seat-of-your-trousers operation."

"Glad they're *your* trousers." The captain grinned.

"Mattress should muffle the blast," the lieutenant said.

"Blast?"

"Smallish," the captain said. "Hopefully just singe you. Put his shoes back on."

The troops took up positions on either side of Kincaid, grabbing the bomb suit below his waist.

"On five," the captain said. He counted slowly. "One, two, three, four, *five*." They yanked Kincaid forward by the suit and fell toward the door as the detonator charge burst the mattress. Cotton, feathers, and stuffing fogged the air with a pungent burn.

"Anyone hurt?" the captain said.

"No, sir."

"Fine here, sir."

"Inspector?"

"Leg's killin' me," Kincaid said through his helmet.

They pulled Kincaid to his feet and helped him to his waiting wheelchair at the front door.

"Get him to the hospital," the captain told Brugha.

"No need," Kincaid said. "I'm fine."

He stayed the night in the hospital, insisting word of the incident stay on this side of the border.

"IT'S HERS," KINCAID SAID, sitting in the O'Connell's living room.

"You're sure?" Constable Brugha said.

"I saw her wearing it."

"It's a lovely bracelet," Sister Grey said. "And quite expensive, from the looks of it."

"The mysterious boyfriend," Kincaid said. He handed the transparent evidence bag to Constable Brugha.

"I'm sorry to be the one who found it."

"We're glad you did, Sister," Brugha said. "It gives us some direction."

Sister Grey took Kincaid's hand. "I know this may mean—"

"I'd best be off," Brugha said. "Queen Street wants my report by tomorrow."

"Queen Street?" Kincaid asked.

"RUC station assigned to the case. Castlereagh barracks had it, but with the bomb—"

The hallway phone rang. "Inspector—back home ringing," Mattie O'Connell said. "Let me see if I can budge this over to you."

Mattie brought the phone along its cord and Kincaid took the receiver.

"Got another one, Adam," McDermott said.

"John?"

"Left in full view on the Ha'penny Bridge."

"Another victim? You're sure?"

"Killer or killers only left the head," McDermott explained. "Spent some considerable time positioning it on one of the wrought-iron spikes."

"Male?"

"Male. Looks to be about forty. Caucasian. Neck tattoo. And one of those kerchiefs stuffed in his mouth. We'll try for a dental ID."

"What did it say?" Kincaid asked.

"What did what say?"

"The kerchief. The manutergium."

"Oh. I have the crime scene photo here. Let me see. Looks like *pea pend it*."

"Pependit," Kincaid corrected, his voice faltering.

"You okay, Adam?" McDermott said. "You sound a little—I don't know—off kilter."

Kincaid lowered the receiver and let it drop from his hand onto the couch.

"How's the leg?" McDermott said. "Getting around better?"

Sister Grey picked up the receiver. "John. Jane Grey here."

"Yes, Sister. Good to hear your voice. What happened to Adam?"

Grey put her hand over the receiver. "Can I talk to him if you won't?"

Kincaid didn't look up. She leaned down. "Stop feeling sorry for yourself," she whispered.

"John—Adam's indisposed at the moment," Grey said. "We found Marta's bracelet."

"Bracelet? Where? How do you know it's hers?"

"Adam saw her wearing it. We found it here. There was an explosion—"

"Where? Anyone hurt?"

"Shaken, but otherwise fine."

"A bomb?"

"Tried to be."

"*Everyone's* fine? Who was there?" McDermott said.

"Everyone's fine."

"Why wasn't I told? You need to—"

"Because no one was hurt," Kincaid said loudly enough for McDermott to hear.

"The bomb was either a dud or a party favor," Grey said.

"Oh good lord," McDermott said. "A bomb is a bomb, especially up there. What's this about Marta's bracelet?"

She paused and looked at Kincaid, who heard McDermott's panicked voice. He took the receiver back.

"I saw her wearing it," he told McDermott. "Several times."

"How in the name of Janey Mac did you find *her* bracelet up there?"

"It was in the home of an itinerant bookkeeper. She may be one of the victims. We haven't identified her—"

"Why not?"

"Nothing left to identify," Kincaid said.

"That far gone, eh? You think it's Marta?"

"The bookkeeper's name is Mary Clery."

"I see your point," McDermott said. "But—I'm at a loss. I've no idea what to say or think."

A knock at the door interrupted them.

"Constable Brugha, no doubt," Mattie said. "He's always forgetting something."

But a woman stood at the door.

"I'M MAKING DELIVERIES," SISTER de la Guerra told them. Three brown paper packages sat on the coffee table. "Laundry plus." With a letter opener, she unpacked a dark green camouflage jacket.

"Looks like a military uniform."

"Provisionals," de la Guerra said. She looked at Sr. Grey. "IRA."

"And how do you deliver uniforms to terrorists?" Grey asked.

"They're not all terrorists," de la Guerra said. In the other package, she unfolded another jacket.

"British Army."

"Terrorists," Mattie O'Connell said. "I'm sorry, but they are."

And a third.

"RRG."

"Another republican group." Sister de la Guerra watched Kincaid pick up the jacket. "Open it," she said. "See the red thread." She took it from him and folded it open across the table. "Press it along here."

"Padding, insulation," Kincaid said.

With the letter opener, Sister de la Guerra slit the thread. Along with some stuffing, she removed a thin sheet of tracing paper. Mattie watched intently from behind.

"Laundry receipt?" Grey said.

De la Guerra unfolded it, to a diagram with arrows, distances, directions, coordinates.

"Looks like a map," Sr. Grey said.

"They all," Sr. de la Guerra said as she was unfolding the other jackets, "have them." She slit the red threads and with two fingers, carefully withdrew the maps.

"Go way outta that," Mattie said.

"You're investigating what—abuse allegations?"

"Yes, Inspector," de la Guerra said.

"On whose orders?"

"I'm not permitted to say."

"Government? Or Church?"

"Church. That I can say. And very high up."

"And you discovered these. What *are* they?" Kincaid asked.

"I believe troop and police movements," de la Guerra said.

"The laundry is providing intel and counter-intel?" Kincaid asked.

"Intel?"

"Intelligence."

"Yes, Inspector. In these Troubles, everybody's carrying something. Guns, bombs. Information."

"Who set this up? Who's in charge of it?"

"I don't know. I only found out when one of the threads busted. I thought it was something left in a pocket. Before washing, we check all the pockets, turn in anything we find. The Agency's bookkeeper—"

"In the business office?"

"Yes, her. I surmise she brung the maps in. Other info—intelligence, too. Orders, commands, even gossip. Seamstress sews the papers into the coats—it's coats, mostly, but sometimes trousers—after cleaning, just before packaging, late at night I'm certain, when none of us is allowed out of our rooms."

"Nic Cionnaith and Clery?"

"I don't think Ms Nic Cionnaith has anything to do with it."

"What do you know about the Agency?"

"Sends temporaries, I think they're called," de la Guerra said. "Probably sent the seamstress. Or seamstresses."

"What did she look like? The bookkeeper, Clery?"

"Dark complexion," de la Guerra said. "From the distance we have to keep."

"We?"

"Laundry room workers."

Kincaid leaned back on the sofa and looked at the maps and uniforms. "So is this bookkeeper our faceless victim?" he asked.

"Faceless?" de la Guerra asked.

"Unrecognizable, rather," Sr. Grey said.

"Or is it Marta?"

Twenty Four

On this quiet Saturday morning, Brugha and Kincaid waited in and unmarked Ford Anglia on the street across from the Sisters of the Atonement building. Another car drove past, slowed, and as it turned into the car park, Brugha raised a pair of binoculars.

"Woman," he said.

Kincaid looked through the binoculars. "Hat, scarf. Can't tell much."

The car parked, the woman emerged, went toward the building. Brugha got out and hurried up the sidewalk and driveway.

Kincaid watched the driveway, checked his watch. About fifteen minutes later, he slid over to the driver's side. He craned his head around, looked out the sides and back of his car. He opened the front and back driver's side doors and from the front seat worked his wheelchair out the back door. It fell on its side on the pavement.

"Shit," Kincaid said.

He leaned down and tried to grab the chair but couldn't reach it. He looked around the car, found a long flashlight, and struggled to move the chair with it. No good. He eyed the binoculars and grabbed them and threw out the neck strap like a lasso that hooked the wheelchair's small front wheel. He pulled the chair to the driver's door, leaned out as far as he could and pulled it upright. He unfolded the frame, locked the wheels, and swiveled himself out of the car, inching his butt into the chair.

He pushed away from the car doors and quietly closed them. He looked around, listened, then wheeled himself to the car park, where he read the woman's license plate, the same one on Mary Clery's unpaid parking citation. Was he about to catch up with Marta?

He studied the door to the office and the glass window in it. The hallway looked dark from here. He wheeled up and tried the door—locked—and pushed himself up high enough to look into the building. Dark. He could have banged or honked the car horn, but who knew where Brugha was or what quiet subterfuge he might interrupt? If he was in the building, he didn't enter through this door, but maybe through a back or side door.

Kincaid wheeled himself to one side of the building and looked around the long brick wall. Grass, shrubs, and flowers abutted windows. He tried to wheel onto the grass but the tires sunk and he grasped the wall and pulled himself back to the asphalt.

On the other side of the building he saw a short concrete corridor that led to a big steel door with no window, knob, nor handle, only a bolt lock. He wheeled up to it and looked at the lock. Probably some kind of utility room.

He started wheeling back to the carpark, then heard the utility room door knock against its jamb, as though an air current from inside pushed against it. He heard a big fan start and looked up at the roof. The door moved again. It was either locked and loose against the jamb or unlocked.

Kincaid looked in the narrow space between the door and where the bolt latched into the jamb. He couldn't see anything, so he moved aside and let enough sunlight in. He did not see the bolt. Probably the most locked-looking door on the premises was, in fact, unlocked.

He looked around for something sturdy he could wedge between the door and the jamb. Twigs on the ground were either too thick or too thin. What he had in his hand, car keys with jagged edges, might pry the door open just enough to get his fingers behind it.

Kincaid pressed the key between door and jamb and tried to use it as a lever. The door moved, but not enough and every time he relaxed tension, it closed. He looked at the bottom of the door, felt down to determine how much clearance it had with its sill and threshold. About a finger's worth. He hunted around and found a thick enough twig. He bent over, forced the twig between the door and the threshold. His legs hurt with the effort. He tugged on the twig, which pulled the door back barely and held it slightly open while he pushed the key back into the jamb. He forced the twig farther under the door and as he tugged on it, the door opened wider. A few more tugs and between his key and the twig, he was able to get his fingers around the door and open it the rest of the way.

He wheeled into the boiler room where exhaust fans pulled out warm air. He maneuvered around burlap sacks and tools and shelves through another door into a dark, silent hallway. He wheeled past offices and a conference room. A sign—LAUNDRIES—loomed over the locked door at the end he, Brugha and Sr. Grey had earlier passed through. He turned and wheeled toward the other end of the hallway, turning a corner before another locked door with a sign, RESIDENCE. He followed a light from what looked like Nic Cionnaith's office.

He peered in and knocked at the open door. "Miss Nic Cionnaith? Constable Brugha?" He wheeled into the room. "Constable?" He looked out the window across the lawn toward the cemetery. "Anyone here?"

He opened a folder on Nic Cionnaith's immaculate desk, thumbed through the papers in it, starting with a handwritten note, *Mary,* on top. Invoice to the Ministry of Defence, Procurement Executive, marked "Returned for Purchase Order Number." Looked like a bill for British Army uniform laundry. Invoice to something called RRG for more laundry. Invoice from Kellen and Sons Funeral Directors. Letter introducing new detergent vendor.

Kincaid returned everything to the folder and set it back on the desk. He looked around the office, at file cabinets, a painting of a misty Irish seascape, and Ms Nic Cionnaith mugging for the camera on the Carrick-a-rede rope bridge, precariously grasping its shaky handrails.

"Any eejit who would try to cross that brazen thing deserves to fall," O'Connell announced one night after the second of two dinners they had shared, when the conversation turned to sightseeing.

"It's spectacular," Mattie had said. "You must see it while you're here." She frowned at her brother. "You don't need to cross it to enjoy it."

Kincaid looked down at desk drawers, went to open one. A hurricane of glass, splinters, and plaster roared through the hallway. The shock wave threw him out of his chair. He landed on the floor near Nic Cionnaith's desk, as a fire alarm blared and stinging, burning dust fogged the air. The blast must have deafened him because he couldn't hear and he was too disoriented to know why his leg was in newly-agonizing pain.

He pushed himself up on his forearms and struggled to crawl beneath the desk. Coughing, choking, gasping, Kincaid pulled a coiled cord and a handset flew off when the heavy telephone hit the floor with a loud clang. Kincaid dragged the phone toward him, pressed a plunger, heard a dial tone. He had no idea what he was calling in.

"WHERE'S BRUGHA?" KINCAID ASKED first thing he could open his eyes, this time in a hospital outside Belfast.

The doctor looked in his ears. "You hear me all right?" he asked.

"Did you hear me?" Kincaid said.

"I heard ya." The doctor pushed away on his stool and went around the bed. "But I'm the one askin' the questions." He scoped Kincaid's other ear.

"Where's Brugha?" Kincaid asked again. "Where's Constable Brugha?" He raised his voice.

"Adam." Sr. Grey walked in.

"Do I have to guess why everyone is dodging my question?" Kincaid asked.

"Constable Brugha," she began.

"He didn't make it," the doctor interrupted. "I'm very sorry."

"What?" Kincaid asked.

The doctor spoke louder. "Your partner didn't make it," he said.

"What are you—"

"He died in the blast, Adam," Sr. Grey said. "The one that almost killed you."

"Wha—where—"

"He didn't suffer," the doctor said. "For what little that may be any comfort." He pushed back the stool and stood. "He'll be here a while," he told Sr. Grey. "You'll be here a while," he told Adam, loudly. "That leg wound needs to heal."

"Did you get it all?" Sr. Grey asked.

"All the metal," the doctor said. "There may still be some debris. We need to watch for any signs of infection." He left the room.

"Inspector Kincaid, my lord," Grey said.

"Brugha is dead," he said.

She came to his bedside. "I know, I know."

"How?"

"From what I gather, it was a car bomb."

"Car—anyone else—"

"No one but you. How did you come to be in the sisters' offices?"

"Brugha followed a woman into the building."

"I don't understand," Grey said. "They found you in the front office, him—well—"

"I got in through a utility door. Where did they find Brugha?"

"I don't want to be indelicate—"

"Out with it, Sister."

"I'll just say, outside. They found Constable Brugha outside, where he was apparently examining the mystery woman's car."

Kincaid lay silently, staring out the window, wondering if Marta Carney had just committed murder.

"**SIR THOMAS MORE, LAYMAN** and philosopher." Sr. Grey sat next to Kincaid's hospital room bed, reading from an encyclopedia. "Sentenced at Westminster Hall. Here's where it gets interesting." She looked at the detective. "Still with me?"

"Get back in the saddle," Kincaid said. "Isn't that what the Americans say?"

"Right back," she agreed.

"What if the horse won't let you?"

"What if Hogan had said that?"

Kincaid wrinkled his eyebrows.

"*Two Mules for Sister Sara*. But they were really donkeys." Grey smiled. "I am a huge Clint Eastwood fan."

"Haven't seen it, I'm afraid. American films—"

"You remind me of Hogan," she said. "He saves a nun from bad men and they side with the revolutionaries in a strange land."

"And the nun falls in love with him?"

"That would spoil the story."

"Not if I don't plan to see it."

"Maybe I'll take you." Sr. Grey smiled and turned back to the encyclopedia. "As was customary for executed traitors, Sir Thomas More's head was displayed on a pike."

Kincaid leaned over the bed, toward the sister.

"On London Bridge for a month," she continued. "Left for . . . his—"

"May I?" He extended his hand.

"Daughter Margaret to recover," Sr. Grey concluded, handing him the text.

Kincaid looked at an artist's sketch of the beheading, and the famous portrait of Thomas More by Hans Holbein the Younger. He looked at Sr. Grey with palpable amazement.

"Does McDermott know?"

"That's *your* thunder."

"He wants to visit this week. I don't want him to. Perfect reason for him to stay in Dublin. You need to call him."

"Why me?" Grey said.

"It's your thunder now."

"Dodger."

". . . **SPECIAL BRANCH AND THIS** is Corporal Robin Jackson, Ulster Defence Regiment, Eleventh Battalion."

"Craigavon way," Jackson said.

But Kincaid only heard "Special Branch" from the man hovering over his hospital bed. He looked at their identification cards.

"Special Branch?" he said.

"We know CID has already interviewed you," RUC Special Branch Sergeant Clarence O'Fall said. "We had some questions of our own."

"I don't know much about *your* special branch," Kincaid said.

"We handle—for lack of a better term—intelligence, for national security purposes. The Defence Regiment helps in that regard. Much like the Guards."

"We have nothing like the UDR," Kincaid said. "Maybe that's why Sergeant O'Connell was skeptical."

"About what?"

"*Your* Special Branch."

"So we both suffered Kev's skepticism, may he rest with the Lord," O'Fall said.

"We got on fine."

"That's not what I heard," O'Fall said. "As for whatever he may have said about us—internecine jealousy. Special Branch calls many, but chooses few."

"Do the good sisters clean your dirty laundry, too?" Kincaid asked.

The Special Branch man glanced at Corporal Jackson, then bored his eyes into Kincaid, gripping the bed's handrail tight enough to turn his hand and fingers white. "Look, Mr. Kincaid —"

"Inspector Kincaid. *Detective* Inspector."

"We are as devastated as the rest of the force over the untimely deaths of our three constables," O'Fall said.

"Two constables and a sergeant," Kincaid said.

Jackson coughed. "You mentioned a license plate," he said.

"License plate?"

"To the CID detectives."

"I don't recall any license plate."

"It had twos."

"How do you know?"

"We know. Four twos. That's a restricted plate. Do you recall the letters?"

"Is that the car exploded?" Kincaid asked. "They didn't say."

"Yes. The plates would help ascertain motive," O'Fall said. "But they were lost in the blast."

"Bombers weren't after the constable," Jackson said. "We don't think, anyway."

"Brugha, we mean," O'Fall said.

"Constable Brugha," Kincaid said.

"They weren't after him," Jackson said. "He probably opened the car door. You were both there investigating something. Isn't that correct?"

"You know it is, I'm sure."

After an awkward silence and some foot shuffling, "If you should remember anything else," O'Fall said. He laid a business card on the tray table next to the bed.

"I'm already working with the CID," Kincaid said. "Won't they share what I tell them with you?"

Jackson and O'Fall searched each other's eyes. "Not necessarily," O'Fall said.

Kincaid stared at the card. "The plate belonged to a Mary Clery. Brugha filed a report about her with CID, She was a bookkeeper at the laundry."

"I thought a Ms Nic Cionnaith handled all that?" O'Fall said.

"Not the ledgers," Kincaid said.

"You know where we can find this Mary Clery?"

"She's been missing," Kincaid said. "She may be dead. If you can find Nic Cionnaith—"

"We've been trying," O'Fall said. "Maybe she's missing, too."

Twenty Five

"Adam?" It was Sr. Grey on the phone, a few days after Kincaid's two-week hospital stay. "There's something wrong over here."

"Where? Where are you?"

"The abbey. We think something's happened to Mother Stephanie."

"We?"

"De la Guerra and I. She was put out of the Atonement home, so she came here. After the bomb—"

"Have you called the RUC?"

"No. I don't want to alarm the other sisters. And I don't want too many questions asked of de la Guerra."

"I'm supposed to be recuperating," Kincaid said.

"I know. But—"

"What's wrong, exactly?"

"I can't reach Mother by phone and she's not answering any knocks. The door to her room and office is locked."

Kincaid considered and with a drawn-out sigh, "All right. I'll see what I can do."

"I heard," Mattie said from the kitchen of her home. "I'll drive you over."

"I don't know."

"My brother was a policeman. I understand careful."

SISTERS GREY, DE LA GUERRA, and another nun met Mattie and the Inspector at the abbey gate.

"This is Sr. Caprice. She has a master key," Sr. Grey said.

Kincaid wheeled onto the grounds, Mattie following.

"May I have the key?" he said.

"I need to take you," Sr. Caprice said.

"It would be best if you all stayed here," Kincaid replied.

"I understand, Inspector. But we have our rules. And you're out of your jurisdiction."

"Can Sister Grey take me instead?"

Sister Caprice hesitated.

"She's as close as we have to another policeman," Kincaid said.

Sister Caprice relented and handed Grey the keys.

"Police *woman*," Grey said, as she wheeled the detective into the abbey.

They approached a door at the end of a hallway of old oak floors patched with pine. Kincaid looked around, stopping on the doorknob and where the latch met the jamb.

"You've knocked?"

"Multiple times. Caprice, too. She was going to enter, but I insisted we call you first."

"Lady Constable," Kincaid said. He tried to bend down but didn't get far before his legs ached. "I need you to look under the door as much as you can." He moved back.

Sister Grey bent toward the bottom of the door. "What am I looking for?"

"Wires," Kincaid said.

"Oh, dear."

"What do you see?"

"Dust bunnies. Sunlight. The feet of Mother's desk."

"No human feet?"

"Don't be morbid."

"If there's sunlight, there must be a window," Kincaid said.

"Speaking of windows." Grey looked up at the transom over the door. "Anything about to stand on?"

Kincaid looked down the hallway. Nothing.

"I may have something in my room." Sister disappeared, then returned with a chair. She stood on it. Not tall enough. "I'll need a supplement." She returned with some books, stacked them on the chair.

"That looks incredibly precarious," Kincaid said.

"Then you'd best hold it."

He held the chair while she stepped up, and balancing on the assemblage, scanned the office through the transom window. "Looking for wires again?"

"Always," Kincaid said.

"I don't see any. But I do see the window."

"Open or closed?"

"Can't tell."

"If it's open, Mother may have had a visitor," Kincaid said. "Visitors leave bombs in this part of Ireland."

"Are you sure I'd see wires?" she asked. "Wouldn't they hide them?"

"From whom?"

Sister Grey went to step down, wobbled to the point of nearly toppling. He startled her by grabbing her ankle.

"Don't get fresh," she said, grasping his arm and shoulder as she lowered herself. "I can check outside, if you like. The window —"

Kincaid took a book second from the top of Sr. Grey's stack. "St. Dymphna was a martyr?" he said, opening *Dymphna: Virgin Martyr, Princess Saint.*

"Give me virginity or give me death," Grey said. "Dymphna opted for the latter." She looked up at the transom. "Inspector—that other window?"

"Yes, yes. If you can see anything. Looked like a big tree in front of it as we were walking up."

"All the better for access."

Sister Grey went outside. Kincaid kept reading.

So distraught over the death of his young wife and her mother, Dymphna's father the king demanded his courtiers find him a match who looked just like the queen. Fourteen-year old Dymphna was the spitting image of her mother.

"She refused her father's offer of incest," Sr. Grey said, on returning slightly out of breath. "Window appears closed."

"So?"

"So—no one got in that way?"

"What happened? To Dymphna?"

"He cut off—" She stopped. "—her head."

Kincaid looked up from the painting of the lovely young woman holding a book adorned with a shamrock shaped like a cross.

"What's a father to do when a child disobeys?"

Kincaid studied the doorknob again.

"So can we assume the coast is clear?" Grey said.

"There," he said, pointing at the wall. "Stand back there."

Sister Grey stood against the hallway wall.

He put the key into Mother Stephanie's doorknob, slowly turned it, and with excruciating care, as Sr. Grey cringed and closed her eyes, pushed the door open, staying well to the side.

"Sure there's no bomb?" she said.

Kincaid peered in. Looked left, right. "I hope not," Kincaid said. He heard Sr. Grey move. "Just stay there."

"Okay."

Kincaid wheeled into the room. "Déjà vu," he said.

"What?"

"Nothing." He wheeled into Mother Stephanie's living quarters. Desk, bed, dresser, other essentials. Nothing out of place. No sign of break in or struggle.

The door to her toilet was closed and locked.

"Sister. Could use your eyes again."

"So I can come in?"

"Yes. But tread carefully. And look under the bathroom door."

"No wires," Sr. Grey pronounced on peering down.

"Anything else?"

"No body on the floor, if that's what you mean."

Kincaid unraveled a coat hanger from Mother Stephanie's closet and pressed an end into the bathroom door lock. He heard it click, turned the knob, and slowly pushed the door open, again staying to the side.

"Anything?" Grey asked.

"Shower curtain's pulled around the bathtub."

"Anything else?"

"Can't tell from here." He wheeled aside. "Too narrow for the wheelchair."

Sister Grey stepped past him. Her shoes clicked differently when she stepped from the wood to the tile floor. She put her hand on the shower curtain.

"Do I dare?"

"I can call the RUC," Kincaid said.

"But if there's nothing—"

She eased back the curtain, looking away.

"We probably need you to look at it," Kincaid said.

She pivoted, then looked down, gasped, whipped around, put her hands on the sink, and looked down again.

"There is. There is!" She barely got the words out.

"What?"

"Awful, Adam. Just bloody awful. Call the police. The police, their police. *Their* police."

SERGEANT O'FALL AND CORPORAL Jackson met Mattie, the three nuns, and Kincaid outside the abbey.

"Regular police are you now?" Kincaid asked Jackson.

"He's assisting me, Inspector," O'Fall said. He turned to Sr. Caprice. "Ulster Defence Regiment, Eleventh Battalion."

"British Army?" she asked.

"Yes."

"I don't know how comfortable I am having you in the abbey," she told Jackson.

"I'm only helping out until a new constable is found," Jackson said.

"We just need to secure the site for CID," O'Fall said. "Corporal Jackson has specialized training in explosives."

"Explosives?" Sr. Caprice said.

"Sisters of the Atonement," O'Fall said languidly, looking up and around the abbey. "So where is—*this* trouble?"

"Follow me," Kincaid said. Sr. Grey walked with them until Kincaid stopped.

"Sister." He sounded exasperated.

"What happened to Lady Constable?" she asked.

KINCAID LISTENED AND CAUGHT occasional glimpses of Jackson and O'Fall investigating the bathtub.

"I'm not ready for this," Jackson said. He looked away. "I'm really not."

"What do you see?" Kincaid asked from the outer office.

"Blood everywhere," O'Fall said.

"Any visible wounds?"

"We have it covered, Inspector. Best to just stay out of it."

"Looks—" Kincaid heard Jackson say.

"Everything all right in there?" Sr. Grey called from the hallway.

"So far," Kincaid said.

"Brilliant!" she replied.

O'Fall slowly dropped to his knees as Jackson stepped back. Kincaid watched the sergeant peer down, around, into the bathtub. He reached back for a small flashlight and brought it around.

"Whoever did this seems to have used the shower curtain as a shield." O'Fall looked up and took a deep breath. "Against spatter."

"Try moving the head," Kincaid said.

"We don't work for the Guards," O'Fall replied.

"Then do it for the RUC."

"Why?" O'Fall said.

"To see if it's attached."

"Why on Earth would it not be attached?"

"Saint Dymphna," Kincaid said.

O'Fall leaned back from the tub, scowled at Kincaid, turned back to the body and brought his hand around.

"I'm supposed to be on patrol duty," Jackson said.

O'Fall reached into the tub with a handkerchief. From what Kincaid could see of his hand, the head did not move much.

"Push down on a shoulder," Kincaid said. "See if there's . . . separation."

"Head's still attached," O'Fall said curtly.

"THEY PUT ME OUT next day," Sr. de la Guerra said back at the O'Connell house. "Laundry's closed until further notice, but the mothers and babies are getting free room and board anyway."

"Does anyone have any idea of your true identity?" Kincaid asked her.

"As a laundry spy?"

"You should return to your order," Kincaid said. "Mother Stephanie knew just enough to get her killed."

"We don't know that, Adam," Grey said.

"Call it an educated hunch."

"Such a frightening, frightening situation," Mattie said. "This hunch? Would you mind sharing it?"

"Mongilly the mapmaker," Kincaid said. "Mongilly and Brenden Wryth and their network of Magdalene homes. Of course, Mother Stephanie knew. But—"

"But what," Sister Grey interjected, her eyes darting from Kincaid to de la Guerra, finally resting on Mattie, "was Mother planning to do about it?"

Twenty Six

"How do I look?" Kincaid stood at the door of his guest bedroom on crutches again.

"I don't mind tellin' ya, I don't like the idea," Mattie O'Connell said. "Kevin had to retrieve our father from one of their parades." She put a hand on a hip and glared at the gardaí inspector. "You're not marching, are ya?"

"I'm meeting with Rowan Doherty."

"God rest his little sister," Mattie said. "But Provisionals? You don't need a third strike."

Kincaid hobbled over to the sofa. "Not just Provisionals. There'll be other leaders, some he thinks are tied up with Father Wryth. I have to go." He moved the newspaper, sat down, thumbed through it, then looked at Mattie. "Had to—what did you say—*retrieve* your father?"

"'Bout a month before he died. The Orangemen were plannin' their Sunday Parade and they had the brilliant idea to enlist the aid of the former B-Specials, still smarting from the Ulster Defence Regiment takeover. Kevin's father wasn't asked to join—"

"Ulster Defence Regiment? Jackson's outfit?"

"Yes. They deposed the B-Specials, at least as Gordon—our father—saw it. He brooded about it, well—until about the time the Orangemen came along and needed him again."

"Needed him for what?"

"Show of force, mainly. Least, that's what Kev thought. He tried to talk Dad out of it, but there's no man like a new man. And with that new assignment, Gordon O'Connell was like a new man."

"Not wanting his son's interference, no doubt."

"Oh, God no. So they made a lot of noise and cleared the parade route, mostly Catholic, whom Gordon knew because he was one of them. But it angered the Provs—Gordon proving himself another cop traitor, in their twisted eyes. And then they paraded, up to Drumcree church and back. About a thousand of them. Dad wanted to hang around afterward, talk old times, but Kev wanted none of it. You heard about what happened this March? After the rally there?"

"Your brother gave me an earful coming back from the Mitchell place. Vanguard something."

"Rally. Ulster Vanguard rally. Strikes. Mob rule. Electricity cut. Food depleted. Catholics in Portadown under siege for a week. Still be going if not for the RUC. I know the British Army takes credit, but Kev woulda told you, it was all RUC."

"Didn't your PM ban parades?"

"Did. Then lifted it," Mattie said. "Feckin' fickle Stormont. They shoulda left it in place."

The door chimed.

"My driver is here," Kincaid said.

CORPORAL JACKSON SIGHED AS he leaned back in the driver's seat.

"I guess I agree with her," he told Kincaid. "They're already making trouble. You're not going to change things."

"They?"

"Resistance Committee. Provisionals. IRA. Already setting up blockades."

"Mattie says your group took over for the old B-Specials. The Ulster Defence Regiment replaced the Ulster Special Constabulary."

"In a manner of speaking," Jackson said. "I knew Gordon O'Connell. I know how much it killed him to see us come along."

"You know his son?"

"Not as well, but well enough."

"Well enough?"

"I don't mix with Catholics. I know Kevin wasn't a republican, nor was his father. But I don't mix with them. If I had my way, we'd have none in the ranks. But we do, and so I make do."

"So your relationship with Gordon was tense."

"Never forget what he told me. 'I stand for law and order and if you're first name's 'Ulster', you stand for anarchy.'"

"Strong words," Kincaid said.

"Damn right they were."

They pulled off the road in Portadown, County Armagh, though only sixteen miles from Briar Lough, very unlike Briar Lough and the mostly Catholic enclave in which it was situated.

"Let's see—Garvaghy to Park. Been a while since I been here," Jackson said.

"We're meeting in the park, right?"

"That's what they tell me. People's Park. Best they could do for a neutral venue. Ever been here?"

"No. But I've been reading up on it."

"Lord Mandeville gave the park to the people," Jackson said, turning onto Park Road. "One day, it will be beautiful again."

"INSPECTOR KINCAID. GOOD TO see you." A Portadown Station RUC sergeant extended his hand, barely glancing at Jackson.

"You look ready for the occasion," Kincaid said.

"I won't be marching," the sergeant said. "But I will be seen. Mayor Tom Nole, Inspector Adam Kincaid with the Guards."

Nole reached down and took Kincaid's hand. "Investigating those witch burnings, I hear," Nole said.

"I am," Kincaid said.

"Grisly."

"Mayor Nole runs the Portadown Borough Council," the sergeant said.

"Soon to become the Craigavon Borough Council," Nole said. "Another change from on high to add to the instability."

"The rest of our peace party, no doubt," the sergeant said, as well-armed men approached from different directions.

"Could've have just met at Corcrain," the nearby Orange Order meeting hall, one of the men said as they arrived.

"Jim Anderson," the sergeant said. "Adam Kincaid, with the Gardaí." To Jackson, "And . . . you are?"

"I know Robby," Anderson said, taking Robin Jackson's hand. "Too many Robbies. North's got too many Robbies. You have this many Robbies your way?" he asked Kincaid.

"Yes, well. Here comes a Bill. Bill Craig," the sergeant interrupted. "Where's *your* entourage?"

"I figured Anderson there would have enough guns for all of us," Craig replied.

"Always nitpicking," Anderson said.

"Jim is running the UDA while Charlie Smith sits in jail," Craig said.

"UDA," Jackson said. "That's—"

"Ulster Defence Association," Kincaid completed.

"You know your North."

"Bill and I are on opposite sides of the right side," Anderson said. "He wants an independent Ulster. I'm loyal to the Crown."

"I'm not opposed to the Crown," Craig said. "We just don't need the Queen up our arses day and night. Which is—"

Another group of armed men emerged from a stand of trees. "Now it gets interesting," Mayor Nole said.

Rowan Doherty went right to Kincaid. "Best man of the lot," he said. "And the only reason I'm here."

"Least you're not killin' babies," Anderson said.

"We had nothing to do with that," Doherty said.

"That's a crock," Anderson said.

"Gentlemen," the sergeant said. "Can we get down to the business at hand?"

"Which is?" Anderson said.

"You know."

"Portadown Resistance Council closed Obins Street," Craig said. "Catholics don't want the Protestants to march," he told Kincaid.

"Prods can march," Doherty said. "Just not on Obins."

"What's so special about this street?" Kincaid asked.

"Main parade route up to the church," Craig said.

"Which they use to attack us," Doherty said. "Lot of Catholics live up there, Inspector. Around the tunnel and all."

"You stop the parade, you have been warned," Anderson told Doherty. "We're not fuckin' around here."

"Over a thousand Orangemen expected," the mayor told Kincaid. "We don't need a bloodbath."

"Which we'll only have because a' the likes a' him," Doherty said, indicating Craig. "He wants to liquidate us. He said so."

"The fate of an enemy," Craig said.

"How many people you kill on The Shankill?" Anderson asked Doherty. "There was nothin' fuckin' left. Nothin' fuckin' left."

"And McGurk's?" Doherty said.

"What are ya, daft? McGurk's. Maaagurks! Don't start with me, don't start with me."

"Fifteen—"

"Balmoral. Innocents. Wee innocents, blown to bits."

"That wasn't my group," Doherty replied.

"It was Provisionals."

"Not South Armagh Brigade."

"Doesn't matter which brigade," Anderson huffed.

"Gentlemen," Kincaid interrupted. "I really don't care if you kill each other. You've got another enemy in your midst, one with an especially brutal streak who doesn't play with guns and bombs and isn't afraid to attack innocent women." He looked at each man. "Wives, mothers, girlfriends. In their backyards. Maybe their bathtubs. When their men ain't watchin'"

"Charlie warned us about this," Anderson said. "He said—"

"Is this the Charlie cooling his heels?" Kincaid asked.

"Is," Anderson said. "Our leader. Caught runnin' guns. He warned us. Said Wryth would put a curse on all our houses."

"What do you know about Wryth?" Kincaid said.

"Everyone killed been connected to him," Anderson said. "Up this-a-way, anyway."

"Is your head cut?" Rowan Doherty asked. "Lann McLaughlin wasn't connected to that minger."

"Whaddya think they was sewin' in them pelts?" Anderson said.

"That's a thick thing to say. Don't believe a word of it," Doherty said.

"You knew Lann McLaughlin?" Kincaid asked Rowan Doherty.

"She knew my sister of course," Doherty said. "And I'll not have her name sullied by a terrorist."

"Watch your tongue, laddie," Anderson said.

Doherty smirked.

"Did you ever meet her?" Kincaid asked.

"Met her on the pull one night," Doherty said. "She was right lovely."

"And?"

"And it went no further," Doherty said. "Prov wasn't her daddy's kind of Catholic." His sarcastic emphasis on "daddy" caught Kincaid's ear.

"She tell you that?" Kincaid asked.

"Nah," Rowan said. "I could tell. I can always tell."

"Ain't that funny?" Anderson said. "Lann McLaughlin smuggling intel across the border for the Provs and any other Fenian would have it. Wryth arranged all of it. 'Nuthin' like a warm mink pelt to hide cold-blooded murder.' That's what Jimmy Mitchell said about it. Bragged he was gonna stop it." He eyed Kincaid. "You're here, with us, why?"

"Getting to know my witnesses," Kincaid said. "Before they get killed."

"None of us gonna get killed," Bill Craig said.

"He's seen it. He took a bullet for Michelle," Doherty said. "And another for Kev O'Connell."

"I didn't know Michelle Doherty," Craig said. "But Kevin O'Connell was a good man."

"What's going to happen here tomorrow?" the RUC sergeant asked. "Can we all agree, the parade will go on, peaceably?"

"I can't move the barricades," Doherty said. "I won't. But I will promise that if we aren't fired upon, we'll do no firing."

The group broke up with few handshakes and no smiles. Kincaid wheeled alongside Doherty on the way to his car.

"Handled that thing pretty well," Doherty said.

"Practice," Kincaid said.

"Where's your driver? The sister?"

"Out of harm's way."

Doherty looked up to see Robin Jackson walking toward them. "Get the sister driving for ya," Doherty said. "He's dangerous."

"Autopsy report, Inspector," Jackson said, tapping a notepad. "Mother Stephanie was shot. They radioed. Coroner wanted you to know immediately."

"Shot with what?"

"A gun."

"I know a gun," Kincaid said. "Bullet? Caliber? Type?"

Jackson thumbed through his notebook. "Remington model ninety five, point four one rimfire cartridge. It's a rare gun, Inspector. Palm pistol."

"A derringer," Kincaid said.

"Shouldn't be too hard to trace."

"Radio Briar Lough," Kincaid said. "Tell them we may be delayed."

"Delayed?"

"Yes. Now, please. I want a word with Mr. Doherty."

Jackson headed back for the car park.

"Sister Grey carried a derringer," Kincaid told Doherty. "And your man took it."

"Shame gave it back. You saw," he said.

"Did he?"

"I told him to. You were there."

"You told him to return her purse," Kincaid said. "I didn't pay attention if he put the gun back in it."

"Has the sister reported it missing?" Doherty asked.

"No."

"Well, then."

"She didn't seem enthused that I knew about it," Kincaid said. "She wouldn't be permitted such a weapon in the Republic. I suppose she'd be just as happy if I forgot about it."

"Oh, Inspector. Why would Shame keep her gun? We got plenty of guns."

"Your guns aren't easy to trace," Kincaid said.

"So Shame would kill someone, pin it on a nun?"

"I don't know."

"Just ask her: Did she lose her gun?"

"What's your man's full name?"

"Shame. Seamus O'Dowd. He'll be at the parade tomorrow. Keepin' the peace."

SUNDAY, 9 JULY 1972. 8:30 A.M. Adam Kincaid sat alone on the roadside just before the Obins Street bridge, watching men with flags and V-shaped orange collarettes mull and talk and assemble.

"Inspector!" Doherty called out, Seamus walking beside him and snare drums like bullets.

"I wouldn't sit too close to the parade," Doherty said. "We expect tear gas, at least."

Kincaid looked up at Seamus in the morning sun and a slow low-thunder triplet—*boom boom boom*—from a marching lambeg drum. They started moving back from the route.

"I understand you had some questions for me," Seamus said.

"The gun you took from Sr. Grey's purse," Kincaid said. "Did you give it back?"

"Yes. Did she say I didn't?"

"I haven't asked."

"I say I did," Seamus said. "Why would I keep such a wee thing?"

"Lots of reasons," Kincaid said. "*Wee* chief among them."

"What are you getting at?" Doherty said. "Shame here didn't take the sister's gun. Sister's gun—what's a nun doing with a gun anyways?"

"Look around," Kincaid said.

British troops in armored vehicles crawled up Obins Street. Masked men and women on both sides ran up and down the street, lined the bridge, adjusted barricades. A practicing bagpipe whined.

"Someone close to the sister was killed with a gun like hers," Kincaid said.

"You think I did it?"

"Didn't say that," Kincaid said. "But if you kept the gun and someone else got hold—"

"Maybe she did it," Doherty interrupted.

"I'm careful with me firearms," Seamus said. "And I dint take that one. I wouldn't. Men don't use guns like that."

"Hey!" Doherty called out, and ran across the street to an IRA trio walking a barricade toward the bridge.

"Clear the street. Clear the street," a British soldier on an armored personnel carrier announced through a megaphone. "Anyone blocking the street will be cleared. Clear the street!"

"Where can I reach you if we have further questions?" Kincaid asked.

"Through Rowan. But you won't," Seamus said. "I didn't take the feckin' gun."

An armored carrier with a blade on the front roared onto the street from the grass.

"Inspector!" Robin Jackson called, waving at Kincaid.

Seamus looked at him. "No Army fatigues, I see," he said.

"He's with me," Kincaid said.

"The hell he is," Seamus said.

"We're leaving." Kincaid told Jackson, wheeling up the incline, farther from the street. More soldiers and RUC officers passed him. Snare drums like bullets again. Flutes played a melancholy melody. As Kincaid and Jackson headed to their car,

Kincaid heard a woman scream and the loud *pop* of a gas canister sailing across the sky on a trail of smoke and tears.

Twenty Seven

Mattie O'Connell looked over Kincaid's shoulder at the *Belfast Telegraph*. "Nuthin' but troubles," she said. "I thought they promised a peace."

"I didn't hear any promises," Kincaid said. "More like hedged bets."

"Hedged? All they do is kill each other. And now this kidnapping."

Felix Hughes. Catholic. Tortured and mutilated. Dumped in a drainage ditch. Kincaid looked at the photo and story of the man UDA members allegedly attacked. "But not burned," he murmured.

"Because he's a man," Mattie said.

"Maybe." Kincaid sighed. "Not one solid lead." He looked up at the mirror.

"How are your legs?" Mattie asked.

Kincaid took his crutches, rose on them, and hobbled to the mirror. He looked at his face.

"Don't worry," Mattie said. "You're as much a looker as when you arrived."

He turned to her. "What did you mean?"

"Handsome. Good looking."

"Not that, but thank you. After your brother died, you looked at this mirror. You said you didn't want—something about a martyr."

"I'm not a martyr. I've never felt like one. I'm a participant. In my own quiet way, mind ya."

"Not that, not you," Kincaid said. "But maybe—your sorrows? You wouldn't cover the mirrors. No wake. You didn't want—you didn't want to be—"

"A martyr to my sorrows," Mattie said. "I remember."

"Your sorrows might kill you?"

"Not that serious, though I've been feeling like they could. I didn't want to look at them, and have them staring back at me," Mattie said. "No reminders. I promised Kev."

"Not to look at them? At your sorrows?"

"Yes, Inspector. I didn't want to be a martyr to them. A *witness* to them."

The door chimed. Sister Grey rushed into the room.

"I checked," she said.

"No gun?" Kincaid asked.

"He gave it back. It was stolen from my room. Bollocks!" she said.

"Is it possible you lost it?" Kincaid asked.

"I don't know. I don't think so. I don't see how. It was in my room"

"You need to report it missing."

"But if—"

"That's why we need to report it," Kincaid said.

"You don't think they'd suspect *me*?"

"Did you have anything against Mother Stephanie?"

"Adam!"

"I concur, Adam," Mattie O'Connell said. "That's a terrible stretch, especially about a sister."

"Kind of stretch they'll make," Kincaid said. "An unlikely suspect is a suspect nonetheless."

"PAINLESS ENOUGH," SR. GREY said, driving Kincaid back from their unlikely visit with Corporal Jackson.

"You saw how he looked at you."

"He wasn't reverent?"

"He doesn't like Catholics."

"I heard he hates them. How did he ever get on with the O'Connells?"

"Common interest," Kincaid said. "Policing. And his own kind doesn't trust him, so who else does he have?"

"He's just a boy, Adam."

"Twenty three is a man," Kincaid said.

"A very young man. He's feeling his way. He obviously looks up to you."

"He's a wannabe. I've seen that type before." Kincaid leaned forward and readjusted his legs. He moved a crutch out of the way between them. "Bloody things," he said.

"You seem to be feeling better."

"I'm loopy from painkillers. You know where we're going, right?"

"I think I can get us there."

KINCAID AND SR. GREY stood before Rory McLaughlin, sitting in a big new recliner in his front room. His housemaid and caretaker Molly took Kincaid's arm and crutches and helped position him in a chair. She looked at her boss.

"Rory? These police officers are here to see you about Lann."

He didn't look at them.

"You knew he lost his wife," Molly whispered.

"Yes. We heard on the operating table."

"They thought they had brought her back," Molly explained. "Terrible day, that. All those people—and for what? What feckin' . . . Pardon me manners, Sister. I didn't—would you care to sit?"

Sister Grey also took Molly's arm as she sat. Molly looked at her boss.

"Like that all the time, he is," Molly said. "Just sits and stares. Ever since he got back from hospital." She looked at Kincaid and the nun. "I'll leave you now," she said.

Kincaid set a notepad on his lap, took a deep breath, and focused on Mr. McLaughlin. "I don't know if you remember me," he said. "I was here for your daughter's wake. I'm a detective." He waited for a sign of comprehension. "I—" He acted as if he was fumbling in his notepad's blank pages. He feigned reading. "Your daughter—Lann—she may have been involved with a terrorist group." He stumbled through the words.

"He can't like hearing that," Sr. Grey whispered.

"They were—allegedly—smuggling maps and other intelligence out of the country. In mink pelts," Kincaid continued.

McLaughlin slowly turned to them.

"We don't know what kind of intelligence, exactly," Kincaid said. "Probably papers, between pelts stitched together."

McLaughlin looked at his hands. "No," he said. "No." Louder. "No!" Loud enough to startle his guests.

"We don't know for sure," Kincaid said. "But when we do, we may have a motive for her murder."

"Can we really say that?" Sr. Grey asked.

"Her murder wasn't like the others," Kincaid said. "What we found may have been a crude attempt at copying by an impatient killer armed with newspaper stories and a knife."

"Agnes would never do that," McLaughlin interrupted. "She would never—" He sighed.

"She may not have known what was in the pelts," Kincaid said.

"Would others," Sr. Grey asked, "come in contact with your pelts? Before you shipped them?"

McLaughlin grunted and looked up. "Agnes," he said.

"Who is Agnes?" Kincaid asked.

"Agnes, Agnes." Agitated. "Agnes." Loud. Molly appeared at the doorway.

"Agnes?" Kincaid asked.

"Agnes again," Molly said. "Mr. McLaughlin—"

He pointed. Leaned forward and pointed. Thrust his finger.

"The post?" Molly asked.

Rory McLaughlin pointed again. "Agnes."

She took a week's worth of mail from a small table near a lamp. "I give it him every day. We move it here when he's done."

"Agnes?" Sr. Grey asked, as Molly set the envelopes and papers on McLaughlin's lap. He licked his thumb and forefinger and started into it. He pulled out a folded sketch, unfolded it, and handed it to Kincaid.

"Is this Agnes?" Kincaid asked.

McLaughlin found an envelope and handed it across to Sr. Grey.

"A letter," she said. "Were these together?"

"Mm hmm," McLaughlin said.

"Adam." She handed it to him. He read.

Agnes Tuum morietur. Ibi fuerunt alii. Ibi erit magis.

"Something about Agnes and death," Kincaid said.

"Agnes Tuum. *Your* Agnes," Sr. Grey translated. "The envelope is addressed to Mr. and Mrs. McLaughlin."

Kincaid looked at the illustration with the letter. "A young woman, lambs at her feet," he recited. "Angels overhead."

"Anything else look familiar?"

Kincaid looked both pages over.

"Insular calligraphy," Sr. Grey said.

"The Book of Kells," Kincaid murmured.

"Miss Lann's name wasn't Agnes. No surname, no nickname remotely like that," Molly said. "They can't be meanin' her."

"He seems convinced they are," Kincaid said, looking at her father. "I'm inclined to agree, though I don't yet know why."

"YOUR AGNES DIE," SISTER Grey read aloud, a Latin dictionary beside her. "There have been others. There will be more." She looked up at Kincaid, on the O'Connell's sofa. "My best translation."

"*Your* Agnes. Whose Agnes?"

"Who's Agnes?" Mattie said. "Maybe a pet name. A nickname?"

"Lann McLaughlin affectionately known as Agnes. The envelope *was* addressed to her family." Grey looked at it, in a fresh transparent evidence bag.

"Posted from Belfast," Mattie said. "A jilted boyfriend there, perhaps? Rowan Doherty."

"He has a solid alibi, backed up by his men," Kincaid said. "I don't figure him for this anyway. Not with his sister's involvement around here, if for no other reason."

"Darren Larkin, then," Grey said. "I think of pet names like lovey or sweetie or dearie. But Agnes?"

"It means something to the killer—or killers," Kincaid said.

In another evidence envelope, Sr. Grey studied the illustration, the lambs, the angels. "Is there a Saint Agnes?" she asked. The ringing telephone interrupted.

"I DON'T HAVE TO tell you how it looks, certainly," said RUC Special Branch Sergeant O'Fall, sitting in Sergeant O'Connell's office chair, Robin Jackson standing beside him.

"Seems hasty to conclude anything at this point," Kincaid said. "If it was her gun, it was obviously stolen—"

"How many derringers are shooting Mother Superiors?" O'Fall said. "The bullets must be from Sister's weapon."

"What's the motive?"

"Some kind of internal intrigue, certainly," O'Fall said. "I'm only just now beginning to understand Sister's mission on our two soils. She sounds, for all intents and purposes, like a republican spy."

"Corporal Jackson doesn't like Catholics much," Kincaid said. "Are you in this camp, too?"

"I've done nothing to disparage her," Jackson said.

"Maybe not directly," Kincaid said.

"What are you suggesting?" O'Fall asked.

"I'm suggesting it's strange you aren't passing this case to CID and SOCO. I'm suggesting it's strange Special Branch has taken up a perch in this station."

"Sister Grey will be treated justly and respectfully," Sgt. O'Fall said.

"Sounds like you're preparing an accusation," Kincaid said.

"We're not accusing the sister of anything," O'Fall said. "But we will need her fingerprints."

"She lost her gun. We reported it. To Corporal Jackson, in this very office."

"We know, we know, Inspector," O'Fall said.

A standoff stifled the three men.

"It would be good if you would bring her in without trouble," O'Fall said. "We aren't needin' the press to report we're out manhandlin' nuns. Get enough bad press as it is."

"LIKE AN ALIEN INVASION over there." Kincaid hobbled into the O'Connell's house.

"I been hearin'," Mattie O'Connell said.

Kincaid hung up his jacket.

"I see you drove," Sr. Grey said. "Thank God you didn't get into a collision."

"Gotta get back in the saddle sometime," Kincaid said. "You've got me fixated on American Westerns."

"I thought those men were just in till Kev and Brugha could be replaced," Mattie O'Connell said. "We don't need the British Army policing our fair county or their Special Branch surrogates."

"What did they say?" Sr. Grey asked.

"Maybe that was the plan all along," Kincaid said.

"To occupy our station?" Mattie called from the kitchen.

"What did they say?" Sr. Grey asked again, placing her hand on Kincaid's forearm.

"They want your fingerprints," Kincaid said.

"Fingerprints?"

"Surely you're not going to hand her over," Mattie said, returning with tea. "The only *other* thing Brits are good for," she said, smiling at Sister Grey.

"What choice do I have?" Sr. Grey asked.

"I don't trust these people," Kincaid said.

"Sounds conspiratorial," Mattie said.

"Someone wants me out of the way?" Sr. Grey asked.

"You, me," Kincaid said. "Could be the killer. Could be the new constabulary. Such that it is."

"My fingerprints will be on the gun, should they find it," Sr. Grey said. "Surely they must know that."

"Surely," Kincaid said.

"How convenient," Grey said.

"Yes it is," Kincaid said. "It most certainly is."

"CONSTABLE BRUGHA HAVE FAMILY?" Kincaid asked Mattie. "He never told me, or said anything about his person."

"Confirmed bachelor," Mattie said. "I bugged Kevin that we should fix him up. I have a cousin in Antrim." She looked at Kincaid directly, straight in the eyes. "After the loyalists shot Victor Arbuckle, Kevin decided it was best to hire young constables without families. Victor left a child and a widow."

Kincaid laid his head onto the pillow and stared at the ceiling.

"Constable Arbuckle was just twenty nine."

"I know," Kincaid said.

Mattie handed a book to him. "I took the liberty," she said.

Agnes of Rome. Kincaid looked at the cover. "She's petting a lamb."

"Lambs in every picture I could find of her," Mattie said. "Encyclopedia's in Portadown. Found the book in Lurgan."

"You've gone above and beyond. Thank you."

"Wasn't hard. Asked the librarian, 'Have you any books on St. Agnes?'"

"So you'd heard of her?"

"I, well—after Sister asked. It sounded like a saintly name." She looked over Kincaid's shoulder. "You'll find as you're reading that Agnes was martyred. At first, they tried to burn her at the stake, but the pyre refused to burn. Miracle, right? They tried beheading her, but that didn't work, either. They stabbed her in the throat, finally. Lann was fifteen. This girl was thirteen."

"You've read the book, then," Kincaid said, looking up at Mattie.

"It piqued my interest. I felt I had to."

He turned back to the pictures, turned the pages, saw a bust of the Roman Emperor Diocletian, read a quote from *Alban Butler's Lives of the Saints*.

"'At last, terrible fires were made, and iron hooks, racks, and other instruments of torture displayed before Agnes, with threats of immediate execution. The young virgin surveyed them all with an undaunted eye; and with a cheerful countenance beheld the fierce and cruel executioners surrounding her.' They killed St. Agnes why?" Kincaid asked.

"Refused to bed a man," Mattie said. "Brutal dictators with evil in their hearts. Young girl, pure as a lamb."

"*Our* Agnes," Kincaid said.

The hallway telephone rang. Mattie answered it. "It's for you."

"Who is it?" he asked.

"Wants to surprise you." She brought the phone to him.

"Adam! So good to hear to your voice."

"John!"

"You sound surprised. I know, I should have called a lot earlier. Greevey's been badgering me. 'Adam will think we've forgotten him.'"

"How are you?"

"How are *you*? Leg—legs—healing all right?"

"Out of the wheelchair, mostly. Using crutches. Getting ready to find other quarters before I wear out my welcome. How are things at Phoenix?"

"Under the gun," McDermott said. "We need you back. Home. In the office."

"I can't."

"Can't?"

"I can't come back. Not yet."

"It's not optional, I'm afraid," McDermott said. "We finally got a positive on that bridge victim."

"The one who lost his head?"

"The same. British Intel man. Assigned to Operation Banner. No dental records to be found. Greevey had the brilliant idea to have him all shined up for a photo. Sent it round to all the papers. Somebody recognized the tattoo on his neck. Said he used to have a beard. They knew him as Charlie Mangan."

"That's excellent news," Kincaid said. "But Sister Grey's in trouble and I can't leave yet."

"I thought Grey had returned to her convent," McDermott said. "Didn't the other sister—della—"

"De la Guerra. She was reassigned after the laundry bombing."

"What's Sister's trouble?"

"Long story."

"Why haven't I—we—heard about it? Grey works for us, as much as for the Dymphnans."

"It's not like this is the North and you're in the South and I can barely walk," Kincaid said. "Not to mention the mayhem."

"I wasn't trying to be officious," McDermott said. "What happened?"

"A derringer was used in a recent homicide."

"A palm pistol?"

"Yes. And Sister Grey's derringer, palm pistol, whatever you want to call it, has gone missing."

"Jaysus. What was she doing with a derringer?"

"Derring do."

"Don't be cute."

"Stormont let her have it. They have laxer laws than we do. Meanwhile, there's a new crew in O'Connell's office. Don't trust the lot of 'em."

"Sounds grim," McDermott said. "Can't her order hire a good solicitor?"

"What about us?"

"We—"

"We don't have good solicitors?"

"Not up there." McDermott stopped. "Another reason to come home."

"Not without Sister," Kincaid said. "They may detain her."

"Shit, Adam. What am I supposed to tell Greevey?"

"Tell him we drew some Special Branch prick and a wet-behind-the-ears volunteer with an army group called the Ulster Defence Regiment. Ever heard of it?"

"Yes," McDermott said. "The head on the bridge."

"He was part of UDR?"

"Working with British Army Intelligence. Press is calling him *Our* Thomas More."

"Funny they should put it that way."

Twenty Eight

"Seamus, it seems," Rowan Doherty told Kincaid at a cafe in Briar Lough, "has fled our little fold."

"When did you discover this?"

"A few days after you confronted him about the sister's gun," Doherty said.

"No idea where he went?"

"None, though I have my suspicions."

Kincaid frowned at him.

"You said you thought Special Branch might have shot the abbess?"

"It's a possibility," Kincaid said.

"Special Branch is always lookin' to throw a little blame our way," Rowan said. "If they knew we knew about the sister's firearm—"

"How would they know?"

"If Seamus ratted us out. Turned evidence. Or defected to the other side."

"To the loyalists?"

"I've had me suspicions. He was spotted up The Shankill way, maybe ta meet Billy Spence."

"Gusty his nickname?"

"Brother's nickname. Gusty and Billy."

"Why would Seamus meet with your opposition?"

"The Balmoral showroom bombing. I think it broke him" Rowan said. "He never killed before. I don't know what he did, but he was there. He was part of it. But it wasn't our brigade."

"Maybe like most civilized people, he didn't like the idea of infants being blown to bits," Kincaid said.

"Like most civilized people," Doherty agreed. "Gusty and Billy swearing revenge ever since. Seamus may have seen redemption in their pitch."

"They recruit from their enemies?"

"To get a hand like Shame, they surely would. They'd walk in the front feckin' door." Doherty sipped his coffee, looked at his hands, rubbed a palm across his fingers. "After UVF bombed McGurk's, we all swore we'd pay 'em back. They got fifteen. We got four, maybe five at Balmoral."

"Civilians."

"Aren't they always?"

"Why civilians and not combatants?"

Doherty narrowed his eyes. "Because it hurts more."

Kincaid leaned back and looked down.

"You got no right to judge us," Doherty said. "Your own force, your own police are in this up to their bloody blue necks."

"I don't believe that."

"You don't, eh?" Doherty said. "Why don't you ask more questions? Why don't you ask why they won't hand over Father Brenden Wryth? After what you been saying, after what I been learning, he must have been the reason we knew about Balmoral in the first place. And the reason Gusty's group knew about McGurk's."

"That much intelligence and counter-intelligence. From a priest. Seems more than a little far-fetched," Kincaid said.

"Fuckin' children and gettin' away with it is a powerful motivator for a man like that." Doherty stretched his arms as he tried to crack his knuckles. "About a mile from McGurk's there was a prison break. Crumlin Road Gaol. Some of our men broke out. Well, not ours specifically, but republicans. British Army and RUC swarmed the area for two days after. Then, just a couple hours before loyalists hit McGurk's, police pull out. After everything I've learned about Wryth, I can't but think he's the reason Spence's boys knew just when the law planned to leave."

"I admit," Kincaid said, after some consideration. "It is a strange coincidence."

"More than. Way more than." Doherty rubbed his face with both hands. "After McGurk's, Seamus came in with a map," he continued. "The Shankill. Said it was in a coat. Sewed in. Just back from the laundry."

"Sisters of the Atonement?"

"I don't know. Maybe," Doherty said. "All we cared about was the map. We were so angry. And there it was, the road to our revenge, with a blood-red X on the Balmoral Furniture building and a date, one week to the day after McGurk's. We figured the map came from the Belfast Brigade, trying to coordinate support. These things never came with more than a route and a date. Because you knew what to do."

"Why didn't you go?"

"Why didn't *I* go? My sister is why. I was on my way outta here. Outta all this because of Michelle. Then, they killed her."

Kincaid sighed, turned his head, looked out the window at the sun on the wet cobblestone street.

"I begged Seamus not to go," Doherty said. "But he's young. I'm an oul man to him. I convinced the rest of the men to stay. If Belfast wanted Balmoral, Belfast could have it."

A waitress came round for more coffee. Kincaid nodded; Doherty waved her off.

"Don't need any more to wind me up," he said. "There were people screamin' and cryin' and the babes—'just lumps, just lumps.' And blood. 'Numbness and blood.' That's all Seamus could remember."

"IT WAS WRENCHING," KINCAID told Sister Grey on their way to the Briar Lough station barracks. "I don't see Seamus O'Dowd stealing your gun or using any gun to kill anyone, let alone a nun."

"That leaves *me*, Adam."

"Never admit anything," Kincaid said.

"I'm not in the habit of lying. Obviously."

"It's *not* a lie to *not* admit," he said. "You have to get a good solicitor. *Now*."

"You did a pretty good job."

"Now that they have your fingerprints—"

"They will find them on *my* gun."

"If they find it. Without a ballistics match, and no apparent motive, they'd have a tough time convicting you. We can only hope they either don't find it or find the real killer's prints on it. Meantime, solicitor."

"And if I can't get a solicitor, for whatever reason—" Grey said.

"You *will* get one."

Sister considered the advice, and promptly changed the subject. "So the man on the Ha'penny Bridge was one of these Ulster Defence Regiment types? Like Jackson?"

"According to McDermott," Kincaid said.

"What does that mean?"

"It means we—I—need to have another talk with Jimmy Mitchell."

"The fellow from Glenanne?" Sister asked.

"Doherty says his place is a loyalist enclave. If anyone knows what's going on, he does."

"Should you be going there alone?"

"Corporal Jackson's coming," Kincaid said.

"Corporal now, is it? I thought you—we—didn't trust him."

Kincaid pondered. "I want to see how he behaves."

"WHAT YOU SAID ABOUT me," Jackson said. "You had no call."

Jackson and Kincaid were reluctant partners in a Ford Zephyr headed to the James Mitchell farm.

"Maybe not," Kincaid said. "But I have to do what I must to protect a valued garda consultant."

"You have no idea what it was like growing up—here. No idea how what those Prov savages are capable of."

"They've done their share of killing and bombing in the South," Kincaid said. "But you're right. I have no idea what it was like to grow up here."

"Lying in bed, showered with glass," Jackson said. "Me dad boarding up every window, plunging us into darkness. Crowds screaming on the streets. Throwing rocks and bricks. Trying to pry off our boards. An armed gang stormed me da's place of work, lined everyone up, shot them dead. It was only that he was home, protecting us, that he wasn't killed."

Jackson's voice broke.

"Walls shaking, ducking all the time. Bombs going off in places you knew since a kid. Burning vehicles littering the road. And soldiers and helicopters. Everywhere, all the time. Is that civilization, Inspector?"

"No," Kincaid said. "No it's not."

"You know how you can tell if you need to take cover?"

"Gunfire, explosions, alarms, screams."

"Pinging," Jackson said. "Like a bell, not ringing, but vibrating. The bomb goes off somewhere and you're thinking, thank God they didn't get me ma and da and me brothers and sister. Then you hear the pinging and you throw yourself down and cover your head just before the blast wave hits and showers your family with glass. Forget the stones and bricks. The blast waves were the real reason me da boarded up them windows."

BALACLAVA-CLAD MEN STOPPED Kincaid and Jackson at the beginning of the road into Jimmy Mitchell's Glenanne farm off winding, narrow Lough Road.

"What's your business here?" one of them asked Kincaid at the driver's-side window. The inspector produced his garda ID.

"The Guards?"

"I was up here before, a few weeks ago. With Sergeant O'Connell," Kincaid said. "Mr. Mitchell should remember."

"The sergeant was killed?" one of the men asked.

"Yes. Kevin O'Connell."

"Some would say he had it comin'," another man said.

Jackson passed over his UDR ID. After looking the cards over, "wait," the first man said. He walked up the road, returned in twenty minutes. "Get out," he ordered the two visitors.

"He can't walk," Jackson said, nodding toward Kincaid.

"Then turn around and get the hell out of here."

"I've got a wheelchair," Kincaid said.

"In the boot?"

"Yeah."

"Keys."

Jackson handed over the keys and another man opened the trunk.

"It's here."

"Anything else?"

The man pawed through the trunk.

"Nah."

A third man frisked a seated Kincaid and Jackson, standing beside the car. They got Kincaid into the wheelchair. Men on either side and Jackson behind, Kincaid wheeled the chair down the winding, choppy, macadam road to the farm.

The Special Patrol Group Land Rover Kincaid and O'Connell had seen was now across the yard and clean. Mitchell emerged from the house.

"Haven't ya had enough, man?" Mitchell said, walking toward them.

"And that's supposed to mean what, exactly?" Kincaid said.

"Look at ya."

"Your name keeps coming up," Kincaid said. "You and a fella name of Spence."

"Gusty or Billy?"

"Gusty, mostly."

"You got no jurisdiction here," Mitchell said. "I told ya before, but you're not keen on listening."

"I don't have jurisdiction because you killed the man who did?"

"Kev didn't, neither. We had nothing to do with that anyways."

"No?"

"I'm truly sorry about Kev," Mitchell said. "His dad and me were tighter than a Prod and Taig had a right to be."

"You know who *did* kill him?" Jackson asked.

Mitchell looked at Jackson, as though seeing him for the first time. "And you are?"

"Name's Jackson, Mr. Mitchell," one of Mitchell's masked henchmen announced. "Ulster—"

"Ulster?" Mitchell said. "Off to a good start, anyways. Ulster what, young fella?"

"Ulster Defence Regiment," Jackson said.

Mitchell rubbed his chin. "Ulster Defence Regiment."

"Newest battalion. Eleventh, out of Craigavon."

"He has jurisdiction here," Kincaid said. "Of a kind."

"Maybe he does," Mitchell said. "Maybe he don't. Don't care either way." Mitchell studied Jackson. "Killed the B-Specials, did ya?"

"I wouldn't put—"

"I was a B-Special," Mitchell interrupted. "How do you like bein' a killer?"

"I'm not a killer," Jackson said.

"You were never a B-Special?"

"No, sir."

"You said your group had nothing to do with Sergeant O'Connell's murder," Kincaid said. "Who did?"

Mitchell rubbed his chin. "Persistent bugger, aren't ya?" He looked back at the house. "Follow me."

MITCHELL LED HIS VISITORS and his men into a large but sparsely-furnished room with a big wooden table. A young woman went to pour tea, but Mitchell stopped her with what Kincaid thought an uncharacteristic gentility in his eyes, voice, and touch.

"Something rougher, Lily," Mitchell said. She returned with three glasses and a bottle of whiskey. "Thank you, love." Mitchell gave the first glass to Jackson. Kincaid's glass was third.

"A toast," Mitchell said. "To Kevin O'Connell, a good man cut low before his time."

Jackson and Mitchell raised their glasses. Kincaid hesitated.

"You don't agree?" Mitchell asked.

"Not until I know who killed him," Kincaid said. "And Mich Doherty. And the other people at the wake."

"Mich Doherty I don't give a damn about," Mitchell said. "As for the others: my information suggests that's where you should focus." Mitchell let this revelation set in. "Revenge is what I'm hearin'. For the colleen's betrayals."

"Lann McLaughlin?"

"The same."

"She was already dead."

"Don't matter. More needed to pay, especially her fur trader daddy."

"Rory," Jackson volunteered.

"Smart lad," Mitchell said. "They never should've got involved with Brenden Wryth. Tradin' secrets with the enemy just to protect his sorry arse."

"What secrets?" Kincaid asked. "Which enemy?"

"Gardaí. Your people. IRA, Provs," Mitchell said. "That nun he had workin' for him worked a deal with the mother and baby homes. Shippin' maps, letters, cables, memos, whatever they could get their feckin' hands on. Sent 'em through the laundries. Then somebody had the brilliant idea to sew things into coats and pelts. Easier to get across the border. Everyone's checkin' uniforms. No one's checkin' furs."

"So some group fired on the McLaughlin burial, what—to put an end to this?" Kincaid asked.

"Revenge what's done, prevent what's not," Mitchell said.

"Which group?"

"Which group, what? Killed 'em? Doesn't matter. Coulda been loyalists, coulda been republicans. All the same where killin's concerned."

Kincaid looked at Jackson, busily taking notes.

"You *will* let me see them scribblings before you're off," Mitchell said.

Kincaid subtly nodded.

"Yes, sure," Jackson said.

"Good boyo ya got there," Mitchell told Kincaid.

"One other question," Kincaid said.

"Don't test my generosity."

"Ever heard of a fella name of Seamus O'Dowd?"

Mitchell considered. "O'Dowd. O'Dowd. Always loved the name Seamus. Thought if I ever had a son a me own . . . O'Dowd, O'Dowd. Can't say that I have. Which foot?"

"Foot?" Kincaid asked.

"*He* knows," Mitchell said, eyeing Jackson. "Which foot does he kick with?"

"A green foot," Jackson said without hesitation. "A left foot."

Mitchell eyed Kincaid and leaned toward him. "Then why in *the fuck* . . . " He pounded his palm on the table. " . . . would you ask me about this Seamus O'Dowd?"

"He may have defected," Kincaid said.

"Death," Mitchell said, "is the only defection."

Twenty Nine

Sketch paper with victims' names and occupations lay before Kincaid on the O'Connell's kitchen table. **Physician. Monsignor. Accountant. Solicitor. Psychiatrist. Furrier's daughter. Nun. Abbess. Sergeant. Lady Constable. Constable. British military.** And the unidentified bookkeeper:

Marta??

Kincaid felt Mattie's presence.

"My victims," he said.

He started laying out another set of cards. **Bartholomew. Andrew. Oliver Plunkett. Thomas More. Agnes of Rome. Dymphna.**

"My martyrs," he said.

Mattie picked up the card marked "Furrier's daughter."

"I don't believe what James Mitchell told you," she said. "Not for a minute. Lann was a good girl."

"They needed money," Kincaid said. "Her father was in debt. She wanted to move to Dublin. Set her sights on Trinity."

"I know what it means to need money. But I still don't believe it, not of Lann McLaughlin."

Kincaid moved the three "cop" and abbess cards aside.

"Really?" Mattie said.

"Different M.O."

"Shot, you mean? And blown to bits."

"Mother Stephanie I'm calling a murder of convenience," Kincaid said. "Constable Brugha took a bomb meant for someone—or something—else."

"And my brother? Mich?"

"We can't rule out paramilitaries," Kincaid said. "Kevin knew his life was under constant threat, as much if not more from his own people. Repub—"

"Catholics," Mattie interrupted. "Catholics." She turned away, folded her arms, looked downcast and alone. "What's this I hear you're thinking of returning to one of our local inns?" Mattie said. "You're perfectly welcome to stay here. Besides, you're recovery isn't complete."

"I'm imposing," Kincaid said. "On both you and whatever good will your neighbors may have toward a Catholic cop."

"I cry every night," Mattie said. "I cannot spend my days in the same despair consuming my nights. If you weren't here, I'd have nothing else but four empty walls and a houseful of memories."

"I've got to consider—"

The phone rang and Mattie gladly ran into the hall to answer it. "He's here," she said. "Inspector—you've a phone call."

"Adam. John."

"Let me guess," Kincaid said. "Greevey is furious I've so far defied him."

"Always. But that's not why I called. The head on the Ha'Penny."

"Charlie something," Kincaid said.

"Charlie Mangan. The girl recognized him."

"Girl?"

"One we interviewed over the killin' of that chancer her mam was with."

"Alyson?"

"That's her name. She saw the photo in the papers."

"I thought you got the victim's name through channels."

"Did. Scotland Yard. More than happy to provide it, they were. In some kind of pissing match with the Operation Banner crowd."

"Then what did this—Alyson—"

"Right. What did she tell us? She told us Charlie Mangan was the one with Marta. The man with the dog. The man Alyson saw before Marta disappeared."

"Hold it, hold it," Kincaid said. "She's sure about this?"

"He had a beard before. Just like the other witness said. But the tattoo didn't lie. Her mam brought her down. Took statements from both. It was definitely him."

"Thought her ma never saw the bloke."

"Saw him come and go. Said the chancer used to talk to the fella."

"Dan?"

"Dan Faunt. Mam's boyfriend," McDermott said. "Befriended Mangan, apparently."

"What does this mean for Marta?" Kincaid said.

"No premature conclusions."

"The man she was with is murdered gruesomely. She vanishes. Woman who might be her turns up with her face beat to a pulp. What conclusions would you consider premature?"

"You can't conclude Marta's dead, Adam. The killer may want you to *think* she's dead. But you can't conclude anything. You know that."

"I don't know a feckin' thing" Kincaid said. "I'm learning how much with every passing day."

"I—WE—REFUSE TO be cowed, Inspector. By these—terrorists." Sisters of the Atonement Prioress Catherine spoke over construction workers sawing wood, positioning drywall, moving wheelbarrows, raising hammers and dust. She stepped across a low stack of two-by-fours, started down a hallway, then turned to Sister Grey and Kincaid still standing on the other side of the lumber. "Oh. I'm so sorry," she said.

"Quite all right," Kincaid said, leaning on his crutches.

The prioress waved two workers over. "Can you relocate these?" she asked them.

"I can assure you, I knew nothing about this dreadful scheme," Mother Catherine said in her partly-rebuilt office. "When Sister de la Guerra—"

"You've seen her?" Sr. Grey asked.

"No," the prioress said. "She telegraphed."

"From where?"

"She didn't say. I didn't ask. You didn't know?"

"She left about a week ago," Grey said. "I didn't know anymore than that."

"Gone into hiding, perhaps? I'm sure she felt quite threatened. Mother Stephanie. The bomb here. By the way, Inspector, you have my deepest sympathies, both for your own injuries and for the death of your friend, the constable. Brugha."

"Thank you," Kincaid said. "I wanted to know—" Sister Grey tugged his jacket, shook her head. But he persisted. "I wanted to know how well you knew Mother Stephanie."

"Mother Stephanie. A fellow woman of the cloth. I knew her, but not well. I encountered Sister Mongilly a time or two, when Stephanie was her superior."

"Really? In what capacity?"

"In passing. I may have spoken with Mother Stephanie a time or two. But we were not close."

"You're here in Belfast, she near Briar Lough," Kincaid said.

"She did not approve of our mission," Catherine said. "She made no secret of it. I tired of apologizing years ago and didn't plan to start again."

"Adam—must we rehash what is obviously an uncomfortable subject?" Sister Grey asked.

"I have no problem answering questions," Mother Catherine said. "So long as you don't think *I* killed her."

"Mother Stephanie didn't approve of Sister Mongilly's activities any more than she approved of this laundry," Kincaid said. "The smuggled maps were a particular sticking point."

"The maps, which I knew nothing about," Catherine said. "After I learned from Sister de la Guerra what had been going on here right under my nose—"

"What did she tell you?" Kincaid asked.

"What *didn't* she tell. How and when the maps arrived at our office. How they ended up carefully stitched into the clean laundry of soldiers, policemen, and terrorists. How my order unwittingly aided the deaths of innocent people. And all because of Mary Theresa Mongilly and, from the looks of things, her relationship with either my office manager, our weekend bookkeeper, or the both of them."

"What of Miss Nic Cionnaith?"

"I've been unable to reach her since the explosion," Mother Catherine said. "I don't think the authorities have had any better luck. What of the woman you and the constable saw that day?"

"Never identified," Kincaid said. "But CID did confirm the license plate number belonged to your weekend bookkeeper."

"Fine, then," Mother Catherine said. "Maybe these will move things along." She handed Kincaid a manila envelope. He pulled out tracing paper—maps, routes, roads, movements, markings, letters, numbers—as detailed as any army—or loyalist or republican brigade—might find useful.

"Fools who blew up this place probably thought that was all destroyed. But there was a small safe. One of our kind police officers brought it to me. It normally had money in it—petty cash, sometimes a valuable or two. The lock was damaged, so I took it to my brother's house and banged it open."

"Mother Catherine!" said Sr. Grey, gazing intently at the treasure from the hidden safe. "How rather dashing of you."

"I wish I could say it was the most excitement I've ever had," she said. Then she looked around. "But alas—I cannot."

"JUST WAIT UNTIL MOTHER Catherine hears my gun was used to murder Mother Stephanie," Sr. Grey said on their way out of the building.

"I'm glad you didn't feel the need to brag," Kincaid said.

"Me, the soul of humility? Speaking of bragging, what *did* you learn from that little squish Mr. Jackson during your sojourn with the gang from Glenanne? You still haven't told me."

"Mitchell took a liking to him."

"His blue eyes are rather charming—for a corpse," Grey said.

"He's young and impressionable. Wasn't that *your* thinking?"

"We'll see after he arrests me."

"He's not going to arrest you."

Kincaid stopped abruptly at the new door frame to the entrance the blast destroyed. He grabbed it and gasped.

"Adam," Sister said. She put her hand on his back. "Adam!"

"I'm—" Kincaid said.

"You need to sit," Grey said.

"I don't." He looked down the hallway. He turned and leaned into the door frame and looked up. He started sliding down the frame.

"Oh dear God." Sister Grey grabbed his arm and steadied him. "Are you all right? Are you faint?"

"No, yes. I don't know," Kincaid said, breathing heavily, almost panting, losing his grip on his crutches.

"I can't support you," she said.

Kincaid steadied himself.

"The wheelchair's in the boot," Grey said.

"Just—let me rest. I'll be all right. Let me rest." He stumbled.

"I'm going to get your chair. I'll not have you fall in the carpark."

Grey took the keys from Kincaid's trousers and ran. At the car, she struggled, managed to yank the wheelchair out of the trunk, opened it, and hurried to Adam, who seemed marginally steadier. She locked the chair's rear wheels and helped him into it.

"Still feeling faint?"

"Dizzy."

She waited.

"I'm okay," he said.

She wheeled him to the car and helped him into it, and quietly told Mattie to keep an eye on him after they returned to Briar Lough.

"ADAM?" MATTIE APPEARED AT the bottom of the stairs to her temporary bedroom. She stared in the dark across the living room toward Kincaid's closed bedroom door.

"Darn iron," it sounded like, coming from his room. She walked toward it and listened at the door. Mumbling, groaning, maybe the word "no." She heard him toss in the sheets. "Darn iron!" suddenly, and the sound of bed covers hitting the floor. She knocked at the door.

"Adam?"

"Uhh," he said.

She opened the door and peered in.

"Did I wake you?"

"No," he said.

Mattie entered and looked at him best she could.

"Darn iron?" she asked.

He turned on the small lamp next to the bed.

"Darn what?"

She approached him. He looked at her face in the light. "A new name for Norn Iron?" she asked. "Or maybe just gurnin'."

"I'm sorry," he said.

"May I?" She followed his eyes and sat on the bed. "You look feverish." She touched the back of her hand to his cheek and forehead. "Those wounds aren't raging, are they?"

"No," he said.

"Darn iron," she said. "Did it burn ya?"

Kincaid smiled into her brown eyes, miraculous beneath her softly-lit amber hair.

"Darian," he said. "Dominic Darian."

"And why would you be callin' poor Dominic when you have me just up the stairs?"

"He was a priest. I was his altar boy."

"And he's givin' ya nightmares?"

Kincaid looked through the dark at the door.

"Would you like some water?" Mattie said. Before he could answer, she was up. She returned with a glass and a coaster. "Sit up. Don't spill it."

He sipped and stared.

"You were an altar boy?" she asked.

"*His*," Kincaid said, setting the glass on the coaster. "Altar boy."

She looked at him quizzically. "Sounds like he owned you," she said. When he didn't respond for a while, "What happened to this Father Darian?"

"I don't know," Kincaid said. "He built a new church. The town fell in love with him. Then he was gone."

"He never said goodbye?"

"Not to me," Kincaid said. "I was probably the reason he left. Me, and a few others."

"Why would that be?"

Kincaid turned away. Mattie took his hand. "Did he do something to you?" she asked.

He breathed deeply and moved his legs.

"If you don't want to—"

"Yes," Kincaid said.

"What?"

Nothing.

"Did he hurt you?"

"Indirectly."

"Oh, Adam. I'm so sorry. Did you tell anyone?" she asked.

"Me mam," he said. "She damn near disowned me."

"Go away! Your own mama. The woman you've been trying to reach from our phone?"

"Why do you think I haven't reached her?" Kincaid asked. "Nurses tell me she's asleep every time."

"Your own mam," Mattie said.

"My future was over before it began, as far as she was concerned. I entered the seminary to make it right."

"The seminary? You were becomin' a priest?"

"I didn't finish," Kincaid said. "That just compounded things with my mother."

"Sounds like the right decision, regardless what she thought."

"Darn iron," Kincaid said. "I never could pronounce his goddamn name."

Thirty

"And you believe Mr. Mitchell?" Rowan Doherty asked Kincaid over lunch at the Briar Lough cafe.

"I've no reason not to," Kincaid said.

"I can think of plenty of reasons."

"Mitchell was losing his head over the mere suggestion," Kincaid said. "Seamus O'Dowd is not at Glenanne."

"Then where the feck is he? Why would he just vanish like that? Seamus is one of my most reliable men. He wouldn't just up and take off."

"Maybe he didn't. Maybe someone took him. Maybe he's dead."

"Perish the thought, man," Doherty said.

"Could he have joined another group—some other faction? Official IRA, Saor Éire?"

"He left the officials to come with us. I don't know why he'd go back," Doherty said. "Saor Éire is a creature of your country. And Seamus is no communist."

"Any other republican or nationalist groups? What about disaffected Catholics?"

"Ah. You mean like Mulvaney and Chesney?"

"I've heard the names."

"Seamus already turned Father Chesney away," Doherty said.

"Over what?"

"Payback for Felix Hughes. You heard the UDA shot him?"

"The accordion player?" Kincaid said.

"Mindin' his own business. They threw his twisted body into a ditch. Chesney came to us with a revenge plot. It was Seamus told him no."

"What about Mulvaney?"

"Missing since he ratted out Chesney. He's the one I'd peg for dead."

KINCAID COULD BARELY SEE Sr. Grey behind the stack of books she was carrying in from her car. He stood up to help.

"Are those the photos we were talking about?" she said.

"They are. Here, let me—"

"No, no. Just sit. I'm fine."

The books toppled onto the O'Connell's couch. She looked at the phrase the recovered manutergia spelled out in several autopsy photos.

O bona crux diu desiderata et concupiscenti animo praeparata suscipe discipulum pependit in te

"Seems we're still missing some words," she said.

"*Eius qui,*" Kincaid said. "The one."

"The one," Sr. Grey said. "Killer referring to himself?"

"Or herself," Kincaid said.

"A woman strong enough to hoist a crucifix? Have to have a partner," Grey said. "Or partners."

"Maybe the final victim is The One," Kincaid said. "Maybe Wryth himself. Were these books any help?"

"Perhaps." She opened one to a book-marked passage. *"Lógmar muince,"* she said. "A Dubliner named John Carey said this on the way to the gallows back in 1594."

"On what charge?"

She read. "Aiding and abetting—a priest, of all things. He took the noose, kissed it, and called it a 'precious collar'. *Lógmar muince."*

"What about the priest?"

"The priest he assisted was hanged with him. And drawn and quartered. They called it the Traitor's Death."

"Who did they betray?"

"The Protestant Queen, Elizabeth. Daughter of Henry the Eighth. You know—Off-With-Her-Head Henry."

"John Cornelius," Kincaid said, looking at a sketch in the book. "The aforesaid aided and abetted priest."

"Who, on his way to the gallows, uttered—"

"O bona crux—"

"Like Saint Andrew. 'Oh good cross,'" Grey continued, "'long desired and prepared for the yearning soul, take up the disciple of The One who hung on you.' Pope Pius declared Father Cornelius a martyr about fifty years ago. John Carey, too."

"More martyrs." Kincaid thumbed through his stack of index cards. He wrote on a blank card, **John Cornelius.** "What was the other fella's name again? The aider and abetter?"

"John Carey," Sister Grey said.

Kincaid wrote **John Carey**, too.

"So Terence Byrne, the hanged accountant with *Lógmar muince* in his mouth, is *our* John Carey. And *our* John Cornelius?"

"Father—" Grey jumped at loud pounding on the front door. "Good heavens," she said. "Scared the habit right out of me."

"Sounds familiar," Kincaid said. Sister Grey looked at him through more pounding.

"Like what?"

"Like cops," he said, sliding across the couch to look past the curtains.

"Mattie?"

"Gone for the messages," Kincaid said. "Go upstairs, close the door, don't come out till I tell you."

"What's going on?"

"Just go."

Kincaid grabbed his crutches and walked with studied feebleness toward the front door.

More pounding.

"I'm comin'," he said. He opened the door.

"Inspector Kincaid." Sergeant O'Fall went for his identification.

"No need," Kincaid said. "And Corporal Jackson." Kincaid kept them at the door, leaning forward on his crutches, as though he could topple at any moment.

"We need to speak to the sister," O'Fall said. "She's not at the abbey. We figured we'd check here."

"Speak to her about what?"

"I think you know."

"Corporal?"

"It's not my idea, Inspector," Robin Jackson said.

"You find the gun?" Kincaid said. "You know—the wee derringer Sister Grey used to shoot the Abbess in the bath with no discernible motive?"

"We have to ask her some questions," O'Fall said. "That's all."

"Who says?"

"We need to talk to the sister," O'Fall said. "Do we need to push you aside to do that?"

"She's not here," Kincaid said.

"Then let us in. Show us."

"This is not my house."

"No, it's my house," Mattie said, coming up the walk with a bag of groceries. "You wouldn't be doin' this, Clarie O'Fall, if my brother were here." She pushed past the men and looked at Kincaid. "O'Connells and Special Branch don't get on," she said to him.

"Got on fine when I was saving Kev's arse," O'Fall said.

"You weren't Special Branch then," Mattie yelled from the kitchen. She saw Sr. Grey peeping out from the stairway door. She jerked her head, shifted her eyes, and Grey closed the stairway door. Mattie went back to the front door and stood beside Kincaid.

"You were welcome here once," Mattie said.

"Yeah," O'Fall said.

"So what happened?" the inspector asked.

O'Fall hesitated.

"Tell 'im, Clarie. Tell 'im *your* side," Mattie said.

"I—"

"You been tellin' it for years," Mattie said. "Why stop now?"

"Kev and I was partners," O'Fall began. He hesitated. "I got the brunt of it." He stepped back and slowly raised his shirt above a long scarred burn that snaked around his side to his stomach. "Ten hours surgery. Three weeks in hospital. Six months agonizing pain only relieved by enough morphine to constipate a horse." O'Fall turned to Jackson, then back to Mattie and Kincaid. He lowered his shirt. Kincaid adjusted himself on his crutches.

"We was delivering a message to a bereaved family, Kev and me, only they weren't bereaved," O'Fall continued. "Hell, they weren't even a family. We thought they didn't have a phone—most didn't, that's why we called on 'em. But they had a phone. Used it to coordinate the thing. The setup, the ambush. Fire and bombs. It's the only thing these feckin' Fenians understand."

"The RUC delivers news to people their families can't reach. Births, deaths, invites," Mattie told Kincaid.

"*Used* to deliver," O'Fall said. "Republicans bombed us out of that business."

"He saved Kev's life," Mattie said. She peered around the corner to make sure Sister Grey was upstairs. "Even though Kevin was a feckin' Fenian. Right, Clarie?"

The sergeant shuffled his feet, looked back at Jackson, looked down the street.

"Let them in," Mattie said.

Kincaid hesitated.

"It's all right," Mattie said. "Whatever they're looking for, they won't find it here."

Kincaid hobbled out of the way. O'Fall and Jackson stayed put.

"Are you coming in or not?" Mattie said.

"Kevin O'Connell was a good man," O'Fall said. "Best partner a cop could have had."

"Then why did you try to drum him out?" Mattie said. "You save his life, then try to kill him?"

"That wasn't me," O'Fall said. "It was Artful Tongue wagging the Hunt report."

"You went along. Trying to impress Sir Arthur after rolling around in Peacocke's mess like a happy hog."

"That's not true. I worked with the Chief Constable on the welfare department. We worked on the Benevolent Fund. Kev and I knew better than most—"

"Kev and you nothing. Stormont needed scapegoats. You needed something to step on, to ascend that higher rung," Mattie said. "Kevin wouldn't go along, so you stepped on him."

"It was either—" O'Fall stopped. Mattie came to the door and looked straight at him.

"What, Clarie? Finish your story. Your side. Tell the inspector about the choices you made. How you donned your shiny blue uniform while everyone else stayed green." She looked at Jackson. "Have you told your little friend?"

"Inspector," O'Fall said, slipping around Mattie with a business card and a scowl. "For the sister. We need to talk to her."

Mattie intercepted the card, crumpled it, and dropped it on the steps.

"You shouldn't have done that," O'Fall said. "It's obstruction."

"We know where to find you," Mattie said. "We don't need your little road sign."

O'Fall and Jackson turned and walked toward the street. Jackson looked back and saw Inspector Kincaid precariously retrieving the card.

"WE NEED TO GET back," Kincaid said. "Home."

"With me, a fugitive on the lam?" Sr. Grey said.

"You're not a fugitive. And you're watching too many American movies."

"I will be, if I run," she said. "A regular desperado. How would that look?"

"A lot better with a proper solicitor," Kincaid said.

"I have to defend my honor, prove my innocence. Here. I'll get someone local. My order—"

"We have many good solicitors here," Mattie said. "I'm sure you'd have no trouble finding one."

"They get a mind, they'll jail her," Kincaid said. "Planning a defense would be that much harder."

“And it won’t be from Dublin?” Sr. Grey said.

“Someone may be trying to discredit us, slow us down here,” Kincaid said. “What about Sister de la Guerra? She ups and leaves, right after the murder.”

“She had no idea I carried a gun,” Grey said. “And why would she kill Mother Stephanie, who was kind enough to put her up after the explosion that killed Constable Brugha?”

“Why would you kill Mother Stephanie?” Kincaid asked.

“Why would anyone?” Sr. Grey said. “She had Mongilly under her wing for a time. Maybe she got too close to something.”

“Maybe,” Kincaid said. “But it doesn’t change the fact we need to get back to Dublin. We can’t deal with this here anymore.”

“It’s going to be terribly lonely,” Mattie said.

“You’ve been a wonderful host,” Kincaid said. “I only wish we could have met under clearer skies.”

“Yes, well. I’m used to the clouds,” Mattie said. “You and Sister have been a welcome parting.”

Sister Grey hugged her.

“When do you leave?” Mattie asked.

“Tonight,” Kincaid said. “I’ll tell McDermott to have a border greeting party and a solicitor at the ready.”

“JOHN SOUNDED CONFUSED,” SR. Grey said. “Or maybe just excited.”

"Confused," Kincaid said. He clicked on the car's high beams through a dark stretch of road. "I had no intention of returning yet."

"I hope we haven't jeopardized this case," Sr. Grey said. "Over me."

"The only people jeopardizing the case are the people framing you," Kincaid said. "Once we get that sorted, we may get some real answers."

"How will we do that from Dublin?"

"Not from Dublin. I plan to come back here. If they'll have me."

"You can return Caprice's car, then," Sr. Grey said. "I doubt she ever expects to see it again."

"Very generous of her."

"It *was* Mother's car," Grey said. "Caprice started driving it after—" She paused. "I'm fleeing the law in Mother Stephanie's car. The woman I supposedly shot."

"With her blessing, I've no doubt," Kincaid said. "The driving, that is. Not the shooting."

A bright blue light flashed in the rear view mirrors.

"Oh dear. Are they after us?" Grey said.

Kincaid pulled over as an older-model Land Rover parked behind.

"How will we explain this car?" Grey said. "The stolen getaway car?"

"Sister." An exasperated Kincaid rolled down the window to a blinding flashlight that turned toward the ground. Robin Jackson leaned in.

"I've been instructed to escort you to the border," he said.

"Have you now?" Kincaid said.

"I have."

"Well, then." Kincaid went to put the car in gear. Jackson reached across and grasped his hand.

"Only you, Inspector."

"What do you mean, only me?"

"Sister stays. Until we get this sorted."

Kincaid looked at Grey. He turned back to Jackson. "I'm not leaving without her," he said.

"That's not up to you."

Kincaid and Grey saw more blue lights behind the Land Rover.

"The Chief Constable approve this?"

"I don't know," Jackson said. "I'm too low."

They heard footsteps approaching. Another man joined Jackson. A third stood next to the passenger side.

Grey took Kincaid's hand. "I'll be fine," she said.

Kincaid stared ahead.

"We'll take the car back, Inspector," Jackson said. "Please don't make this any harder than it already is."

"Adam," Sr. Grey said.

Kincaid hugged her and stood firm outside the car, watching while men he now recognized as Ulster Defence Regiment escorted the nun to a waiting car. Jackson slipped behind the wheel of Sr. Caprice's car. The third man drove Kincaid and his suitcases the roughly sixteen miles to the border in the Land Rover.

"ADAM!"

Kincaid stood on his crutches as McDermott approached him from two gardaí cars in the lights of a military checkpoint. The superintendent reached out for a handshake, but Kincaid just stood. A garda picked up the detective's bags.

"Don't you wonder where Sister is?" Kincaid asked.

"I know where she is."

"No help for her, then?" Kincaid said.

"We'll do what we can," McDermott said.

Kincaid watched the garda load his bags, slam the lid of the boot, stand and wait in the headlights.

"You wore out your welcome," McDermott said.

Thirty One

Kincaid lay in his own bed staring at the ceiling. His weeks-empty Dublin flat smelled musty but looked clean. He turned toward knocking at his door but didn't move to answer it. He heard the door open.

"Don't get up," McDermott said from the front room. "Wherever you—" He appeared at Kincaid's bedroom door. "Knock, knock."

"I'm not due back till Monday," Kincaid said.

"I know. I brought food."

"I'm not hungry."

McDermott sighed. "Rather lie in bed all day, waiting for the world to happen."

"I'm not waiting for anything."

"Then letting it pass you by."

"I think I'm allowed."

"Allowed what, pray tell?"

Kincaid looked at his friend. "To mourn."

"Mourn? Who—" McDermott stopped. "The sister?"

"And Baldwin. And Marta. And Kevin O'Connell. His partner, Constable—"

"I understand, Adam."

Kincaid turned his head to McDermott. “Brugha. And Mich Doherty, a fine officer. And a woman, with her own station. Can we claim such a thing here, in the Republic?”

“I don’t know, Adam. I don’t track every garda outpost.”

Kincaid coughed and turned back to the ceiling.

“We’ve arranged for a criminal law solicitor to speak with Sister Grey next week,” McDermott said. “Out of Portadown.”

“Her gun—if it was her gun—was used for some reason,” Kincaid said. “If that reason somehow involved the authorities, I don’t see how she can get a fair hearing.”

“She hasn’t been charged, Adam. If they can’t find her gun, they may even release her. It’s so ridiculously far-fetched that she would have had anything to do with the abbess’s death in the first place.”

“I’m going back,” Kincaid said.

“Back where?”

“The North.”

“Why?” McDermott asked. “Sister Grey is, or will soon be, in good hands.”

“We were making progress.”

“You returned empty-handed.”

“We found a pattern. We were working an angle.”

“Oh, the martyrs? Maybe. Sounds plausible, even. But the *why* is still missing, Adam. Why would someone—or someones—replicate the murders of famous martyrs? Until we answer that question, where are we, really?”

“I need to go back,” Kincaid said.

McDermott leaned against the door jamb. “Then give us something. A reason to send you back.” He sighed. “We will take care of Sr. Grey. Even call in political favors, if need be. But if we’re to bring her back to Dublin, solve these crimes, and keep whatever semblance of peace we can muster, we can’t get off on the wrong foot.”

“Keep the peace,” Kincaid said. “Isn’t that the real motive? We don’t want the Troubles here?”

“In case you haven’t noticed,” McDermott said, “they already are.”

KINCAID LOOKED AT A report on his desk at Dublin Castle about the death of Charlie Mangan.

“We think he killed Daniel Faunt,” Greevey said at the doorway.

“Chief Inspector.” Kincaid went to stand reflexively, fumbling with his crutches.

“No, no. Sit.” Greevey stepped forward. “You feeling up to being here?”

“Didn’t you want me here?”

“If you’re in pain, psychic or otherwise—”

“I appreciate it, Chief Superintendent. But I’m fine.”

“Well, then. Mangan, we’ve discovered, had motive, means, opportunity. He could see Faunt’s bathroom from Marta’s bedroom window.”

“He was *in* her bedroom?”

"We think so."

"Mangan knew about the electrical work?"

"Probably planned to drown Faunt. Or shoot him, originally," Greevey said. "Razor was convenient. The way Faunt complained all the time, Mangan probably knew about the faulty breakers, too."

"Then Mangan ends up dead. Rest of his body ever turn up?"

"No." Greevey pulled a chair out and sat. "You gave us a fright, Adam. A couple of frights. Terrible frights."

"That wasn't my intention."

He reached across the desk and squeezed Kincaid's arm. "We've missed ya," he said. "I have a little get together planned. A welcome home. At my home."

"Thank you, sir. But—"

"No buts. You're the guest of honor, and a well-deserved honor it is. You made a tremendous impression. Shillington was disappointed he never got to meet you."

"I heard I'd worn out my welcome."

"Oh, that. Just John, being hyperbolic again. And stop fretting over the sister. She has excellent representation. Solicitor hired a young barrister for her first court appearance—"

"Court appearance?" Kincaid said.

"He's mid thirties I'd guess. Just took the silk. Lavery, I think his name is."

"What's the cause for the court appearance?"

"I'm not clear on that," Greevey said. "But in the North, Queen's Counsel is an impressive credential and Lavery has it. I'm not worried."

"It's Special Branch, sir, that's after Sister Grey," Kincaid said. "So I am worried. The sergeant working the case has a history with Kevin O'Connell. He was none too happy about our being there."

"Didn't you insist Sister stay here?" Greevey said.

"Lot of good that did."

"Yes, well. Anyway, I hear this Lavery fellow is a marvel, and will insist the Criminal Investigation Division take the case from Special Branch should any charges emerge. Which I doubt."

"I wish I shared your optimism," Kincaid said.

"You do, otherwise how could you do this job? Speaking of which, about this report." Greevey picked it up. "Why was Charlie Mangan calling on Marta Carney?"

"You've learned nothing else?"

"Only that Daniel Faunt probably knew, or had an inkling as to why, and that may be why he's dead."

"You said this Mangan was in the Ulster Defence Regiment," Kincaid said.

"Yes. Just left the British Army," Greevey said. "Probably wanted to keep his hand in things."

"Why here?"

"Mangan was a newly-commissioned training, intelligence, and security officer for the UDR. We think he was here gathering intel."

"Through Marta?"

"Maybe he was using her. Knew that she knew things."

Kincaid turned the report's pages, looked at a sketch of neck wound positions, photocopies of crime scene photographs, Mangan's height, weight, and other Scotland Yard-provided details.

"And still no body," he mused. "Says here Mangan had been known to the Yard since at least sixty seven. Why?"

"Operation Banner," Greevey said.

"Normally, I'd understand that," Kincaid said. "But Operation Banner didn't start till sixty nine."

"**HAVE YOU MET HIM** yet?" Kincaid asked Grey on the phone.

"What a nice surprise. And hallo to you, too."

"Sorry. Just anxious."

"Scared to death here."

"Greevey says you've got the best representation we could find," Kincaid said. "Have you met him?"

"Mr. Lavery?"

"The barrister."

"Thursday," Sr. Grey said. "I hear he's marvelous. Mattie says her brother dreaded being examined by him, which is an excellent sign." Sr. Grey took a deep, exhausted breath. "I've stolen your old room," she said. "I hope you don't mind."

"The abbey—"

"Got their car back. But not me. Didn't want a murderer in their midst. Caprice and I had an uncomfortable exchange. Can't say as I blame them. But still—"

"I thought clergy weren't supposed to judge."

"Most judgmental lot of all," Sr. Grey said. "Why do you think we have Confession? Anyway, don't feel bad for me. Mattie insisted and—I love Mattie. She's so upbeat."

"A little too upbeat."

"Adam!"

"That doesn't surprise you?"

"I hear her crying. She screamed at the telephone the other day, When I asked her what was wrong, she ran up to her room saying something about Kevin."

"I heard her crying. Maybe I'm being too—"

"Judgmental?"

"I hear it's going around. Optimism, too. Greevey's trying to smother me with it," Kincaid said.

"Beside telling you I have the finest barrister—*I've* heard in *both* the South and the North—what else is he pushing?"

"That Charlie Mangan knew the layout of the flat Dan Faunt shared with Marisol and her daughter Alyson."

"And he knew this how?"

"Marta's flat. Binoculars or a rifle scope could have done the rest."

"That must be hard to hear."

Kincaid let the receiver slip from his mouth.

"Adam."

He said nothing.

"I'm baffled about Marta's Houdini act, too," Grey said. "But what if she vanished of her own accord? To escape the same people who killed Mr. Mangan."

"You had her running off with a boyfriend before."

"I have her doing things under her own volition," Grey said. "That's a theme you may have noticed about me."

"I find either of those theories as hard to believe as you murdering Mother Stephanie," Kincaid said.

"Hope my captors share your—optimism," Grey said. "I am frightened, Adam. Fear isn't something I often feel and even less often admit. I've never felt more alone or more alien in my own United Kingdom."

A FAMILIAR BOOMING VOICE startled Kincaid as he reached for an appetizer at the end of a table of hors d'oeuvres.

"You remember His Excellency," Greevey said, placing his hands on both their backs.

"I do," Kincaid said. He shook Bishop Gerry McCarthy's hand.

"Francis tells me your trip to the North was fruitful," McCarthy said.

"Francis," Kincaid looked at Greevey. He hesitated. "Yes," he said. "We found a pattern. We have an angle."

"We?" McCarthy said.

"Sister Jane Grey," John McDermott added, taking an appetizer from the table. "She's been an enormous help."

"Indeed?" McCarthy said. "What patterns and angles did the sister's keen eyes discern?"

"If I share that, these two fellas may sack me," Kincaid said.

"Mustn't have that," McCarthy said. "I heard you were once a seminarian."

"Did you."

"I did."

"I was." Kincaid looked at his two bosses. "Who told you?"

McDermott smiled and sipped a drink. "It wasn't me," he said.

"Sixth sense, Gerry?" Greevey asked.

"Father Kane, maybe," Kincaid said.

"Kane," McCarthy said. "Haven't seen him since he transferred."

"Father was very forthcoming," McDermott said. "Very helpful, very forthcoming."

"Kane's a good man," Bishop McCarthy said. "I'm sure his parish was sad to see him leave, especially so soon after Monsignor Gwynedd passed."

"Why did he leave?" Kincaid said.

"I'm not his prelate, so I've only heard rumors," McCarthy said. "He wanted a younger flock. He was a youth minister with no youth to minister." McCarthy sipped the froth off the top of his beer. "I heard another rumor, too."

"Well, then. I hope it's a good one," Greevey said.

“I hesitated to say anything, until I heard your doings in the North might have crossed paths with Brenden Wryth,” McCarthy said to Kincaid. “Is that true?”

“More or less,” Kincaid said.

“Monsignor Gwynedd was his prelate years ago. *Many* years ago,” McCarthy said.

“That is interesting,” McDermott said. “What do you think, Adam?”

“Wryth would have been a young man then,” Kincaid said. “Just starting out.”

“Yes,” McCarthy agreed. “Just starting out.”

“I DON’T MIND TELLING you,” the librarian said. “The loss of Marta Carney has been keenly felt.” Her brisk pace tapped the Long Room floor. “So you think another look around may help?”

“I don’t know,” Kincaid said, leaning on a single cane now. “How did they get Baldwin’s body in here? We’ve been assuming through the rear door. Why didn’t Marta see anything before she discovered the body? Or did she, and that’s why she’s missing?”

The librarian searched the room with her gaze, the ceilings, the shelves, the busts of great men, the numbered stalls. Her eyes finally lighted on Kincaid.

“No construction work going on? Ventilation shafts left open? Wall openings for wiring and such?” he asked.

"No, Inspector. We would have shut the library. We take great measures to protect the collection around any construction work."

"Murder squad thinks Dr. Baldwin was brought in during the night."

"I heard that," the librarian said. "But I don't know why Marta didn't see him. How could she have missed—the scene?"

They stopped at Stall H and Peter Scheemakers' bust of James Ussher, Archbishop of Armagh and Primate of All Ireland.

"O Lord, forgive me, especially my sins of omission," the librarian said, quoting Ussher's famous last words. "Good a place as any to leave you," she told Kincaid. "If you have any questions —"

Kincaid entered the stall and gazed at the books. He set his cane aside, started up the ladder, felt pain in his leg, but kept going. He went to the top, looked beyond the stall across the room. He went down the ladder and at the bottom, slid it along a runner. A handsomely-bound book caught his eye.

Immanuel, or the Mystery of the Incarnation of the Son of God. By James Ussher. He opened the book and read.

A notable wonder indeed, and great beyond
all comparison. That the Son of God
should be made of a Woman: even made of
that Woman which was made by himselfe.

He turned more pages and stopped, at a transparent sheet over a colorful illustration. With the book, he stepped out of the stall and limped down the center aisle as quickly as his injured leg allowed.

"I have a question," he told the librarian. "Is this tracing paper?" He opened the book to the transparent sheet.

"Oh, no," the librarian said. "It's archival interleaving, used to protect delicate illustrations and antiquarian pages."

"Could it be used to trace something?"

"Trace?"

"If I wanted to reproduce this picture."

"Well, it wouldn't be," the librarian said. "But I see what you're getting at. Our scholars, translators, students of the book —they use archival-grade tracing paper."

"For what, exactly?"

"Well—they sometimes trace words with unusual lettering or oddly-shaped typefaces, or even pictures. We do not allow photocopying."

"Would Marta have used anything like this?"

"In a rare volume? Absolutely not," the librarian said. "Marta was *particular* careful. If she wanted a copy of a page, she would have photographed it. No flashbulb, of course."

"What about The Book of Kells?" Kincaid said.

"Archival interleaving came along well after that," the librarian said.

"No, I mean. Tracing the letters."

The librarian frowned at him as she put her hand on the Ussher book. "I can return it," she said.

Kincaid relinquished the book and walked to the front of the Long Room and limped up the spiral staircase. He ducked through the openings in the shelves that formed a continuous tunnel through the second-story stalls to the other end. He stopped at each opening, looked up, sideways, checked the shelves, the floor, the ceiling, any windows.

Pain prompted him to lean on his cane and better leg and he felt something give. The floorboards squeaked. He looked down. Balancing on a shelf, he knelt down.

A pattern of dust and wear revealed a square panel made of floorboards. He pressed his car key into a narrow gap between the panel and the rest of the floor. The panel moved and he raised it. He lowered it and hunted for his new pocket knife. Its hooked bottle opener looked best so he stuck it into the gap and raised the panel completely. It covered an opening large enough for a person to slip through, to step on the bookshelf ladder in the first-floor stall below. He replaced the panel, stood, and looked over the railing along the main floor. He read LITERARIA INSTRUXIT directly beneath.

Kincaid returned to the spiral stairs.

"Find what you're looking for, Inspector?" the librarian asked as Kincaid descended.

"About half of it," Kincaid said.

"Just let me know," she called after him.

In stall TT beneath LITERARIA INSTRUXIT he searched the floor. He walked each floorboard, pressing in. No give. He leaned against the low center bookshelf with the slanted book stand that ran the length of the stall. His leg hurt and he let his weight drift. He looked down, at a small section of unpolished, rough wood floor boards. He eyed the line of the bookshelf and saw that it aligned with the edges of the unpolished section.

He pushed on the shelf. It budged. He pushed again, pressing his good leg against the base of the shelf on the opposite wall. The bookshelf moved from the polished floor boards, exposing a larger rough area that included gaps. Kincaid bent down and pressed against the gaps with his pocket knife, revealing loose boards. One came up, followed by another. And another, until he exposed a second person-sized opening.

"Inspector?" the librarian said at the end of the stall.

"I think I found the other half," Kincaid said.

"I'LL BE DAMNED," MCDERMOTT said, standing next to Kincaid and peering down through the opening in the Long Room stall floor. "You found one of the mythical tunnels." They saw a flashlight and heard voices. A Technical Bureau examiner peered up at them.

"You'll never believe what's down here," he said. He held up a dusty bottle of wine in his gloved hand.

"And the mythical wine cellar," Kincaid said.

"Old shelves and old bottles. I'm not a wine person, so—"

"Where else does it go?"

"Bell tower, a corner cranny in the Parliament Square, the other library."

"So plenty of ways to get in and out unseen," Kincaid said.

"Especially at night, Inspector."

"Marta wouldn't have seen Alex Baldwin," Kincaid said. "He was far enough out of sight if they brought him through here."

LONELINESS. KINCAID WAS ADMITTING the condition for the first time since Marta's disappearance and Baldwin's death.

"You think you have an inability to commit?"

"No," he had told Marta during one of their after-work visits to Bloom's Pub.

"Is that why she left?"

"I don't know," Kincaid said. "I thought I was ready to marry. I think she knew otherwise. But I don't know."

Looking into the tunnel at the Long Room prompted the memory, of the dark hallway, the office doors, the noise, the whimpers, cries, screams. The memory Baldwin helped him examine, also at Bloom's.

Kincaid looked up from his whiskey about halfway through this discussion, pursed his lips. "I'm not your patient, goddamn it."

"Maybe you should be," Baldwin had said.

"It was a woman," Kincaid told Baldwin. "I always see a woman."

"Maybe the way your subconscious tries to make sense. You see a woman comforting a lad."

"Comfort . . . isn't what I saw."

"I understand. Marta's a comfort, isn't she?"

Kincaid's eyes acknowledged him.

"And no wonder," Baldwin said. "She understood you, I think. I'm surprised she isn't the woman you almost married."

IN HER ABSENCE, AND Sister Grey's peppering—*Were you an item? I'm dying to know*—Kincaid saw the logic in the pairing. Maybe that was the lure of the North. The feeling that Marta was there, somewhere, reinforced when he experienced Marta's wise yet congenial qualities in Mattie O'Connell; and Jane Grey, sharp, sarcastic, persistent. Marta was certainly the most introverted of the three, but certain qualities they all shared. This Dublin flat seemed empty now, being home as good as being lost.

The ringing telephone found him.

"Mr. Lavery is *wonderful*," Sister Grey said. "Everything Phoenix Park promised."

"I'm relieved," Kincaid said. "How's it looking?"

"Much better than it was. Mr. Lavery is a very precise man. He doesn't let assumption and innuendo creep into conversation. He's holding their feet to the fire with every recitation."

"So you'll be back in Dublin soon."

"I'm counting on it," Grey said. "But maybe not soon."

Kincaid told her about the Long Room discovery, and with it, a possible motive for Marta's disappearance and even death. Maybe she was aiding the killers, even. As Marta on this side of the border, Mary on that side.

"You're obsessed with this unlikely doppelganger," Grey said. Well, I have news for you. I overheard Mr. Squish—"

"Mr. Squish?"

"Mr. Jackson. Who insists on being called 'Corporal.'" I'm sorry, Adam, I don't like him. Or maybe it's that I don't trust him. Probably doesn't matter."

"Back to the overhearing."

"During our meeting with Sergeant O'Fall and a woman—some kind of investigator, criminal division, I think. Mr. Squi—Corporal Jackson was talking to this woman in the hallway. About Mary Clery."

"And?"

"They were talking about her body. Every limb pulled from its sockets. Burned at the stake. The unidentified victim. The woman without a face."

"Any idea how they know it's her?"

"They were talking about her teeth. Which means, Adam, that it can't be Marta Carney. Mary Clery is not Marta Carney. And Marta is still alive."

"THEY'VE SENT NOTHING OUR way about identifying this

Mary Clery," McDermott told Kincaid in the office. "And they haven't returned my calls."

"This is the first I've heard of any of this," Mother Catherine told Kincaid over the phone about the same subject. "You'd think the authorities would at least have the decency—"

"So no one's been by to interview you."

"Not since the blast," Mother Catherine said. "If I thought I'd been fooled before—"

"I think your life could be in jeopardy," Kincaid said. "Can you find somewhere else to stay?"

"Wouldn't they just follow me? Track me down?"

"At least go to the RUC."

"What did you do with those maps?"

"I have them," Kincaid said.

"You didn't turn them over?"

"No," Kincaid said. "I have trust issues with the people who replaced Constable Brugha and Sergeant O'Connell. And I didn't have time to seek out anyone else."

"WHY AREN'T YOU TAKING my calls?" Kincaid asked his mother. She turned away from the window and watched as he steadied himself into a chair.

"What happened to you? You're gimping about like a cripple."

"I was shot. And then bombed," Kincaid said. "If you'd have taken my calls—"

"I told you about police life," she said.

"If you knew what I knew about priest life—"

Evelyn turned back to the window, to snowflakes so sparse they were almost individual. "Where's the girl?" she asked.

"What girl?"

"The girl. The one you were here with the other day."

"You mean Marta."

"I don't remember her name."

"She left the Guards."

"Smart girl."

"She's gone missing, mum. We don't know where she is."

"She ran away. From you, do you think?"

Kincaid's cane slipped off the arm of the chair and hit the tile floor. He jumped, looked at his mother, lost in thought.

"Somebody will trip on that," she said.

Thirty Two

Kincaid stood at a mirror in a Dublin Castle lavatory. The voice after the door opened startled him. "We got a call from Marta's old neighbor. The woman with the daughter."

"Marisol." Kincaid parted a red eyelid.

"Says a suspicious car has been lurking outside Marta's flat." McDermott looked in the mirror at Kincaid. "Getting enough sleep?"

"Guards still paying Marta's rent?"

"We are. Landlord is still leaving it be."

"What's suspicious about the car?" Kincaid almost turned away from the mirror.

"Not the type of car generally seen in that neighborhood. *Or* the overactive imagination of a habitual imbiber."

"Don't be so hard on her," Kincaid said.

"She *was* a big help with Charlie Mangan."

"You want me to drive round and have a look?"

"I asked Fields to go with you. He will be armed. Just a precaution."

"Should I be?"

"You are armed, Adam."

Kincaid turned to McDermott, who tapped the side of his head.

"The other victims," Kincaid said. "Were they in any court proceedings?"

"Which other victims?"

"Crucifix Killer. All Saints Slayer. The Republic's share."

"In the Courts?"

"Yes."

"Circuit, district, criminal? Which?"

"I don't know."

"They had no convictions, if that's what you mean," McDermott said. "The Monsignor—Gwynedd—had some traffic things. But—"

"I don't mean that. I mean, were they ever *witnesses*? In any kind of proceeding."

"We can find out. Another common thread?"

"They weren't mapmakers, or map transporters, not like in the North," Kincaid said. "But they were killed like martyrs just the same. *Martyr* means *witness*."

KINCAID AND FIELDS HEARD the muffled, unmistakable pops. Fields ran up the stairs. Kincaid hobbled up them, landing on the second floor as Fields bent down to someone in the doorway of Marisol's flat. He stood and raised his sidearm. Kincaid watched him enter the apartment.

"All clear, Inspector," he heard.

Kincaid bent down best he could to Alyson. Her eyes stared past him. He put his fingers on her neck. "Poor girl," he said.

"Went out through the fire escape," Fields said, emerging from a bedroom.

"Her mother—"

"No one else here, Inspector."

Kincaid stood and stepped carefully over Alyson and went to the bedroom window, which overlooked a leafy, quiet back street.

"Shall I call it in?" Fields asked, a telephone receiver in his hand. Kincaid stared out the window. "Inspector?"

"That look like a BRW over there?" Kincaid asked.

"From here."

"You see it pull up?"

"No. But I wasn't looking."

"We're here on a suspicious car call, and you're not paying attention to the cars?"

"My apologies, sir. I was examining the fire escape."

Kincaid looked at Alyson. "Did you get the time we heard the shots?"

"Yes, Inspector."

Kincaid looked back out the window. "Don't call it in. Not yet."

"But sir. She's—"

"Wanting us to find her killer," Kincaid said to Alyson. "Go downstairs and get the plates on that BRW. Keep your sidearm poised."

"Think it's the killer's?"

"Everyone's at work. And it's certainly out of place in this neighborhood."

"Not many around, period," Fields said. "I've only seen a couple."

Kincaid watched from the window until he saw Fields on the street peering through binoculars. He heard footsteps in the hallway. Marisol? He went to stop her before she saw her daughter's body. He stepped over Alyson and into the hallway but it wasn't Marisol he saw.

"Back away please, sir." The bearded man turned to see Fields at the hallway stairs with his sidearm drawn. "Gardaí, sir. Now please, put your hands over your head and back away."

"I've done nothing wrong," the man said, his voice low and sparse.

"I followed him in, Inspector," Fields said.

The man fidgeted but kept his hands at his sides.

"Hands over your head." Fields moved in, turned the man around, stood him against the wall. Kincaid walked up to them and stared at the bearded man's eyes.

KINCAID AND MCDERMOTT PEERED through the interrogation room window.

"No name, no ID, no fingerprints on file," McDermott said. "Think he pulled the trigger?"

"Or showed up to make sure the job was done. What about the car, the plates?"

"A BRW registered to 'BRW Limited.'"

"The car maker?"

"We checked. But it's not them," McDermott said. "Their legal counsel expressed concern about the use of their name."

"Car was parked across the street from Marta's place," Kincaid said.

"That's what Fields said. We haven't found it yet., but even if we do, we've got nothing tying it to any crime."

Kincaid looked at the suspect. "Why no solicitor?" he asked.

"Says he has nothing to hide."

"Does he remind you of anyone?"

McDermott studied the man. "Not right off. Someone in mind?"

"A clean-shaven someone with innocent spectacles." Kincaid bent his head toward the window glass.

"Who? The suspense is killing me."

"It's just a hunch," Kincaid said. "I don't want to say anything until I know more. Mind if I—" He nodded toward the room.

"All yours," McDermott said.

KINCAID SAT ACROSS FROM the suspect.

"I told you. Them. My name is Robert. Robert Mann." The man paused. "Why are you staring at me?"

"When did you change it?" Kincaid asked.

"What do you mean, *change it*?"

"To Robert Mann."

"I haven't changed anything."

"How about the beard?" Kincaid said.

"A man has a right to wear a beard."

"I just wondered when you started wearing it."

"You must be crazy, hallucinating, or confusing me with someone else," Mann said. "I've sported a beard for years.

"ANNE ASKEW," SR. GREY said over the phone. "Our first *Protestant* martyr."

"Did you know martyr means *witness*?" Kincaid asked.

"Among other things."

"I didn't. Until Mattie told me."

"Anne Askew refused to be a witness. Her tormentors wanted her to out fellow Protestants, including Catherine of Aragon, the Queen. She was tied to the racks, knees, shoulders, and hips ripped from their sockets. She had to be carried to the pyre."

"Was Mary Clery Protestant?"

"I've no idea. Mr. Squish and I aren't talking anymore."

"So you haven't shared this theory?"

"Of course not. Well—I did share it with Mr. Lavery. He was positively captivated. He even added a few details, including Anne's bravery as the flames surrounded her. She refused to scream, even in all that pain. She was also a great challenger of male rule. Mr. Lavery is quite the historian."

"Just so long as he's quite the barrister," Kincaid said. "McDermott talk to you yet?"

"About what?"

"He wanted me to wait."

"Wait about what?"

"To tell you," Kincaid said.

"Well, you can't wait now."

"We walked in on a shooting. The girl, Alyson."

"Oh no," Grey said. "Was she hurt?"

"She was killed."

"Oh dear God."

"Fields and I were checking on a suspicious car."

"The getaway car?" Grey asked.

"Hard to say. It was outside Marta's place. Been showing up, said Alyson's mam. It was gone by the time Fields and I emerged with our suspect."

"So you have someone in custody? What about the weapon?"

"Can't find it, nor any evidence he used it. So—we won't be able to hold him for long," Kincaid said.

"He have a name?"

"Robert A. Mann."

"How onomastically convenient," Grey said. "How—I hate to ask—but how is Marisol—that was her name, right—how is she taking this?"

"Hysterically. She's gone to stay with family in Spain."

"Poor woman. First her man, now her child. Was this related to Marta?"

"I thought so, at first. But none of the dots connect."

"So this Mister Mann—not Alyson's killer?"

"McDermott doesn't think so. And I have my doubts. But he was in Alyson's building, right after the shooting."

"She was shot—my God. In her own home," Grey said.

"Answering the door."

"Well who is he, Adam? This apparition?"

KINCAID AND MCDERMOTT SAT and stood, respectively, in Chief Inspector Greevey's office.

"No more information about the Clery woman?" Greevey asked.

"I've been in regular touch with the RUC, sir," McDermott said. "The Special Branch is like a—how did Adam put it—a *rogue state*."

"How did Special Branch end up with this case?"

"Same way they ended up with Sister Grey," Kincaid said. "By hijacking Sergeant O'Connell's office. I hear tell they like the County Down location, with its republican majority. Makes a good perch for IRA intelligence gathering."

"Pardon the pun, but this is beyond the pale," Greevey said. "Friendly cross-border relations—"

"Only help Provisionals and other IRA scum, in their mind," Kincaid said.

"Just keep doing what you can, then," Greevey said. "Not why I called you in here anyway."

McDermott looked at Kincaid as Greevey opened a folder on his desk and passed each man the same copy. "That's a summary of testimony Alexander Baldwin gave during a hearing in the criminal courts. As you can see from the top of the sheet, the defendant was one Brenden Robert Wryth."

"Baldwin?" McDermott said. "Some kind of expert witness?"

"For the defense," Greevey said.

"Defense?" Kincaid said.

"I thought you'd be surprised," Greevey said. "I certainly was. Dr. Baldwin made mincemeat out of the case our department spent over a year helping build. Wryth walked. His victims—well, I can't imagine how they ended up."

"Says here Dr. Baldwin found no evidence of psychological harm to the victims," McDermott said.

"Harm that was, in fact, evidence of sexual abuse," Greevey said. "No harm, ergo no abuse."

"I don't believe it," Kincaid said. "Somebody fabricated this thing." He tossed the document onto Greevey's desk.

"I understand how you feel. I guarantee the rest of the department—many of them his students at Templemore—will be in a state of catalepsy—"

"You have to release this ráiméis to the entire department?"

"Ráiméis or not, it's motive. SDU has to have it. CDU has to have it. Technical has to have it," Greevey said. "The whole department's got to know."

"The press, sir?" McDermott asked.

"It doesn't have to go to the press."

"Leave the man's reputation in tatters, this bloody rubbish, if it goes anywhere," Kincaid said.

"It was your idea," Greevey said.

"My idea?"

"Wasn't it Adam's idea that we look at old court files?" Greevey asked McDermott, who nodded slowly.

"So you found this and suddenly it's a motive for the man's murder?" Kincaid said. "A man beloved by gardaí across this entire country?"

"It was his professional *opinion*," Greevey said. "He wasn't an advocate here. He was just an expert witness who examined some victims. *Alleged* victims, I suppose I should say."

Kincaid tried to calm his thrumming fingers. "Fine, then," he said. He stood, slowly, his leg hurting more than usual. "Destroy his legacy. He's out of our lives, anyway."

"Adam, we aren't destroying his legacy," McDermott said. "Your hunch about some sort of vigilantism *may* be right."

ORIGINALLY, THE TWO PHYSICIAN victims—one a psychiatrist, the other a generalist—had no apparent connection to the Catholic Church. But now that Baldwin emerged as a witness in a case against Wryth, Kincaid wondered how Dr. Robert Boyd fit the role as witness. He reviewed the old files—patient and hospital records, witness statements, photographs, fingerprints, the sparse physical evidence tucked away in folders and boxes. An offhanded comment scribbled in a detective's notes caught his eye.

I wouldn't have handled it that way.

"Been hearing great things about you," Detective Sergeant Philip Casey told Kincaid over the phone. "Long time since the Boyd case. Seems like eons ago."

Old notes, what was the context, Casey asked. Looked like interviews at a hospital, or a clinic.

I wouldn't have handled it that way.

"I don't know why I just jotted that down," Casey said. "You made Inspector."

"I did," Kincaid said, while he thought *I may be seeing why you haven't.* "Could the remark have come from another physician?"

"I don't think so," Casey said. "I may be absent-minded on occasion, but I'd have followed up that sort of comment."

"What about from a nurse?"

"Would I have followed it up then?" Casey took a deep breath. "It pains me to admit, with a few years hindsight, probably not. Especially if she was speaking about a doctor, like Boyd."

KINCAID AND A BANGHARDA stood on the rain-dashed steps of a Sheriff Street flat watching children run and scream, kick a half-inflated ball, scurry in and out of a burned car, and rip the cotton from a tossed-out couch, chasing each other with the wet, dreary snow.

"Look at them kids," the bangharda said. "Haven't changed a bit."

Kincaid breathed in the pungent, spicy smell of port and wine stored in nearby warehouses.

"That, neither," the bangharda said. She looked at the key in the door. "Back then, I always let myself in."

The door opened inward to a young-but-grim looking woman whose face ignited. "Fin?" she asked. She stepped back. "Oh, Fin. Ain't you the fine thing."

"Maggie O'Hearn, I want you to meet Inspector Kincaid. *Detective* Inspector Kincaid."

"Pleasure. Thank you for meeting with us," Kincaid said.

"I can't believe me eyes," Maggie said to Fionnuala. "All this time, and such a fierce cut ya bring. If only your mam—"

A different ball, mud-greyed and tight, hit Fionnuala in the leg.

"Hey!" Maggie yelled at the kids.

The bangharda kicked the ball right back.

"Come in, why don't ya." As they stepped inside the doorway, to dry heat, cramped furniture, and old cooking smells, "you didn't say you'd be bringing an *inspector*," Maggie said.

"Inspector Kincaid is in charge of a very big case," Fionnuala said. "Maggie and I grew up together."

"Like sisters, we was." Maggie hugged Fin. "Ask your mam, rest her soul."

"I was in Laurence's Mansions, Maggie in Brigid's Gardens," Bangharda Fionnuala said.

"Terrible lot of difference that made. Ah, it's so good to see you. So good."

Kincaid cleared his throat and shuffled pen and notepad.

"Yes, well. I can take a hint," Maggie said. "What might I be helpin' you with? This very big case? Is that why you're here? I don't know how I could help with anything like that."

"Your daughter," Kincaid said.

Maggie's face changed. Fionnuala intervened.

"Lilly must be thirteen by now," she said. "I haven't seen her sweet face—"

"Lilly is dead," Maggie said. "She died last year. She was fourteen."

"Oh dear God," Fionnuala said.

"I'm very sorry," Kincaid said. "I don't—"

"How did she die?"

"By her own hand."

The revelation almost toppled the tall bangharda. "Why—why didn't you say anything?" Fionnuala gasped. "Why didn't I know?"

Maggie pressed her fist into her cheek and pushed away a trickling dampness. "You're gone a long time," she said. "You've moved on."

"That's no reason—"

"Garda." Kincaid touched Fionnuala's arm.

"It's all right," Maggie said. "I've grieved, I've let her go. But how on Earth did Lilly bring you here? Fin's letter only mentioned her doctor—"

"Robert Boyd," Kincaid said.

"No, if that's what you're to ask me. No," Maggie caterwauled. "He didn't report it. He didn't say a damned thing, just let it by, like nuthin' ever happened."

"So Boyd did examine Lilly?" Kincaid said.

"Examined her and then some. She was bleedin' mind ya, bleedin' out here." Maggie waved her hands between her legs. "Gave her something to stop the bleeding, he did. But he didn't care how it happened. Told us not to make too much of it. That the Church would take care of us, but only if we was quiet."

"So he gave her a shot, pills, what type of medicine?" Kincaid asked.

"It was pills. I don't think Lilly could have stood no shot. Not like that. Not like she was."

"How long after she saw the Father—"

"He left her for dead," Maggie said. "Right here. Right here in this god-forsaken flat."

"So you rushed her to hospital?" Kincaid said.

"As quickly as we could. Godforsaken flat, maybe, but me neighbors are all family. No one could believe what happened. He come to put the ashes on her forehead. He come to administer a sacrament." Maggie was close to hyperventilating as the realization re-dawned on her.

"Wryth?" Kincaid asked. "Was that his name?"

"Brenden or Brandon," Maggie said. "Father Brandon. Wore glasses."

"Did you report any of this to anyone but Dr. Boyd?"

"We wasn't allowed. No. Not allowed to say anythin'. I wish Fin had been here. I wish to God Fin had been here. Look at her, so tall and strong. And me, so small and weak."

Fin took Maggie's hand and squeezed, in a discreet way that look both professional and loving.

Kincaid finished jotting down these notes.

"You were never interviewed by the Guards?"

"No, Inspector. The only person even talked to us was the duty nurse that afternoon," Maggie said. "The one you talked to."

"The nurse, the nurse. If you don't remember, but—do you remember—the name of the medicine Boyd gave your daughter?"

Maggie looked away, took some time to think. "Started with a T," she said. "Seemed like a long name."

"Tranexamic acid?" Kincaid said.

"Maybe. I don't remember. I just remember the doctor said it was for heavy vaginal bleeding. And that's what Lilly had."

Thirty Three

God, the flat again. And on the eve of the discovery of such a horrible miss. Kincaid tossed his soft-leather briefcase on a chair. Nothing on the telly so he turned on the radio. Poured a scotch neat. Sat in the bigger chair, sipped, stared out the window at the night. So tired. He closed his eyes.

So Boyd was the first victim of the Crucifix Killer, bloodless like the rest, but because he was strapped to the cross, not nailed. The others got doses of tranexamic acid, the same coagulant Boyd prescribed Lilly O'Hearn to make her bloodless, too. Coincidence? If not, how did the killer know what medication she took?

Time now for the groovy bábóg from Spidéil, said Terry Wogan, on the clear signal that swept out some of the loneliness and interrupted his train of thought.

"You remember that famous introduction," another voice intervened. "Seán Bán Breathnach was the innovator behind *Popseó na Máirte,* the revolutionary music show Mr. Wogan introduced for twenty six weeks, three years ago. Seán talks to us now about his decision to join the newest entry in Irish radio, Raidió na Gaeltachta . . . "

Thoughts. Sleep. Keys.

Key. The key in the O'Hearn woman's front door. "I always let myself in," her childhood friend recalled. Why not the killer, too?

Kincaid's eyes fluttered open when he felt something hitting his leg. Hitting it harder, till it hurt. Kicking it. He jolted up. A hand restrained his shoulder.

"There, now," the ski mask said.

Kincaid recognized the voice of the short man from the train stop near Newry and it showed.

"Remember me, do ya?"

Three other masked intruders surrounded him. Kincaid tried to stand, but another masked man pressed his shoulder. "No need ta get up for us," he said.

"As we was sayin' Garda Kincaid, you have someone we want. Harborin' a fugitive from the North, you are. Me mates and I want him returned."

"We don't have Brenden Wryth," Kincaid said. At least, not officially, he thought.

"That's funny," the short man said. "You was just speakin' to him. Marchin' him across Synge Street, near your mot's place."

"That individual has been identified," Kincaid said. "His name is not Brenden Wryth."

"What?" the second intruder said. "Running under an alias now, is he? Didn't used to have a beard, either, especially not a big, bushy, hidey one like that."

"We could force the issue," the short man said, leaning into Kincaid's face. But another small person, slight in build, laid a gloved hand on the short man's arm.

"Adam." A familiar voice. The small hand pulled off the mask. Kincaid gasped.

"Marta," he said.

"You *do* have him," Marta said. She took off a glove. "But you might not know it because most pictures of Brenden Wryth are decades old. And the newer ones are grainy garbage." She turned toward the window onto the street below. "Then again, you do have an uncanny eye for faces. You don't see any resemblance between the bearded Robert Montgomery Mann and the boyish Brenden Robert Wryth?"

"You know that's his alias?" Kincaid asked, breaking his open-mouthed stare. "How did you get—" He thought about saying "involved with these terrorists" but settled for attenuated tact. "Involved?"

"The same way you did," Marta said. "Only I *left* the law to make things right."

"Maybe what I mean is—why?"

"Oldest motive known to man or woman," Marta said. "Revenge."

"For what? Did he harm you?"

"Do ya need to be tellin' him anything?" the short man said. Marta ignored him. She took off her mask.

"Brenden Wryth molested my sister," she said. "She was his first victim, best anyone can tell."

Kincaid shuddered under the pressure on his shoulder.

"I didn't know you had a sister. I don't know what to say."

"You really don't know, do you, Adam? You don't know how this monster will slip the bonds of justice once again, especially if he's allowed to stay with the guardians of justice."

Seamus O'Dowd removed his mask. Kincaid looked up at him.

"You—"

"Justice, Inspector. Me. All of us, when we were lads. Altar boys, mams who wanted priests. Easy prey."

"Why do you think we took up arms?" the short man said.

"Charlie Mangan was protecting Wryth," Marta said. "Or rather, Wryth's map-making scheme. For the British government, or at least, under their shadowy auspices."

"Are you the ones doing the killing, then?" Kincaid asked. "Did you kill Mangan?"

"No, Adam," Marta said.

"Then who's doing it?" Kincaid said.

"Why do you think I know?"

"A hunch," Kincaid said.

"Well—your hunches are somewhat legendary," Marta said.

"What about Alyson, the girl?"

"We figure the man you have in custody for the girl's death," Marta said. "But you'll never prove it. You won't find powder residue on his hands because he wore gloves. You won't find the gun because it's at the bottom of a river. You won't find the man, because he's a practiced phantom, ever so skilled in evading justice."

Kincaid tried to stand, only stiffening the pressure on his shoulder. "You're involved in this up to your neck, Marta. Necks have a funny way of getting noosed and chopped, if you haven't noticed."

"I'm not directly involved," Marta said. "I have no interest in sending a message. But I understand those who do."

"Those, who? Who are they?"

"I doubt you'd believe me, so why does it matter?"

"How much more unbelievable can all of this get?"

Marta walked to the window and looked out over the street. "*Camera stellata.* Have you heard the term?"

"Something to do with photography?"

"A camera is a chamber, Adam. Stellata refers to the great stellar out-there." She looked up at the night sky. "The stars. A star chamber. Do you know what that is?"

"Vigilantes," Kincaid said.

"I prefer—" She turned to him. "*Extra-judicial enforcers.* As it was four hundred years ago, when a Star Chamber in England made sure the well-connected did not evade justice."

"Are you part of this?" Kincaid asked.

"We—" the short man said.

"Shut up," Marta said.

"I just think he should know—"

"I said, shut up."

“You quit the Guards over the Heavy Gang,” Kincaid said. “So what—so you could form your own—heavy gang?”

“So I’m a hypocrite? That’s what you’re thinking?” Marta said.

“I’m thinking you’re an accessory to multiple homicides. You had access to The Book of Kells. The lettering. You could have copied it. Traced it.”

“I would never do that,” Marta said.

“Or looked the other way when one of your gang came up from the tunnel, just like I’m sure you did when they brought Baldwin in.”

“That’s a heavy charge.”

“And the manutergia, the carefully-reproduced lettering?”

“I would never use tracing paper on a rare text,” Marta said.

“It had to have been traced.”

“Not by me.”

“Somebody close to the Book, with access to it, had to—”

“My hands aren’t that steady, Adam, to trace from a photograph or heaven forbid, the text itself. Too many years in the Gardaí, I suppose. Too many bombs, ringing in my ears. Ask Sister.”

“Sister Grey?”

“That bombing case we worked. I couldn’t even copy the threat letters,” Marta said. “She had the steadier hands, even under rubber gloves. Speaking of explosions.” Marta went to the front window. “Adam.” She looked at the other men. “Let him stand.” He stood, stretched, and tried to shake the pain from his leg. She nodded him over to look outside. "You recognize that car? The one under the street light?"

"The suspicious BRW," he said.

"Which stands for Brenden Robert Wryth, who would be missing it now if he weren't in Garda custody," she said. "Seamus?"

"Eight, sharp," he said.

"Wait with me, Adam." She tugged him back from the window.

The blast sent a fireball into the air that cracked the window and scorched the leaves and forced a wave of heat close to their faces. Alarms flared with distorted sounds as the flames settled and the car burned.

"We don't have much time," Marta said. "So I'll be brief. If we don't have Brenden Wryth, also known as Robert Mann, in our custody one week from today, a larger explosion will occur. Much larger."

"So you'd kill innocent people just to get this wanker?" Kincaid said.

"We already have, Inspector," the short man said.

"Really." Kincaid looked at Marta. "Is that true?"

Marta looked at the short man. "You open your fat mouth one more time—"

"Is it true?"

She turned away. Kincaid grabbed her shoulder. "Did you kill Kevin O'Connell? Mich Doherty?"

She shrugged him off.

"Did you?"

"That was IRA, killin' a couple traitors," the short man said. "No secret, when you know who you know."

"What about Iain Brugha?" Kincaid asked.

The way Seamus O'Dowd was staring at the floor suggested the answer.

"You did, didn't you? You murdered an innocent man, you and these hooligans." Kincaid lunged at Marta, spun her around, and stumbled. She fell back against the couch. Seamus pulled a pistol. All three men were upon him.

"What's happened to you?" Kincaid said. "You kill innocent people—"

Marta wiped blood from her lip.

"Nothing innocent about the Royal Ulster Constabulary," Seamus said. "Or the Guards."

Marta pushed herself up. "Let him go." When they wouldn't, "Let him go!" she insisted. "He's our messenger." They left him standing in the middle of his living room. At the door, "One week, Ad—Inspector," Marta said.

Seamus went to put away his pistol. He looked at it, then showed it to Kincaid. "I gave the sister back her gun," he said. "I'm not a liar."

After the door closed, Kincaid hobbled to a locked drawer, took out his own pistol, grabbed a cane, hurried with a limp. Down the hall, elevator too slow, down the stairs, gripping the handrail but nearly slipping twice. He rushed through the lobby and into the street. He felt the heat from the burning BRW, smelled gas and scorched rubber, heard a siren in the distance.

MCDERMOTT AND FIELDS SHOWED up at Kincaid's flat less than an hour later. Fields inspected the living area while Technical Bureau dusted for fingerprints and in the street below, photographed the remains of Wryth's car.

"Outlandish claims all around," McDermott said. "Wryth has been causing havoc for years. Why didn't the Gardaí or the RUC ever connect him to this Mann fellow?"

"Why didn't we connect him to Lilly O'Hearn?" Kincaid said. "Or Charlie Mangan? Or Marta?"

"Marta. I can't bloody believe it," McDermott said. "Any of it. A terrorist now?"

"A week," Kincaid said. "That's how long we have."

"I'm sorry about the girl, Lilly," McDermott said. "And Alyson Penner, too. Terrible tragedies and I'm sorry we missed out on helping them."

"I'm sorry, too," Kincaid said.

KNOCK KNOCK. MCDERMOTT AT Kincaid's office door. "And guess which solicitor handled the deed poll for the name change."

"Ruadhán Moloney."

"One in the same," McDermott said. "In the employ of the Catholic Archdiocese."

"Friends in high places."

"So Brenden Wryth started over as Robert Mann," McDermott said. "With help from a Church solicitor."

"No doubt prompted by Monsignor Mulvaney blowing the whistle in Armagh," Greevey said.

"But true to form, rather than turn him in, the Church cast him out," Kincaid said. "Wryth would be dead or in prison if it weren't for his maps and his clients."

"Sure that's not why this group wants him?"

"It's not why Marta wants him," Kincaid said. "Maybe the others."

"And why does Marta want him? I still don't quite grasp that," Greevey said.

"Wryth molested her sister," Kincaid said.

"I didn't know she had a sister."

"I didn't either. Marta said she was Wryth's first victim."

"So she *is* part of this ritual execution squad," McDermott said.

"She said some kind of star chamber was responsible. But she wouldn't admit being part of it," Kincaid said.

"One thing's for certain: we're not handing Wryth over to Marta and her gang," McDermott said. "They want him North, they'll have to settle for extradition. We have nothing we can hold him on here, anyway."

SISTER GREY CALLED TO announce no forthcoming charges over the murder of Mother Stephanie Teresa.

"I'm relieved," Kincaid said. "I never thought they'd charge you, but—"

"You can't imagine how relieved I am," she said. "Of course, if they ever find my gun—"

"You're coming back straight away," Kincaid said.

"I am. A few things to take care of here first."

"Yes?"

"Loose ends."

"The Order must want you the hell out of there."

"Nice way to put it, Adam. Yes, it has been hell. And I want the hell out of here. But first things first. So—what's *your* big news? McDermott insisted *you* tell me."

"Marta and Wryth," Kincaid said. "She showed up, unannounced. We found him. And the missing connection in the Boyd murder."

"Tell me."

He did. Everything. Right up to Seamus O'Dowd's comment about returning her gun.

"I'm so sorry, Adam," Grey said. "Sorry to have left you alone to face a grieving mother. And those wolves. No to mention that sicko Wryth. The Guard's aren't turning him over to Marta, surely."

"If we let him walk, it would be just the same."

"But the Gardaí isn't releasing him, right?" Grey said.

"Not yet," Kincaid said. "But a crafty solicitor can easily show we have nothing to hold him on. Most of his crimes, *reported* crimes anyway, occurred in the North."

"Where he hid amid the chaos, camouflaged in spoils from the war," Sr. Grey concluded.

Thirty Four

"There will be no handing over of Wryth," Greevey told Kincaid and McDermott.

"I've already explained that, sir," McDermott said.

"Did you communicate our position to Marta?"

"Her group is not backing down," Kincaid said.

"We'll extradite him," Greevey said. "Let the North deal with him."

"In one week?" McDermott said. "The Gardaí Commissioner has to sign a warrant from the North. Which he would be unlikely to do even if he had one to sign."

"Why not?" Kincaid asked.

"Political offense exception," McDermott said. "We cannot extradite political prisoners."

"Molesting children is a political offense?" Kincaid asked.

"Not the molesting," McDermott said. "The map making."

Kincaid went for copy of the 1965 Extradition Act on a bookshelf next to his desk.

"I have to agree. Wryth could have picked a lot of ways to buy protection," Greevey said. "With the maps, he picked a political way. We cannot extradite if the offense is political or connected to politics."

"The terrorism loophole," McDermott said.

"The court might even grant Wryth political asylum," Greevey said. "I'd hate to risk that outcome."

"We can't keep holding him without a proper warrant, regardless," McDermott said. "Adam?"

"I'm reading."

"Then you see how convoluted it all is," McDermott said.

"Ever get a provisional warrant?" Kincaid said.

"Never," McDermott said.

"I handled one a few years ago," Greevey said. "Don't recall the circumstances."

"Urgency," Kincaid said. "Section Forty Nine," he read. "A justice of the District Court, on the sworn information of a member of the Garda Síochána not below the rank of inspector —"

"At least we have that covered," McDermott said.

"If said inspector-or-above-rank person has reason to believe a warrant has been issued by a judicial authority in the North for the arrest of a person accused of an indictable offense under the law of the North, but that the warrant is *not yet in his possession* —"

"It says that?" Greevey leaned in.

"And that he has received a request made on the ground of urgency by or on behalf of a police force of the North for the issue of a warrant for the arrest of that person—"

"We've received no such request from the RUC," Greevey said.

"No, we haven't," Kincaid said. He re-read the passage. "But it says by or *on behalf of* a police force. If I made the request, based on Wryth's connection with the witch burnings, Sister Mongilly, the rest—"

"You'd have to testify, Adam," Greevey said. "Swear an oath."

"Barrister would have to get into the facts of those killings," McDermott said. "And attack the details of Adam's investigation, if he were to have any chance of proving the warrant request frivolous."

"I can swear that Sergeant Kevin O'Connell wanted Wryth," Kincaid said. "So did Constable Michelle Doherty."

"It's a gamble," Greevey said. "The High Court could still rule political offense. We have to overcome any possibility Wryth could be granted asylum as a political prisoner."

"Why don't we just bring Marta and her group in?" McDermott said. "Put an end to this madness."

"We know how large her group is?" Greevey said. "Any idea the identity of its members?"

"I only know one—Seamus O'Dowd, PIRA man. The others wear masks."

Greevey rubbed his chin. "Okay. Then I think our best chance is to get him out of our jurisdiction."

KINCAID SAT ACROSS FROM Brenden Wryth, alias Robert Mann, taking notes in the interrogation room at Dublin Castle.

"Brenden Robert Wryth," Kincaid said. "BRW."

"A car. So what?" Wryth smirked.

"A car they blew up. Your car," Kincaid said. "Masked bunch. Wants you back in Northern Ireland."

Wryth fidgeted, looked away, feigned disinterest.

"They want me to turn you over. Or they blow something else up."

"What the fuck am I supposed to do about that?" Wryth said.

"Nice language for a priest."

"Who said I was a priest?"

"The deed poll Ruadhán Moloney handled."

"Moloney, Moloney. Am I supposed to know him?"

"Just know that he died a wretched death," Kincaid said. "For helping you."

"I know what you're getting at," Wryth said. "It's why you're holding me." He extended his hand and placed it over Kincaid's knuckles. The detective stopped writing. The other man's hand felt rough. "I'd remember such things if they were true," Wryth whispered. "A Father remembers," and his voice dove into a nearly-inaudible whisper, "all his boys."

Kincaid withdrew his hand, paused, then jammed it into Wryth's neck.

"Adam." McDermott opened the door.

Kincaid retracted. Wryth coughed, rubbed his throat. A man and a woman walked in behind McDermott.

"Inspector Kincaid," the man said. "I hope you weren't assaulting my client."

"Barrister, Adam," McDermott said. "Solicitor, too."

"Brian Porter," the man said, extending his hand.

"Kay Booth," the woman said, also shaking Kincaid's hand. "Mr. Wryth's solicitor."

"I thought you didn't need representation," Kincaid told Wryth.

"I don't know these people," he said. "I didn't hire them."

"A benefactor hired me," Kay Booth said. "I hired Mr. Porter."

"And this benefactor is?" McDermott asked.

"Privileged," Booth said. "Even Mr. Porter doesn't know."

"I don't need a barrister," Wryth said. "My name is Robert Mann and I've done nothing wrong."

"You're about to be extradited and your name has only been Robert Mann for what—two years, give or take?" Booth said. "Unless you want a one-way ticket to Belfast in shackles, you'll permit us to do our jobs."

Kincaid looked at McDermott. "Guess I'd best tell Marta," he said.

"Marta?" Wryth asked. Kincaid stood.

"You know her, too?" Kincaid said.

"I'd have to see her. Girls," Wryth drawled, "do not serve on the altar."

KINCAID MET MARTA IN St. Stephen's Green. "This man is slime," he said. "I can't see why anyone would take up his case or his cause."

"The Church isn't paying his lawyers," Marta said. "They've washed their hands of him."

"His solicitor said a *benefactor,*" Kincaid said. "Who has the money to mount a vigorous habeas. I need to show urgency to the court if you want him extradited."

"You want me to testify we're going to bomb Dublin Castle unless the North gets him back?" Marta asked.

"Is that the plan?"

"No. But it always sounds more urgent when government buildings are threatened."

"I'd arrest you right now if you weren't holding us hostage," Kincaid said. "I hope you know that."

"I know it."

"So what do I do? Tell them you killed Brugha. That you mean business."

"The RUC constable?" Marta said. She hesitated. "We didn't kill him."

"But you know who did."

"Charlie Mangan may have had something to do with it."

"Your boyfriend," Kincaid said.

"He wasn't my boyfriend. He was a source—of convenience. He led me and my ragtags to our target, never suspecting a demure librarian."

"If he wasn't your boyfriend, how did your bracelet end up in Belfast? Where I almost lost my arse because someone wanted someone—Mary Clery—dead."

"I lost that bracelet. Maybe Charlie took it." She pursed her lips and looked away. "When Mary Clery went missing, the British Army sent Charlie up there to keep an eye on their investment, as Mary had before him. Mary, the perfect little daffodil—who could kill a man with her bare hands. Charlie said they were shocked when she vanished."

"Must have taken more than one man to rip her to shreds, then," Kincaid said.

"From what I know of her, that's an understatement," Marta said.

"I figured the office manager, Nic Cionnaith, for the eye keeper. Know anything about her?"

"Charlie didn't like her. Complained the Agency hadn't sent Clery's replacement."

"The temp agency."

"British Intelligence too, Adam. Just like Mary, just like Charlie. *He* thought Nic Cionnaith had made him, that she was RUC. Special Branch. Whatever."

"I don't think so," Kincaid said.

"I wondered if she wasn't British Intelligence herself," Marta said. "Wondered if that wasn't why she got testy with Charlie, acting like he shouldn't question the state of things, acting like it wasn't his *place*."

"Apparently someone agreed with her," Kincaid said.

Thirty Five

Kincaid pulled the maps and sketches from the envelope Mother Catherine rescued in the convent blast. He set various crime scene photos next to it.

"Inspector?" A uniformed police woman stood at his office door.

"Good morning, Garda Shire."

"Good morning, sir. Superintendent McDermott asked me to drop this by."

Kincaid took the folder.

"He said it's all they could get without a judge's order."

"Thank you." She stood while Kincaid read. "Disbursement inquiries to Offices of Terence Byrne, Chartered Accountant."

Some kind of lawsuit. Case files sealed. Note in pen next to solicitors' names, "Handled cases for the Archdiocese."

"Inspector."

He looked up. "Yes."

"This may seem a foolish question."

"No such thing," Kincaid said. "Question away."

"You never call me bangharda. Why not?"

"No need for the longer word," he said.

"Others use it."

Kincaid tapped his pencil. "They're old school," he said. "Back in the fifties—"

"When the TDs worried about us being horse-faced?" she said.

"And 'frumpish.'" Kincaid said. "I think that was the Dáil term."

"And plain. And not too good-looking, lest we run off with a man."

"You're a garda," Kincaid said. "No different word required."

She smiled. "Thank you, Inspector." And disappeared from his doorway.

Kincaid dialed McDermott's office. "What do you make of these court documents?"

"Some kind of settlement," McDermott said.

"More like a payoff."

"Aren't they all?"

"Nothing names the litigants," Kincaid said.

"I asked for anything with Byrne's name on it. I figure he wrote the checks, maybe helped structure the payments."

"How long for a magistrate's order?"

"Too long. Litigants would fight it. If the Church is involved, could take months, maybe longer."

"I'll try his brother again," Kincaid said, staring at the maps and crime scene photos.

"I REALLY DON'T KNOW how much more I can add, Inspector," Terry Byrne's brother explained at his home.

"You said your brother was an idealist."

"I didn't use that word, but I agree with it."

"He never expressed concern about clients, you know, finagling books, padding accounts, cheating on taxes? The things accountants see?"

"Those *are* the things accountants see," his brother said. "Common things. Terry wouldn't have mentioned them, at least not to me. He already thought his job was routine." He picked up a pipe on a smoking table and stuffed it with fragrant tobacco. "You think someone killed him to cover something up?"

"We think someone killed him because *he* covered something up."

"Terry?" He lit the pipe. "That's thick, Inspector. My brother was honest as they come."

"He ever mention the Archdiocese?"

"The Church? Now they're coverin' things up?" Before he set the pipe stem between his lips. "Mind?"

"It's your house." Kincaid looked across the room, at bookshelves, a filing cabinet, desk drawers.

"Your brother leave anything behind you could share? Anything connected with his work?"

"Everything went back to his clients or into the fire," the brother said. "To hear you talk, I'm glad it did."

A STENOGRAPHER SAT POISED to type Kincaid's testimony before the Dublin Metropolitan District Court. The detective inspector never took the grayish-white wigs and ceremonial vestments on the barristers and judges as seriously as tradition demanded, and so as not to betray this sentiment, he looked at everyone else in the room.

"If it please, My Lord," the barrister representing the Gardaí said to the judge. He looked at Kincaid. "What is your rank in the Gardaí, Mr. Kincaid?"

"Detective Inspector."

"And you are swearing under oath that, on behalf of the Royal Ulster Constabulary, you are requesting a warrant for the arrest of the man presently in Gardaí custody, Robert Montgomery Mann, formerly known as Brenden Robert Wryth?"

"Objection," Barrister Porter announced. "If it please My Lord, this man's *previous* identity has yet to be ascertained."

"We've provided the court with the relevant materials in the Section Twenty Five D supporting documents," the Gardaí barrister said.

"Objection is overruled," the court declared. "The witness may answer the question."

"You are requesting a warrant for the arrest of the man presently in Gardaí custody, Robert Montgomery Mann, formerly known as Brenden Robert Wryth?"

"Yes," Kincaid answered.

"You do not yet have the RUC warrant. Is that correct?"

"It is."

"Yes or no."

"Yes, that's correct," Kincaid said. "No, I don't have the warrant."

The barrister lowered his eyes. “Tell us about how you came to be involved with an RUC investigation of matters concerning Brenden Wryth.”

And so Kincaid did, detailing his conversations with Kevin O’Connell and Mich Doherty, and the status of both North and South serial homicides: investigations open, cases linked. O’Connell, he insisted, would have arrested Brenden Wryth had the opportunity presented.

“And your request is urgent?” the barrister continued.

“Yes.”

“Why is it urgent?”

Kincaid looked at McDermott, Mr. Porter and Mrs. Booth at their respective tables. Wryth was not in the courtroom.

“Inspector?” the Gardaí barrister asked.

“Mr. Wryth is a serial child molester,” Kincaid said. “He is suspected of at least three such offenses and one homicide in the Republic.”

“Objection, My Lord,” Porter declared. “The DPP has not charged my client with any crimes.”

“Sustained,” the bench commanded. “The witness will stay to the facts.”

“Again, Inspector Kincaid. What’s the urgency?”

“You have to ask?”

The barrister lowered his eyes and leaned toward Kincaid. “I’m on your side,” he muttered and stepped back.

“Wryth will re-offend,” Kincaid said loudly.

"My Lord," Mr. Porter interrupted. "I object to this entire line of questioning. It calls for ridiculous amounts of speculation, propped up by incendiary innuendo."

"So noted, so sustained."

The Gardaí barrister handed Porter, the judge, and Kincaid a copy of the pathologist's report on the death of Alyson Penner.

"Could you please explain to the Court the contents of that report."

"Markings and trauma consistent with sexual abuse were found on the body," Kincaid explained. "We believe that may have been the motive for her killing."

"My Lord. Objection. There is no physical evidence linking my client to that young woman's murder, or any other harm to her person, and he has not been so charged."

"Objection so noted, and so sustained."

"You found Mr. Wryth at the scene of the crime, did you not?" the Gardaí barrister asked Kincaid.

"We did."

"Objection again, My Lord. The State has no evidence my client possessed a firearm, the weapon used in this young woman's murder. And the girl could have been molested by her mother's boyfriend, or another individual."

"Noted and sustained."

"Boyfriend's name: Dan Faunt. Is that correct, Inspector?" the Gardaí lawyer asked.

"It is. Yes, I mean."

"And he was killed some time ago?"

"Yes."

"But the trauma on the decedent was recent, according to the pathologist."

"Yes," Kincaid answered.

"Could someone else have killed Alyson Penner on Brenden Wryth's behalf?"

"That's one theory," Kincaid said.

A few more questions later, and Mr. Porter presented his case. Initially reluctant to hire a barrister because he was guilty of no wrongdoing, Mr. Wryth only consented because he had no other way to fight this frivolous extradition request.

Porter kept to himself, meanwhile, that Wryth's mysterious benefactor insisted Porter *not* attempt to confirm or deny any RUC interest in a warrant for Wryth so as *not* to alert Belfast's Royal Courts of Justice to Wryth's detainment in the Republic.

Instead, Porter used the strategy Greevey feared, portraying Wryth as a valuable counter-operative in the war against IRA murderers. The child molestation charges, he insisted to the court, were trumped up to take this political refugee out of the fight.

Since Wryth's alleged crimes were never reported in the Republic, and therefore any physical evidence and witness statements were ostensibly locked away in Northern Ireland evidence rooms and file cabinets, the court was forced to discount Kincaid's testimony. Brenden Wryth, the court thereby declared, was a political refugee and therefore, a free man.

“BLOODY BASTARD,” MCDERMOTT SAID.

“He will be,” Kincaid said. “I’m sure that was the benefactor’s plan all along.”

“I suggested we put him into protective custody.”

“And true to form, Barrister Porter objected.,” Kincaid said.

McDermott looked at a report on Kincaid’s desk. “If your vigilante theory is correct, this so called free man could lead us to the All Saints Slayer.”

“I’m tempted to let them both be,” Kincaid said. “Killing all the accomplices. The criminal mastermind must be next.”

Kincaid’s phone rang.

“Greevey,” he told McDermott with his hand over the receiver. “Commissioner’s up in arms.”

“What else is new?”

“Body parts showing up at border stations. A hand here, a foot, an arm.”

“DEFINITELY HUMAN,” GREEVEY TOLD them in his office.

“Prints?”

“Waiting.”

“No indication of why. No calling cards with the packages.”

“I suspect we’ll know why when we know who,” Kincaid said.

Rapping on the door interrupted.

“Bangharda Shire,” McDermott said. “Looking lovely today as always.”

"I wish I had lovely news, Chief Inspector. Scotland Yard just received a leg."

Thirty Six

Kincaid studied the Polaroid photographs arranged on his desk. His instructions to each jurisdiction: position the body part for maximum exposure of each tattoo.

"That's one way to do it," McDermott said as he walked in.

"I didn't want to wait," Kincaid said. "Coroner's backlogged and getting each puzzle piece here—"

"Puzzle piece," McDermott said. "Funny way to put it."

"Our puzzle had all his fingers," Kincaid said. One hand was open to a tattooed palm, the other spread to tattoos on top of each finger that together formed a letter.

"Elaborate," McDermott said. "Different color inks. Where have I seen this before?"

Kincaid handed McDermott a crime scene photo from the Gwynedd murder.

"Ah, yes. The altar towels."

"Fingerprints come back yet?" Kincaid asked.

"No match. Our dismembered mystery man remains a mystery."

"Interpol empty-handed, too?"

"Nice pun, Adam."

"Some kind of spy? British Intelligence?"

"SDU is exploring that angle," McDermott said. "Most plausible possibility is Charlie Mangan—or the rest of him."

McDermott examined the photos of the body on Kincaid's desk. "Looks like it's waving or pointing."

"Has to be positioned this way to read the tattoos."

"D,I,S,C,I,P,U,L,U,M," McDermott read. "*Discipulum*. Another Latin word?"

"Means 'follower'. Of the good cross. *O bona crux,*" Kincaid said.

"Well then—the All Saints Slayer has stepped up his game."

"Or *her* game," Kincaid said.

KINCAID'S OFFICE PHONE WOULDN'T let him focus. First, Garda Fields with news of the surveillance.

"No movement outside Wryth's flat," Fields reported.

"You're sure he's still there. Didn't go out some obscure fire escape."

"Absolutely, Inspector."

"Any deliveries? Messages, whatever?"

"No. Place must be well stocked."

Next, the medical examiner with news the dismembered victim's body was complete and in one location and if the Inspector wanted to review it—

"Can you photograph it from above?" he asked.

"You mean, like an aerial shot?"

"Like a crime scene photo."

"It's on the table, sir."

"Positioned so each tattoo is clearly visible?"

"The fancy letters? We'd have to spread him out, Inspector. Autopsy table's too narrow."

"On the floor, then?"

"I can check."

Thirdly, a charge nurse called from his mother's care home.

"She was asking about you," the nurse said. "If I knew how you were doing."

"I can't recall the last time she asked about me," Kincaid said. "What are you feeding her?"

The nurse chuckled.

Finally, Sister Grey, returning his call.

"Busy connecting the dots, I take it," she said.

"Mattie O'Connell said you'd been held up," Kincaid said.

"Sister de la Guerra. You remember her."

"She turned up?"

"She wasn't really missing, just incommunicado. Fearful, and with very good reason."

"How is she?" Kincaid asked. "What's she doing?"

"She needed my help with her report on the Magdalene Laundries. One of the loose ends I was telling you about. How are your dots connecting?"

"I called about Wryth. You've heard by now."

"That he's a free man. Sickening."

"We're watching him round the clock," Kincaid said. "He's not completely free."

"But he must know his days as a caged bird are numbered," Grey said. "That the cat will inevitably succeed."

KINCAID LAY IN BED thinking about dots. In the Republic, Moloney the attorney for the Archdiocese, who handled Wryth's name changes and, as Kincaid last week uncovered, "settled" with some of Wryth's victims. Byrne the accountant, who structured the "settlements," payoffs in Kincaid's mind. British spy Mangan, the map mastermind's keeper, who murdered Dan Faunt to protect his charge's identity. Monsignor Gwynedd, Wryth's first prelate, what—a co-conspirator? Another enabler? Or a witness who chose to remain silent? Dr. Baldwin, whose testimony helped free the abuser from the Republic's criminal courts, doubtless reducing the Archdiocese's liability for Wryth's abuses. And his first homicide, Dr. Robert Boyd, silent witness to a brutal penetration.

Witness. Witnesses. "I didn't want to be a martyr to my sorrows," Mattie had told Kincaid. "A *witness* to them."

The dictionary said martyr means witness. Witnesses, murdered like history's most famous martyrs.

In the North, more dots. Lann McLaughlin and Mary Clery, map smugglers. Mary Theresa Mongilly, mapmaker. Each woman a handmaiden in Wryth's self-protection racket, murdered with medieval mania. Mother Stephanie Teresa, someone who knew too much, saw too much, but killed unceremoniously with a tiny pistol at close range. And Constable

Brugha, felled by a bomb doubtless meant for the prioress Mother Catherine, the safe recovered in the debris, or both.

Kincaid's phone rang. Two twenty three in the morning, his clock read.

"We have movement, Inspector," Fields told him.

KINCAID PARKED AT THE end of the next block, then walked toward Fields' car. The garda emerged from an alley about halfway down.

"Marta and company?" Kincaid asked

"Maybe," Fields said. He looked up the street at an armored Land Rover. "Piglet up there."

"Not exactly discreet."

"Do we go in?" Fields asked.

"Is the back covered?"

"Yes, sir."

"People coming and going from the building?"

"No one resembling Father Wryth."

"Are you sure?"

"From the night vision, binoculars. We can only get so close."

"McDermott know?" Kincaid asked.

"He does, sir. He told us to hold off until you came down."

"Get backup and check the truck. Then we may go in."

The piglet didn't move. Backup arrived and lit it up with spotlights.

"Empty, Inspector," Fields told Kincaid. "Could be wired."

"Get EOD out here," Kincaid said. "Don't go into the flat until they've cleared it. Keep the street blocked until Technical takes the truck."

Less than an hour later, it was clear Wryth was gone.

MARTA TELEPHONED KINCAID THAT morning.

"Did *you* take him?" Kincaid asked.

"If I took him, would I be ringing you?"

"I should have locked you up when I had the chance," he said.

"On what grounds?"

"Making a threat against the Republic. Bombing a car in a public street."

"Wryth wasn't turned over nor was he extradited. Was the threat executed?" she asked.

"Not yet," Kincaid said.

"I didn't ring to have this discussion," Marta said.

Kincaid started to speak but she interrupted.

"My wee sister was six when Wryth assaulted her," Marta said. "She tried to commit suicide when she was a teenager. Mam and Dad sent her to a boarding school outside London. Everyone thought it best she get out of Dublin."

"Where's your sister now?"

"When is Grey due back?"

"On her way as we speak," Kincaid said. "So what happened? Did your sister, was she, did she recover?"

Marta sighed as though she might cry. "I've always been the protector," she said. "The bangharda everyone thought would be the first woman commissioner. But with a secret like that? Think about it, Adam. With the power the Church wields. I find it ironic that guarding people like my sister meant leaving the Guards." She blinked and opened her eyes wide to clear them. "Does Grey know about Wryth?"

"That the courts let him go."

"But not that he's vanished?"

"She's in transit," Kincaid said. "McDermott talked to Mattie O'Connell about it."

"First you hear from Sister, let me know," Marta said. "She and I need to catch up."

KINCAID OPENED HIS EYES during the wee morning hours. Got up, set a piece of tracing paper over the coroner's aerial-style photo of the tattooed corpse on a white tarp re-membered on the floor.

Connected the dots.

D—I—S—C—I—P—U—.

Took one of the tracings Mother Catherine found, overlaid the two, studied the near perfect fit. He next pulled road maps of Dublin and County Armagh around Briar Lough from a drawer in his desk. He originally thought the tracings were roads to places loyalists or republicans were battling. Roads to hideouts like James Mitchell's farm in Glenanne. Roads to churches, police stations, army barracks, strategic positions. These were, after all, the maps Lann McLaughlin and Mary Clery smuggled. The maps Sister Mongilly drew.

But the safe keepings unearthed after the Sisters of Atonement explosion were none of those things. They were rough maps of the All Saints Slayer crime scenes in Dublin and the Witch Burnings in County Down.

The dots on the autopsy photos seemed to connect to some as-yet-unknown crime scene, letters on a foot, ankle, leg, and stomach marking a continuous road. As for the Latin word, a brightly-embellished L on the palm side of a curled thumb connected to a U on the tip of a middle finger. The hands were outstretched. But the final M was spread across four toes. Place the toes next to the middle finger? The foot was dismembered, after all. Kincaid turned to his Polaroids, placed the toes next to the fingers.

If the body was a land mass, beyond the body, the sea?

Kincaid remembered a picture of Miss Nic Cionnaith on holiday by the sea. He remembered Mattie O'Connell raving about the same place. On a proper map, it had the vague outline of a slender hand with curled thumb touching the toes of a dismembered foot. It lay north of all the crime scenes.

Kincaid left a message with Dublin Metro dispatch, told them exactly where he was going. Told them to relay the message to John McDermott. Woke the Chief Superintendent of County Antrim, insisting he notify all RUC offices in the area. Then packed a few belongings and set off on the three-hour drive north.

Thirty Seven

Bucketing down, as Kincaid turned onto A2, the coastal route known as Whitepark Road. The downpour would slow whatever backup arrived. They planned to meet in the village of Ballintoy, RUC cars marked and lighted, drive toward the coast and park as close to the bridge as they could, then walk the rest of way. Kincaid waited in his car until an RUC Land Rover pulled up beside him.

"Still not a titter of wit," Sergeant Clarence O'Fall shouted through the rain. "Get in." Kincaid hurried around to the passenger side. "Surprised to see me?" O'Fall asked.

"A bit out of your jurisdiction."

"Not for Special Branch." O'Fall turned. "Station sergeant says this is the quickest way. Hope I don't get us stuck."

They drove along another road to an opening in a broad green field, bumped and skidded down the grass toward the coastline.

"Where's Mr. Squish?" Kincaid asked, unable to resist Sister Grey's jab.

"Who?"

"Corporal Jackson."

"Haven't seen him." His voice sounded final, so the Inspector didn't press. They slowed, parked, turned off the headlights. O'Fall handed Kincaid a second flashlight.

They walked down a long path with steps to a steep wooden staircase where two dozen stairs descended to a narrow landing before the Carrick-a-rede rope bridge. Kincaid shined his light down the steps, then started down, as steady on his legs as he had been in months.

"Not planning to cross?" O'Fall said.

"I'm still recuperating." At the bottom, Kincaid shined the flashlight along the rope handrails, then along the sparsely-planked walkway.

"See anything?" O'Fall yelled down to him.

Careful to avoid slipping, Kincaid bent down. He shined his light on the underside of the bridge.

"Wryth's long gone, if he was here," O'Fall said.

"He wouldn't jump," Kincaid said. "He'd hang."

"If you see something, you're a better man than I," O'Fall said. They kept looking, O'Fall from the top of the steps, Kincaid from the bottom, lighting one end of the slender bridge to the other. Kincaid walked back up.

"Chief Superintendent's office said you were sure," O'Fall said.

"I am sure it will happen. Just not when."

"We can't stake anything out in this."

"Weather's supposed to clear tomorrow, early afternoon," Kincaid said. "Station sergeant said he'd be back in the morning."

THE RAIN STOPPED AT dawn, leaving the skies heavy with dark clouds. Kincaid left his room in Ballintoy with the pitter-patter of the final drizzle, drove to the trail head, walked as quickly as he could to the bridge, through mud, around puddles, ghosts of pain haunting his gait.

Near the path down to the bridge, he heard voices. Father Kane was first to emerge.

"Inspector Kincaid," he said. "Sister said you might come."

"Grey?"

"Yes. Said we should expect you."

"Where's Marta? Marta Carney?"

"Back in Dublin, I suspect. We did the hand-off at the border as planned."

"Where is Wryth?"

"You just missed the most glorious sunrise service," Kane said.

"Brenden Wryth. *Where is he*?"

"The body, are you meaning? Or the blood?"

Kincaid started to push past him, but Kane grabbed his arm, looked him in the eyes with surety. "I owe you," he said. "I want you to know. I'd have told you sooner, if you weren't a garda."

Kincaid kept on, Father Kane calling after him. "Had it not been for your bravery, no telling what might have become of me." Then at the top of his lungs, "I was the altar boy."

Kincaid stopped.

"Whose attack you interrupted."

As Kane turned away, Father Robert Parrodus, deep in conversation with Siobhan Nic Cionnaith, almost bumped into Kincaid on the embankment. Neither recognized Kincaid, who nearly collided head on with Fr. Lochlann Shaughnessy.

"Oh! We've met, haven't we?" Shaughnessy said.

"Inspector Kincaid." Sister De La Guerra was beaming as she emerged from the wood stairs.

"What's going on? What are you all doing here?"

"Janie said you'd be here. I'm sorry you missed it."

"Janie?"

"That's how she wanted to be remembered. To her friends."

"Jane Grey?"

"Yes. Of course. Who else."

"What do you mean, *remembered*?"

The sacristan from Fr. Parrodus' church came up behind Sister De La Guerra, put a hand on her shoulder, which she grasped like an old friend.

"Jane said she would tell you," Fr. Shaughnessy said. "Did she not?"

"The bishop is still down there," the sacristan said. "He and the monsignor celebrated."

They walked past Kincaid.

The detective hurried down the steps to the narrow spit that opened to the rope bridge. In celebratory vestments, Bishop Gerry McCarthy and a priest were packing away a traveling Mass. A pistol lay in a second open leather case.

"Inspector Kincaid," McCarthy boomed.

"Where's Sister Grey?"

"I don't believe we've met," the priest said. He put out his hand. "Fallon Mulvaney."

"Where's Grey?"

Monsignor Mulvaney looked over the water's edge, the one hundred foot drop to the rocks and water beneath the bridge. Kincaid grabbed him.

"What the hell happened?"

"Your hands, Inspector."

"I'll throw you off if you don't tell me."

"Unhand him," McCarthy said, aiming the pistol.

"Father Wryth received the noose, like John Cornelius before him," Mulvaney said. He yanked his arm back. "Sister Grey followed."

"She hanged herself?"

"She let herself go. No noose required."

Kincaid stood in stunned silence.

"She found peace, Inspector," the bishop said. "Which is more than I can say for the rest of his victims."

"Inspector!" O'Fall trotted down the steps. Bishop McCarthy closed the pistol away in its case. "Some kind of service?" O'Fall said.

"A funeral mass, apparently," Kincaid said. "A burial at sea."

"I don't think that's legal," O'Fall said. To Kincaid, quietly, "Anything? I asked the people up there. No one has seen anything."

"It's high tide," Kincaid said. "There's nothing left *to* see."

Before Bishop McCarthy ascended the stairs, he handed Kincaid an envelope and a lavabo towel from the seaside service, this one engraved with the missing phrase.

Eius qui.

The One.

"There's a letter for you. Sister Grey insisted," McCarthy said. "Kane said you'd understand, too. But I opposed it," and he lowered his voice so O'Fall wouldn't hear. "I wanted you dead."

Kincaid stepped away and as his leg started to give, he leaned against a rock, removed the contents from the envelope: tracing paper filled with Book of Kells characters, a map to the Carrick-a-rede, and a typewritten letter with Tipp-Ex white fluid corrections.

Bishop McCarthy pushed past him and O'Fall, Monsignor Mulvaney following. He watched the two men of God climb the steps.

"What do we do?" O'Fall asked, "Is there—anything—"

Kincaid was staring now, his mouth half open. "No," he said. "There's—" His head and eyes fell to the letter he was gripping in the wind.

"IT'S NOT EVERY DAY, nor every life, that one gets to attend one's own funeral," Sister Grey's letter began. "Mine was beautiful, fitting, and dare I say, an act of loving yet vigilant closure, where all in attendance, including me, saw justice served and nightmares ended. A timeless melodrama, where you, certainly the finest investigator on the Island and one of the finest men I've known, attended each riveting scene.

"We, his fearful victims and frustrated peers, began with the enablers. Without them, the perpetrator would never have been so successful. Having followed our warnings—our *indictments*, as they were—the presses and their gory narrations, each enabler approached his or her sentence in a state of full horror and overdue remorse, which we ascertained after allowing for any last words.

"We were, of course, amazed by the intricate web our spider had weaved, across two countries with strands in a third, England, my adopted homeland. But we were ever vigilant, pruning the silk where necessary (I do regret Brugha's death) and defending our ground (Mother Stephanie got too close).

"My sister—whom you must now know is Marta Carney—and I chose to do it this way, one foot in the system and one foot with those sworn to destroy it. Though not a one of us—who called our Church a spiritual home and our State a moral center—had faith in any system, we had no choice but to avail ourselves of the system's resources, including, dare I say, you.

"You're probably wondering what my last words were, what remorse I expressed, why I, too, had to die.

"Firstly, I suborned the destruction of the Atonement Sisters' offices, which led to the death of your colleague, when those papers Mother Catherine found, but that we could not, were Siobhan's intended targets.

"Secondly, I murdered a defenseless human being in the most defenseless position imaginable, naked in a bath, then lied about the loss of my little gun.

"But those crimes pale in comparison to my failure to come forward, my failure to finger that bastard, my silence all those years, and the lives and well-being it cost, including, nearly, my own.

"Had I only the courage, there may have been no more victims, including victims like Mary Teresa Mongilly, perpetually trapped in the kind of endless co-dependency I narrowly avoided.

"I am The One, Adam. Brenden Wryth's first victim. And I am (or was) a ruthless, sociopathic operator whose superficial charm fooled even you. I know that's hard to comprehend. But once the darkness surfaces . . .

"Now you have the final act. I left the script with Mattie O'Connell."

Kincaid looked across the water, waves roiling the surface, wind lapping at the sheets, eager to rip them away.

The letter was not signed.

Thirty Eight

"Adam!" Mattie O'Connell leapt. "Come in. Come in."

"You got my message."

"Our new Constable got it to me," Mattie said.

"When did O'Fall give up the post?"

"Last week, thank God. She's a woman, Adam. Our new station sergeant. I never thought I'd see that day."

"Mich Doherty—"

"That's Greene. Not Briar Lough. Ours is a more conservative village. A woman, Adam. Sister didn't find it all surprising. Women can do anything, she told me. And *this* woman would like to get my treasured guest something. Tea? Something to eat?"

"Tea," Kincaid said. "Thank you."

"I need to tell you," she said, taking his jacket, "they arrested the men who killed Kev and Mich."

"I've been waiting to hear that," Kincaid said. "Which group?"

"Saor Éire, they think. The old resentments—" Her voice cracked, she rubbed her hand on her blouse. "The old resentments over betrayal of church and country. Some will not abide Catholics and republicans in the Royal Ulster Constabulary. Like Gordon and his kin before him, Kevin dealt with the threats and the hate his entire career."

Kincaid smoothed his palm along her arm. "I'm sorry," he said. "You don't know how much."

She gathered herself and led him to the sofa. "Please," she directed.

"Are they sure?" Kincaid asked. "Will the charges stick?"

"Always the question when these paramilitaries are involved. I hope so. I dearly, dearly hope so," Mattie said. "I need closure. I need peace. I'm weary of looking over my shoulder."

"What about under your car," Kincaid said. "Your brother taught me—"

"I don't drive, thank Heavens. Haven't had to, but I may take it up." She went into the bedroom and returned with a book. "This is the book Sister left," Mattie said. "I assumed she forgot it and meant to give it her when I saw her again."

"Yes," Kincaid said. He stared at the book.

"What is it?"

"Sister Grey is dead," he pronounced.

"Dear God. How?"

"As I was told, she threw herself off the Carrick-a-rede bridge."

"Why on Earth did she do that?"

"She was involved in a covert effort to avenge serious crimes," Kincaid said. "Her conscience was killing her."

"Re—eally?" Mattie said. "What kind of crimes, or are you allowed—?"

"Serial child molestation," Kincaid said. "And its enablers."

"I'm not sure I—enablers? Who would enable such an awful thing?"

"People who helped Brenden Wryth cover up the crimes, evade justice, leave this country for the Republic," Kincaid said. "They're all dead now. Wryth, too. They claim to have hung him."

"Kev would have arrested him in a minute had he ever surfaced. So the oul bugger finally met his fate—"

"I wouldn't call it fate so much as premeditated homicide. And with a degree of planning and execution the likes of which I've never seen," Kincaid said.

"Sister Grey was involved in this?"

"Up to her proverbial neck."

"Oh." The word escaped Mattie's lips as more sigh than exclamation. "But they're all—dead now? These vigilantes?"

"No, not them," Kincaid said. "The people who helped Wryth. His co-conspirators. Some of them were the witch burning victims Kevin was investigating. Some of them died in my jurisdiction, by equally heinous means."

"So the people who did this—are still alive, still free?"

"For now," Kincaid said. "Maybe forever. They left very little evidence in their wake."

"And Sister Grey—in this house—I just—I can't believe it."

"I'm as shocked as you are. A veteran homicide detective, and I hadn't an inkling."

"And Grey wanted you to come back here."

"Apparently." Kincaid flipped over the copy of *Murder on the Orient Express*.

"For that book?" Mattie said.

Kincaid thumbed through the front of the book, the back, looking for anything else Grey may have written.

"Have you read it?" Mattie asked.

"Years ago. As I recall, everyone—" The teapot whistled and Kincaid's eyes followed Mattie into the kitchen. He saw the mirror out the corner of his eye, crooked, moved, somehow out of square. He set the book down and heard the cup and saucer rattle as Mattie walked them in.

"Everyone, Adam?"

"Was—guilty," he said, staring at the mirror. "In the book, everyone was guilty."

Mattie set down the tea.

"Is that why you didn't cover it?" Kincaid said. "Too weak to handle the weight?"

"The mirror, you mean? I hadn't noticed," Mattie said. "Kev took care of those things."

"Nail in plaster," Kincaid said. "If it doesn't penetrate the lath behind . . . Looks like it's getting ready to pull from the wall."

Kincaid felt his leg throb. He grabbed the sofa arm and pushed up.

"Leg still bothering ya?" Mattie asked.

"Cramps up. Just need to stand a while, walk it out."

He walked around the sofa to the mirror.

"Oh, don't worry about that."

"I don't mind," Adam said. "I'll put a new nail up."

"No need—" The phone in the hallway rang. But Mattie didn't move.

"Your tea's getting cold," she said.

"Your phone's getting hot."

She stood firm but the phone kept ringing and finally she swiveled with a reluctant lurch and watching him on the way to the hall, answered it impatiently.

Kincaid tried righting the mirror, but it wobbled and moved and so he lifted it off its nail and as he lowered it, a narrow cubby appeared. He jumped and almost dropped the mirror at the voice behind him.

"For Kevin," Mattie said, aiming a Webley 0.38 handgun at the Inspector. "Step away, please, Inspector. Kevin taught me to shoot."

Kincaid backed away.

"He built that little press after the Hunt Report disarmed the police. They reversed that decision, but the press stayed." Mattie pressed her case with the Webley. "Why did Sister send you here? Don't lie to me, now."

"You want her exact words?"

"I want to know. I need to know."

"She said she left the script here, with you. Matilda O'Connell," Kincaid said.

"The script for what?"

"All these killings, apparently."

"She left that book," she said, nodding at Christie's classic. "That's all. Don't lie to me. I'll shoot you dead and walk away from this place, for as you must know, as the sister *must* have told you, I am a dead woman if I stay."

Kincaid slipped around to the couch and lowered himself back onto it painfully and gradually. "She said nothing of the sort. Said nothing about you at all."

Mattie hung back, gun still poised.

"Do you know what it's like living on a policeman's wage? What it's like having no education, no employable skills, having to live off your brother because you can never find steady work?" Mattie walked around the sofa and stuck the barrel into the back of Kincaid's head. "I kept *an eye* on him," she whispered. "I spied on him." She withdrew. "Where are they? Where are they?!" She walked around to the front of Kincaid, arms stiff, both hands gripping the gun, eyes square on her target.

"Where are *who*?" Kincaid said.

"The vigilantes."

"I don't know," he said.

She leaned in and patted his trousers, his shirt with one hand. She took the jacket from the coat rack and patted it, glancing out the window, staring out the window. She extracted his car keys.

"You're the reason Brenden Wryth eluded the RUC," Kincaid said.

"You're giving me too much credit. I only helped around County Down," she said.

"The North's main Catholic stronghold, the place most eager to get Wryth out of circulation. Now you're marked for execution."

"I did what I had to do," Mattie said.

Kincaid picked up *Murder on the Orient Express*. "Everyone is guilty," he said. "Jane Grey brought me back here—"

"Are you one of them? Are you going to kill me? Or are you here to arrest me?"

"I can't arrest you," Kincaid said. "You know that."

Mattie looked out the window. "Clarie, then. He's coming to arrest me."

Kincaid heard her in the bedroom.

"Since I don't wish to be burned at the stake, or interned at The Maze, I can't stay," Mattie said. She emerged with a suitcase. "I thank you and Sister Grey for alerting me," she said. She opened the front door but stood away from it, looked out. Up the street, down the street, across the street, revolver in one shaky hand, suitcase in the other.

Kincaid leaned up and saw her scurry down the path to his car. He pushed himself off the sofa and went to the open door. Suitcase at her side, she looked in the back seat. With Kincaid's luggage, no room. She hurried around, unlocked and opened the trunk.

The blast blew him off his feet, sending glass and metal shrapnel and cloth and burning upholstery into the house and the air, shattering windows and setting a tree on fire.

And sending the last enabler in pieces up and down the quiet road.

Thirty Nine

"Your sister used me. You used me," Kincaid told Marta on the phone in his Dublin flat, during their last-ever conversation. "And you have the audacity to *check on* my well-being?"

"I wanted to make sure you weren't hurt," Marta said.

"You don't read the papers? Watch television? I even used your phrase: star chamber. *Camera stellata.*"

"I wanted to talk to you in person."

"Then come over."

"You know I can't."

A song Kincaid overheard on Marta's radio filled a pause in their conversation. A song about armored cars, tanks, guns, missing sons, Belfast streets, crying children, soldiers dragging fathers from their beds, men imprisoned without due process of law, blood.

"Charlie Mangan is the owner of those body parts," she said. "You'll never prove that because you'll never get his prints. I thought you should know."

"When you rigged the bomb, had you followed me to the border stop? Or were you and your heavy gang at your sister's funeral?"

"How would I know," Marta said, "about such things as bombs and gangs?"

"No one's listening," Kincaid said. "Your friends must have known I wasn't using the trunk. That my luggage was in the back seat. If you didn't plan to harm me, that is."

"I—"

"And what if I had used the trunk?"

She didn't say anything. He held the receiver away, then put it very close. "My luggage went up in the blast, along with my bangs and eyebrows," Kincaid said through gritted teeth.

"I'm sorry to hear that, Adam. Deeply sorry." Marta sighed and Kincaid heard the lowness in her voice. "I know you don't want to. I know you want to focus on the justice and rightness of the thing, right now, today. But think of all the people Wryth ruined. He ruined me, Adam. Ruined my family."

"You know good and well I've never ignored any of that. My mam never forgave me for leaving the Church. She refused to believe I caught someone like Wryth in the act."

"At least she's still alive. And you still have a chance," Marta said. "Our daddy—he hung himself. He left no note, but Janie and I knew. We knew why. He had failed in the most fundamental duty of a father: to keep his child safe."

"So the ends justify the means?" Kincaid said.

Marta's voice stiffened. "Good night, Adam."

KINCAID WAS READING A letter by lamplight in the dark of his flat next to crystal glass of whiskey.

"I'm so glad you write back," he read. "I wondered if you would. The waiting was killing me. You asked why I came over to you in the pub and I didn't answer. I will tell you my answer, but only if you meet me. In person. Until then, I remain,

"Kateryna Myelovych Fyodorovna Tereshchenko

"(So you won't confuse me with anyone else you adore)."

Kincaid couldn't help but chuckle and it felt good. He was so, so tired. That little bit of release—like that night, when he told her he adored her in *The Mikado*. He was rarely that forward with his personal feelings, especially with women.

When the phone rang about two hours later, he thought it might even be Katerin. All the reporters swarming the Star Chamber Slayings called him at Dublin Castle, or stopped him on the street, or even once in Bloom's Pub, where he sat alone looking at Baldwin's preferred bar stool from Marta's favorite table.

"Mr. Kincaid," the nurse began.

KINCAID STOOD BEFORE HIS mother, her hand in his, caressing the top of it with his thumb. Her mouth was open, her eyes closed.

"We close them," the nurse said, interpreting the doubtful look on his face as the skepticism of a homicide detective used to the blank stare of the newly deceased.

Kincaid leaned down and kissed his mother's forehead. As he stood again, the wrapping paper caught his eye, and the unwrapped gift in its midst.

"It's lovely," the nurse said. "She stared at it for just the longest time."

"She adored their story," Kincaid said. "Their windblown journey to our shores."

AS KINCAID REARRANGED A small suitcase, an old woman chattered.

"So you're going to visit your girl?" she said. "You've been exchanging letters? She's your girl all right. You write. And she sings! How wonderful for you."

Kincaid smiled. "She's only a friend," he said. "She's not actually my girl."

"A right colleen she is, and you're saying she's not your girl? Is she famous? What's that you have there?"

Kincaid moved his mother's gift away from his socks. The old woman leaned in for a closer look.

"The last present I gave my mam."

"Your mam? Why you poor lad. How sad she didn't like it."

"She died," Kincaid said,

"Oh."

He held up a stained-glass Monarch butterfly mounted in a case trimmed with twenty-four karat gold.

"I take it back, then," the old woman said. "She must have been thrilled."

"They were her favorite."

"I don't think I've ever seen that kind of butterfly here. I did when I lived in the States, but never here."

"We saw them in the south when I was a boy," Kincaid said.

"County Cork, County Kerry?"

"Mostly. No one knows how they get there, but my mam said they blow with the wind across the Atlantic. We're going to see if we can find some."

"You and your girl, then? Your friend, I mean. Hope she's not disappointed."

"We'll find one, maybe two, at least," Kincaid said. "This is the best time of year."

"How do you know where to look? Them are big counties."

"My mam and I found them along the water," Kincaid said. "Katerin and I will be searching by the sea."

"Katerin. Ahh. What an exotic name," the woman said. "And a right couple detectives you'll be. Just to be safe though, say a little prayer. Let your mam know you're here that way, too."

Kincaid half-grinned. "Of course," he said, looking at the Monarch. "My mother always wanted a priest."

Notes

Barker, Alan. Shadows: Inside Northern Ireland's Special Branch. Edinburgh and London: Mainstream Digital, 2012

Brady, Conor. The Guarding of Ireland: The Garda Síochána and the Irish State, 1960-2014. Dublin: Gill and Macmillan, 2014

Breen, Suzanne. *'Glenanne gang murders case file was a page and a half... we felt their lives were seen as worthless,' says Eugene Reavey.* Belfast Telegraph, January 04 2021

Butler, Shane and Jordan, Tony. Alcoholics Anonymous in Ireland: AA's First European Experience. DrugsandAlcohol.ie, 2006

Cassel, Douglass, et. al. Report of the Independent International Panel on Alleged Collusion in Sectarian Killings in Northern Ireland. Notre Dame, Indiana; Notre Dame Law School, Center for Civil and Human Rights, October 2006

Commission to Inquire into Child Abuse. Final Report. Dublin: May 20, 2009.

Doherty, Richard. The Thin Green Line: The History of the Royal Ulster Constabulary, 1922-2001. South Yorkshire, UK: Pen and Sword Books, Ltd., 2012

Jordan, Hugh. *Revealed: The ex-RUC officer suspected of brutal Reavey brothers' murders,* **Sunday World,** September 29 2021

Marry, Pat. The Making of a Detective: A Garda's Story of Investigating Some of Ireland's Most Notorious Crimes. Dublin: Penguin, 2019

Marsh, Courtney. An Garda Síochána: Culture, challenges, and change. Dublin: Trinity College, School of Social Work and Social Policy, Doctoral Thesis, 2020

McKay, Susan *Families of the Troubles' victims must learn the truth.* **Irish Times**, Jun 13, 2008

Mulholland, Peter. Justice and Policing and Orange Parades: Towards a History of Orange Violence and Corruption in Northern Ireland. January 2010

Neville, Stuart. The Ghosts of Belfast. New York: Soho Crime, 2016

Pierce, Colm. Sheriff Street Dublin 1989 Volumes I and II,

Raidió Teilifís Éireann (RTÉ). Documentary about Sheriff Street in the 1960s.

Urwin, Margaret; Meehan, Niall. The 1972-73 Dublin Bombings. History Ireland, May-June 2018

Young, Connla. *British government officials 'knew about loyalist Glenanne Gang', former RUC officer claims.* **Irish News**, 28 August, 2017

Miscellaneous online references, including Wikipedia, the Irish Times, Belfast Telegraph, Garda.ie, Justice.ie, Irish Mirror, RTE, RoyalUlsterConstabulary.org, PSNI.Police.uk, Ulster Special Constabulary, et. al. Re: Ulster Special Constabulary, Royal Irish Constabulary, Loyalist paramilitaries, Border Campaign, The Troubles, Partition of Ireland, Irish War of Independence, Saints and Martyrs appearing in the narrative.

Thank You!

Thank you for reading The Trouble. If you are so inclined, we'd greatly appreciate your thoughts on the book as a **rating or review** on Amazon or Goodreads.

Reader ratings and reviews enhance the reading experience for everyone, and have become the number one way new readers discover new books. But they are also hard to come by, and always an honor to receive.

JOIN OUR MAILING LIST
https://heartbeatbookstore.com

Contact Us

Heart Beat Publications, LLC
POB 125
Columbia, Mo 65205
marketing@heartbeatpublications.com